Shahbano Bilgrami is a published poet, children's book author, and freelance editor whose debut novel, *Without Dreams*, was long listed for the inaugural Man Asian Literary Prize in 2007. She lives in Upstate New York with her husband and three daughters.

THOSE CHILDREN

SHAHBANO BILGRAMI

HarperCollins *Publishers* India

First published in India in 2016 by
HarperCollins *Publishers* India

Copyright © Shahbano Bilgrami 2016

P-ISBN: 978-93-5264-157-4
E-ISBN: 978-93-5264-158-1

2 4 6 8 10 9 7 5 3 1

Shahbano Bilgrami asserts the moral right
to be identified as the author of this work.

This is a work of fiction and all characters and incidents described in this
book are the product of the author's imagination. Any resemblance to
actual persons, living or dead, is entirely coincidental.

HarperCollins *Publishers*
A-75, Sector 57, Noida, Uttar Pradesh 201301, India
1 London Bridge Street, London, SE1 9GF, United Kingdom
Hazelton Lanes, 55 Avenue Road, Suite 2900, Toronto, Ontario M5R 3L2
and 1995 Markham Road, Scarborough, Ontario M1B 5M8, Canada
25 Ryde Road, Pymble, Sydney, NSW 2073, Australia
195 Broadway, New York, NY 10007, USA

Typeset in 11/15 Electra LT Std Regular at
Manipal Digital Systems, Manipal

Printed and bound at
Thomson Press (India) Ltd

In loving memory of Amma,
Sakina Haider Bilgrami,
from those children
she left behind.

PROLOGUE

21 May 2—

My Dear Son, Aftab,
Beta, you Can, no Doubt, imagine with what FEelings I write this letter to you so sOOn after the Tragic and untimeLy demise of N. Your Ammi, your brothers, and your doting sister, Durdana, Join with me in extending our profoundest SYMpathies.

I trust the Children are well. They ~~sHOUould~~ *should take this in the spirit of our great religion: everything happens for a reason, and that reason is the indisputable will of the great Almighty God.*

It has, in fact, been more than a dECade since we saw them last. They must have grown. You and N made such a concerted effort to keep these precious buds (now, surely, sprouting tendrils!) away From their native rOOts, and us, that I daresay I wouldn't recognize THem if I saw them strolling up our road. I cannot begin to compreHEend your reasons for preferring to keep them immured in the strange customs of their adopted land, but – well, I'm sure you had your reasons. I know your Ammi and I, tHough nOt in favour of the alliance, would have welcomed your offspring and, in time, you and N, too, notwithstanding her very different BAckgrounD. I only hope that it is not too laTE to teach the CHildren our culture and our WAys. And as for poor n – well, she has met her Maker at last. May ALLAH shower her with blessings.

This is, in fact, why I am Writing to you, to persuade you – even order you as a FAather – to come home, bring yOUR family, live witH us as you should have done years ago. America is no place for a widower and four motherless children. Little ~~Fati~~ Jamila, with her unfortunate condition, would be far happier heRE with her Dadi, who can show her ways in which to make herself usefuL.

Please don't disappoint mE.
Abba

The four of us sat around a small fire in the middle of a treeless clearing, the stars above, the heat and hunger of the flames in our eyes. No one spoke. The letter lay on the dark grass, dangerously close to the blaze but not close enough for those of us who wished it into the fire. We were surrounded by night sounds, heavy and muted, the buzzing of insects, the hooting and rustling of creatures of the wild. These creatures, moles and squirrels and black-eyed raccoons, watched us from the dark, effortlessly crossing the line between forest and suburbia to make nests and burrows and lairs in picket-fenced gardens such as our own.

Above, the stars; below, the growing unease, like a freshly inflicted wound, swelling. We hated the author of that letter, our grandfather. He was a crotchety, doddering, wizened old greybeard, so remote in our minds he may as well have been a mythic fire-breathing beast. There he hunched, in a corner of the world far-distant from our own, pounding out missives on a dusty pre-Partition typewriter, an instrument of torture that was about to change our lives.

'I'm sorry.' It was Jamila. She shrugged wearily as if the responsibility lay with her. Sadly, she often ended up as a ninety-pound pretext for getting the family in and out of all sorts of scrapes. She pointed bitterly to the letter.

'Oh, come on. You mean that melodramatic reference to "little fatty Jamila"?' Raza asked. Fatima clapped her hands to her mouth, suppressing a laugh, while Raza continued, 'He'd have written that letter anyway. He's like that.'

'How'd you know?' I asked, my ten-year-old's curiosity getting the better of me, even though questioning Raza, my big brother, was something I rarely did. And rightly – for his heavy hand landed on my head, but not before he had pulled me roughly onto his lap and I stared, above his wide shoulders, at the stars, and beyond them to a place where I imagined our mother was.

'I just do,' he said. 'I've heard enough of the stories.'

'What kind of stories?' I asked excitedly, sliding from his lap onto his long legs, which, impressively hairy like a grown man's, lay half-buried in the grass. I began to fiddle with his toes, curled in his sandals, trying to pry them straight.

'No, Chhoti. Not those kinds of stories. Not like ours,' Fatima said, looking at me in a way she had only recently begun to adopt, wistful, even maternal, although she was nothing like our mother had been – small-boned and short-statured, soft around the elbows and the knees, a woman with no sharp edges, just a comforting wholeness that kept us together through good times and bad. In fact, Jamila, who now sat hunched over with her head buried in her knees, resembled her most, which was just one of the many reasons why I loved her best.

'Oh.' I was disappointed. Then I remembered why we were here, out in the garden, under the black sky. Bright yellow light fell at a distance from the far right, the last window on the second floor of the brown-bricked house that we had lived in since Amma and Baba moved to America in 1979. This was the house where Fatima, now eighteen, was brought as a squalling infant days after an icy birth, our immigrant parents bewildered by the clinical aloofness of the hospital staff, the conspicuous absence of family. I realized that it was only a matter of time before Baba noticed that we weren't in our beds. 'What about,' I began cautiously, 'the game?'

Jamila's head shot up. All of a sudden, the usually fluid features of her face fell, mask-like, into place. She looked determined, even queenly, as she waved her arms, signalling for the rest of us to draw closer to the fire till our faces were red with the heat. I put my hands on my cheeks and felt them burn. It was happening again. We were being pulled into another world by our imaginings. The thrill of becoming someone else, someone greater, more powerful, took hold of me. Heart pounding, I waited for her to speak.

'The letter,' she motioned imperially as the great and powerful Lady M. The rest of us kept our heads bowed in deference as Raza approached her with the letter, made of a flimsy blue material that resembled tissue paper. Grabbing the letter and crushing it in her hand, Lady M looked at each of us in turn: Timmer, Dag and myself, Little Furry. 'Listen, people,' she began, 'are we all united on this?'

We nodded our agreement.

'Hands over the fire,' she commanded.

All four of us placed our right hands one on top of the other over the blaze. Mine, being the smallest, was right at the top. I held my flowered skirt away from the flames.

Lady M continued, 'We make a pact today, now, that we will not leave this house. Things will not change. We cannot allow them to.'

'We are one,' Timmer, Dag, and I said in unison like the dutiful minions that we were.

Smiling, Lady M threw the crushed letter into the fire. We watched as it was first licked, then swallowed, by the flames.

Baba never saw that letter that was addressed to him, but that night, even as I helped my brother and sisters put out the fire and heap soil, bits of grass, and leaves over the burnt patch in our garden, I could feel it. The long, hot summers that we were accustomed to, the ones that culminated in a white light as sudden and as brilliant as a camera flash, were coming to an end. A chilly wind blew through the garden, tugging relentlessly at everything that was frail, rootless.

We were destined, despite our games or, perhaps, because of them, to live from now on in a land of endless summer.

CHAPTER 1

It's easy enough to laugh now, decades later, but our games seemed more real than our actual lives the year that our mother died. When I think back to that evening in August, to the garden beneath the stars, and to those children intent on play-acting, it is always with a strange mixture of pity and exhilaration. We thought we were the heroes of our own destiny, exerting our will over a random and cruel world, a world where mothers were taken from children and letters derailed lives.

It was a year of unbelievable change, Amma's loss the first in a series of events that took us from our comfortable suburban life to an unfamiliar city halfway across the globe. As children, we were obsessed with returning to Chicago. We didn't realize how many good things were to come out of this displacement. My earliest impressions of our new home – some real, some snatched from fantasy and dream– and of the family in it were to have a lasting impact on us all. Over the years, though my perspective has changed, I still remember what it was like to be that confused ten-year-old girl who had just lost her mother.

✳

Jamila sat wilting in the nominal shade of a leafy, flower-clustered champa tree, lulled into a stupor by the oppressive heat and the nauseating perfume of the flamboyant white-and-yellow blooms that threatened to fall into the massive bowl of garlic bulbs on her lap. I was certain that this was not where she had expected to find herself just six short weeks after the ritualistic burning of the letter. She looked at us unhappily.

Raza was lying face down on the dusty and dirt-stained cushions of the cane sofa that Dada often used in the early evenings as Tea Central. He affected sleep.

Fatima and I were going over some material in preparation for fifth grade, a thin glossy-paged alphabet book with alien letter-forms, curvy shapes with dots and dashes in unexpected places representing the first letters of objects that I could recognize but had to re-learn in Urdu. It didn't help that even Fatima only had a vague idea of what the symbols represented. I knew it would take months for me to catch up to the rest of my class.

Suddenly, Jamila overturned the steel bowl on her lap, scattering the bulbs all over the tiled patio, and wailed miserably, 'I have failed you all!'

Fatima and I rushed to capture the errant bulbs as they rolled this way and that. A few of them found their way down the steep driveway, through the half-open gate, and from there onto the busy street just outside C44, our dada's crumbling stronghold.

Once the centre of a respectable Karachi suburb, C44 had become an anomaly in the midst of an encroaching commercial thoroughfare where everything from toilet seat covers to education was haggled over, bought, sold, or bartered. Anwar Chacha, the scrawny bare-chested chowkidar, blocked the way out, his bony arms folded across his white-haired chest.

'Nahin, Bibi, nahin. No outside. Strict orders,' he said, grinning.

We only had a moment to glimpse a few of the garlic bulbs roll into the door-less opening of one of the makeshift tenements opposite us, and a scramble of childish hands emerging from the dark to lay claim to them.

By the time we returned to the patio, Raza was kneeling next to Jamila, his arms wound tightly around her. She was shaking. I felt oddly frightened of her as we joined the circle and huddled like football players, staring at each other's faces through the occasional bursts of light that seeped in through the cracks.

'Look, Jamila,' began Raza, breaking the silence, 'just put it out of your head that you're responsible for our coming here.'

'Besides,' added Fatima, 'now that we're here, we have to make the most of it. And we will. You know we always manage to. We've got our games and each other. Remember, you're our leader…'

Jamila shook her head emphatically, her features contorted as the tears fell, her slender body trembling with frustration.

'You are, Jamila! You are!' we all whispered, pulling each other closer till we had formed a tightly-knit ball, a globe, a spinning universe of our own that protected us from what was now an unpleasant reality.

✳

Even before we had left our beloved suburban home in America's midwest, there was a feeling that the vacuum left by our mother's death would inevitably cause some cataclysmic change in the way we led our lives. In the months after she had gone, we tried, like shipwrecked sailors, to construct a convincing replica of the existence we had left behind in a house that quickly began to resemble a deserted island. We went to school, ate our meals, slept, woke, slept again according to the same rhythms as before, threw ourselves into television, friends, sports, or random entertainment, studied and passed, till our own play-acting had become a practised deception meant to convince others that we were exceptionally brave.

Baba often stood by his desk, an uncertain hand brushing the grey of his uncombed hair as he quietly watched us fast-forward through the traditional grieving period of forty days. He didn't know how to handle us in this new, hyperactive phase; we seemed unnaturally excitable. We rolled around the carpet in hysterics at the laugh tracks of our favourite television shows. Sometimes, when we had enough self-awareness to step out of our roles, we would even feel sorry for him: the perplexity was so apparent on his face that he looked like one of those sad mimes who performed to vacant street corners.

Relatively free of parental supervision, Fatima and Raza spent most of their spare time out of the house, scheduling visits and study sessions that went on till after Baba, Jamila, and I finished our quiet and lonely dinners on the narrow oak table where, as a family, we once enjoyed boisterous mealtimes. In an effort to make the food edible (most of it consisted of defrosted dinners from the local Indian restaurant), Baba would feed us in turn while softly singing to us in Urdu or in English, stringing together disjointed phrases and melodies snatched from songs with words he only half knew. The worst nights were when he would make no effort at all, putting our trays on the floor in front of the TV while he sat in a corner, head flung back, eyes closed, a restless hand nervously fiddling with the remote.

One day, as Jamila and I sat washing our doll collection in the tub of the upstairs bathroom, we overheard Baba on the telephone. He didn't sound like the Baba we knew.

'Here, Jamila,' I said, as I finished rinsing my Barbie's golden hair in the sudsy water, covering her glossy plastic nakedness with a paper towel, 'you hold this. I'll be back in a second.' I slipped out of the bathroom and stood at the top of the stairs. I could hear Baba clearly now. His voice cut through the mid-afternoon silence like a blade:

'I have said it once, and I will say it again. I'm not interested.'

There was a long pause.

'I understand what you're trying to say, but I won't put my children through that. They've been through enough.' I could hear him tap his foot impatiently as the person on the other end went on a few seconds longer.

'Look, I don't care what it'll do for science. I will not have them experimented upon and tested just because their mother died of cancer.'

I went back into the bathroom baffled by what I had just heard. Amma had died of *cancer*. Baba had only ever said that she was ill because God loved her so much He wanted her back. I had never heard the word 'cancer' in any of these discussions. The look on our poor father's face, I remember, always belied the forced bravado of his descriptions, the faltering victories – they've removed the feeding tube, she sat up at sunrise – all the more pathetic as we watched her swift decline. Turning to inspect Jamila's progress with the dolls, for once I wished I hadn't eavesdropped on a conversation.

After almost a month of this kind of fractured living, Jamila broke down. Baba had reluctantly gone to the office after two months' absence to sort through a mound of pressing correspondence. Perched on a bar stool in the kitchen, I watched with fascination as Raza clumsily strained a large pot of spaghetti in a steel colander over the sink, the steam rising in his face and clouding the large window that overlooked our front yard. Fatima and I exchanged glances. It was hard not to laugh: he was a hulking football player, but he couldn't even manage to drain a pot of pasta.

'Typical,' she muttered, as he heaved the strained pasta onto the counter, the strands of spaghetti emerging medusa-like from the colander and spilling over the sides.

'What do you mean?' he responded irritably.

'You always—' Fatima stopped in mid-sentence and suddenly asked, 'What was that noise?'

I had never heard anything like it before. I was convinced it was a ghost, the white-sheet-black-holes kind that flickered malevolently down the corridors of haunted houses at Halloween. My brother and sister raced upstairs with me following somewhat reluctantly behind. 'Is it a ghost?' I asked anxiously as I crawled up the stairs on all fours like a baby, something which I sometimes did as my birthright, being the youngest of several siblings.

When no one answered, I made my way towards the bedroom that I shared with Jamila, stopping just before the entrance as another low moan came from within, and I wondered, for the second time, whether it was a ghost, or an animal, or something more frightening still which couldn't yet be identified.

'Come in, Chhoti,' Fatima called. 'Don't be scared.'

I saw Jamila rolled up on the floor, rocking back and forth. The only reason I recognized her was because of her pale-pink jogging pants and yellow t-shirt. Otherwise, with her hair undone and her head locked into her knees, she looked nothing like herself. Every few seconds, she would lift her arm and point to the ceiling, calling out – and now it was clear: 'Maaa!'

That's what she called our mother.

'Hey, it's okay,' Raza coaxed, wrapping his large arms around her entire body and exerting enough force to stop her from rocking. It was a while before she was still, her body heaving sporadically not from hysteria, as before, but from a hoarse, painful sobbing that made her sound like a gutted animal. I stood by the door, transfixed by the sight of her, nervously rubbing my goose-pimpled arms in order to warm some life into them.

'Ferzana, come here,' Fatima called out again. This time I ran straight into her arms without looking at Jamila. 'Raza,' she said, 'we can't do this anymore. We need each other. We can't pretend that we don't.'

He nodded.

It was then that our special games began. We replaced one kind of play-acting – that we were brave and invincible – with another: games in which we became characters larger than ourselves, sometimes superhuman, sometimes villainous, acting out scenarios that were as impossible as dreams, often more tangible to us than our real lives, which over the course of one winter and one long illness, were derailed.

Jamila, whom I later learnt had thought she had seen the ghost of our mother that day, became our leader – the indomitable Lady M.

Although Baba never actually saw the letter that Dada had sent owing to our expert interception, it would take more than a secret bonfire to ward off the inevitable. Several weeks after the dutiful condolence calls from relatives far and near, some even attempting to simulate tears as they bewailed our family tragedy, there was a concerted effort from Baba's side of the family (and the letter was only part of it) to convince us to return home.

Of course, we had never known any other 'home' but this, our brown-bricked house with its picket-fenced garden, its squared-off neatness distinct, we liked to think, from the hundreds of more-or-less identical houses that flanked it on either side, across the street, down the road, or even in similar suburban settlements across the length and breadth of the country. It was special, we thought, because over the years Baba and Amma had made careful additions to it to accommodate our growing family and its particular needs – a study for Amma, a library for our books, a playroom that later served as a classroom for Jamila but, in fact, it was really only special because it was ours.

After several weeks of respite, the stillness of our once-quiet afternoons was marred by persistent overseas telephone calls. Like a fire alarm, the telephone's ring tore through our house until poor Baba, the only one brave enough, shuffled up from the basement to speak to his relatives in Pakistan. His voice, soft at first, rose to a yell as he fought to be understood over the static. Closed doors, blaring electronics, and even my fuzzy ear muffs couldn't block out the sound of him attempting to justify our American way of life to his parents:

'Ji, Abbaji, you're right. Absolutely. But isn't it a little early to uproot the family?'

A pause.

'I know there will be support. You have all been an immense support to us, but I'd have to talk to the children first—'

'Well, it isn't easy. They're used to this life. It'll be a big change for them, especially for Jamila. I'm afraid it might upset them further.'

And, finally, he gave in.

'Right, Abbaji. I'll see what I can do,' he sighed. The four of us were huddled at the top of the stairs when this final admission was blackmailed out of him.

Raza immediately bounded down the stairs to confront our surprised father while the rest of us trailed behind. Burning letters evidently had a cathartic effect, but as a practical strategy it was sadly lacking.

'Baba, you can't do this to us!'

'Beta, I'm only thinking about it right now. It isn't easy – the five of us together here. Perhaps Dada is right. Look at it as a new beginning.'

'Baba!' wailed Fatima. 'I was going to start college next fall!'

Jamila and I appeared visibly distressed although we didn't speak a word. Our older siblings continued, like pygmies beating at the breast of a mighty Titan, to argue themselves hoarse. Baba nodded but remained unperturbed.

Once the subject of our 'return' was out in the open, there were several family meetings on the subject, some conducted with grace – at least the ones presided over by Baba – some hijacked by a kind of communal hysteria that left us panic-stricken and tearful. It didn't seem fair to expect us to move so soon after our mother's death and that, too, to a country we were completely unfamiliar with. It wasn't as if we hated our country of origin, only that we knew it from afar and hadn't spent enough time immersed in the sun and the wonder of it to appreciate that it represented more than just a name on a map and a loose cultural affiliation.

Before we left our beloved home, there were farewells, and then there were farewells.

Once I knew that I was permitted to take all of my toys with me – even the broken dolls and incomplete tea sets, and the clown with the missing nose that always made Jamila laugh – I was immune to the rest of the process which, though distressing in a way that I couldn't express, had its obvious advantages. For example, overnight our house spored brown cartons like a fungal growth that spread from the basement upwards, till even our bedrooms and bodies smelt of musty cardboard. I spent hours crawling in and out of the larger boxes, or building towers with the smaller ones, cottages, castles or igloos, till eventually each and every one of them was packed and sealed, labelled and put away. Duct tape, too, afforded me many hours of pleasure, my fingers tangled in yards of sticky brown as I mummified my Barbies and one or two hapless teddy bears. It was only when I was discovered trying to tape my hair up in imitation of the colour treatments I had seen at the hairdresser's that the rolls were finally confiscated from me.

The last day of grade four fell on an absolutely gorgeous day in June, and I remember it well because, despite the weather, I distrusted it, thinking that it would end with a spectacular thunderstorm as summer days so often did. Standing in the playground in my favourite printed dress, I waved to a few of my friends and their mothers as they left the school grounds and hoped that they didn't realize it was for the last time. Instead of taking the bus home, Baba had come to pick me up. Holding my hand tightly in his, we went inside to say a final farewell to my teacher, Mrs Thorndike. After the initial pleasantries were over,

Baba shook her hand and reminded her that I wouldn't be returning for fifth grade.

'Oh, yes! That's right,' she said, looking at me oddly. 'We'll be very sorry to lose her. Fayrzana' – that's how they all pronounced my name – 'has such a wonderful imagination, don't you, dear? Well beyond her years! She's such a little storyteller!'

'Yes, yes, thank you,' Baba answered eagerly, oblivious to her tone which even I, at ten, could tell was not entirely without irony. He looked at her expectantly, as if waiting for more. Instead, she said, 'I hope you've thought this through, Mr Mahmud. Isn't there a warning out for that place? I mean, is it safe to take your family there?'

'Well, yes, I have thought it through,' Baba said, somewhat taken aback. His hand tightened around mine. We were both perspiring.

Mrs Thorndike gestured vaguely to the south-east section of the world map on the wall. 'A lot of crazies near the equator, eh? Must be the climate out there. Heat gets to their heads, poor dears!' I'm not sure if this was offered as a joke to lighten the mood, but it had the opposite effect on Baba, whose expression turned a shade darker as he clenched his teeth and stared right through her.

'Yes, well,' Mrs Thorndike muttered, 'just joking, of course. I'm sure you'll be very happy there.' She pulled me towards her and crushed my head against her bony ribcage.

'Bye, Mrs Thorndike,' I mumbled into her breast, trying my best to hold my breath so that I wouldn't have to smell her.

Baba and I stood there awkwardly for another second. During that brief pause, I stared hard at my classroom, the desk where I'd put my head down to rest during quiet time, the bright posters on the walls, the bulletin board pockmarked with pins, the blackboard where I once had to write 'I won't lie to the teacher about a mouse in the potty' seventy-five times.

And then the second passed, and we walked out into the playground where the asphalt was already speckled with the heavy drops of rain that fell from a now overcast sky.

That same day, I would later learn, Raza sat in a darkened auditorium in another part of the school district waiting for the final bell of the academic year to ring. In his arms lay Clarice, Fatima's best friend, her hair untidily falling on either side of her weepy face and her long bare legs tucked under his. Suddenly, she twisted around to face him and asked, blue eyes wide and voice trembling, 'If I visit you in Pakistan, will I have to wear a boor-ka?'

At home, Fatima sat in her room with Jamila, both of them staring blankly at the pale lilac walls. All of Fatima's books, papers, clothes, and other personal items formed a large mound on the floor where she had dumped them the night before, paying little attention to neatness or order. She was the last of the family to pack. It was almost as if she thought she could stop the move by refusing to acknowledge the existence of its most literal symbol – the cardboard box. At last, her face wet with tears, she began angrily stuffing her belongings into cartons. And thus, her quiet rebellion ended with no other witness than her younger sister who, halfway through the proceedings, fell asleep where she sat.

Perhaps that was just Jamila's way of escaping.

'Well, boys,' Lady M drawled, 'looks like we've done it. And in record time.'

We scanned the house, now empty of everything except a half-eaten bag of potato chips and a few crushed soda cans that the movers had left behind.

'Yes, Lady M,' bowed Dag. 'The loot's been loaded onto the truck. We better hurry if we want to make our flight to the tropics. They probably have an alert out for us already. The cops are on our tail.'

'Right as usual, Dag,' Lady M replied, raising her arms so that her cape concealed everything except her eyes. 'Do you ladies have any objections?'

'Nope. Let's get out of here, guys.' Timmer, her cat's eyes shining, catapulted herself through the front door, beckoning the rest of us to follow. 'Fast. Before someone finds the goods missing.'

As the rest of us stepped outside, I wiped the doorknob clean of fingerprints and then, with a last look for any obvious signs of tampering, closed the door softly behind me. Our getaway car stood waiting at the base of the hill.

It was as if we had never been.

CHAPTER 2

'Meat! Meat! Meat!' Dag exclaimed as he cannily observed the various inhabitants of C44 from the vantage point of an upstairs window, from where he could see the entire garden laid out like a checker board with its patches of grey and green, its few stunted trees rising out of the ground like dwarves, and the cemented patio an interruption that wound its way around the base of the entire structure, ending in a small black gate that led out into an abandoned alley.

'Down, boy, down,' Timmer laughed gleefully. 'You'd think you were about to tear into them!'

'What a wonderful idea,' he replied, his eyes still hungrily scanning the ground below for prey as he smiled into his wide shirt collar. Within a few minutes, however, all movement had ceased and there was nothing left of the busy morning but a matted crow cawing nastily to its mate.

'Well, I can tell you what I'd like for a snack,' Lady M piped in. 'Someone small and furry!' With that all three of them pounced on me as I sat sniffling in a corner, my tears soaking through the giant 'Alif' and the pinkish pomegranate on the first page of the Urdu alphabet book that I was supposed to master before classes started. It wasn't long before the alphabet book was tossed aside and I was rolling on the cold marble floor fending off their bites and tickles.

'Little Furry, have you completed the tasks that were assigned to you last week by Lady M?' asked Dag, suddenly stern.

'Well, Raza—' I began.

'I was talking to Little Furry,' he snapped.

'Yes, yes, I have,' I hastily replied, getting back into character. I went on to tell them how I had performed a complete reconnaissance of our new hide-out – code name C44 – investigated who lived where, and made a list of potentially suspicious characters that could jeopardize our mission, which was, of course, to return home to Chicago. Perspiring, I wiped my face with the edge of the kurta that Durdana Phupo had forced me to put on earlier that morning. (It was scratchy and stuck to my skin, aggravating my eczema; I wanted to pull it off and run around in my underwear, but that, I was told, was *out of the question*.)

'Good. Good. Good.' Lady M dusted herself off and reclined majestically on one of the hard cane beds that we were all slowly getting accustomed to. Crossing her legs and closing her eyes, she continued languidly, 'Go on, Little Furry. Tell us everything you know.'

In the early days, we knew little. The first few weeks were like trying to reacquaint ourselves with the world, for the world we had left behind in Chicago was nothing like the one we were now faced with: there was heat and dust, and perpetual sunshine; there was noise of a kind we had never heard before, the crows and the rickshaws, donkey carts, rustling coconut palms; there was a house with relatives whose names we did not know and whose love we suspected because of a long history of distrust.

In the first few weeks, we re-learnt the fundamentals of living: how to talk in our grandfather's house, that is, always in Urdu; how to walk in our grandfather's house with a dignified gait, not scrambling like wild things; what to eat in our grandfather's house, which was whatever was served, and not just 'Amriki' food; how to dress in our grandfather's house, and this meant mostly in shalwar-kameez, so no more fitted jeans for poor Fatima.

The only constant in all of this, of course, was Baba. Unfortunately, he too was going through a period of adjustment, and like a lab rat removed from its obstacle course and then returned to it, spent his days wandering through the high-ceilinged rooms of his childhood home in a kind of trance, trying to seek comfort in the known. Initially, he marvelled at everything he saw:

'Array, Abbaji, what a fantastic split unit!'

'My God, I can't believe they're showing that on television!'

'Well, there definitely is a freer press.'

'I had no idea that dating had become commonplace here…'

'Salma Chachi's wearing a hijab now? At her age?'

And so, Baba was no help at all. An absence of two decades had transformed the city of his youth from the relatively orderly metropolis it once was to a kind of ravenous urban sprawl that existed outside of its population and threatened, with its voracious appetite, to swallow it whole – roofless slums, unfinished buildings, palatial homes, skyscrapers, hovels and all. Sometimes I would amuse myself by imagining him emerge from the dry underbrush of the garden at C44 dressed in the khaki of a big-game hunter, binoculars and camera in a strangulating twist around his neck, guidebook in hand, renegotiating the once-familiar streets of his city like an awed and bewildered tourist. Only the streets that he marvelled at weren't just the congested thoroughfares that crisscrossed our neighbourhood and threatened one day – and not too far off in the future – to rise from beneath the foundations of our family home and tear through it, but a new society and a recycled form of politics that had completely changed the way things were done.

For example, in order to get from point A to point B, the city municipality had built overpasses and underpasses that cut through points in the metropolis notorious for traffic delays. These massive structures rose from the midst of crowded markets on squat, grey pylons, streaked with dust and graffiti even before being officially open to the public. Sometimes, in a quirk of city planning, it was possible for the eighth-floor window of an apartment building to be at eye level and within a few feet of speeding traffic, wild-haired children reaching across the divide to grab a mango from the back of a Suzuki. However, like the drab skeletons of long-extinct creatures, the flesh of these structures – the decorative tiling, the fancy railings – quickly fell away as substandard materials purchased from siphoned-off funds sank beneath the monstrous tonnage of car, bus, truck, and land cruiser. Often, decades-old ways of life reasserted themselves: the railings of the new bridge would sprout a vegetable bazaar or a super highway would serve as a cattle crossing.

Over the years, the city had also been given a fine coat of paint, its dusty and filigreed historic buildings tucked away behind modern structures, but no longer visible to the uninformed observer. The skyline was all but dominated by large shiny towers that mirrored the traffic on the lit overpasses that looped and whirled around them. Aggressive commercialism was rampant, with mega malls and cineplexes replacing the quieter entertainments of the past, like strolling by the sea front on a Friday evening, sipping Coke through a paper straw. Cell phone companies and an explosion of television networks with crews of cameramen, news anchors, reporters, actors, and interviewers of varying abilities and political agendas had changed the nature of human interaction. Baba looked on, bemused, as his seventy-four-year-old mother emailed a recipe to her eighty-eight-year-old cousin. It was as if, like a lottery winner, the city had shrugged off its dusty threadbare cloak and donned a glittering evening gown, hoping for revolution when the essentials underneath – the beating heart, the blood in the veins, the soul – remained the same.

These changes, however, were not out of the ordinary. What disturbed Baba most were the subtle – and not-so-subtle – differences in thought. This had begun before he left Pakistan in the late seventies and had continued to gather momentum despite the outwardly secular face of politics after Zia's rule.

One day, the four of us sat in the TV lounge, trying to while away the afternoon by *not* watching TV, which, according to the rules of the house, was out of bounds until Dada had seen the evening news. It was then that we overheard the following conversation:

'Do you remember Rizwana Hameed, Abbaji?' Baba asked reflectively, almost as if he had just thought of, and spoken, the name simultaneously without analysing the consequences.

'Who? Botswana? Botswana who?'

'Abbaji,' Baba coaxed patiently, 'could you please put on your hearing aids? Why'd we spend money on them when you hardly ever use them?'

'Bahee, they make a bloody ringing noise in my ears, so I can't hear anything anyway!' Dada grumbled and swore for another few seconds while struggling to push the tiny bean-shaped plastic aids into the wizened holes that were his ears, buried under the tufts of white hair that framed either side of his rosy balding scalp. He asked again: 'Who?'

'Rizwana. Rizwana Hameed. The girl who went to college with me. Her father was an old friend of yours from your days at Aligarh. Colonel Arif's daughter.'

'Yes, yes. What about her?'

'I saw her the other day at the Gymkhana. Apparently she never married?'

'No,' Dada's eyes, wrinkled round the edges like a sea turtle's, widened as he focused beyond his son's greying head to the quarter-slice of kitchen doorway visible from his favourite chair where a smudge of pink-and-yellow confirmed the lurking presence of an eavesdropper near the stove. It was Dadi, of course. (Little did he know that the four of us were also listening just a few feet away.) 'Why?' he continued. 'Were you impressed by her credentials?'

'What does she do?' Baba asked innocently.

'Haven't you seen her on television?'

'For God's sake! Am I the only breathing adult of marketable age in this city who is not on television these days? Apparently there's a channel for everything now, even for – ' Baba exclaimed, exasperated, leaving his sentence so deliciously open-ended that Raza couldn't help but whisper what sounded like 'mass debate' into Fatima's ear, another one of their adult jokes which Jamila and I didn't find funny at all but which seemed, nonetheless, relevant to the discussion.

'And no,' Baba could be heard continuing, 'I have not seen her on television. What remarkable talents does she have that she has to display them for all the world to see?'

'Beta,' Dada intoned solemnly, disapproval evident in the acid inflection of his voice as he explained without the slightest trace of irony that Rizwana was the host of a religious programme where scholars from various denominations came together to quibble over the finer points of religious jurisprudence.

Baba sat up in his chair. 'And you're telling me that you watch that show?'

Dada sheepishly replied, 'I want to see the other party proven wrong – as they mostly are, time and again.'

'Well,' Baba said emphatically. He struggled to compose himself before another outburst might lead him to say things he would later regret and then repeated 'well' as more of a final statement than a prelude to further discussion. With a parent's inscrutable talent for knowing when his children were near, he kept quiet for our sakes when he could have, perhaps, said more.

Baba and Dada could go on for hours on this subject and others, but my attention wandered as their voices continued to rise and fall. Politics and religion, culture and identity, race, ethnicity, and the like were far less important to me than the mission recently assigned. Being small of build and fairly invisible to the adults around me because of my age – too young to be singled out for inappropriate clothes or wild behaviour, for example, too old to be fed, bathed, or dressed – I was always the spy, the intelligence-gatherer, the snoop, slipping in and out of doors like a masked thief.

Climbing stairs and peering over banisters, overhearing conversations or simply observing tableaux – my relatives in various states of quiet self-reflection, unaware of being watched – I acquired a childish grasp of the mechanics of the household we had joined, the emotional and psychological underpinnings of the complicated kingdom over which Dada presided. For kingdom it was, with Baba as prince regent, younger princes Jamshaid and Shahbaz with their dukedoms, and Durdana Phupo the languishing princess, often seen looking at herself in the mirror above her bare dressing table, this piece of vanity a reminder of a short-lived but intense bloom that had long since passed.

The compound at C44 was arranged around a dry, grassy patch which served as a communal garden and was meant, when the units were originally constructed, to be a playground for all of the cousins – now mostly grown up – to romp around in. In fact, owing to the shortage of water and the indifference of the Mahmuds to gardening, this area, with its rusting swing dangling from a pole like a hanged piece of automotive machinery, was never used precisely because it was barren and uninviting, crisscrossed several times a day by the various inhabitants of the compound. Any effort to beautify it was in vain; it remained stubbornly unattractive for most of the year, rising to dubious glory after a rare monsoon deluge left dusty leaves and limp flowers dripping and briefly erect.

Baba, being the eldest, stood to inherit the main house, where his parents currently lived with his sister, Durdana Phupo, still single and caught up in a fantasy of her own making, leading a grown-up life from within the suffocating confines of her childhood bedroom, stale in its lace and little-girl pink. Her unit, which lay to the left of the main house, was occupied by our family, the other two units by our chachas – my father's younger brothers, Jamshaid and Shahbaz – their wives and children. These three units, identical in structure, were each painted in the favourite colour of their owner so that, from the height of say a coconut palm, or better still, a helicopter, our rectangular plot looked like a child's open paintbox, the beige of the main house offset by squares of pastel blue, yellow and pink.

Jamshaid Chacha and his family owned the blue house, where a quick reconnaissance on my part revealed an astounding surface clutter, a preponderance of bric-a-brac collected over the years on numerous trips abroad facilitated by Jamshaid Chacha's work with the national carrier. I had never seen so many souvenirs in one place. Their drawing room showcased a thimble and spoon collection, an assortment of figurines, and a series of mounted plaques that commemorated the cities they had seen or passed through, fleeting impressions consolidated in brass or wood and remembered forever as that, and only that – Paris for the Eiffel Tower, San Francisco for the Golden Gate, London for Big Ben. Although, as a family, they had spent most school holidays busily travelling the world, collecting visas like trophies at a time when that was still possible, their outlook remained myopic and parochial: other countries were always measured against the moral righteousness of Pakistani life, the natural beauty of its northern areas, the delicacy of its cuisine, the purity of its peoples' hearts. No country, as a consequence, ever matched up.

Like Jamshaid Chacha, whose beard had recently taken on a life of its own, trailing well below his shirt collar and threatening to lay claim to his chest and belly; his son, Aslam, a twenty-four-year-old graduate student at the prestigious City Business Institute, sported a small growth on his chin, its curly tendrils proclaiming his beard more pious than his father's for being virgin. Why, I wondered, did the men flaunt their hair and the women conceal theirs? Shahana Chachi and seventeen-year-old Parveen wore hijabs that matched their outfits, their faces pale against the shock of colour they chose in compensation, the swirls and floral motifs of their shalwar-kameezes visible from my bedroom window and across the garden. When I asked my equally-bearded Dada why this was so, he nearly choked on his chai, uncurling one of his arthritic index fingers and pointing me away in the direction of the kitchen where, presumably, someone would provide me with the answer I was seeking.

Our younger chacha, Shahbaz, present at the time, also spluttered over his tea, wiping his chin with a starched napkin and whispering, 'I'd be careful what I ask him so early in the morning. Not quite the time for religious controversy, hmm?' I had no idea what that meant. I only remember my breakfast plate of andaa-paratha at the end of the meal: a few lonely pieces of egg still floating on a lake of salt-water. As far as I knew, there was nothing wrong with asking questions. In fact, we were always encouraged to. Dada I could understand, but Shahbaz Chacha, too?

The fact was that I had developed a childish infatuation with Shahbaz Chacha and his young bride, Tania, whose sunny yellow house was a welcome refuge from the bleakness of our own. He was an architect, his wife a miniature painter, and together their living space was cluttered with all manner of captivating objects: one-haired brushes and jars of gold-leaf paint, rulers, reams of paper, bright spotlights under which sparkled miniaturized scenes of battle or love, or modern reinterpretations depicting Karachi and the sea, moored boats, tangled markets, smudged cityscapes – entire stories waiting to be unravelled by me as I lay on their sofa on hot summer afternoons. It was too much to bear that he, the master of all-that-was-cool, had scolded me.

That Jamshaid and Shahbaz, by virtue of being our chachas, were Baba's brothers was self-evident. In the first few weeks of our arrival, however, I had pieced together a theory about the Mahmud siblings who, being four, were an inverted image of ourselves – three boys and a girl. Dadi's partiality for the youngest, Shahbaz, wasn't strange at all; it was exactly as it ought to be, particularly as, inside-out, he was irresistibly attractive, his hair and his eyes, the warm tan of his skin, the loose relaxed motion of his limbs like a California surfer's, with the same carefree recklessness of confronting waves head-on. He was different from his other siblings though. It was true that my brother and sisters were not identical in appearance or personality either; Jamila was like our mother but in most ways looked nothing like us, while Raza, rare in most families, had drawn all of the good-looking genes to himself, leaving little for us girls except our 'wheatish' complexions and dark curls. Still, when standing side-by-side in a police line-up, we looked like siblings, something beneath the skin proclaiming our kinship like an alarm, the sameness of the blood conjoined to produce us rising scarlet in our veins. The three older Mahmuds had this shared quality, too, but Shahbaz Chacha none of it, and that's what was strange.

By the third week of our arrival in Pakistan, I had convinced myself that Shahbaz Chacha was not our uncle by blood, that he was either an impostor or a changeling, had been switched at birth, adopted or – and this terrified me most – was possessed by a demonic spirit. My siblings, it must be said, had a far more plausible theory although it smacked of scandal.

'So,' Lady M sat up, 'what you're saying is — Shahbaz is not an uncle?'

'Exactly how did you figure this out?' asked Dag, his lizard-like green-brown eyes flashing haughtily as he swatted a fly away from his sleeve.

'It's just a feeling…' I trailed off, suddenly unsure of myself and wondering if I had said something wrong. This theory of mine was supposed to have brought me importance in our world of make-believe, but it seemed to be doing the opposite. 'Look,' I retaliated, 'he just doesn't look like the other Mahmuds. And his personality — well, the only way I can describe it is "happy".'

Timmer howled in delight, and I felt somewhat vindicated.

'Do you think,' Dag began cautiously, aware of the shock-value of what he was about to say, 'do you think that he might be a love-child?'

'Whose?' Timmer gasped.

'Whose do you think?' Dag turned away from us to look out of the window and across at the beige house, its straggly shrubs and bougainvillea glowing fiercely in the unflinching light of an August afternoon.

CHAPTER 3

A week later, the four of us lay sprawled on our beds, naked toes wriggling pleasurably after a day spent in socks and sweaty PT shoes. Through my half-closed lids the world looked like a split watermelon. I felt comfortably full, drowsy. I imagined the grey fan above me an albatross (a word I had been forced to learn that very day from Fatima's obsessive recitation of Coleridge for English class), its expansive wings carrying with it a weight of air and sea, leaving my flesh damp and my nostrils full of the metallic scent of silver-tailed fish. This faintly acrid odour, like the residual smell of eggs on a poorly washed plate, overlay all the other scents (both good and bad) Karachi had to offer. It was a scent, I realized, that was slowly becoming a part of me, much the same way as the sharp, smoky Chicago air had earlier found its way into my blood.

'So then,' Fatima began abruptly, 'I'm standing there, just another uniform in the crowd, and everyone is singing the national anthem, right? I look to my right and to my left, and all I see are rows of uniforms – bent heads, bored heads, a few patriotic heads rising high above the rest – and from a distance, I see Raza, who's already made several friends (all girls, of course), whisper something into the ear of a pretty Pathan.'

'What?' I mumbled, opening my eyes to take in my siblings in the sunlight: Fatima sitting up with her knees pulled under her chin, Raza lying sprawled across two beds, arms folded against chest, and Jamila sitting on the edge of her bed, legs dangling.

Ignoring me, Fatima went on to describe the headmistress, with her narrow, high-cheeked face rising sepulchrally out of the black drapery of her gown, scanning the assembly and eventually coming to rest, with terrible purpose, on Fatima herself, her palms now wet against the polyester-cotton of her sticky shalwar.

'Why was she staring at you? What happened?' I asked.

Apparently, as the students neatly filed into the sandstone building and from there, in noisy knots, to their respective classes, Fatima had felt a hand on her shoulder and had allowed herself to be steered in the direction of the small closet that served as Mrs Altaf's office. An imposing glass-and-teak structure that housed a collection of dusty leather-bound tomes from the British Raj covered the entire back wall, its bars, slats, and reflective glass like the unwelcoming façade of a jailhouse. Fatima stood in front of the headmistress's desk, her uniform and skin one. Suddenly, the headmistress rasped:

'Fatima Mahmud.'

It had been a statement, not a question.

'Yes, ma'am.'

'Are you,' Mrs Altaf had demanded, 'one of those children?'

'I – I'm not sure what you mean,' began Fatima, her hand travelling upwards to the dark curl she tugged on when nervous.

'Oh, you know,' the headmistress had snapped meaningfully, a slow-spreading smile stretching her aged skin to the limits of its elasticity till her face looked like the x-ray of a skull. 'You know. You people come here full of yourselves, speak with a twang and expect all the world to admire you for what you don't know – your language, your religion, your roots, your culture, your—'

'But I have a brother!' Fatima had interrupted, exasperated at last that she was being singled out while Raza was safely in class, flanked, no doubt, by a posse of admirers.

'Don't interrupt me.' Mrs Altaf rose from her seat and turned away from Fatima to face the bookcase. 'Are you a Pakistani?'

'Yes,' Fatima had responded immediately, although it was something she had never considered before. Uncomfortable at last in her foreignness, her thoughts had turned, once again, to our mother.

'Do you know the words to the Star-Spangled Banner?'

'Yes. Well, maybe not all the—' Fatima had fumbled as her eyes strained to focus on the black of the headmistress's gown, now just a dark wave against the bookshelf. Mrs Altaf didn't bother to turn around as she issued this order:

'When I see you in assembly tomorrow morning, I expect you to know the words to your own national anthem. Our Quami Tarana. Understand?'

'So,' Fatima ended in a monotone, 'that was my day.'

'Poor you. Now if you'd spent half as much time meeting people as you do describing them, maybe you'd make a friend or two.'

Fatima's jaw dropped. 'Stop being a jerk, Raza.'

'I'm not a jerk. Just ask the girls.' Raza had, of course, made friends with all of the girls in the class, except a few of the truly pious ones who affected disinterest.

'And don't worry,' he smiled smugly as he raised a palm to display several scrawled telephone numbers. 'It won't be long before they come running, too. After all, which of their Lord's bounties will they deny? Definitely not this one.'

Our brother, we had to admit, was the kind of boy whom you could easily mistake for the princely angarkha-clad figure on horseback in a miniature painting: regal in bearing but with a trace of cruelty, his bow-and-arrow poised to shoot a beautiful long-legged gazelle. For though he was good-looking in the hyperbolic sense of fairytales, as sisters we knew him too well to think of him as completely pure of heart. He was the kind of boy we would want to protect our closest friends from, not because he was deliberately cruel but because his good looks sometimes made him reckless. Fatima was the worst affected. Because they were only a year apart, they had to share so much more than we did – the same school, the same teachers, sometimes even the same friends. An immaculate academic record was small solace to Fatima when even her best friend Clarice called from overseas to speak to her brother instead of herself.

'That reminds me,' Fatima began slowly, 'why does Clarice call you and not me?'

'Clarice who?'

Jamila interrupted, 'More. Tell more. Then what?'

It wasn't Fatima's fault that her storytelling had an element of the melodramatic. It was a characteristic that we all cultivated in our descriptions of the outer world for the benefit of Jamila, who looked forward to the afternoons and the brief time we had together before we dispersed for homework or chores. Her anticipation of these story sessions was paralleled only by her eagerness to play Lady M. Fatima stood up and did a comical imitation of Mrs Altaf, while Raza listed, in order of appearance (quite literally), the girls whom he had already captivated. I told her about my fifth-grade teacher, Mrs Nasim, who was only twenty-two-years-old and had just returned from the summer holidays with mehndied hands, a new silk-and-polyester wardrobe, and gold bangles, all of which made her incredibly glamorous to me. 'And,' I enthused, 'she's even teaching me the Quami Tarana!'

'What! You, too?' Fatima asked, bemused.

'Yes, and I have to translate it as well. So I know what I'm singing. I'll teach you.'

Fatima pushed her face into a pillow.

Jamila, whose hair had been oiled and tightly braided, had spent that tepid August morning in the kitchen. As part of Dadi's efforts to make her 'useful', she had been asked to help prepare dinner. It was an effort. There she stood, her stooped frame over a large steel bowl of shami kebab masala, frenziedly manipulating the soft brown mush in her clumsy fingers, while Dadi spun flawless discs like a magician and tossed them into a tray. Bewildered by the pressure, the need to place the hara masala exactly so in the middle of a perfect cup-shaped disc and then spin that disc in the palm to smoothen the cracks, Jamila at last rebelled in the only way she knew how: with slow deliberation, she rose from her chair, let out a yell, and overturned the entire bowl so that the mixture landed with a monumental splat on the freshly-Phenyled floor.

'Array, larki! What are you doing?' Dadi looked uneasily through the doorway to the TV room. 'Stupid girl! Is this any way to behave? Look at the waste!' She moved a step away from Jamila and the table, dramatically pulling her ears and muttering 'Tobah' so that when Baba finally walked in, looking sleepy and confused, he thought she had lost an earring. It only took a second to understand what had happened. Wrapping Jamila protectively under his arm, he escorted her out of the kitchen.

The three of us looked at each other and then at Jamila as she finished her story, conveyed through words, and where those failed, gesture and facial expression.

'I'm sorry, Jam,' Fatima said quietly, putting a hand on her shoulder.

There was a knock, and the four of us turned to the door. 'As-salaam alaikum.'

Fatima's face fell. The guttural Arabic inflection of the greeting could only mean one person, our cousin, Aslam, whose recent adoption of a more 'Islamic' pronunciation had rendered most of what he said unintelligible. For some reason he had taken to joining us in the afternoons on days that he didn't have class. I sat up and stared at him. My eyes focused on his beard. The last few times we had met, I had had to resist the urge to run my fingers through its curls. In that moment, I realized that this beard obsession had to stop.

'So,' he began somewhat awkwardly, 'How are you all liking school here? Made any friends?' He turned to Fatima but seemed to look through her and beyond.

'Friends and Fatima? Not a chance. She's a loner. A social misfit.'

Fatima glared at Raza but kept quiet.

'I can't believe that. Not her. She's such a decent girl.'

His defence of her only deepened Fatima's scowl. I noticed her sit up primly. 'I have homework,' she said abruptly and left the room, her dusty book bag over her shoulder.

'Aslam Baee,' (I still hadn't mastered 'bhai'), 'May I – may I touch your beard?'

Aslam obviously did not know how to respond to this.

'Ferzana, what's wrong with you?' Raza asked.

I realized that I had once again uttered the unacceptable and was hastily trying to apologize when Aslam backed out of the room and bounded down the stairs.

'Well, Chhoti,' Raza said drily, 'at least you got rid of him for us.'

At dinner that night, the entire family gathered at the main house. Dadi puttered around the table like a wind-up toy, directing Salima to bring more of this and less of that. Dozens of hands grabbed and passed, with fingers deep in bowls of salan and rice, while elbows and knees fought for space as if a giant multi-legged creature had taken over the underside of the dining table. I watched as the cook brought a balloon-like roti straight from the tawaa and placed it in front of Dada, who flattened it with one imperious slap of the hand.

'Didn't that hurt?' I asked, seeing the steam rise from the shredded remains of the bread, but no one heard me because I was sitting (despite protests) some distance away in the 'children's area', a resurrected bridge table set up for Jamila, our cousin Parveen and myself. Parveen raised an eyebrow. I could sense that she, too, resented the seating arrangements.

About halfway into the meal, I made another effort at conversation:

'Parveen, do you play pretend games?'

Parveen looked baffled. 'What kind of games?'

'You know, imagine that you're something other than what you are. Have you ever wished you were a boy?'

'No.'

'Or a bird?'

'No.'

'How about—'

'No, Ferzana, no.' Parveen didn't seem particularly communicative. I looked over at Jamila for support but she was busy with her spoon, holding it unsteadily between thumb and forefinger as she carried it to her open mouth. Slipping off my chair, I crawled in between the tangle of adult legs to a clear spot beneath the main table, grinning into the darkness and relishing my invisible participation in what was going on above. The table vibrated with the clatter and thump of dishes, cutlery and glass.

'Dekho, beta,' Dada was saying, 'I have nothing against them.'

'Come on, Abbaji,' Shahbaz Chacha protested, 'We haven't seen them in a decade. Don't you think that we owe it to the children? To Najma Baji?'

I stiffened. This was the first time in the month since our arrival that our mother's name had been mentioned by anyone other than our immediate family.

'Shahbaz,' Dada said, 'Not in front of the children. You'll upset them.'

Fatima and Raza's legs shifted beneath the table. I stared at Fatima's feet in their silver kohlapuris and focused intently on her slender toes. I convinced myself that I was absorbed by them, by the fact that they were slightly crooked, the third toe a little longer than the first, and that for the moment they were all that mattered.

Meanwhile, I waited for Baba to speak.

'Jamshaid Bhai,' Shahbaz Chacha continued, 'don't you agree?'

There was much coughing. 'Look, Shahbaz, it isn't for us to say what's right. Let Bhai Jan decide. Alamdar and Salaar are his in-laws.'

Still no response from Baba. Swivelling on my bottom, I examined his dark-trousered legs, his toes wrapped tight in maroon Peshawari sandals. His feet looked like two swaddled babes, I thought, but they provided no clue as to what was going on in his head. Sorry for Baba, I hugged his knees.

Within an instant, everything changed. It felt as if the table had come crashing down on my head, my ears ringing with the brittle snap of breaking glass and plate. A magician's trick gone wrong, the surface contents pulled along with the cloth, I watched everything fall, the spinning forks, the streaked plates, the deeply stained red-and-blue ajrak napkins, even a clear stream of Ruh-e-Afza (Dada was partial to the sugary drink) falling in slow motion like a shard of ruby-coloured glass. The world is falling, I thought, the world is falling, and as if in counterpoint to my refrain, I could hear the repetitive rise and fall of two syllables, hysterically exaggerated in the voice of Durdana Phupo:

'Choo-haa! Choo-haa!'

A mouse? I only experienced an instant of pure terror before I felt myself being shaken. A pair of firm hands gripped me by the shoulders and pulled me out from underneath the table. I squinted in the bright yellow light and tried to locate my siblings. I realized with relief that they were near, that I could feel the warmth of their protective hands, one on my knee, the other at my shoulder, a third by my feet.

'Tumhari larkiyaan paagal hain, kya? Are your daughters crazy?' Dada demanded, his voice raised in anger.

'That's enough, Abbaji.' Baba finally spoke, but by now I wished he hadn't. As I turned around and looked up at him, I realized with a start that he seemed a decade older, his mild features distorted with uncharacteristically strong emotion. I placed my hands on his forehead and pushed the flesh away in an attempt to smoothen the furrows, but with an abrupt jerk of the arm, he threw me off and walked out of the room.

CHAPTER 4

Amma and Baba had met several years before they were grudgingly allowed to marry. (Or at least that is what we had been told.) In 1977, Baba travelled with a group of friends from the coastal city of Karachi northwards by train and by bus to Swat, where the moustachioed Imran, a fellow student, had his family home in Mingora. Imran, like Baba, was completing his B.Com. that year and planned to return to Swat to manage the Pine Cone Inn, a ramshackle guesthouse that his father owned in nearby Kalam. Presenting it as a reconnoitering expedition, a 'case study' for his fellow classmates to solve, Imran persuaded his father to allow the six of them to spend a few weeks at the Inn and use their recently acquired knowledge of business models to turn it into a profitable enterprise.

Predictably, none of that happened. As soon as they reached Kalam and settled into the Pine Cone, a dusty, sky-blue eight-passenger minivan groaned its way up from Miandam, halted at the Mountain View, and spewed out a botany professor, six female students, and a skinny-legged chaperone in churidar-pyjama universally known as

'Baji'. The Mountain View was across the Swat River and clearly visible from the upper windows of the Pine Cone. The day the minivan disgorged its passengers, Baba was on the roof of his friend's hotel, the flares of his bell-bottoms flapping in the cool mountain breeze as he smoked a hand-rolled cigarette and tried to imagine what life after graduation meant – a scholarship to the US, perhaps, which was what he wanted, or settling in, as was Imran, to the humdrum of local small-time business. There was a commotion down below as the girls disembarked and immediately ran this way and that oohing-and-aahing at the contrast of jagged mountain and azure sky, the icy blue whiteness of the swiftly-flowing river, the clusters of frail huts leaning against each other for support against the gusty wind. Baji shrieked in protest, her arms flailing like shafts of sugar cane as she called out to them in vain. Amused, Baba watched from above and across the river while the girls scattered like a bunch of brightly-coloured marbles, his now-forgotten cigarette smoldering beneath a Bata loafer.

All of a sudden, one of the girls, a petite long-haired beauty (clearly our heroine), turned to look up and caught Baba staring. With a disdainful toss of the head, she motioned for the others to follow and ran into the hotel. Within seconds, they had all vanished. Baba looked around and was embarrassed to find that, like himself, the valley's entire male population was perched, poised, or angled sniper-style to witness these six young women entranced by Swat's natural beauty.

The remaining tale is, like most love stories, uninteresting. They met, perhaps, by accident at one of the shops that lined the one narrow road that led through the tiny village upwards into the mountains, haggling over the same dark shawl, or fighting over the last handful of dry fruits. They might have bumped into each other in a shadowy corner of the deeply fragrant forest that lay behind the Pine Cone, Amma busy over a rare plant while Baba admired her bent figure, the graceful curve of her neck, exposed by the upsweep of her thick black hair. Who is to say that there might not have been a downpour, the exchange of wet clothing for sheets, and a provocative dance around a fire, Bollywood-style? Whatever the details, there must have been sulks and quarrels and tender moments, too, promises made and broken, then made again beneath a pendulous alpine moon and, eventually, the crowning moment – a kiss.

The end. Or the beginning. For me, it was usually the end. The limits of my imagination could go no further into the grown-up world of intimacy that belonged to my parents before I was born. The 'Swat Affair' was, by far, the most romantic of the stories I had invented to explain my existence and that of my brother and sisters, embellished with ever greater detail over the years as my imagination, always outstripping my years, dictated. After all, Baba and Amma meeting, marrying and moving to America was all to forward one cause: procreation. In other words, *us*. 'Jab main pehda hui', or my birth, was a seminal event in my ten-year-old life. That and the death of our mother.

But the 'Swat Affair' was only one of many possibilities. Another of my favourites involved Baba as a young placard-wielding student protester, Amma his revolutionary side-kick. His curly dishevelled hair rising Afro-like above the crowd, I saw him in a wide-collared snug-fitting polyester shirt in psychedelic contrast to sensible beige trousers, while Amma, in pastel-pink mini-kurta and bell-bottomed shalwar, carried a notebook and pencil, recording injustices against the student community for an underground newspaper. What they were protesting against or for was not immediately clear to me – changes in educational policy, solidarity with left-wingers (as Fatima suggested, whatever that meant) – but it usually involved them in a crowd, sometimes at the forefront being lathi-ed or behind a podium addressing a rapt audience. Somewhere along the way, in between a peaceful rally and a hunger strike, an accidental touch in the semi-darkness of the newspaper's inner office may have ignited other, more passionate, feelings...

'Their pure love a perfect example of the union of the personal and the political,' Fatima interrupted, waving her arms theatrically. 'Ferzana, have you been borrowing Durdana Phupo's Mills & Boons? You know Baba told you not to read them.' (I had this habit of reading books that were expressly forbidden. I found them irresistible.)

I frowned in mid-sentence. 'I'm telling a serious story. What do baboons have to do with it?'

'Never mind.'

'Come to think of it, Fatima,' Raza said, 'it's not so far-fetched. I'm sure Amma would've approved of this version,

Chhoti. It's one that does justice to her dad.' Our Nana was a prominent left-wing radical, the editor of a controversial newspaper published in the 1950s, who had been jailed repeatedly for publishing anti-government material. Sadly, it was all we knew about him.

'Thank you,' I beamed, turning to Jamila, who was still waiting for the next instalment. 'There is,' I hesitated, somewhat dampened by Fatima's negativity, 'another version that I rather liked.'

Jamila nodded in encouragement.

It was Chaand Raat. A sliver of shiny moon gleamed from behind the heavy clouds above Karachi and its stormy sea coast. Amma's brothers smuggled her out of the house and into their rusty 1968 Toyota Corolla to drive through the market, try on bangles, and see the lights, which flickered tremulously on wires that swung jauntily in the breeze. Crowds roamed the streets of Saddar, mostly men, some burka-clad women, a few young girls dressed in the fashion of the times (churidars or bell-bottoms and short kurtas), presenting slender wrists to shopkeepers whose tables gleamed with bangles in an array of extraordinary colours. Amma tried on several before choosing a set of light pink ones, her thin wrists effortlessly passing through the hooped glass, her arms iridescent with silver dust. An hour passed in making small purchases (a mehndi cone, new suits for each of them), time enough to take in the noise and the lights, and to observe the eager acquisitiveness of shoppers, their self-indulgence hard-won after a month of fasting. To celebrate further, they left the glowing market behind in their reconstituted car, painstakingly put together out of miscellaneous spare parts, and crossed the main road, taking a right at the large roundabout where the cinema was located.

As they settled into the dusty maroon seats of the Novelty and sipped green Pakola through paper straws, Salaar suddenly let out a whoop of excitement, jumped to his feet, and began waving his arms. Amma watched as arms were raised in greeting from the opposite end of the theatre, followed by hoots and howls, and the eventual appearance, seconds later, of a breathless young man in partially wet clothing.

'I see you got caught in the downpour earlier this evening!' Salaar exclaimed, embracing his friend and then turning to Alamdar and Amma. Apologetically, he continued, 'Wait, let me introduce you. This is the friend I was talking about – the one who helped me with the car when it broke down. Aftab, meet my brother Alamdar and my sister Najma.'

Baba nodded at Alamdar and ignored Amma until he was comfortably settled in the seat next to her. Then, it all happened at once: the lights dimming, followed by the magnified image of uniformed schoolgirls singing the national anthem to a hooting crowd, the heraldic trumpet of a Hollywood opening, and the flash of a wrist, a simple girlish wrist in the half-light of the projector's beam, the blinding shimmer of bangles. When next he turned to look, it was not her wrist, but Amma herself who stared back at him, her kohled eyes shining in the darkness like a cat's. They sat side by side as images flickered on-screen and characters' lives unfolded beneath the scrutiny and pressure of the lense, voices rose and fell in orchestrated despair, an entire community's troubles neatly resolved at the end of a customary two-hour delay. Once the film was over and the appropriate catharsis reached, everyone filed slowly out of the theatre. Amma and her brothers drove away in their rusty blue Corolla. Baba stood for a long time on the pavement in front of the theatre, puffing on a cigarette, its smoke rising snake-like into the darkness.

'A filmi beginning,' said Fatima sarcastically.

'I thought it was rather good.'

'Ferzana, you know how you can find out how they met once and for all?' Raza called from the bed by the window.

'How?' I asked.

'Go. Ask. Baba. Ha. Ha.'

I could tell by his voice that he was being patronizing.

It was obvious to the others that that was the easiest way to put a stop to my conjecturing, but I was scared to ask. After the incident at the dining table, Baba had changed. I overheard Dada talking to Dadi and our uncles about a suspected 'breakdown'. Like a car, only worse, was how Raza later explained it to me. Apparently, it was not uncommon for human beings to stop functioning. It was a little like a wind-up doll that loses its animation once its internal springs work out their tautness. No, it wasn't death, Raza hastily reassured me, just a breakdown of the system that makes us happy and productive (which was close enough to death in my mind). Whatever it was, it was worrying, and I had spent the last few days making up stories in order to avoid the inevitable meeting with him. This human wreck, I felt, was my fault, but I knew I wasn't up to the task of putting him back together even though, as my father, I wanted him whole.

My strategy, as a consequence, was to avoid him. After a few days of some strenuous engineering on my part, involving tiptoeing, wall-hugging, and (in one instance), a cloak of invisibility, I realized it simply did not matter. Even when Baba was there, eyes half-closed, sitting at the breakfast table, his tousled head slumped over one hand, the other hand around his cup of chai, his face betrayed an absence. There was no life in him. The moment I realized this – and it was a specific moment – I panicked.

It didn't help that around the same time Amma was officially banned from household conversation. My fault, again. My unchecked habit of asking questions brought me eventually (as it always did) to Baba's armchair, once a bloated American specimen, now a battered cane one placed squarely in the sun. Baba had recently taken to sitting outdoors for hours on end, even in the sweltering heat, and could be seen from the courtyard-facing windows of all four units, a pathetic figure in his white kurta-pyjama. I studied him for a few seconds, imagining his expressionless face and limp body as a child's scattered puzzle that had to be put back together again.

'Baba,' I began tentatively, resting my chin on the cool skin of his forearm, 'I was just wondering…'

'Wonder,' Baba spoke softly, 'don't forget to wonder.'

I stopped in mid-sentence. A little confused but on the whole encouraged by this gentle interruption, I blurted out:

'Baba, where did you and Amma meet for the first time? Well, the others…' I continued, alarmed as I noticed his face alter, 'the others said I should ask you.'

I could hear a lone crow cawing from somewhere above my head, beyond the concrete roofs of C44 and farther still, into the bluish haze that haloed Karachi.

Baba didn't respond at once. He didn't have to. His face passed through a series of conflicting moods, settling back eventually into the unnerving blankness of recent days.

I waited patiently, hoping I would be rewarded by confirmation of one of my imagined scenarios. Swat, a political rally, on the set of a film (neither were actors, but who knew?), a railway station in the hills… A muffled sound brought me out of my reverie. By the time I realized that Baba was speaking to me, Dada had already come up from behind, pulled me far enough away and, stooping over me so that I couldn't see my father, warned sternly, 'Ferzana, do not speak of her in front of him – or at all.'

It was only later, while I stared at myself in the rusty mirror above our bathroom sink, that I remembered Baba's one-word answer.

It turned out, for all my imagining, that our parents met in a *library*. A library of all places!

'So, Little Furry, what have you found out about Shahbaz? Birth certificate? DNA results? Anything concrete about his origins?' demanded Lady M. 'If we can prove that he was born of a scandalous union, it would tear this precious, tight-

knit family apart and mean we could make good our escape.'
The four of us sat in the dark, a lone candle in a chipped
china plate feverishly fighting its own demise at the centre
of our circle.

'How am I supposed to—' I asked, looking blankly at one
face after another.

Fatima hissed, 'Ferzana, it's a game. Play along, okay?'
Her shadow clawed its way across the opposite wall as she
pulled herself up and glared at me.

'Lady M,' I cleared my throat, 'my investigations have
yielded nothing so far, but I hope in time to be able to extort
information from a secret source within C44.'

'There are no secrets among us,' Dag intoned solemnly.
'Who is the informer?'

I quickly ran through the possibilities in my mind: Dada
(definite no), Baba (definite no; questionable mental state),
Dadi and Durdana Phupo (unpredictable and, therefore,
dangerous), Jamshaid Chacha and his shrouded wife (lacking
imagination), Parveen, Aslam ... Aslam. 'The gentleman
in question,' I began cautiously, 'is someone whom I am
confident of being able to... bully.' I said the last word with
impressive force, indicating that I knew perfectly well what
it meant.

'And his name?' asked Lady M with an impatient flick of
her wrist. The candle, drawing its last breath in a blaze of
wax, left us in complete darkness.

'He is the Keeper of Photographs,' I shouted above the
rattle of the overused generator, which someone outside
had suddenly yanked into action. Early on, I had realized

that the Mahmud clan, headed by Dada, was obsessively concerned with recording its own history. In addition to Dada's meticulously-drawn family tree, an extensive photo library was kept under lock and key in the main unit. The only person who had access to this room was our cousin Aslam.

'A name please,' Lady M insisted.

'Sloth. His code name is Sloth. And I have reason to suspect that he is hostile to my investigation. I will have to use all my powers to get him to cooperate.'

Timmer suddenly laughed. 'Sloth. That can only be one man. Get it out of him, Little Furry. Spare no torture.'

CHAPTER 5

By the time I met Salaar and Alamdar Hussain, they were almost old men to my ten-year-old self, at least in their late forties, if not early fifties. I was told that they had once made an historic journey to the United States in the late summer of 1986. Because that was several years before my birth, I felt the need to investigate. I ended up discovering three or four partially discoloured Polaroids in a box of Amma's keepsakes. The first of these showed the two brothers, their wavy hair practically to their shoulders, their beards unruly, one sporting an ill-fitting spandex jogging suit (borrowed from Baba, no doubt), the other in a white kurta-pyjama, standing in front of our fireplace in Chicago. In the second, they stood on either side of a laughing Amma, her body bent under the weight of their burly arms as they humorously posed in front of a billboard advertising Miller Lite. The third showed each of them proudly displaying a runny-nosed toddler – Salaar with two-year-old Fatima in pigtails, Alamdar with a wailing bare-bottomed Raza.

I took out my magnifying glass and examined the pictures further, trying to look beyond the watermarks and the predigital photography to what these unknown uncles of mine were like in their prime. Although five years apart in age, they were virtually identical. Salaar, the older one, was heavier around the face and belly, his taste in clothing similar to Baba's (hence the borrowed jogging suit). That was where the similarity ended, however. Unlike Baba, who was gentle and retiring, Salaar was goodnaturedly ferocious, like the trained bear who, with his master, had once been shooed from our gate by Anwar Chacha. My younger mamu, with his wild, broad-shouldered look, had the physique of a village pahlwan. Resembling the dark hero of a pulp romance, he nursed an unmentionable sorrow, giving him an endearing neediness that offset his physical strength.

It was peculiar, I thought, that these two men had never married. From what I had gleaned from Dadi and Durdana Phupo (eavesdropping, of course), Pakistani men who didn't marry were most certainly deviant in some way, and it worried me that my uncles might be thought so. They were my mother's brothers: I needed them to be perfect. I thought of the man I once overheard Dadi and Durdana Phupo discussing in whispers, the son of an old neighbor, who had begun wearing silks during the day and in whose bedroom a cache of cosmetics had been discovered. Men and make-up just didn't go together, they whispered to each other in shocked tones, although their smiles indicated that there was at least some part of this story that they found amusing.

My mamus had remained celibate for noble reasons, I decided peremptorily, putting it down to one of those things that I was too young to understand and didn't much care to investigate. (Like the fact that Fatima and, lately, even Jamila, had begun smuggling brown paper packets into the bathroom.)

Salaar and Alamdar's one and only foray outside of the subcontinent would remain a reference point in all of their conversations. In the month that they had spent in the United States, they had gathered enough anecdotes to satiate their appetite for foreign travel. Their woes began at customs and immigration. It weighed heavy on Alamdar that they would be away from Karachi during Muharram, even though Amma reminded them that there were majlis in Chicago. When Salaar wasn't looking, Alamdar secreted a dagger and a couple of other complicated devices of self-flagellation among his shirts and underwear. The discovery of these weapons led to an intense two-hour-long interview with a US Immigration Officer who couldn't, for the life of him, understand how these weapons were used for religious worship. Alamdar, in his most persuasive English, clarified, 'Sir, I use these daggers to beat myself up.'

This and other tales were gradually revealed to us over a period of several years after that initial meeting, which took place on a Saturday afternoon during the first September of our return.

'Now look, Chhoti,' Shahbaz Chacha cautioned, as he held my hand and guided me across the courtyard towards his unit, 'this is a big secret. Do you understand what that means? You're not to tell anyone about this.'

I frowned. 'But why do we have to keep it secret?' I asked, ignoring his patronizing tone.

'There are reasons. You'll understand when you're older. And it won't always be like this. It's still early days.'

'Early days?'

'Baba, you all – you're all upset, of course, over your mother's ...' he stuttered, his grip on my hand loosening as he looked up at the blank sky for assistance, from Allah, I wondered, or from Amma herself, whom I always imagined floating just above our heads. None, of course, was forthcoming. Shahbaz Chacha was no better than the rest, I thought bitterly. He was just like all of the other cowardly grown-ups we had met at the Imam Bargah in Chicago or the polite strangers on the airplane who had asked us why we were moving. Or like the relatives who had gathered us into their arms when they received us at the airport in Karachi but couldn't bring themselves to mention our mother's name.

'Death?' I said coolly, completing his sentence and looking up at him in time to catch him falter, his swinging surfer's gait at once slower, more deliberate. I realized with a pang that I had hurt him, but before I could say anything, we had reached his unit. Mumbling an awkward yes, he nudged me into the drawing room where Fatima, Raza, and Jamila sat stiffly on the takht, immobile like the stylized figures in the miniature painting above their heads. They gasped as I stumbled into the room.

'Ferzana!' wailed Fatima, pointing an accusing index finger at my person.

I glanced down at my clothes. I must have spilled something on the dress Fatima had changed me into because there was a strawberry-shaped smudge above the sash. I pressed my thumb gingerly into the stain on my stomach and brought it up to my nose. It smelt like lunch.

Tania Chachi wrapped her sari pallu tightly around her shoulders as she ran towards me, scooped me up, and was rushing me into the powder room when the front door bell set everyone fidgeting.

'They're here!' she whispered nervously as she tinkered with the tap above the sink until a thin trickle of water made its way down the edge of the basin. Using this and a cake of soap, she rubbed the stain on my dress until it had almost disappeared. I tried to stand still as she worked, but my instinct for espionage made it impossible for me not to strain, balancing on one foot as I stretched my body as far as it would go in order to catch a few words of the exchange, rising steadily in pitch, that was taking place in the next room. Either there was a crisis, or my mamus were fond of shouting.

It was, I was soon to realize, the latter.

I entered the drawing room behind Tania Chachi, trying to wrap myself up in her sari pallu so that no one could see me. Unfortunately, chiffon, even the darker variety, was not good camouflage material. For a second I saw light, and then my face was pressed up against damp cloth, so close that I could almost distinguish the warp and weft of it, my eyes straining against blindness to concentrate on the magnified grain, the pattern of the weave. Suddenly, I took a deep breath and then fell limp, as if someone had placed a chloroformed rag to my face. That scent. It was unmistakeable.

Amma was in the room.

When I pulled myself away from their joint embrace, I knew the two men before me. They were older than in the photographs, perhaps a little heavier, now beardless, their immaculately pressed trousers belted high on their waists, their shirts damp around the collar and the chest, both staring at me like I was a creature out of a storybook. My eyes widened as I saw Alamdar suddenly raise an aqeeq-adorned hand to his chest and beat wildly at it while moaning something unintelligible, his face twisting spasmodically as he fought to master his grief.

Salaar glared at his brother and growled, 'You'll scare the children! Get a grip, aymakh.' He crouched till he was at eye-level and then opened his arms wide to me. I fell into them a second time, looking over his shoulders at my three siblings, standing in an awkward line before the takht, their expressions somewhere between embarrassment and disbelief, their adolescence for once, I thought smugly, a disadvantage to them. I burrowed deeper into my mamu's embrace like a small animal in search of a permanent nesting place. I knew I liked this man. He was, after all, my mother's brother.

Alamdar used a crisp shirt sleeve to wipe his wet face, took a deep breath, and settled sheepishly into a nearby chair, folding his large body into its frame in an attempt to disappear.

'And Aftab? My friend? Where is he?' Salaar began, looking over my head to Shahbaz Chacha, perched on the arm of an adjoining chair, staring distractedly at a pale chhipkali that had managed to slip in between the mosquito screen and the half-open window to escape the heat of the wilting garden.

'Salaar Bhai, we thought it best that he didn't know – he's ... upset.'

'Haan, of course. Of course, he's upset. Who wouldn't be? He lost his wife,' said Salaar. 'But I can't understand why we haven't seen him since his return to Karachi.' After a moment of silence, he continued haltingly, 'We did what we could for Najma. We followed our own traditions. We weren't sure whether anyone here believed in marking her death,' his voice broke, 'the way that we're accustomed to.'

'We're not allowed to talk about Amma here,' I blurted out.

'Ferzana!' Shahbaz Chacha snapped angrily, glaring at me with meaning, as if I had done something truly terrible. Suddenly everything I loved about him – his honey-gold looks and casual manner, the way he swiftly lifted me up, up, up till I screamed in the sunlight and pulled at the elephantine leaves of the stunted coconut palms – was obscured by this complicated development in our relationship; the third time, in fact, he had disappointed me since our arrival. Perhaps, I thought nastily to myself, he wasn't a changeling. The Mahmud traits had been in him all along, temporarily obscured by a few good-looking genes. My eyes began to burn. I could feel my heart through the thin cotton of my summer dress and clutched at it as if it would betray me.

There was a moment of awkwardness as we all looked at each other – Jamila at Salaar, Alamdar at Shahbaz, Fatima at Raza, and I, who couldn't see anything except a blur of water and colour, squeezed my eyes shut so that I, too, could disappear.

And then, as the perfect antidote to the moment, something magical, something phantasmagoric happened when I opened my eyes next:

The tea trolley was rolled in.

One of the charms of our return to Pakistan was our introduction to this fantastic piece of mobile drawing room furniture, which, whenever it made an appearance, was laden with lemon tarts, samosas, fruit chaat, sandwiches, pakoras, and an ever-changing variety of treats that instantly demanded that everyone's complete attention be focused on the all-important task of consumption. In this instance, Tania Chachi's beatific smile as she gracefully poured tea, distributed cups and saucers, offered snacks, passed spoons, forks and plates and insisted on seconds reminded us that in every social exchange in Pakistan the human animal had a specific function: to eat, of course.

Within twenty minutes, the room had changed. The bold, uncompromising colours of Tania Chachi's décor had softened with the light of early evening, and people sat in quiet clusters, talking. The paintings, too, had shifted, their sharp lines and jewelled tones now smudged, the scenes they depicted fluid and relaxed, a stylized face suddenly animated by a stray shaft of light. I watched, fascinated, as a scene from one of the paintings, transformed by a trick of light and shadow, appeared to swirl and dance, the old Sufi mystics it depicted pirouetting like wobbly bearded ballerinas. One of these wizened old creatures, dressed in loose white robes and a lopsided turban, paused to wink at me slyly before resuming his spinning, his skirt floating around him like a parachute.

'Look, Jamila,' I pointed, 'see those dancing men?'

My sister looked at the painting and nodded. It was difficult to say whether or not she could see what I saw, but we usually had a way of understanding each other. A few seconds later, she laughed and clapped her hands. Maybe that sly old spinner had paused in his heavenly revels to wink at her as well.

I leaned back on the takht till my head rested on a cushion and stared at the high ceiling with its peeling paint and spidery cracks. I traced one of the wiggly lines with my finger in the air when I spotted the pale green chhipkali again, this time near the curtains directly above me. My skin goose-pimpled as our eyes locked.

Suddenly I heard Fatima's voice near my ear whispering: 'Ferzana, get up. We can see your panties.'

I sat bolt upright. For a few seconds I was too mortified to think. Then, very slowly, I surveyed the room. Raza was engrossed in explaining the rules of American football to Salaar, who kept confusing it with soccer, maintaining all the while that cricket was, by far, the more gentlemanly sport. Fatima and Tania were now huddled over their tea cups on the yellow settee, joined at the head and knees, laughing over a whispered joke. Shahbaz, with his arm around Jamila, stood near the trolley dropping cocktail-sized lemon tarts into her mouth. Alamdar looked on, smiling into his plate, which was heaped with sandwiches and chilli sauce. And there, through the window directly opposite me, the champa bush had grown a beard. I was safe; no one, other than Fatima, had seen my frilly underwear.

All of a sudden, I jumped to my feet and rushed towards the window. Without a word of explanation to the others, I ran out of the drawing room and through the screen door that led out into the garden. I gasped as the setting sun slapped me hard on the face. Looking up at the sky and threatening it with a clenched fist, I scrambled towards the bushes on the left and was just in time to see a flash of white moving across the lawn. I was, I reminded myself, no longer an ordinary human child with an ordinary human child's limitations. Gone was the fragile, undeveloped body, the credulous mind. With incredible speed and stealth, gathering momentum as I sprinted, I morphed into a sleek animal of prey in pursuit of my target.

Across the courtyard, through the front door, and up the stairs. There was the door, its brass handle gleaming in the darkness. I opened it without a knock. I could see him at his desk, his back towards me, bent over a book, the light from his reading lamp barely there as the last rays of the setting sun filtered in through the curtains. I grabbed his head from behind.

'Array, array! What's going on? Stop pulling my hair!' he howled as he swivelled to face me. 'Here I am studying and you come at me like a screaming churail? You little witch!'

'No. I am not a witch, Sloth.'

'Sloth?' His face was blank. 'What's that?'

'What were you doing outside the window? Spying?'

'What're you talking about?'

'I saw you spying on our secret family reunion.'

The Sloth's eyes narrowed. 'So it was them? Your mother's brothers?'

I had given away too much. Stupid, stupid me.

'What if Dada were to find out? Or your Baba? Does he know?' The Sloth stood up so that he was at least two feet above me, the edge of his curly beard brushing the top of my head. 'That kind of information could push your abba jan over the edge, hmm?'

'You won't breathe a word, understand?' I slipped into my skin again, pulling myself up. I could feel my sinews tighten, the muscles of my arms and legs flex, and my courage return. Suddenly I became someone else, someone invincible. 'Don't you dare tell anyone,' said Little Furry.

'Not that easy, Chhoti,' the Sloth whispered, as he lifted me up so that we were at eye level. I raised my knees and placed my black Mary-Janed feet on his hips to lever myself out of his grip, but it was no use: he was stronger than me.

CHAPTER 6

Closing my eyes, I felt the wet wind lick my ear. I was flying. My winged ship was over the city of Karachi, now cruising low over Kemari, its boats and fishing vessels and colossal tanks sitting stolidly in dark, oily water, rocking imperceptibly as the breeze rippled the sea. I breathed deeply and felt like I was inhaling fish, the kind that float in ocean water, big, glassy-eyed, silver-finned or rainbow-coloured, the bold kind that swim right up to you and stare you in the face. Again, a gust of warm wet finny air, and my hair, open now, floated behind me like seaweed, or like the legs and antennae of a waterborne shrimp. I knew, when home, I'd stick my tongue out, curl a strand of hair around my finger, and put it in my mouth and taste salt. That was the way my new city was.

Past Kemari and now through Mai Kolachi and across the salt flats to the row of shops that curved past you as you raced, their tempting signs beckoning empty stomachs to nihari, tikka, haleem, pizza, donuts, hunter beef, chaat, and early morning nashtas of aloo-poori. The signs, all a blur, one giant neon board proclaiming, like Pinocchio in the

Land of Toys, the delights of gorging and excess. As this
area receded beyond the curve with the lonely beachfront
park to the right, I felt the wind underneath my winged
ship raise me higher and higher till I was racing through
wet clouds, my face damp with yet-to-fall rain. There was a
knocking. Suddenly, I lost control and felt my ship swoop
to the left, then to the right, then down, down, down in a
stomach-upheaving descent till – there! – my feet skimmed
the surface of the sea. I opened my eyes:

Earthly traffic lights and regular, hum drum, on-the-way-
to-school early morning sounds. The knocking that had
pulled me out of my imaginings was caused by a small-fisted
little girl draped in an oversized grey chador, her yellowing
hair haloing a perfect chocolate-brown face.

'Ferzana,' Fatima said, 'don't look.'

I couldn't help it. I had to. She was probably the same age
as I was. I sat up and stared harder. She opened her fist and
revealed a pink palm like a quietly blooming lily opening its
petals to the sun.

'What does she want? Shake hands?' I asked through the
closed window, nodding my head and smiling.

With an irritated flip of her hand, she pulled her chador
over her mouth and made a lewd gesture at my receding face,
which I had now, in brazen defiance of Fatima's warnings,
pressed right against the window pane.

Fatima and Raza laughed. Khyber, the driver, who had
been watching my exchange with the little girl through the
rear view mirror, chuckled into his bushy mustache as he
turned into the school gate.

'I'm no expert,' Raza said, 'but I think she gave you the equivalent of the finger.'

Before I could ask what that was, we were already scrambling out of the car, Raza's heavy hand on my back propelling me to the primary section, where glamorous Mrs Nasim was showing off her new raw-silk outfit to a group of middle-aged teachers and to Joseph Sir, who taught chemistry in the senior school and who was standing to one side looking on appreciatively. As we walked towards them, I noticed with surprise that our arrival was causing quite a stir: the female teachers began to pull themselves up as if reporting for active duty; stomachs were sucked in, chests thrust out, and a desperate few tried unsuccessfully to rein in their ample buttocks. A nervous hand flew upwards to settle a stray hair. Mrs Nasim's voice trailed off as she saw us approaching. She emerged from the centre of the circle like a self-conscious starlet, bracelets and anklets and lockets tinkling with each mincing step. Simpering, she took my hand from Raza's and led me into the classroom, disdainfully sidestepping a few latecomers who were dragging their school bags in the dust, mere underlings to my queenliness.

On the way home from school, I busied myself by looking at my Urdu textbook, starting from the end and reading backwards. When I reached the letter that looked like a fat comma with two beady eyes, I tried to guess the word from the illustration next to it. It was a realistic rendition of a gaunt old man wearing a peaked cap on his head, his torso and shoulders stiff beneath a buttoned grey shirt that rose as high as a turtleneck. This was a difficult one. I suddenly made the connection, though, and exclaimed in excitement as I pointed to the word: 'Zayeef!' Finally, I thought with elation, these symbols were starting to make sense.

Fatima, who had been staring out of the window, turned to look. 'Hmm … No, Chhoti, that's not zayeef. Look, it begins with a different letter,' and she placed her finger on the fat comma. 'This is the Quaid-i-Azam, the person who founded Pakistan, and this,' she flipped a page or two, 'this old man illustrates the word "zayeef" which means old.'

'But the Quaid is old, too, right?'

'Was old. He's dead now.'

It took me a while to digest this. He was dead. So was Amma. Did that mean that they were in one and the same place? I felt scared for my mother if she had to live in the same house as this gaunt, stern-looking man. Suddenly, I realized that his picture was everywhere, on television (when we were allowed to see it), and even hanging above Mrs Nasim's desk in our classroom. Perhaps it wasn't such a bad thing for Amma to be with him. All things considered, he seemed like somebody who was likely to receive preferential treatment.

It was frustrating, though, that these symbols, which should have had some meaning for me by now, were just as perplexing as they were when I first started my lessons. I had tried to memorize the letter shapes by likening them to objects – the ح looked like Fred Flintstone's nose, the ط like a single-leafed stem, the ک like a hockey stick, ل a candy cane. I always managed to remember ں because it reminded me of something rude that I wasn't allowed to say, point to, or even remotely suggest in company, although in private I teased my sisters mercilessly about their 'swollen' appendages. I looked down at my beautiful flat chest and felt happy.

Just as I peered out of the window to see if I could recognize any Urdu characters on the store signs, everything went black and the car growled ferociously before burrowing deep beneath the ground. Several vehicles sped by us in the dim half-light, like determined moles darting towards their burrows, with hundreds more, maybe even thousands, above our heads, rocking the earth with their tremendous tonnage. Seconds later, we were out in the blinding sunshine again. I turned to look at Fatima. I knew she hated these tunnels, and we had to go through one in order to reach C44 from school. This time, she was bent over, her head between her knees. After several minutes in the bright September air, she sat up, rolled down the window, then wrapped her arms around herself as if she were trying to hold something in.

'Raza,' she said hoarsely, 'Raza!'

'What?' I could see the top of his golden-brown head bobbing up and down from where I sat directly behind him. As usual, his ears were plugged, and he was listening to music.

'Raza,' I pinched his shoulder. 'Fatima's not well. Look at her!'

'Don't touch me, Ferzana.' Then, turning to Fatima, he inquired in a bored monotone, 'What's up now?'

'I don't want to scare you-know-who,' (it was no use, I knew whom they were referring to), 'but these goddamn tunnels are driving me crazy! I feel like I'm drowning.'

'Have you ever heard of claustrophobia?'

'I've never had it before.'

'Things change.'

'You'd think I'd know that,' she replied sarcastically.

I looked on, anxious to be of help. 'Fatima, don't worry,' I said, with a maternal pat on her arm. I was using the adult voice I had perfected in private, and continued, 'Just think of it as closing your eyes for a few seconds.'

'Thanks, but I've tried that. It's the sounds. The roaring in my ears, the voices. It's as if people are calling to me for help. Like they're drowning.'

I was silenced. I could feel the skin on my arms tingle in the scorching sunlight, goose-pimpling either because we had emerged out of the darkness or because I was unnerved by Fatima's description, I couldn't tell which. My adult voice abandoned me.

Raza snapped matter-of-factly, 'Of course you hear voices and noise. It's the traffic above us, dimwit.' He plugged his ears again.

I edged closer to Fatima and took her hand in mine. I knew that in some situations we women had to stick together, and this was definitely one of them. Within a few seconds, the tears began to fall, but silently. I raised a timid hand to brush them away from my sister's face.

When we reached C44, my older siblings disappeared. The compound, along with its four identical units, was labyrinthian enough for anyone to lose themselves in if they chose to. Suddenly alone again, I wondered what to do as I pulled my schoolbag out of the backseat of the car. I felt a hand on my head and looked up gratefully at Khyber, who smiled down at me with his niswar-stained teeth. Before I could speak, however, his back was already to me, a hand travelling towards the pocket that contained his little packet of tobacco. I watched him vanish behind Dada's unit to a part of the compound I hadn't seen yet but which everyone referred to as the 'servants' squatters'.

I ran upstairs to where Jamila was sitting on the bed reading a comic book. She, for one, was happy to see me. She pulled me down on the bed next to her and tickled me. Once done laughing, we lay side by side squinting as the sun streamed in through the windows and I described how I had been escorted into the classroom by glamorous Mrs Nasim. She raised her arms as if to ask why, but neither of us had an answer. It was a question that warranted further thought. I resolved to puzzle over it just before falling asleep that night, a time I generally devoted to untangling the day's events.

After Jamila, the next in the rounds was Baba. These days, I was nervous to approach his door because I was never sure what I'd find on the other side. Some days, he was happy to see me and gathered me into his arms like he used to, asking me about school, listening to my stories (mostly truthful, partly fanciful), or just cradling me quietly as if I were an infant in need of comforting. Other days, he was distant and unapproachable. Today, as I stood outside his door, I could hear the monotonous drone of the air conditioner, which meant that he was most likely asleep. I didn't bother knocking but still spent several minutes leaning against the door, staring at my white uniform shalwar ballooning around my sneakers as the wind from the fans on either end of the corridor filled it with air.

The afternoons were quiet and, at times, lonely at C44. Most of the adults fell asleep, a habit which I thought they should have outgrown by now. (I personally detested nap-time.) Fatima and Raza were busy with their homework or sometimes helped Jamila with her reading and writing. Shahbaz Chacha and Tania Chachi worked till late in the evening, although I couldn't understand how drawing, of all fun things, could count as work. I never dared visit Jamshaid Chacha's house in the afternoons because I was afraid of another encounter with Aslam. Eventually, bored of staring at my shalwar, I stepped out of it, and walked from our unit to Dada's. I could hear voices in the TV room.

Durdana Phupo and Dadi were on the cane sofa, their legs crossed, cups of tea in front of them. It looked as if Durdana Phupo had been crying because her long face was longer still, as if someone had yanked her chin and extended it by several inches. Dadi wasn't wearing her glasses, which she had folded and put on the table next to her. Without them, she suddenly looked old and frail, not the domestic powerhouse she usually was.

'Who is it, Durdana?' Dadi asked, putting her hand out blindly for her glasses. 'Accha. Tum ho. Come in, come in. Here,' she patted her ample lap, 'this is the place for you, chottu.' I sank into it and rested my head on her shoulder.

'Array, where's your shalwar?' Durdana Phupo exclaimed, grabbing one of my naked limbs.

'Shalwar ko chhoro. Forget her clothes. We need to focus on you, Durri.' Dadi's tone of voice startled me. I looked up at her face from below and could only see several soft, wrinkled double chins, topped by a nose. Her face, from this angle, looked like an upside-down ice-cream sundae.

'Ma, please.'

'Durri, you're unhappy. You're forty-one, for God's sakes. I was the mother of—'

'Ma, please. Enough. I like my work. I'm not one of the bosses, but I have a respectable position in the accounts department. The men I work with leave me alone.'

'Well, that's the problem right there!'

'I meant they're decent. Most of them are married, anyway.'

Dadi rolled her eyes and threw her hands up in the air.

I settled down to take a nap. I had overheard this conversation one too many times. I felt sorry for Durdana Phupo, having to justify her continuing presence in the home that was hers since birth.

'Madam Shaista is a fantastic boss,' she continued earnestly, as if for the first time. 'Amazing! I've never seen an MD so committed to her work. And she looks after us girls. I don't know how she manages to look so fresh after flying in from London or Tokyo.'

'Your own freshness is what you should be worrying about, Durri, not hers.'

But Durdana Phupo carried on, as if she, too, were flying above Karachi in my winged ship, the fresh and fishy sea air blowing her chador off her head, her hair, now free, streaming behind her like a majestic banner that proclaimed her devotion to Madam Shaista of Alpha Pharmaceuticals. 'It never ceases to amaze me how gracefully she handles the men, even the chauvinists. I remember Farooqi Sahib once disagreed with her on the budget. You should have seen her rebut him! The other board members were speechless ...' By the end of her eulogistic outburst, which lasted a full five minutes, she was reduced to staccato praise, so that when I opened my eyes (who could sleep with all the noise?), I heard 'Brave!' 'Principled!' 'Feminist!'

'Phupo, what's "feminist"?' I asked, sitting up. 'Is that a woman who loves women? Because I remember there were some ladies on TV once who were kissing each other.'

That silenced Durdana Phupo. She halted in mid-praise, a little breathless from all the talking. Dadi shifted in her seat to take a better look at me. 'Beta, what kinds of things did they teach you over there? Can you imagine, Durdana, and she's only ten? Tobah.' I realized that Dadi's earlobes, which hung low, were a consequence of her pulling on them so often. 'Durdana!'

Durdana Phupo had not moved since I had contributed to the conversation and, even now, sat extremely still on the cane sofa as if she feared she might tumble out of her winged ship and free-fall to earth.

'I want you to meet a divorcee your Shahana Bhabi has recommended for you. He's in his forties. He has two children—'

'Ammi!'

'Durdana, don't be a fool. Look at your age.'

Poor Durdana Phupo looked down obediently as if her age, like a slave's brand, were seared onto her stomach. I was fortunate, I thought to myself, that I was only ten. I prayed I still had many years to go before I, too, was hounded out of the house.

Suddenly, I felt Dadi's body soften under me as she moved towards Durdana Phupo, extending her a conciliatory hand.

'Beta,' she began quietly, 'please try to understand. Before, you were my only worry. Now I have others to think of, too. Jamila will always be with us. As for Aftab and Fatima, the sooner they are settled with nice spouses, the better.'

Durdana Phupo nodded in agreement.

I scrambled off of Dadi's lap and stood before them in my shalwar-less state, my brain issuing instructions to my tongue to protest, or at least to question. Then I realized that it was no use. They would not talk to me as an equal.

'Kya hai, chottu? What's the matter, silly girl?' Dadi asked.

Instead of answering, I flew out of the room, my bare feet hardly touching the cool marble floor.

CHAPTER 7

The Sloth and I had settled upon a meeting place where the exchange of information for our mutual benefit could take place without third-party intervention. At ten o'clock that night, Baba imagined me in bed, the way I usually lay asleep, arms and legs flung about, mouth open, a trail of saliva fast-trickling down my chin, my body resembling a child's abrupt crayon scribble. Instead, however, of a girl abandoned to sleep, I was wide, wide awake, slipping into my day clothes – the darkest I could find – pulling a mask, which I had fashioned cleverly out of an article of clothing, over my head, and stealthily creeping down the stairs. Once out in the darkness, the musty fragrance of our wilting garden with its steaming half-dead champa and raat ki rani left me momentarily paralyzed. For a second I thought of decay, then of Amma. I blinked into the darkness like a blind person, raising my arms in front of me and pummelling the air, so wet that it was palpable like clay in my hands.

Suddenly, the compound was illuminated, the tubelights over each porch flickering weakly as someone at the back switched on the generator. I froze. The whole garden began reverberating with the din, and in the half-light I could see the leaves of the bushes, the bushes themselves, even the earth in which they grew, quaking. Under the cover of this tremendous roar, I was, once again, Little Furry, arch-snoop, supreme sleuth, super detective, an agile gymnast vaulting across the lawn. Somersaulting the last two or three yards, I landed expertly on my feet in front of the rusty swing, where the Sloth, a book in hand, waited. Dressed in a white shalwar-kurta, he sat on the swing like a coy village girl from the Basaant tableau I had seen on TV, legs crossed, head cocked to one side. He stared dreamily at the cloudy night sky as the swing rocked gently beneath him.

'All you need is a string of mogra around your neck and two braids.'

'Excuse me, Ferzana?'

'I'm Little Furry.'

'Call yourself whatever you want. Do you have what I asked for?' He jumped off the swing and could see me clearly now, the flickering light from the nearest entrance playing hide and seek with us in the moonless dark.

'What's this on your head?' he asked, pulling the mask off and holding it up to the light. 'Is this what I think it is?'

'No, no, it's not. Give it back! I have to give it back – '

Wordlessly, he slipped it into his breast pocket. 'So, where's the information I asked for?'

I pulled out a piece of paper, unfolded it, and then continued to stare at it uncertainly.

'Chalo. Hand it over.'

'You won't use it to hurt her, will you?'

'Does it look like a weapon?'

'No,' I answered, crushing the paper in my hand before finally relinquishing it.

'If this isn't right…' the Sloth threatened, jumping off the swing and grabbing me by the shoulders, his face within inches of mine, so that I could, quite easily, make an attempt to slip my hand into his breast pocket if I dared. But before I could try, he had stepped several paces away, as if suddenly aware of the inappropriateness of this exchange, of the imbalance that existed between us, man and child.

'Theek hai,' he muttered. 'Thanks for this.'

'Hold on. What about what I had asked for?'

As he turned to go, he pulled a red velveteen pouch out of a pocket deep within his kurta and threw it at me. 'Remember to put them back exactly where you found them once you're done, otherwise I'm a dead man.'

I squatted, pulled open the pouch, and shook its contents onto the grass. A set of brass teeth smiled ghoulishly at me from below, as if the earth itself were laughing at me for my brazenness.

I picked up the brass key and pushed its sharp teeth into the soft flesh of my palm.

Early the next morning, there was a commotion at the front gate. I pulled myself out of bed and staggered to the window, half-asleep. A battered Suzuki was spitting out a trail of black exhaust as it puttered its way out of the narrow service lane in front of C44, leaving in its wake a forlorn group of three, a

mother and two children by the likes of it, several nondescript
bundles tied with packing rope, and a crate of – I squinted
in the early morning light – odd-shaped kitchen utensils. I
wondered who these newcomers were and whether the four
units within our compound could accommodate yet another
unhappy family.

For, even at a distance, it was easy to imagine the three
individuals on the uneven, potholed slope that led out of
our driveway and onto the street as somewhat distressed
by their circumstances, dumped unceremoniously in front
of a firmly shut gate, the top prongs of which looked like
a snarling monster's fangs. I was standing at my window,
comfortably within that monster's gaping maw, waving my
arms in a mad effort to ward them off when I realized that
they weren't looking my way at all but were staring at the
pavement as if its ugly concrete would open up and provide
tunnel access to the house. A few minutes later, as I bit on
my foamy toothbrush and hopped to the window with one
foot in my shalwar, I could see the top of the woman's head
within the compound in close confabulation with Khyber's,
both leaning intimately towards each other, while the two
young boys struggled to drag their belongings up the drive.
Already a crowd of inquisitive spectators from the settlement
across the street and from the small dhabas that lined the
road had gathered at the gate, a few of them suspiciously
close to the crate of kitchen utensils which the boys had yet
to bring in. Suddenly, the crowd scattered amid gasps as an
armored vehicle swerved recklessly past our gate, its gigantic
wheels crushing the crate and leaving the two boys, who had

run back at the sound, disconsolate by the roadside. I opened the window a fraction and could hear them wailing, 'Our radio! Babaa, our radio!'

By the time we drove out of the gate, there was nothing left of the family's possessions on the road, the early morning traffic of car, bus, truck, rickshaw, donkey cart and stray bullock ensuring that whatever had survived the collision had now been crushed to a fine dust. I rolled down my window and pulled myself up so that half of my body was outside. I scanned the ground to see if I could distinguish radio parts in the accumulation of junk that the road had washed up, like drift wood, in front of our house, but there was only a mound of fruit peels curling in the sun.

'Ferzana, inside the car!' Fatima pulled me from behind by my ponytail.

'I wanted to see if I could find that sad family's radio.'

'Sad family?'

I glanced up at the rear view mirror, where I could see a sliver of Khyber's suntanned face, his blue eyes focused on the road. I edged forward on my seat so that I could capture more of him in the mirror, turning my head to the far right so that his entire face and then parts of the outside world – bright, hard images like shattered bottle shards – were visible in that constricted space, the swift movement of the car causing the trucks, shops, palm trees and pastel-coloured houses that we passed on that rocky road to click by like the images in a toy ViewMaster. Staring up like that into the rear-view mirror, I became totally absorbed in this world of glass, so much so that I lost my balance and fell forward as the car lurched over a giant speed breaker.

This time Raza pulled off his earphones and turned around to face me. 'Ferzana,' he scowled, 'do you want to see yourself flying head-first through this thick pane of glass?' He pointed to it. Of course, I mutely shook my head in the negative.

'Sit back and don't move for the rest of this drive. And put your seat belt on, you idiot!'

Silently, I obeyed, tugging on the disused seat belt, which, with great resistance, I eventually managed to pull across my narrow lap and into the buckle. I closed my eyes and tried to imagine I was in my winged ship again, but this time it sulkily refused to rise more than a few feet off the ground. It was the seat belt, of course, I thought to myself. Who could blame my poor ship for being offended that such mundane safety measures were required even aboard an imaginary aircraft? One of the pleasures of our drives in Karachi was the freedom of movement, the feel of the bumpy road, the unbridled speed with which we raced to and from school in the unfettered glory of our beltless bottoms. And no one could appreciate this as much as I could, having been a prisoner of the dreaded booster seat just a few years before our arrival in Pakistan. I folded my arms across my chest and didn't move till we had reached school, where, as usual, a gaggle of female teachers awaited my entrance into the classroom.

On our way home from school, I finally mustered up the courage to ask Khyber about the new family. He explained that his wife and children had travelled from up north to come and live with him in the city.

'Does that mean they'll be living at C44?'

'Well, yes.'

'But there's no space.'

There was an awkward silence. Fatima quickly intervened, 'Ferzana, of course there must be space. Dada wanted Khyber to have his family here.' Then in an English undertone, 'Less extended holidays in the village, if you know what I mean.'

I nodded wisely as if I understood the implications of this, and then responded, 'Oh, yes. I'm sure there'll be enough room in the servant's squatters.' And, as usual, before I could spend more time in my adult voice, 'grow' into it, so to speak, my siblings burst out laughing and spoiled the mood, making me feel like an imbecile.

Tuesday evenings were sacred at C44. They were observed with greater religiosity than even Juma prayers on Friday. For on Tuesdays at 5:30, Dada and his cronies gathered at Tea Central, the collection of weatherworn cane furniture that clustered in no particular order on the cemented patio that led out onto the courtyard. From our bedroom window, this group of men, now in their late seventies, clad in crisp safari suits, flush with aftershave, regimental in their walk even after decades of retirement, looked like a disgruntled group of Green Sea Turtles congregating to feast on sea grass. Being the youngest, I was always greeted with shouts of 'Array, Chhoti!' 'Little lady!' 'Princess, how are you?' if I accidentally happened to pass that way. I was happy with all the attention and pleased to perch on one lap or another (Uncle Raff's, who was in kidney failure, was the boniest) so that they could imagine me as their own little Laila or Sofia or Zara, far away in some remote western metropolis, hostage to school schedules, visas, and that vile species, the overprotective parent.

'No one has time for us,' Uncle Raff groaned as he shifted in his seat to redistribute my weight on his knees, 'except, that is, for this little lady.' He winced, patting my head and gently bouncing me up and down on his lap like a baby.

Dada ignored this comment and instead launched into a discussion of the 'situation', which always meant something dire, something worse than being buried alive with mites tearing into your flesh or plunging headfirst into the middle of the Indian Ocean without a lifejacket. Karachi was always in a 'situation', apparently. For Dada, it was a perpetual state of chaos and disorder, a collective madness brought on by bad governance. Spluttering into his tea, he blamed the extremists, not just the Kalashnikov-wielding, explosive-throwing jihadists, but also the opulent, westernized and (according to him) decadent elite. The 'situation' was fuelled by extremists of both persuasions, a schizophrenic tug-of-war between the fundamentalists and the modernists. 'Where will it end?' he asked, arms raised in mock-perplexity. 'These bloody bastards in politics (Uncle Raff covered my ears) think we've forgotten, but it's all Russian roulette, a recycling of criminals in power…'

'Well, Sikander, the army had its turn,' began Uncle Raff hesitantly, 'several times over. We did no better, did we?' He turned and posed this question to me while joggling me on his knees, hoping, perhaps, for a change of subject.

The third cane chair grunted as Uncle Shahnawaz pulled himself up out of layers of perspiring fat, his smallish head and beaked nose emerging tentatively above his double chins as he broke the silence with his trademark falsetto: 'Sikander's right, Raff. Who else'll get us out of this blasted mess?'

'I'm not sure I have the answer to that,' admitted Uncle Raff with a sigh. 'Does anyone?' He looked around vaguely as if he had forgotten where he was, his dark irises darting from face to face in momentary bewilderment. I planted a wet kiss on his leathery old cheek, taking one of his hands in mine and grasping it tightly as if to say that I stood by him.

Dada, who was used to being the focus of these evening discussions, paused mid-sentence. He stared at me distractedly, and then said, 'Ferzana, shouldn't you be doing your homework?'

'Don't have any, Dada.'

'Well, go and help Dadi and Jamila in the kitchen then. Bring some more pakoras.'

'Oh come on, Sikander!' protested the other two, Uncle Raff's arms forming a protective belt around my waist. 'We won't give up without a fight!' he yelled with bravado as I raised my legs and kicked at the air like a wild stallion.

Dada's scowl deepened, but instead of responding to the challenge, he blew noisily on his tea cup before taking a long sip.

'How's Aftab?' asked Uncle Shahnawaz.

'Hmph,' Dada grunted.

'Baba won't talk anymore,' I said quietly.

'Hain? Sikander, how is he? How's the boy?' Uncle Shahnawaz repeated.

'He's going through a bad patch.'

'Only natural,' commented Uncle Raff.

'Natural or unnatural, I don't know,' Dada replied, 'but ...' he suddenly sat up, 'I think I have a solution. In fact, I've been working on something for the last few weeks.'

We all waited with interest. I, in particular, was curious to know how Dada could put his son back together again when the rest of us had failed.

'Remember Arif? Colonel Arif? Malir Cantt. Ordinance Depot?'

'Arif, haan. Of course. He's now in the US, living with his son in Newport,' nodded Uncle Raff.

'Well, what do you think of his daughter, Rizwana?'

'The one on TV?' Uncle Raff shook his head, then continued, 'Stirring up religious controversy, that's what. Don't like her much. People are even beginning to question her credentials. These days everyone thinks they're an authority on something or another.'

I knew from experience that when Dada's scalp turned pink it didn't bode well for anyone present. I feared for poor Uncle Raff. My grandfather sat up in his chair and adopted a bullying posture, pushing his chest out and placing his hands squarely on his arthritic knees before responding gruffly, 'Raff, tum bhi nah. You're so credulous. People say all kinds of things. They're jealous. This girl is perfect for Aftab. About the right age, too.'

I tried to process what this meant. It only took a few seconds, but it was enough. An image rose in my mind of the five of us as members of a new family, her family, Baba and Raza standing proudly behind the four of us women, identically hijabed, as we smiled as a unit for our annual portrait. I imagined Baba's history with Amma erased, the reel of film whining as it was made to flip back on itself, the delightful mountain tryst, the political rally, even the first meeting in the university library now figments of my imagination, our shared lives over so many years nothing but a collection of faded photographs that once told a story, the captions gone, the albums out of sequence.

No Amma. Another Amma. Either thought was unbearable.

Uncle Raff looked concerned. 'Chhoti, what's the matter?' he whispered into my ear, but I was already in mourning, mourning for what had passed – our lives before Amma's death – a time which was both unreal as well as preternaturally real, bright in our collective memory like a piece of overexposed film.

CHAPTER 8

Closing my eyes, I felt the wet sea breeze wrap itself lovingly around my waist, tugging at my nightdress as it worked its way upwards, making the loose cotton billow outwards like a ship's sail. For a moment, I forgot why I stood outside the entrance to my grandfather's house in the middle of the night, and breathed deeply as if the only purpose of my night-time prowl was a hedonistic tryst with Karachi's irresistible salt-water breeze.

I could hear nothing except the familiar, the eternal movement of tiny creatures in the garden, busy with their own lives, in the to-ings and fro-ings of food collection, egg-laying and mating, their sounds magnified a hundredfold in the stillness. I imagined I was back in our garden in Chicago, my knees deep in grass, my eyes closed: the sounds were the same, almost. A heavy humming, the weight of nature's constant productivity dripping slowly, like honey from a comb. Again, I saw the four of us around the fire, our expressions fierce and determined, the words of Dada's letter smoking skywards as Lady M raised her arms above her head like an enraged sorceress. But the desperate click-clicking of a chhipkali as it narrowly missed being sliced off at the tail by a random predator and the dampness of my skin brought me back to the present and Karachi, a city unlike Chicago in many respects but one: they were both mine now.

Suddenly, I felt someone shove me from the back. Before I knew what was happening, I had fallen face first into the grass. My eyes, within inches of the moist earth and its multitudinous inhabitants, focused on the nearest blade, behind which sprouted an indeterminate number of legs that belonged to some nocturnal creature on the prowl for a midnight snack. I scrambled to my feet in haste, brushed the dirt off my white nightdress and raised it above my knees to examine the damage. A few scratches, maybe a bruise or two in the morning – nothing that a super hero of Little Furry's stature could not bear. Still, I felt within me a superhero's powerful rage, and turned around to face my adversary with fists raised.

Lady M gazed at me apologetically. Ignoring my combative stance, she motioned for me to follow her into the house and then disappeared into the darkness. It was true; there was very little time before fajr, when the household would rise for prayers, and we had a great deal to accomplish before then. I slipped through the screen door, dodged the shadowy obstacles in the living room, and vaulted up the stairs behind Lady M. When she reached the top, she motioned for me to pass her the key. I pulled out the velveteen pouch the Sloth had given me from the pocket of my nightdress and reluctantly handed it over to my leader.

Within seconds, the door was open and we entered one of the strangest rooms I had ever seen. It was a tiny, suffocating cubicle with no windows. Now, when I think back to it, it was easy to imagine the room as the aperture of a camera, a dark, airless, lightless hole that ravenously drew everything to itself, then flung it all out again in a multitude of iridescent reflections. Our flashlights cast random dots of light against three walls lined, from floor to ceiling, with shelves. These consisted of albums of different shapes, sizes and colours, forming a bizarre railway track of a silhouette across the room. Each was labelled neatly and consistently, rigid and precise in the fashion of an army cantonment's archives. We looked at the shelves in awe: so this was a record of the Mahmud family's collective life over – Lady M peered at the first volume – the last sixty years. Lady M flashed light on my face and I on hers; bewildered, we wondered where to begin. Finally, she motioned me towards the end of the last shelf, while she pulled out one of the first volumes, sat cross-legged on the floor and began flipping pages. The idea was to find early photographs of Shahbaz Mahmud in an effort to determine whether his parentage was, as we suspected, *suspect*.

In the habit of reading 'backwards' from Urdu class, I began with the final volume on the shelf, which was still incomplete. As I flipped page after page, I recognized several photographs that Baba must have sent to Dada in the last year, including one of Fatima's, her curly black hair falling, like a horse's mane, down hunched shoulders. Then, a sequence of photographs of the four of us in our yard in Chicago. The greens and golds of the trees in our old garden shimmered beneath the glare of my torch, and as I stared, I could almost imagine those branches moving as they had on that day, millions of leaves, like the emerald shards of an amazing celestial chandelier, shuddering each time the wind blew. I traced our features with my index finger, slowly, deliberately, trying to x-ray our faces to delve beneath the flesh, find connections in the bone, in the cut of chins, the placement of eyes in the hollows of skulls. Did we, too, resemble the Mahmuds whom we were about to join, thousands of miles away in distant Karachi?

These photographs were taken on our last day in Chicago, but poor Baba would have done better to have left our departure unrecorded. There we were – faces grim, jaws clenched. There was an unnerving shot of me looking at the camera askance, the dark circles under my eyes accentuating my pale skin, my hair yanked back from my high forehead, so that – even to myself – I looked like the stock horror film menace, one of those creepy children who, with the help of dark forces, secretly engineer their family's downfall. Pure evil, I thought to myself, giggling. My attention was caught, a page later, by Raza and Jamila, arm in arm, both refusing to look directly into the lense, followed by a wistful one of Fatima focused on a point far away, past Baba and the camera, past the place of our birth and the city of our childhood, to a point thousands of miles away, the jagged edge where land met sea.

'Little Furry,' whispered Lady M, who had heard me laugh, 'could you please concentrate? We only have half an hour before sunrise.'

I pulled another album off the shelf. Working backwards had its advantages. As I flipped from volume to volume, from last page to first, I watched the members of our family magically grow younger, stronger, and in some cases, more likable, the stiffness and decorum expected of age falling away to reveal real people – elastic grins, arms draped casually around each other in the well-worn clothes of outdated fashion, they were friends and cousins and youngsters clowning around on sagging charpoys or wrestling on the grey sands of Hawk's Bay.

By the time I had seen four or five albums, the Mahmuds of Pakistan had become familiar, even downright lovable, creatures. I peered at them in the '80s, tracing their features in the dim glow of the flashlight with my index finger, a child's game: spot the Mahmud in the crowd. It was easy enough to recognize Durdana Phupo, even though she had undergone numerous transformations in hair, dress, and make-up over the years. In these photographs, for example, she sported a frizzy perm and fluorescent hoops and bangles, but her hawked nose, which always made her look undeservedly severe, her dark eyes and heavy-set eyebrows set her apart from her softer-featured cousins. Her brothers, on the other hand, were chameleons. They blended into the background with their beiges and their greys; what was distinctive about them – their long hair, drooping moustaches – was the fashion of the time. Every hirsute young man of that era was decked out in identical, nondescript, form-fitting trousers, large-collared shirts, or short white kurta-pyjamas.

By the time I had reached the tenth album from the end, I had almost fallen asleep. Drowsily, I propped up my chin on the torch, which I had carefully balanced on top of one of the albums. It was only natural: after a dozen pages of wedding groups, of people in different configurations of relationship and importance, the tiny, virtually unrecognizable faces had begun to merge. The only individuals who truly stood out in these photographs were also the confectionized centerpiece, Jamshaid and his eighteen-year-old bride (younger than Fatima, even!), who resembled plastic dolls, their finery, their expressions, and their toothy smiles identical in almost every image.

I yawned loudly. 'This is boring,' I said over my shoulder to Lady M, who didn't bother to reply. I realized that she was busy working, so I continued rifling through my album, an occasional image catching my interest and forcing me to pause. There was one photograph, for example, of Dada in his military gear, his salt-and-pepper hair clipped smartly behind his ears, his khaki uniform bright with coloured strips and golden dangling things, which I assumed, with awe, were medals for brave conduct. In another photo, I saw him with two comrades, and I squealed with delight as I suddenly recognized Uncle Raff, his shoulders wide above a solid frame, his face a youthful, fuller version of what remained of it today, his brown locks golden in the reddish light that the '70s cast on its images. This reddish quality made everyone look peachy fresh, so that in one photograph, thirty-something Dadi, wrapped in a printed chiffon sari with flowers in her hair, looked as glamorous as a film star.

'Little Furry,' whispered Lady M urgently, 'come look at this.'

I crawled over to where she sat, focusing my torch light onto the same page as hers, so that all of the tiny black-and-white images shone with reflected light. Impatiently pushing my arm away, Lady M pointed to a miniscule photograph off to one corner, with a neatly printed, handwritten, one-word caption underneath: 'Dhaka'.

'What's that mean?' I asked dubiously, as I stared at the baby in the photograph, who, even in black-and-white, looked golden, with its tight curls and bare chest lit by early morning light, a towel loosely draped around the waist, its skin still dewy.

Lady M shrugged. 'A name, perhaps?'

I wondered why she had singled it out. I squinted at it, and then suddenly realized where I had seen those eyes before.

'Shahbaz Chacha!'

Lady M nodded. 'This is the only photograph of him as a baby in the entire collection. Isn't that weird? There are more photographs of Baba as a child, even though he was born over a decade earlier.'

That was strange. One of the benefits of being the youngest, as I well knew, was being the most photographed in the family. The ratio of my photo albums to those of the rest of my siblings was a steady 3:1, rising to 4:1 in the first year, when I was (so I've been told) at my most irresistible.

'Do you know,' I began slowly, my eyes still focused on the photograph of baby Shahbaz, 'there's something else that's been bothering me ...' For the last half hour, while my thoughts were occupied with the Mahmud family history, my subconscious was grappling with a vague absence that, dozens of albums later, had now become clear to me. A giant worm, it seems, had eaten into the entrails of the photo library and had made off with that part of the family history which most interested me.

'Lady M,' I asked softly, 'why aren't there any photos of Amma and Baba's wedding?'

Her eyes widened in the dark. I could see the panic in her face, too. Before we could discuss this further, there was movement in the room next to ours, the sound of water running, slow steps shuffling across marble. Within seconds, dozens of voices in various stages of the azaan, some melodious (was there a budding musician amongst the muezzins?), some painfully off-key, a few cracked with strain or fatigue, infused the morning air, along with the brazen cawing of crows awakening from slumber. Lady M and I pushed the albums roughly onto the shelves, paying no attention to order or importance, scurrying down the stairs just as Dada was heard calling for breakfast.

'Ferzana,' Dadi said sharply, 'why do you look like you haven't slept all night?'

I raised my head, which I had buried in my folded arms, and mumbled, 'Nawwatchma.' I was sitting on one of the cane chairs at Tea Central, the afternoon sun searing the back of my neck, exposed to the elements because of my habitually high ponytail.

'Kya?' she asked again.

I cleared my throat and squinted at her before repeating, 'Nightwatchman.' I half expected her to pull me to my feet and demand an honest answer of me, for we had used him as an excuse for sleeplessness so often that it had almost become a joke among us siblings. It was true that the nightwatchman's high-pitched whistle was a sleep-deterrent, but how that same whistle, blown strategically throughout the night, was going to ward off dakoos and madmen was beyond me. Besides, he was the tiniest, skinniest Pathan I had ever seen. Unless he hid a giant's strength in his wiry arms and legs, it was unlikely that he could really protect the entire neighbourhood, let alone himself.

In any case, I allowed myself to be led inside.

'Yahaan aao, beta,' Dadi coaxed as she pulled me onto her lap so that my head rested in the warm spot beneath her ample belly. 'Tell me this. Why didn't you eat lunch today? It was aloo gosht, your favourite.'

I closed my eyes and forced air through my nose so that it sounded as if I were falling asleep. It worked. After a few minutes of caressing my head and exploring my ears and eyebrows with her index finger, Dadi picked up one of her ladies' digests and settled down to read. I, too, was happy for a place to rest my head. I had been fretting over the absence of my parents' wedding pictures all day long, and had decided that Baba was the only one who could explain away my worry. I had fidgeted until the final bell, pushed my things into my schoolbag, and even slipped out of the classroom without saying goodbye to glamorous Mrs Nasim. When we reached home, I saw Baba padding across the compound in his rubber chappals. He barely stopped for me, running his fingers through my hair and mumbling something about taking a nap before he left me standing there in the garden.

I closed my eyes tightly till I felt the tears come. I kept my insides, the part of me where all the sadness was, as still as I could so that Dadi would not notice that I was crying. I had done enough of that already, and it didn't help at all. Nothing changed.

A few minutes later, Dadi shifted underneath me, and below her, the sofa. Someone else was in the room.

'Ammi,' Durdana Phupo said, 'look at her face.'

I thought, at first, that she had noticed I was crying, or that I wasn't really asleep. Then, to my surprise, she continued, 'Doesn't she look just like Najma?'

It took all my self-control to prevent me from sitting up.

'Haan, beta. She does. A constant reminder to that poor son of mine. No wonder he avoids her. These days he doesn't even shave. Is this what they call "naarwiss breakdown" in English?'

'I don't know, Ammi. Depression, perhaps. Maybe we should make an appointment with a psychiatrist. I hate to see Bhai Jaan like this.'

'Naa. None of that. Your Abbaji would never hear of it. Besides, what can doctors do when his trouble is in the head—'

'—and in the heart,' Durdana interjected. 'Madam Shaista once told me that everyone in the West sees a therapist or a psychiatrist.'

'Well, they need to. We don't. We have our religion to see us through the hard times,' Dadi snapped with finality.

I barely followed what they were saying. I kept repeating 'I look like Amma, look like Amma, look like Amma' to myself, turning the words around and around in my head like a precious new toy in the hand. I imagined my photograph next to the one of hers under my pillow and used a finger to travel across her face, outlining her features, the dips and curves of her cheek bones, the shape of her chin, the rise of her nose with its slightly prominent bridge, then used the same finger to go over mine. Yes. I had it, too, the cheekbones, the nose – I raised my hand surreptitiously to my face – and perhaps even her most precious asset, her smile. And all this time I thought I had lost my mother when she was inside me. But then, as Dadi and Durdana Phupo's conversation turned to other topics, another one of Madam Shaista's corporate triumphs, no doubt, I remembered that because I looked like Amma, I was also a constant reminder of her absence. Fortunately, before I could focus on this for too long, the previous night's weariness caught up with me. Once again, I fell asleep in Dadi's lap just as she was expertly steering the conversation towards marriage, Durdana Phupo's, Baba's, Fatima's and the world's.

CHAPTER 9

'Ferzana, come here, please.' Mrs Nasim intercepted me as I was leaving the classroom, an envelope in her hand. I noticed that it wasn't of the standard-issue school variety.

'Don't worry,' she whispered, bending forward so that I could see the lace of her black undergarments beneath the sheen of her polyester-blend kurta, month five of the banishment of cotton from her wardrobe post-marriage. 'It's for Raza.'

I took the plain white envelope in my hand and stared at it, wondering all the while why it wasn't addressed to Baba. 'Mrs Nasim,' I began in a rush, 'I'm not sure how you found out that my Baba isn't well. If this is about me, I know he'll want to read it.'

Suddenly, Mrs Nasim's gorgeous smile vanished. She placed a set of red nails on the envelope as if to snatch it away as she said, 'Ferzana, this envelope is for your brother and has nothing to do with you' and, after an uncomfortable pause, 'or your Baba.'

This only served to confuse me further. I saw her turn away from me in obvious disdain, raising a silken sleeve to wipe the blackboard with a sponge, her large gold bangles cascading down her arm and forming a glut near her damp armpit. She continued to rub the blackboard vigorously, even after the day's spellings had disappeared in a haze of chalk dust. Thinking I had been dismissed, I began sidling out of the room, my eyes wet and my throat tight. I raised the envelope to my nose and was about to wipe my face with it when Mrs Nasim suddenly appeared in front of me, all manner of metal adornments tinkling with her sudden movement.

'Look, sweeto,' she began softly, 'just take this letter to your brother. He needs extra Maths tuition. I wrote down a few numbers for him. Kissy?' she pulled my wet face into both her hands and kissed either cheek. Then, opening a jar on her desk, she took out a shiny toffee and waved it in front of my eyes as if she were hypnotizing me. I accepted the peace offering, stuffed the envelope into my schoolbag, and made my way to the car, where Fatima, Raza and the driver were listening intently to the radio, the newscaster speaking in rapid Urdu of city happenings – in this case, a protest by lawyers at a public memorial and yet another round of load-shedding for huge chunks of Karachi.

When we reached home, I took the envelope out of my schoolbag and straightened it out on the bed. I pointed to it, and Jamila held it up to the light. Of course, we both wanted to see what was inside, even though we knew this was only acceptable when we were play-acting, sometimes not even then. Before we could decide what to do with it, Raza and Fatima walked into the room arguing over the car, pausing in mid-sentence when they saw Jamila and I perched on the bed, the envelope between us.

'For you,' I said simply, pushing it towards Raza.

He tore it open, pulled out the thin sheet of white paper almost black with curly scrawl, scanned it rapidly, then tore it in half and threw it away. Fatima, Jamila, and I all rushed to pick up the pieces, but he was quicker.

'Well, well, well. Why so curious?' he said, crushing the shreds in his fist.

'Who sent it?' Fatima asked, trying to pry his fingers open. 'Another one of your admirers?'

'Mrs Nasim!' I shouted, the relief of finally sharing a secret with someone too much for me to contain, my body shaking with the sheer exhilaration of complete disclosure.

Raza smiled and said nothing.

Jamila and I returned to our positions on the bed, our hands automatically rising to our ears to block out our older siblings' shouts. But no; this time, Fatima suddenly became tearful, running her hands through her thick curls and raising her eyes to the ceiling fan, which spun wildly on its loose hinge as a surge of electricity coursed through it.

'Why would Mrs Nasim send you a note?' Fatima wailed, clearly distraught. 'It's just not done. Why is it so difficult to tell what's right and what's wrong now?'

'Why bother? It's my business, not yours,' Raza snapped. 'Just a bit of harmless fun. Happens all the time.'

'But she's different. She's a teacher!'

'Fatima,' I spoke up timidly, 'Mrs Nasim said that Raza needs Maths tuition.'

'Ferzana, you don't understand. None of us do. We don't have anyone to talk to now that Amma's gone and Baba's dead.'

My fingers dug deep into the bed, then searched for Jamila's. It comforted me to feel the warmth of her hand in mine, her damp palm, skin to skin. It took several seconds, but I eventually stopped shaking. Jamila, too, was visibly upset.

'What are you saying?' Raza began angrily. 'And in front of these two? Don't you have any sense?'

'Well, he's dead to us, isn't he? He's not there for us. He's the only parent we have left, and he spends most of his time locked up in his bedroom or moping around in pyjamas.'

Raza stepped over to the window and stared out at the courtyard. Another flock of crows was noisily picking at the remains of a chunk of goat and bone that Dadi had thrown out that morning to ward off the evil eye, which she was convinced had its demonic hold on Baba's nervous system.

'Don't you remember?' he said. 'We have each other. We have our games.'

Was it my imagination, I wondered, or was he already disenchanted, like a grown-up weary with the day's work, forced to re-read the same fairytale to a besotted child, the magic of its perfect closure, its just rewards and punishments lost on his jaded mind after the hundredth retelling? His voice, monotonous and unconvincing, continued: 'Look, it's important for the four of us to stick together. We have to take care of each other. And we'll work on Baba, too.'

Fatima, calmer now and feeling guilty for having put Baba to his imaginary death, wiped away her tears with the back of her hand and came to the bed, putting her arms around us. She whispered, 'Lady M and Little Furry don't get scared, right?'

'Right,' I agreed with enthusiasm. 'You have to hear this – we've gathered a ton of information over the last week…' However, before I could proudly detail our findings, Fatima was in the hallway with Raza, pulling out a piece of paper from her pocket and urging him to follow her downstairs.

Frowning, I stared at my feet, my toes splayed, each crucified in its rubber chappal, my painted nails chipped from their daily incarceration in white socks and PT shoes. My eyes travelled from my feet, a golden brown, upwards to my chalky legs and grey knees. Since our arrival, my legs had not seen the sun. For causes unknown to me, my shorts and shorter skirts had disappeared, my drawers now full of diminutive shalwar-kameezes with matching dupattas, their frills and embroidery compensating for the theft of my familiar summer wardrobe. I stretched out on the bed next to Jamila, who had pulled up her legs and wrapped her arms around her knees. The bed creaked with her rocking.

'Hey, Jamila, don't worry.' I kissed her and brushed a strand of hair away from her face. Perhaps she, too, was disappointed that no one wanted to hear what we had discovered. I lay down next to her and closed my eyes. Someone needs to take charge, set things in order, I thought to myself. What we needed was a Baba-substitute until Baba was himself again. My thoughts turned, once more, to Dada's plans of introducing Baba to that TV lady with the hijab, his proposed – I pulled on my ears and muttered 'Tobah' in imitation of Dadi – Amma-substitute.

'Jamila,' I said. 'I think it's time you called another meeting.' Jamila stopped rocking. Slowly gathering herself up, her demeanour regal, stately, she raised herself from the bed, and stood to face me. For a few seconds, she said nothing, her eyes focused on a point behind me, the electric blue of the sky through the window, where the browning leaves of the coconut palm flapped slowly in the breeze.

When she finally spoke, it was in the powerful, the commanding, voice of our great leader, Lady M:

'Tonight,' she paused for emphasis, 'we will meet tonight.'

'Ferzana,' Fatima looked at me suspiciously, 'have you seen my black panties?'

I was sitting cross-legged on one of Tea Central's dusty cane chairs, an open workbook on my lap, my stained fingers clumsily wrapped around a leaky fountain pen. The workbook was streaked with my penmanship. Starting out with confidence, the characters on the far right were disciplined, well-curved, and appropriately dotted, but quickly degenerated into a mess of blotchy ink as they crawled their miserable way across the page. I paused at my sixteenth ع and looked up blankly. 'Panties?'

'Yes. You know the ones. I always dry my underwear in the bathroom. I've been missing them for days.'

Suddenly, all of the characters on the page, the well-formed as well as the hopelessly deformed, jumped out at me in the brilliant sunlight, liberated from their paper prison like a host of imps performing a maniacal dance in my mind's eye. I squeezed my eyes shut, but they were still there, x-rayed against a backdrop of nectarine-orange.

'Ferzana, answer me.'

I opened my eyes and looked up at my sister. It was obvious she was tired and upset. I thought uncomfortably of my exchange of information with the Sloth. Curse my need for heightened drama. Why did I always require stage props, costumes, the appropriate setting? To Fatima, I merely replied, 'No, I haven't seen them,' burying my face in my workbook in an effort to appear busy.

'Chhoti, you will tell me what you know, understand? There are these' – she suddenly faltered – 'things happening...'

There she was again, this unfamiliar Fatima, lost, uncertain. Could she be 'breaking down' like Baba? No, no, no, I panicked, I won't let it happen to her. I won't. I stood up, my work falling to the ground, my arms open wide to embrace her, my mind already formulating a confession —

But an exuberant 'As-salaam alaikum' from across the courtyard sent Fatima flying. By the time Aslam reached Tea Central, breathless from the sprint, she had already disappeared through one of the doors that led inside. Disappointed, he glared at me.

'Yes?' I inquired.

'Don't you think you should greet your elders when you see them, or is that not done in America?'

'Hi.'

'Hi-fi! Bibi, learn something about your Deen.'

This was a new word. I would have to ask Shahbaz Chacha or Tania Chachi what it meant.

Aslam tugged at his beard, suddenly thoughtful, his eyes now on the door through which Fatima had escaped. 'Chhoti, I don't want to fight,' he said suddenly. 'I want to help all of you. I believe I can. I don't know how Aftab Taya raised you, or whether your mother's religion had anything to do with it—'

'Wait a minute,' I interrupted. 'What do you mean? We're Muslim. Baba is and so was Amma.'

Aslam smirked. 'Shows how little you know, Chhoti. Haven't you ever heard of the terms Sunni and Shia? I thought this was common knowledge for even stupid Americans after 9/11 and Iraq.'

I looked at him blankly. In all my ten years in Chicago, these foreign-sounding words had never entered my vocabulary. This much I knew: Baba and Amma, according to their friends, whom I often heard teasing them over it, had evolved their own eclectic mix of religious belief over the years, derived partly from tradition and mostly from a natural human instinct for what was right. Even I had realized, by the time I was six or seven, that ours wasn't a conventional household; we were not fully 'American' in the sense that our neighbours were, yet we were on the periphery of the Pakistani-Muslim community, whose social gatherings and religious activities (including dreaded Sunday school) bred an insularity that our parents disliked.

'I'm only ten,' I replied in my defence. (This was not entirely true. My birthday had been on the sixteenth day of this month, and I had turned eleven but chose not to celebrate it without Amma. In private, I referred to it as my 'Happy Bad-Day', a day I wanted to forget.)

By now, Aslam had been joined by Parveen, who reverentially cradled a swaddled copy of the Quran in her arms. She whispered, 'Aslam, leave her alone. It's the older ones we should be worried about.'

He nodded, flushing self-consciously before he ventured, 'Parveen, maybe you could persuade Fatima to attend dars with you and Ammi next week.'

Another new word, I thought. In addition to Urdu and the regional languages, it seemed living in Pakistan demanded a working knowledge of Middle Eastern tongues. Disheartened, I picked up my workbook and fountain pen. I realized I had much to learn.

'Allah Hafiz, Chhoti,' Parveen called back as she ran to the car, where her mother was in the driver's seat, her gloved hands on the steering wheel and her dark chador pinned tightly to one side with the help of her trademark brooch, a funny diamante rabbit with long ears and black eyes that Jamshaid Chacha had brought her from Los Angeles.

'Aslam Baee!' I called out in panic as he ran after Parveen. 'Wait! I need my black mask back.' He was already in the passenger seat next to his mother as their white Corolla slowly pulled out of the gate. He rolled down the window and waved but said nothing in response to my request.

Shahana Chachi noticed me standing there too, a little pathetic, perhaps, for she gestured dramatically with one arm as she shouted, 'We're late, beta. We have to drop Aslam to Quran class. Maybe next time. Get yourself a pretty headscarf first.'

The threat was enough to send me running back to my seat, where, even from a distance, I realized that something had changed. My workbook was not where I had left it. In fact, it was now in the hands of an unfamiliar child. His tawny short-cropped hair was golden in the sun as he squatted on the ground and examined my work intently. He scrambled to his feet as he saw me approach. I was surprised to note that he was the same height as me, perhaps the same age, too. He wore an adult-sized yellow t-shirt over greying pants, his feet in grimy plastic sandals. Speechless, I took the workbook from him and was embarrassed that he had seen the sad result of my efforts.

'Who are you?' I asked. Then, quickly recovering myself, I said more politely, 'I'm sorry. Have we met?'

'I'm Shahnaz.'

'Isn't that a girl's name?'

She stared back at me pointedly, not bothering to answer.

'Sorry,' I apologized again.

'That's okay. Easy mistake, I suppose. Everyone thinks I'm a boy. I wear my older brother's clothes.'

'And he is...?'

But Shahnaz, it appeared, was already bored with this conversation. Turning on her heel, she walked away in the direction of the servants' quarters, proudly informing me, with a toss of her tawny head, that she was the driver's daughter.

Later that night, much later, when the rest of the household was asleep and the chowkidar had cycled by at least a dozen times, his sad, tuneless whistle, like an owl's cry, startling the stillness of the garden and disturbing Baba as he slumbered in his room across the hall, the four of us met around the light of a solitary candle.

Lady M revealed what we had discovered of Shahbaz in the photo library – that single image of him as a baby, cryptically labelled 'Dhaka'. Maybe, we suggested, 'Dhaka' was a secret identity. Instead of marvelling at our discovery, Timmer and Dag began howling, writhing on the floor in fits of uncontrollable laughter. Finally, when their hilarity was spent, Timmer revealed that Dhaka was a place name, the capital of a country now called Bangladesh, which was once, many years ago, part of a united Pakistan.

CHAPTER 10

On my very first visit to my mamus' house, a pale green two-storey in the congested heart of an older subdivision of Karachi famous for its sweet sheermal as well as for the Imam Bargah at its centre, I was immediately captivated by a massive portrait in black-and-white on the wall directly opposite the entrance. It depicted an older man with thinning, shoulder-length hair casually sitting on a bench surrounded by trees in a park or a garden. His kurta sleeves were rolled up to his elbows, one pyjama leg slung across the other, his sockless feet in Oxfords. He was smiling through his eyes, not his lips, his entire face a study in suppressed merriment. Mischievous, a friend of tricksters and frauds, he looked as if he had just hoodwinked a pair of little boys into trading their chocolate for a bowl of bitter gourd. I decided immediately that I liked him and assumed that ours was a relationship not only of kindred spirits, but also of blood. This man must be my Nana, I decided, long before we had been formally introduced.

Our trip to this part of the city to visit our mother's side of the family was secretly arranged by Shahbaz Chacha who had proven himself a consistent ally, notwithstanding a few incidents, which I eventually put down to lapses in good judgement, and forgave. We set off that Sunday morning on a 'tour' of the old city, which Shahbaz Chacha persuaded Dada was necessary for our full integration into Karachi life, although we had already spent six months in the city and had seen a fair part of it. Miraculously, no one objected and Baba, when told, briefly looked up from his newspaper (it was last week's) to nod his head, wishing us a safe drive but showing no desire to participate. And so, there we were, the three of us girls in the back, the windows pulled down and our hair flying, while Shahbaz Chacha and Raza, in front, yelled over the wind and the amplified traffic sounds, and spoke of the city, as it was now, and how it once was when our father's family first moved here.

I listened intently, craning my neck forward so that I was, for all intents and purposes, sitting between them, first looking up at one, then the other, until Fatima, worried for my safety as we mounted a huge speed breaker, pulled me back and held me down. I was intrigued. Like us, who had migrated from one large metropolis to another, the Mahmuds had made their own migratory journey from the northern Indian province of Uttar Pradesh to the southern sea port of Karachi, where they had settled after the Partition. Before I could ask, Shahbaz Chacha explained that the Partition referred to the division of India and Pakistan in 1947 by the British, who once ruled over them. Dada, whom I had always imagined as a giant oak, his roots buried deep and wide beneath the foundations of

C44, so fixed and rigid was he in his routine, had grown up in an entirely different place, a village no less, with a population of a few thousand people. For a couple of minutes, I mulled over this, paying no attention to Shahbaz Chacha's description of the busy thoroughfare we were slowly making our way down, the heart of the business district, its tall buildings rising above the pollution and touching the blue cloudless sky.

It was no less a surprise to me, after countless geography classes and colouring my way through outline maps, that countries, like people, were not stable entities, that they were made and broken, then made again.

Once we had passed I.I. Chundrigar Road, relatively calm on a Sunday afternoon, we drove towards Kemari, a favourite spot of mine, where we paused for a second at the bridge to admire the boats, big and small, the oil containers and cargo ships from the Middle East and East Asia, even tiny fishing vessels, which could be observed jauntily bobbing up and down, faint glimmers on the sea. I breathed deeply at the open window, leaning over Fatima to stare out at the water, which I admired for its deceptively sparkling surface under which lay the debris and rubbish of the city, and below that, miles down, lightless ocean. Again, the smell I had grown to love, faintly eggy and piscine, this time heavy with the fumes of land and sea traffic, filled my nostrils, and I imagined myself climbing out of the car and onto the bridge, then diving deep into the brackish water. The hulls of ships, like whales, above me, below just an eternity of wavy darkness dotted by filtered sunlight.

As if from fathoms away, I heard Shahbaz Chacha say that much of the city was once under water, that large tracts of land were reclaimed and that as little as seventy years ago, heavily congested residential neighbourhoods were blanched sand and rock, an extension of the beach inland for miles. Even the ground upon which our own C44 stood was once a part of the Arabian Sea, instantly conjuring up (in my mind at least) an underwater household, the flippered Mahmuds going about their daily routine through kitchen, bathroom, and bedroom in scuba suits, surrounded by schools of fish, giant sea turtles, and tentacled sea anemones. It was difficult to imagine that our congested neighbourhood, where shops grew like lichen between the crumbling boundary walls of houses and cars, trucks, motorcycles and rickshaws jostled their way through potholed lanes, was once just a stretch of sand and embedded fossil, so quiet and still beneath the sky that only the seagull's occasional call disturbed its calm.

From Kemari we wound our way through one of the older parts of the city, Saddar, with its remnants of nineteenth-century grandeur. The smoke-darkened facades of its colonial buildings rose like masks above the flurry of mercantile activity below, the declaiming shopfronts with their dangling wares, the uneven pavements suddenly sprouting stairs that tripped seasoned hagglers as they fought their way through the crowds, and the appearance, like a mirage, of soaring, glass structures in the midst of these older buildings. Peering upwards as we stalled behind the back of a water tanker, its rear animated with an artist's rendering of Pegasus, its woman's face thick-lipped and heavily painted, I looked above a shoe store to the building's second storey, a mere husk, the ornately carved windows leading onto nothing but air and blue sky.

Less dense on a Sunday morning, traffic was still heavy enough to hamper our progress through the busiest parts of the city. In Saddar, motor vehicles, like wild rodeo horses, lurched their way forwards, their nauseous stop-and-go motion sending my hand to my mouth. I leaned back between my sisters and closed my eyes, reopening them when Shahbaz Chacha pointed out Bohri Bazaar (I had been there once with Dadi to get half a dozen voile dupattas dyed) and later, an open market, where Dadi often went to purchase vegetables and fresh fish. As we drove by, a whiff of something dark, like a portion of ripped earth exhaling its innards, found its way into the car, forcing all of us to quickly roll up our windows and cover our faces with our hands.

'Rotting fish, probably,' Shahbaz Chacha guessed, 'combined with cow manure.' Still, I thought, opening my fingers a crack so that I could see through the pink crease of my pressed palms, I would ask Shahbaz Chacha to take us through some of these places on foot next time.

'When we're home, remind me to show you some photographs of Karachi in the '30s,' he said, his architect's instinct for purity of form evident in his zealous praise of the original buildings that graced the city, even though some were now just crumbling ruins or tenement housing, shalwars, dupattas and underwear drying on ropes strung from one wrought-iron balcony to another, or offices with greying signs for everything from haemorrhoid treatment to children's day cares.

It was, in fact, next to a similar billboard, emblazoned with the words 'Harvard Children's Nursery, KG to Matric', a menagerie of baby animals and stunted-looking children cavorting on its façade, that we finally came to a halt, tumbling out of the car and stretching our limbs, each of us staring in different directions as if to absorb, then consolidate, our perspectives. What we saw was a narrow lane of modest houses or semi-detached units heavily blackened with the exhaust fumes of passing traffic, eventually merging, a few blocks down, into a dusty four-storey office complex, its roof still incomplete and its naked metal stakes jabbing the sky. I thought, looking up at the freshly-painted, minty-green exterior of the narrow house in front us, that Amma as a little girl must have once stood on the roof of this very structure on warm nights, marvelling at the bright lights and moving traffic of the city, the roundabout at the centre of the parallel double-road a child's glittering spinning top. This was our mamus' house, before them, our nana's. It was the house where our mother grew up.

Allowing us enough time to recover, Shahbaz Chacha pressed the doorbell. The white pedestrian gate instantly opened, as if Alamdar Mamu was lying in wait behind the massive potted plants that flanked the entrance. Salaar Mamu, like Alamdar's shadow, immediately emerged from behind, his impatience to hold us in his arms so great that he nearly knocked his brother down. Once the greetings were over, we sidestepped the paint tins and rags near the gate to enter a narrow, darkened corridor that led into an inner courtyard open to the sky with a charpoy and several folding chairs at one end. We could tell that an effort had been made to tidy up the place, stacks of books and newspapers packed neatly to one side, a vase of waxy plastic flowers on a table by the charpoy along with a tray of dry snacks and glasses of sherbat. Several doors led off the courtyard to different rooms in the house, and a winding cement staircase rose straight from its foundation to the second floor, where muffled sounds indicated that either a television or a radio was on.

Shahbaz Chacha immediately launched into a description of our city tour as we settled into our seats, I climbing onto the charpoy and sitting cross-legged at its centre like a Mughal queen. Fatima, glaring at me, stood politely to one side while the adults took their places, eventually perching, along with Raza and Jamila, next to me. I couldn't understand why my siblings appeared so ill at ease. In fact, Fatima looked ready to cry, one hand nervously at her cheek while the other fiddled with a corner of her kurta. I felt happy being there and imagined the house as it was when my mother was a little girl – her and her brothers' laughter animating the now darkened rooms, their rowdy games of hide-and-seek disrupting the serious discussions in the drawing room, popping up like Jack-in-the-boxes in the middle of debates as Nana and his newspaper friends talked of history and politics, books, poetry, and art. This time, however, it didn't take the appearance of a tea trolley to loosen our tongues. Within minutes, Alamdar had pulled out a massive photo album from beneath the pile of newspapers and books, causing a small avalanche of newsprint. Before we knew it, he was sitting amongst us, the jute weave of the charpoy sagging under our bottoms, I in his lap, the album open on mine, our five heads fighting for space as we examined the photographs.

The photographs were in no known order or sequence, and certainly not chronological. A bespectacled fourteen-year-old Amma in a sea of schoolgirls was side-by-side with a tiny, fading black-and-white square, wherein an even tinier figure, our Nana, held a blanketed dot which, Alamdar explained, was Amma's face at three days. But slowly, as we progressed through the album, some pages packed tight with images, others blank except for single photos at their centre, it became apparent that there was indeed a peculiar logic to it, that the photographs had been compiled in order of favourites, Alamdar's accompanying anecdotes one continuous narrative that told of his love for his dead sister.

'Now, see,' Alamdar pointed excitedly, 'this was taken at a school recital. Najma was Heer in the Heer-Ranjha story, and played opposite a big hairy girl named Batul, whom most people in the audience thought was actually a man. A few parents even protested. "Why was a boy allowed onto the premises of an all-girls' convent school?" they asked.' Alamdar, raising his fists, scowled dramatically in imitation of the irate parents.

'Alamdar, don't forget the most important part of this story. Batul was our first cousin and at one time your fiancée,' Salaar interrupted.

Alamdar smiled sheepishly. 'That's the way it is, children, with our biradari, our khandaan. We're clannish. In a way, you're lucky you've been kept out of it. We've always had the pressure of marrying within the family over our heads. In the end, we thought we'd just not marry at all.'

'We were a little unfortunate,' Salaar added, grinning, 'that all the unmarried cousins on offer were either hairy, shrill, or too religious.'

'Brotherly,' I repeated, trying out the word. 'Is that the way to say it?'

'Biradari,' Salaar Mamu corrected. 'The meaning goes beyond family. People with the same roots, cultural affiliation. Like pedigrees, but for people.'

I heard Shahbaz Chacha, who had suddenly gone quiet while we looked at the photographs, laugh softly to himself. He stood up and pretended to look at his reflection in the cracked mirror above the stand-alone sink, which stood to the right of the kitchen.

'As a people, we're obsessed with our roots,' he commented.

'I didn't know that Amma and Baba were cousins,' I ventured.

'They weren't,' Salaar Mamu replied, embarrassed. Suddenly, it was so quiet that I could hear the television upstairs as if it were blaring inside my head.

'Salaar Mamu,' I asked, trying again, 'the large photo in front of the entrance. That's Nana, right?' I was convinced that that irascible old man with the unconventionally long hair had to be him, a kind of Einstein of Pakistani newspaper editors, discovering novel ways of communicating even when political censorship was at its height.

'Oh no, no!' Salaar exclaimed.

Alamdar, shocked, put the album down and turned me around to face him. 'Chhoti, you don't know who that is? Don't they teach you at school?' He then said to Salaar, 'Bhai Jan, I thought they were supposed to. I mean, after all that trouble we went to to persuade the textbook board … Damn bureaucrats!'

'Mamu, ignore her. She doesn't know anything—' Raza began, although I could tell he had no idea who the old man was either.

'Ahh!' I suddenly shouted. 'Of course I know who that is. The Quad, right? Pakistan's founder?' I jumped off the charpoy and ran back to the portrait in the hallway.

A second later, the rest of the family was standing behind me, Fatima hissing under her breath, 'Silly idiot. That's not Jinnah.'

'That, my dear children,' began Salaar grandly, 'is a famous man. And he happens to be our' – he waved his arms to include us – 'relative.'

It was then that we were introduced to a very important (albeit dead) member of Salaar and Alamdar's world, as much flesh-and-blood to them as we were, despite the remoter relationship, for the man in the photograph wasn't my Nana, but his second cousin, the son of a step-sibling of our Nana's father. It turned out that he was not the leader of a state or the editor of a newspaper after all, but a man of letters, a poet – the best, said Alamdar, of his generation who, through his writings, 'roused a slumbering nation to independence'. Receiving two national awards during his lifetime and a host of posthumous honours in both India and Pakistan, the said gentleman was referred to deferentially as our 'poet-ancestor', his name so well known, according to our mamus, that to mention it out loud would be virtually blasphemous. Besides, Salaar explained, everyone already knew who he was.

Ten years ago, the brothers had set up a foundation in honour of their dead uncle's memory, where his original poetry and prose was housed in a one-room library and where his personal effects, like the black-rimmed glasses of the photograph, or his writing desk and cane, were on display for the general public. The proceeds from this venture, along with a trickle of royalties that were still received on his most famous work, were redistributed among the poorer members of his family.

'I look upon it as public service,' Salaar spoke out. 'If we don't promote our national heritage, who will? We need to teach our children to be proud of their roots, even if,' he lowered his voice, 'we're not sons of the soil. Come on. I'll take you there.'

To our surprise, instead of leading us outside and then across to another building, Salaar and Alamdar returned to the courtyard and began climbing the cement staircase that led to the second floor of the house. The sound I had heard earlier was not the drone of a television, it turned out, but a late recording of the poet reciting his work, his undulating voice filling the empty spaces of the room devoted to his life and writings, the wall above his modest desk covered with framed couplets from his poetry, rendered in calligraphic Urdu and, Shahbaz Chacha pointed out, Persian. Delighted, I immediately ran to another copy of the portrait of the long-haired gentleman in the park which hung in a gilt frame above the bookshelf and stared. Jamila joined me.

'So,' Raza asked cautiously, 'how many visitors do you get?' I noticed him give Fatima a look.

'About twenty or thirty,' Alamdar said proudly.

'A day? Not bad!' he exclaimed.

'Well, no. Actually, about that much – well, a few more – a year.'

'That's okay,' I whispered to the photograph. 'I'll visit you oftener than that, you old rascal!' Jamila, who overheard me, giggled.

'Mamu,' Fatima finally spoke up as we wound our way down the steep staircase, 'what did our Nana and Nani look like? Don't you have pictures of them?'

'Your mother didn't have any?' Alamdar asked sadly.

'Well, yes, she had some,' Fatima said, 'but not enough for us to tell what they were really like, especially when they were younger.'

Like Baba's side of the family, Salaar and Alamdar were hoarders of photographs, although not quite as organized. They opened a large suitcase and dumped its contents onto the charpoy. We spent some time looking at these pictures, several from before the Partition even, when Nani, a young girl in cotton gharara, flirted at Nana through the camera, her eyes upon the lens that he adjusted with his hand. Our grandfather was an avid photographer, Salaar explained, his love of journalism partly fuelled by his desire to capture the passing moment. His articles were often accompanied by photographs that he himself had taken, at times these crystallized images more eloquent even than the words used to describe them.

At last, Alamdar pointed to a large black-and-white photograph of a couple sitting on this very charpoy, the man in straight pyjamas, a white cap, like a folded napkin, upon his head, his legs – in fact, his whole physique – unnaturally thin. Next to him, sat his wife, a chiffon kamdani dupatta draped over her head and across her shoulders, her legs tucked under her as she leaned slightly towards him, smiling. A little disappointed, I realized that our Nana didn't look anything like his mischievous cousin. But I was proud of him nonetheless; there was a gentle grace, a considered thoughtfulness to his person that I associated with my mother the ten years I had known her.

'I really miss them,' Alamdar commented softly. 'All three of them.'

'That reminds me,' I began, a little uncertain of myself after the Quaid incident, 'how come there aren't any photographs of Amma and Baba's wedding at Dada's house?' I directed this question at Shahbaz Chacha, who suddenly stopped what he was doing and looked at the four of us quizzically.

'Didn't Bhai Jan tell you? Or Najma Bhabi?'

'What?' Fatima asked in a panic. 'Tell us what?' Raza put a calming hand on her shoulder, while the four of us anxiously looked at our uncles.

'Well,' Salaar admitted, 'there would be no photos of your parents' wedding there. None of us were present at it. You see, they eloped.'

'What?' Fatima was beside herself. 'That's not possible. How come we were never told?'

'That's something you'll have to ask your Baba,' he replied. 'As for the story of how it happened – we better leave that for next time.'

CHAPTER 11

For some strange reason, our cousin Aslam rarely made eye contact with women. Instead, he looked through and beyond them to a vague spot somewhere above their heads. Later, I learned this was his defence against the nafs – the Arabic word for ego or self – a kind of schizophrenic recognition of one's baser urges. It made for awkward conversation, though, and unsatisfactory one-sided exchanges, all of the poor man's energy dissipated in keeping his thoughts pure. With Fatima, however, he had no control over his gaze. He was obsessed with the area directly beneath her collar bone, a section of the body that he found particularly fascinating. This, I learned, was the reason Fatima avoided him, at least the only articulate reason she admitted to among various unintelligible ones, groans, moans, and the like.

As a consequence, it wasn't easy persuading Fatima to accompany us to Dada and Dadi's house early the following Sunday for a cousinly aloo-puri breakfast, a responsibility Dadi had assigned to me the night before, saying, 'Beta, you know her best. Please get her to come.'

The six of us stared at one another, some of us still in our night clothes, I cradling my teddy bear and Jamila, unused to early rising, half asleep, her face buried in Fatima's lap. Raza, one foot thumping out a tuneless accompaniment to the loud static emanating from his earphones, was in shorts without a care for who was present, his hairy man's legs sprawled out in front of him. Sitting directly opposite, Parveen looked uncomfortable as she tried to drag her gaze away from his shapely limbs to the glossy calendar shot of Lake Saiful Muluk above his head. No one, I thought to myself with a knowing sigh, was safe from my brother's charms, not even – though the thought wasn't clearly formed in my mind yet – the glamorous Mrs Nasim, who once, and not too long ago, had been exclusively mine.

I could hear Dada's chappal-shuffle as he paced the entranceway behind us, his back slightly stooped over his walking stick. His gnarled fingers kneaded the beads of the tasbih in his hand as he prayed, no doubt, for the quick arrival of Khyber from Burns Road, arms laden with greasy plastic bags of aloo-puri. Accustomed to having his breakfast soon after fajr, so that he could have his lunch at noon and his dinner at six, so as to be changed and in bed by ten, his body was badly in need of sustenance, his guts squeamishly contracting as per schedule. 'Damn that blasted shop! Why can't they open at a decent hour so we can have our breakfast on time!' he yelled to no one in particular.

Aslam, from his vantage point across the room, continued to stare at Fatima.

I suppose I spoke for all of us when I suddenly asked, 'Where's Dadi?'

The woman who had organized our family breakfast was nowhere in sight. Curious, we sat up and looked around. I sniffed the air and was reassured by the signature morning smells I had become accustomed to – tea bubbling over a gas flame, the lingering sweet odour of the gas itself, the burnt paper used to light the stove – but instead of Dadi supervising its making, the cook stood in the kitchen, leaning with his back against the counter, his stomach jutting out like a pregnant woman's. Parveen, who for the last few minutes appeared to have been lulled into a trance by the blue waters of Lake Saiful Muluk, leapt to her feet and offered to check for Dadi upstairs, thankful for an excuse to escape Raza's legs yet almost tripping over them on her way out.

'Watch where you're going, lady!' he called to her in jest. I could hear her pace quicken as she bounded up the stairs.

'Why aren't you people dressed?' Aslam suddenly asked, directing the question at Raza, who had now casually draped one hairy leg over the arm of the sofa, his shorts riding up his thighs. I realized with a start that while the four of us were still in our night suits, Aslam and Parveen had come dressed for the day, their clothes, if anything, smarter than usual.

'What do you mean? Are we expecting company?'

'No. I don't think so, but there are servants around.' His eyes darted, once again, to Fatima. She was wearing a thin cotton nightie over yesterday's shalwar. 'It's just not appropriate,' he added.

'Well, that's for each of us to decide for ourselves,' Raza replied.

'That's exactly why we're in the mess we're in.'

'What do you mean?' Raza demanded, suddenly sitting up.

'Well,' Aslam snapped, 'the country's in a mess. American-style individualism doesn't work here. Have you seen the craziness on TV?'

'Yes, I have. Not least that weird lady on the religious show that Dada watches.'

'I meant,' Aslam glared, 'the other craziness.'

Raza raised an eyebrow.

'The sleeveless tops, the fashion shows, the drinking and partying? The aping of Western culture?'

'And that's worse than imposing one world-view on everyone? Have you ever heard of the expression "live and let live"?' asked Raza.

'I've heard things,' Aslam changed subjects, 'about you as well. Parveen told me you've got a reputation at school – at several schools – of being some kind of Casanova.'

'Now that's a word I haven't heard in a while. Thank you.'

'This isn't Chicago, Raza. Karachi's a dangerous place. Hurt the wrong girl, someone with money and connections, and you could get yourself killed.'

'I'm not involved in a *single* girl.'

'See, there you go again!' He slapped his knee excitedly and continued, 'You've your family's reputation to think about – you have sisters.'

'You have sisters, too,' Fatima interrupted, 'and I happen to be one of them, so stop staring at my chest!'

I sat up, my eyes widening at the turn the conversation had taken. Jamila's head, just a mass of curls, slowly rose from Fatima's lap, then sank down again.

For a few seconds, Aslam was speechless, his black eyes the most prominent feature in a face the colour of fuchsia bougainvillea.

'I may be Amriki,' Fatima mercilessly continued, 'but I've read the Quran in Arabic as well as English. Doesn't it mention something about keeping your gaze averted when near the opposite sex? Or is that one part of the "Deen" that you've conveniently forgotten? Looks like everyone picks and chooses, even you.'

My sister continued to break him down piece by piece, like a wayward child with a Lego figurine. Pulling off his head, then his limbs, one by one, then the tiny pieces that locked together to form his torso, she finally pulled out his tiny Lego heart.

'You disgust me!' she finished with venom. Seeing his crestfallen face, I couldn't help but feel sorry for him. I imagined her throwing that tiny red plastic heart into the blaze and cackling as it went up in smoke.

'I ... I don't know what you mean ...' Aslam stuttered when he was finally able to speak, his hands trembling as he smoothened the wrinkles in his crisp white kurta. He continued defensively, 'You people – you're misfits here, with your secret games and weird attitudes. And that little one' – he pointed at me so that I stood up, fists raised – 'she's the strangest of you four. You all need psychiatrists, starting with your Baba.'

That was it. I ran up to Aslam, kicked him in the shin, grabbed a fistful of his curly beard, and yanked, yanked hard. The desultory morning sounds of C44, the lazy cawing of crows awakening from slumber, the protracted moan of the tin-dabba wallah announcing his arrival over a potholed road, the scrape and gurgle of tea being poured from a tinny metal pot into cups in the kitchen, were violently torn through and through by his howl, which began somewhere deep within his throat beneath his beard, and then travelled to every corner of the compound and beyond.

Raza gently disentangled my fingers from Aslam's profuse facial hair. 'As you can see,' he said calmly, 'my sisters know how to take care of themselves.' Then to me, he continued in a stern voice, 'Chhoti, apologize.'

Just as I was forming the dreaded word, the front door swung open and the house was filled with sunlight and laughter. Dada swivelled in mid-shuffle and saluted deftly, raising his bald head high above his walking stick so that he looked very tall and debonair. Durdana Phupo, unnaturally flushed, declaimed like a street performer to a quickly growing crowd, which included a rapt Dada, who had forgotten all about his hunger, Dadi and Parveen, Shahana Chachi, Jamshaid Chacha, and us, too, although we were of lesser importance, invisible, in fact, from where they stood. I leaned across the back of the sofa to catch a glimpse of the person over whom so much fuss was being made, but could only see the edge of a voluminous purple chador made of expensive-looking fabric. The downstairs suddenly smelled like a hothouse of mature roses blooming furiously but clearly past their prime.

Aslam, who had been awaiting an apology, and who had been sitting with his sore beard cupped in both hands, suddenly jumped to his feet and ran to join the others as if a rare treat were on offer. The four of us looked at each other bewildered but firm in our resolve to remain seated unless invited to participate.

'Children, come and see who it is!' Dadi called to us gaily.

'Are we having breakfast in the hallway?' Raza muttered grumpily under his breath. Nonetheless, the four of us obediently formed a line and stumbled towards the light. There, in the doorway, was a woman swathed in purple, her figure haloed by the luminescent light that filtered in through the leafy vines that framed the entrance. I rubbed my sleepy eyes and looked again, this time wondrously, at this fantastic figure. A high priestess with her unnaturally tall head piece, she appeared as if she had just descended from the heavens. She brought to mind the images of Christ in stained glass I had seen at my Church preschool in Chicago. Jesus, as I remembered him, was a bearded, white-robed man with light emanating from him in solid streams of yellow glass. Impressed, I squinted to better see her face, which was obscured both by her tightly wrapped chador as well as by the beatific light surrounding her. Within seconds, however, she stepped forward and opened her arms as if to embrace us.

To my surprise, Raza and Fatima gasped. Audibly. I turned from their open mouths to the lady before me, her face now clearly visible. To me, she was just another Pakistani woman in her forties, with nothing much to recommend her except her head dress, which made her look at least six feet tall and extremely imposing. She could have been Shahana Chachi or even Durdana Phupo but for her self-assurance, which made her stride into a room and immediately take possession of it. It was obvious she was accustomed to the kind of welcome she had just received. In fact, she demanded it.

Without pausing an instant, she wrapped her heavily draped arms around the four of us and exclaimed, 'How wonderful! Allah Subhanahu Wa Ta'ala has brought us together at last!' Then, turning to the others, she continued, 'They do look like Aftab – at least the Aftab I remember from college.'

Wriggling out of her embrace, I ran to the dining room where the cook had already begun serving breakfast. Dada had taken his place at the head of the table, one hand poised in mid-air over the dish of aloo ki sabzi. Once the high priestess was seated next to him (a position of honour usually reserved for our Baba), Dada spooned some of the hot mixture first onto her plate, then his own, shocking generosity, I thought, from one so ravenous and unused to sharing. From my place at the children's table, I noticed the lady eating daintily, using a knife and fork instead of her hands like the rest of us.

But what was really fascinating were her features, well-defined even this early in the morning. I was reminded of Snow White's step-mother in an old colouring book I once had. Everything was outlined, from her eyes, which were heavily kohled, to her plump, full lips and prominent cheek bones. Her perfume still clung to my night dress and hands, making my aloo-puri taste bitter. Why were Raza and Fatima so shocked to see her, I wondered. She was just a typical 'aunty' complete with full stage make up. I had met hundreds of them in Chicago as well as Karachi. They were internationally khatarnak, or dangerous, and feared by children the world over, especially for their wet kisses and cheek-pinching fingers.

Once I had finished breakfast, I looked over at my siblings. Jamila was still enjoying her puri, pulling it apart with greasy fingers and then trying to see through its rubbery layers to Parveen, who tried to ignore her. At the grown ups' table, Fatima and Raza were the busiest I had ever seen them: they ate as if this were their last meal, their fingers frenetically forming mouthfuls that they swallowed without chewing. They scarcely looked up, even when spoken to. There was nothing much to hold my interest here, so I left, softly slipping through the front door and out into the unbearable sunshine.

I took a deep breath.

'Suffocating, isn't it?'

Shahnaz, in an oversized t-shirt and pants, stood near Tea Central, her hands in her pockets, one foot astride a chair. 'We were in the car with her. Had to pick her up after getting breakfast. I nearly died. Who knew someone that famous could stink so much?'

'Famous?' I asked. 'Who is she anyway?'

She ignored my question. 'Did you eat all your aloo-puri?'

I thought back. I couldn't be certain.

'Leave it,' she continued, picking at a scab on her toe. 'Let's play something!' With that, she grabbed my hand and raced with me along the boundary wall, where a scraggly row of half-dead flowering bushes grabbed at our ankles with their clinging thorns. It didn't take long for us to exhaust ourselves in the sunshine, finally landing, after an hour's play, on one of the cane sofas at Tea Central, panting like a pair of thirsty pups. I stretched out, my arms and legs akimbo, hoping the extra space between my limbs would allow the turbid breeze to dry my perspiration. I had almost forgotten that in my other life I was a spy and a super hero; it was nice to just be a child and, like a child, lose myself in play, the sheer physical exhilaration of it. Shahnaz and I grinned at each other and shook hands as if we were meeting for the first time. Then, in an instant, she was gone, disappearing behind the main house to the back, where her family was just sitting down to breakfast, a meal consisting of yesterday's roti and dhood-pati.

I looked up to see movement near the entrance to the main house and quickly ran to hide behind one of the coconut palms. I needn't have worried. Everyone was too taken with the high priestess to bother with me. As she emerged into the sunshine, at least half a dozen people stumbled after her, each trying to outdo the other in the business of farewell pleasantries. I heard Dadi assuring the lady that on her next visit Aftab would be there in person to welcome her and that he would be delighted to see her again, that he had repeatedly expressed an interest in meeting her after viewing one of her programmes. Dada, the tap-tap of his cane as regular as a foot soldier's march, pushed past the others and beamed, pointing jocularly at the stranger and insisting that she would be court-martialled if she didn't come soon. 'Your dear father would have wanted it,' he smiled in a final act of blackmail.

At long last, she was safely in the car and being driven out of the gate by Khyber, who had run out of the servants' quarters mid-way through his breakfast. As she drove by, I caught a glimpse of her through the window, the reflection of the blue sky and trees flashing briefly across the glass. She leaned back against the seat and stared straight ahead, looking like the bust of Nefertiti in profile. Once again, I marvelled at her head piece, which rose majestically over her like a diadem. Before the car finally left the compound, I saw her smile to herself. What was she thinking, I wondered, secure in the knowledge that no one could see her? I suddenly felt uncomfortable. There was a connection somewhere, and I was missing it.

As my siblings and I walked to our unit, I overheard Raza and Fatima having the following conversation:

'Why didn't anyone tell us that that lunatic was coming for breakfast?'

'I guess they thought – and rightly – we wouldn't show up.'

'I can't understand how educated people, our own family, for God's sake, can entertain the likes of her. She's like Pakistan's answer to Jerry Falwell.'

'She was performing the whole time. And why was she being so nice to us?'

'Baba went to college with her or something. I'm sure if he remembers who she is, he'll never want to see her.'

I stopped in mid-stride.

'Chhoti, what's wrong now?' Fatima asked impatiently. They all looked at me. No one was in the mood for startling revelations. I kept quiet and resumed walking, although my belly heaved, my greasy breakfast rising to my throat. I wrapped my arms around my stomach and ran to my room, where I threw myself on the bed, face down. It was her. Rizwana Hameed. It had to be. How was it that I didn't see it before?

And that impressive head dress? Well, it turned out to be just what it was, and nothing more:

After all the silly fuss, it was just another bun under a headscarf.

CHAPTER 12

Finding a private corner for yourself at C44 was not as easy as it looked. Yes, there were places to conceal yourself if you hunted for them, enough tucked away recesses for a quick game of hide-and-seek, a temporary refuge from the onslaught of an irate grandparent or a sinister cousin, but no lasting peace to be had anywhere in a compound where, at any one time, there were always at least twenty people. There was no privacy, especially for us children. We shared bedrooms and bathrooms, were subject to surprise visits from our more vigilant relatives across the courtyard, and were not allowed to telephone our friends after maghrib. Of course, being four complicated matters further still, for while we could escape from the rest of the household, there was no escaping each other on the rare occasions that we tried.

Days after our arrival, however, we discovered one spot in the house, a mouldy recess beneath the stairs that led up to the bedrooms, that began to serve as the headquarters of our alternative universe or, when we wanted to avoid everyone, a place for quiet self-reflection. Initially, we girls cringed at the thought of squatting amidst the dust and grime, where months-old newspapers formed towering stacks against the wall, imagining the dark corner infested with rodents, chhipkalis, and miscellaneous multi-legged creatures like the resilient hard-shelled cockroach, whose gigantic size never ceased to alarm when it poked its antennae out of the wide-holed drain beneath our sink. Soon, however, we came to realize that that was the only 'secret' place to be had in a compound almost as hawkishly monitored as a maximum security prison. Like corrections officers, Durdana Phupo, Dadi, and even Shahana Chachi patrolled our unit, periodically performing chaapas, or surprise attacks, to catch us unawares, once scandalized by the sight of the three of us girls in our underwear, casually lying on the bed discussing which we preferred, chikoo or kiwi, the curtains of our large window wide open, Raza sitting at the desk, calm as can be, reading a book. What was our crime? I thought, baffled. Later, I came to realize that it was not for what we had done, but for our potential for mischief-making that we were being watched. We were Amriki, after all. I closed my eyes and saw Dadi's disapproval in the crooked bend of her mouth, her thin lips merging into the wrinkled creases on either side of her jaw so that it looked as if her face were split, like an over-ripe melon.

Over the months, we made changes to improve upon our dingy little corner, sweeping away the dust and cobwebs, adding a small dhurrie and a cushion or two, spraying its far reaches with insect repellent, and leaving a cracked bowl of eggshells to ward off chhipkalis. By the time we began holding our secret meetings there, our mouldy hideout was a thing of wonder, a hermit's paradise, the staircase an arm curved in protection. It was here on a Saturday morning that I stumbled upon Fatima, her face hidden beneath her dark curls, a sheaf of papers in her hand. When she heard me, she raised her head, strands of hair sticking to her wet face, her eyes unnaturally shiny, like a hunted animal's. Realizing it was only me, she pushed her head deeper into her arms. I thought nothing of it, accustomed to being ignored, but remained stubbornly where I was. Then, reaching out, I felt her hands, which she had positioned in front of her like a pair of maces, her large silver rings the spikes. My sister had become unpredictable of late. I thought how best to disarm her and finally decided on the easiest method, a simple hug. Her whole body was rigid like she was trying to hold herself in. But within seconds, I felt her go limp in my arms, her sobs, silent till now, torn out of her throat in loud gasps as she heaved against me.

'What's wrong?' I asked, trying to prise the sheaf of papers away from her. 'Is this about Amma and Baba? Shahbaz Chacha? Fatima, tell me.'

'You wouldn't understand,' she said, pulling away, wiping her face with the back of her dupatta. She stood up.

'Wait. I'll go,' I said, realizing I wasn't helping. I made my way out of our hideout, then ran upstairs in search of Raza and Jamila. When I had reached the head of the stairs, I could hear Raza's voice, clearly audible above the now-familiar cawing. He stood by the telephone table holding the receiver away from his ear. There was static and a high-pitched incessant chatter at the other end, of which he was clearly bored. Suddenly, deciding that he had had enough, he shouted a curt goodbye into the receiver, his final words addressed, surprisingly, to Clarice.

Clarice, as I remembered her, was Fatima's best friend, tall, blonde, and blandly American, the child of tree-hugging hippies who married late and moved from northern California to Albuquerque, then Chicago, where their home-grown business of healing crystals, incense sticks, and alternative medicine attracted tourists to their modest shop at Navy Pier. Clarice, home-schooled throughout elementary, first met Fatima at high school, where they became friends at once despite their obviously different personalities and backgrounds. Clarice had a fondness for the exotic, spending hours at our house trying on Amma's shalwar-kameezes, wrapping tie-dyed dupattas around her thin blonde locks, and sampling our cuisine, which she thought was 'awesome' and 'funky'. I just couldn't understand the attraction. It was only after Amma died that I realized Clarice had more depth than any of us gave her credit for. She was Fatima's friend, and she had stood by her.

'Why didn't you call Fatima?' I asked Raza, unapologetically direct.

'Clarice is crazy. Crazy Clarice,' he said, then laughed. 'Can you believe it? She wants to visit us here! Impossible!' He did something funny with his lips, puckering them up so that I couldn't tell whether he was snarling or smirking. Then, rolling his eyes, he shrugged as if to say 'What is a man to do?'

That was strange and, yes, frankly unimaginable. I thought of Clarice in Karachi, and everything about the place and the girl seemed incompatible. Lanky legs in shorts, tank tops with flimsy straps aside, there were so many other reasons why it would be awkward. Firstly, I was beginning to suspect that Raza, and not Fatima, was her main reason for wanting to visit. That was enough to set my siblings at war. Besides, there was the rest of the family to think about, all fourteen members of it, headed by Dada, our patriarch. It was obvious he had no tolerance for teenage American girls, even his own granddaughters. I visualized my grandparents' look of horror as Clarice, tumbling helter-skelter out of a yellow taxi, stickered suitcase in hand, anorak-clad and bare-legged, began waving wildly from outside the gate and then ran, in full view of the entire neighbourhood, into the arms of my brother.

'Impossible,' I agreed, temporarily forgetting why I had come upstairs.

'She's a crazy one, that Clarice,' Raza continued. 'Sometimes I think I'll wake up to see her looking down at me while I sleep.'

'Okay, forget Clarice,' I said. 'Why is Fatima crying beneath the stairs? Has something happened? Those papers she has – are they about us or anyone in the family?'

'No, I've read those. If I were her, I'd just ignore them.'

'Why? What's in them?'

'Chhoti, you wouldn't understand.'

'I will, I will, I will!' I whined, knowing full well that that was the quickest way of forcing him into giving me an answer. I fell to my knees and held onto his legs, trying not to laugh as his manly hair tickled my nose. (It would not do to spoil the mood.)

'She's upset over a few emails she's received recently.'

'Emails? What kind?'

'You know, secret admirer-type, only they've turned nasty. The man calls himself "Colonel Bogey". That's almost as outdated as Aslam's "Casanova"!' He added gratuitously, 'Amateur!'

'Well, at least go and see her. She's sitting under the stairs crying.'

Raza, who still appeared to be thinking of his telephone call, strolled in no hurry towards the stairs.

Suddenly, I noticed Baba sitting in a corner of the upper lounge, his legs propped up on a stool, an open book before him, so still in his now-habitual solitude that it took a few seconds to separate the white of his kurta-pyjama from the walls, his toes, long and gnarled like the branches of a tree, an extension of the furniture he sat upon. I ran to him, then squeezed my eyes shut in anticipation of the rough feel of his unshaven face against the cheek I had presented for a kiss. I stretched across his legs to grab one of his toes, third-left on his right foot, my favourite because of the feel of the soft skin at the back which, through years of wear, had a raised ridge at the center which I loved to pinch.

'Horrible, aren't they? Your mother always said they were my worst feature.'

I looked up startled, my fingers still curled around his middle toe. Was that an opening, after all these days, months? And was I left alone, sibling-less, to deal with this miracle on my own? My heart pounded within my rib cage like a bouncy ball. I searched for the right answer, something at once sensitive and witty, something that would trigger an exchange of memories and not the immediate and, perhaps, permanent withdrawal of Baba into his private grief. The questions I wanted to ask were obviously not the right ones at this moment (Where and how did you meet? How did you marry? Why was there opposition?), but unfortunately they were all I could think of. Instead, before I knew what I was doing, I lapsed into the inevitable, taking refuge in the comfort of my own childishness. Was it my voice, or another's, high-pitched, sing-songy, that began to lisp out 'This little piggy went to market, this little piggy stayed at home…', my fingers wound tightly around that familiar middle toe? Inwardly, I cursed myself. What was I doing? Was this the path to Baba's emotional redemption? Probably not, but when I looked up I saw him smile the way he used to before all of this happened, his eyes half-closed, lips parted, the lines of his taffy-coloured skin shooting outwards like fireworks in a Fourth of July sky. He looked like himself again, a whole man with all his various parts – heart, mind, body – intact.

I must have done something right.

All of a sudden, we were surrounded. Jamila ran out of the bedroom, Raza and Fatima bounded up the stairs. We all fell upon Baba, and he held us in his arms, stretching them as far around us as he could so that each of us felt the warmth of him on our shoulders. Huddled like that, we children looked at each other in the semi-dark, our faces identical in expression, our expression one of gratitude, frank relief.

✳

'My son has shaved! My son has shaved!' Dadi was chanting, bouncing her hefty weight from one foot to another as she danced around the room. A few of the lighter china decorations in the glass curio tinkled under the pressure of her movement, forming a musical accompaniment to her clumsy performance.

'Ammi,' Durdana Phupo objected, 'it's not as if Bhai Jan hasn't shaved in the last six months.' She stood to one side, hand on hip, observing her mother quizzically.

'But look at his face! His dress! His attitude! Now I can tell your Abba that all of that goat meat I sacrificed wasn't in vain! Chottu,' she said, suddenly noticing me in the room, 'Come, give me a hug! You have your father back!'

I ran into her arms. Her joy was as genuine as ours; after all, she was our father's mother, and who, other than us, could be as disinterestedly happy in his well-being?

I laughed as she raised me above the floor and spun me around, not very high, of course, but high enough for my feet to just graze the carpet, my uniform flying about me with the swish of air. I laughed some more as she put me down, then burrowed my head under the ample girth of her belly, balancing the entire weight of it on my head.

'Silly girl! Come out from under there!' she exclaimed. She lifted up her stomach like a slab of dough and waited till I had pulled my head out.

Giggling, we both fell on the sofa. Durdana Phupo shook her head and smiled at us, looking down as if at two little girls, not one. I nestled my head on Dadi's lap and closed my eyes, settling down for what had now become my customary siesta.

'Durri, you can't imagine how relieved I am,' Dadi began, her soft fingers tracing my eyebrows, then finding their way to my ears, where a few deft fingers went in and out, outlining their shape and gently tickling them. I stretched my legs and pointed my toes happily like a sleeping ballerina.

'Chhoti, move,' Durdana Phupo said as she lifted my legs to sit under them.

'Durri, I haven't been this worried since we were in Dhaka.'

My eyes flew open.

'I know, Ammi, I know. Please don't bring that up. It's been years, and we're just getting through another crisis.'

'Beta, everything brings me back to that time,' I heard Dadi say, her voice unsteady. Suddenly her hands moved away from my face. I opened my eyes and realized that she was crying now, tears running down her face and into my hair. I made as if to get up.

'Chhoti, don't worry,' Durdana Phupo said softly. 'This happens sometimes. She's just relieved your Baba's well.'

'But why is she sad? She should be happy that Baba's feeling better.'

'I am, I am,' Dadi moaned as she fought against her tears, wiping her face with a corner of her chador before binding me to her chest so tightly that her heart pressed against my ear. 'You're too young to know. The past is the past. Yours is the future. Stop filling your head with adult talk – play, sing, be a little girl.'

My instinct was to tell her that she was wrong. That it was unfair of her to deny us the right to find out about our family's past. After our mother's death, we needed anchorage; after being displaced, exchanging the security of our red-bricked house with its garden of familiar sounds for C44, a structure of cement white with the blaze of sun and cloudless sky, we were searching for something to hold on to, to explain to us who we were and why we were here.

Instead, I asked scowling, 'Do all families around here have so many secrets?'

Durdana Phupo laughed as she replied, 'More or less. Besides, think how boring life would be without mystery! Dadi's right, you know. Go and play.'

'But I'm tired,' I grumbled, turning on my side. My face was pressed up right against Dadi's belly so that the tiny flowers on her kurta looked like giant polka dots. I could hear her stomach gurgling, the digestive juices at work breaking down the tea and cake rusks she consumed over my head. Slowly, my face pressed into her like that, my body against hers, the rhythm of her ageing blood and bones and her dragging heart beat pulled me towards her, bound me to her tightly like an African babe wound in cloth to her mother's back. I nestled deeper into her warmth, into the softly sagging tissues that formed her muscles, feeling the droop of her ample breasts over me, the rhythm of her breath rising, falling, rising, falling, lulling me, eventually, to sleep.

CHAPTER 13

Shahnaz and I had discovered early on in our friendship that if we sat side-by-side at the far end of the garden under the particularly thick and hairy undergrowth of an ancient banyan tree and, that too, at the quietest hour of mid-afternoon, we could hear the faint, slightly muted crash of waves against shore. Because we were at least twenty miles from the sea, no one believed us, least of all Fatima and Raza. To them, it was always traffic – the rumble of colossal trucks over potholed roads – or the roar of thunder under black storm clouds, or the forklift that unearthed the mound of trash beneath the old school bridge. But no one could convince us otherwise, our imaginations buttressed by the indelible sensation of moving earth, which we were convinced we could feel if we held our breath and sat deathly still, our toes curling into the sand as it pulled away with the tide, zillions of particles heavy with the weight of salt water. Though the ground where we performed these imaginative exercises was dry as brittle bone, as bereft of moisture as the Thar in drought, it cooled our hot skins to think that we were waist deep in sea water. Although I did not confide this in my friend, I was preparing myself for greater things, future trips to the moon and stars, even a nocturnal visit, perhaps, to my mother.

Thank God for Shahnaz. I could not have survived that first difficult year without her. Notwithstanding certain obvious differences in appearance (she was shorter, fairer, lithe, her hair a rich golden-brown while mine was black and curly), we were both similar, sharing a passion for unreal adventures. It was almost as if I had been reunited with a fraternal twin. It was this quality I valued most in my new friend. I even hoped, in time, to make her an honorary member of the world my siblings and I had created. It would require a great deal of persuasion (for Lady M resisted change) but eventually everyone would realize, as I did, that Shahnaz was just like us.

But it was confusing, our friendship. It was nothing like the friendships I had had in the past, my three or four years' of conscious experience spanning a variety of prized, though tenuous, relationships through preschool to fourth grade. The sniffing and pawing that led, in Mrs Griseman's toddler playgroup, to my friendship with glossy black-skinned Makeeba, for example, or later, my fierce 'best-friend' phase in kindergarten, Beckie McKenna breaking my heart every time she saved a spot for someone else at story time. All of these friendships I could understand. They were mine to do as I pleased with, the coordinates of acceptable behaviour clearly demarcated by the adults in my life. As long as I stayed within these boundaries (i.e. no biting, kicking, or bullying, no pulling of braids or snatching of toys, all of which, of course, I had tried at least once), Amma and Baba didn't interfere. With Shahnaz, it was different. Although Baba didn't care, Dadi certainly did.

Once I was startled out of sleep by the sensation of Dadi's strong old fingers burrowing purposefully into my scalp. And then came her voice, gruff with irritation, as she said to Durdana Phupo, 'Chhoti was with that driver's girl again. Her hair needs to be checked for lice on a regular basis.' When I mentioned this to Shahnaz, her irreverent response of 'So the old hag's never had lice herself, I suppose?' left me momentarily speechless. (Little did they know that I had already had two encounters with these vermin in Chicago, the last in Mrs Thorndike's class, whose stern letter of reprisal, much to my personal mortification, had circulated throughout the fourth-grade classroom.)

When Dadi attempted to complain to Baba about Shahnaz's influence over me, he laughed it off by saying, 'Look at it this way, Ammi. At least Ferzana's Urdu is improving.'

'Urdu?' Dadi spluttered venomously as she slapped Baba's omelette onto his plate, 'Is that what you call it? Do you think that luckless little Pathani can teach us Urdu?'

There were other, less obvious, signs of Dadi's displeasure that manifested themselves in not-so-subtle ways. (Subtlety, after all, was not her forte.) If, after several hours of sweaty play in the garden with Shahnaz I came running in to ask for a drink, there was an incremental shift in the rings that constituted the soft flesh of her face till her lips, thinner than usual, were swallowed altogether by the folds of her double chins. Then, with stiffly moving limbs and great deliberation, the water would be poured and pushed at me in silence. I later realized that the remarks over the need for more homework and extra tuition were at their loudest when Shahnaz and I, like dusky Wee Willy Winkies, tapped at the windows of C44, rousing each sleeping member from their siesta with a different configuration of tuk-tuk-tuk, or when, early on Saturday mornings, we climbed on to the roof and banged our feet against the legs of the rusty disused bridge table. However, as far as school work was concerned, Dadi had no grounds for complaint. I was doing fairly well in all my subjects (yes, even Urdu) and our school, though sometimes derided by her for its 'foreign' methods, was the alma mater of the city's elite.

Over that, too, there had been some controversy. The school, once rising majestically over the congested inner city, had recently been relocated to one of Karachi's expensive suburbs, where its sprawling academic opulence dwarfed the landscape around it, the sea merely an extension of it rather than a setting. Baba, who had grown up on military cantonments and who had spent most of his academic life in Pakistan in government-run institutions, resisted our enrolment at a private school, concerned with the insidious influence of spoilt children. It was Dada who pointed out that the school population consisted mainly of 'Americanized brats' (his words) who watched many of the same American television shows as we once did, via satellite and who religiously vacationed in Houston or San Francisco or New York. Baba eventually gave in, spending three days filling out three sets of forms, having report cards attested, and providing financial statements to the admissions office. After some pedantic quibbling on the part of the admissions officer over our 'inflated' American grades, we were placed in our respective classrooms, a grudging favour, we were told, to the four-star general who had pleaded our case. (Little did Dada know that his distinguished military career and time as a prisoner of war would be required, decades later, as collateral for our admission.)

The term 'burger' was introduced to us soon after our arrival in Karachi by our cousin, Aslam, who was responsible for the addition of dozens of new words (largely of Arabic origin) into our vocabulary. 'Let there be no mistake,' he announced defiantly, 'you and your burger lifestyle won't be tolerated by Dada.'

'Burgher?' Fatima had asked, baffled by his reference to a mediaeval town-dweller. 'Can't you think of a more current insult?'

Aslam, doubling over his beard with merriment, gasped, 'That's not what I meant!' Eventually, of course, we learned to appreciate this word, and its antonym, bun-kebab, for all its striking gradations and degradations, the weight of its condemnation hinging on the absence of chutney or the addition of a cheese slice. Being called either, it appeared, was an insult. Our admission into this school was an unequivocal acceptance of our 'burger' lifestyle.

It would not be an exaggeration to say that the three of us were awed by our new school, for its spacious air-conditioned classrooms, well-appointed gymnasium, swimming pool, generously endowed library, largely foreign-educated staff, and demanding curriculum rivalled that of any private school in Chicago. The buildings for each section – Kindergarten, Junior, Middle School and College – were arranged around a massive courtyard where school assemblies and early morning drills were conducted. Although it was strange to be bound by the school's excessive regulations, irritating at times to be wearing polyester-blend uniforms in the sun, within a few short weeks I was infatuated with Mrs Nasim and had all but forgotten crusty old Mrs Thorndike of Chicago.

Mrs Nasim had several advantages over Mrs Thorndike, foremost of which were her youth and glamour, crystallized in the form-fitting, colour-coordinated outfits she wore to school and the 'chun-chun' that accompanied every movement of her lithesome body, swathed as it was in dangly adornments. It was rumoured that she was the daughter of a former teacher whose many years of service had endeared her to the administration and had enabled Mrs Nasim, with barely a BA from a local college, to join an exclusive staff of senior academics and foreign graduates. If asked, I could not say how she was as a teacher, for the source of all her methods was a mysterious binder full of notes, which she took every opportunity of consulting, particularly when one of us asked her a question not related to the curriculum. Her answers generally ranged from the vague, followed by flapping hand gestures and a penetrating look through the window at the sky and trees, to the rigidly mechanical, uttered in the staccato tone of a robotic device whose 'on' button had been triggered. I realized early on that asking her a question (especially the sort that I was likely to ask) yielded little in terms of meaningful resolution. It was easier to pester the other teachers, Mrs Din and Sir Tariq, who taught Urdu and Islamiyat respectively, and who obviously knew more about the fundamentals of life.

As a big 'apa', however, she was far more interesting than my own sister, Fatima, who was only a couple of years younger than her. Mrs Nasim enjoyed spending time with me and actually sought me out in a crowd of other fifth-graders. When Raza brought me to my classroom in the mornings, she often came out to receive me. At break, Mrs Nasim's bangled hand on my shoulder, I watched the retreating backs of the tail-end of the line as it serpentined down the hallway and through the wide-open doors into the sun. From the tall windows of the air-conditioned classroom I was able to see the burning asphalt, a pure white, with children clustered in wilting bunches across its length and breadth. I, in the meantime, enjoyed a few leisurely chores (arranging books, watering the plants) and spent the rest of the half-hour break sitting with Mrs Nasim and talking about my family. A few times a week I was required to pass tuition notes to Raza. For all of this I was rewarded with fistfuls of toffees from the special jar underneath her desk.

Pester her as I might, Mrs Nasim rarely spoke of her marriage to the moustachioed, earnest-looking gentleman in shiny suits who came to pick her up on Fridays in a rusty '82 Corolla. His perfectly round face reminded me of the merry little children in my Urdu Qaida, for his neatly scraped hair divided his scalp into two equal portions of smooth jet black, curling a little behind his ears. Otherwise, he was as monochromatic as a single-colour illustration. Arm dangling over the side of the car in an attempt at carefree jauntiness, he spent the blistering afternoon awaiting his haughty bride outside the main entrance to the Junior School. I marvelled at his face, which I once caught sight of, so brightening at the sight of my teacher that I thought his two-dimensional self might jump out of the car and skip to her while singing 'Alif, anaar', 'Bay, bakree…'

How, I wondered, had he looked as a bridegroom? Did he wear a sherwani and a traditional pugree of raw silk that clumsily unfurled as he bent to greet his mother-in-law? Did he enter the wedding tent draped in a lavish shawl, his saleem shahees rising like ducks' bills as he stumbled toward the stage? While he ate, did his elaborate moustache get soaked in the hot liquid of the shadi korma? However romantic a scene I conjured up in my mind, he always fell short of my expectations. The fact was it was impossible to cast him as the hero opposite a heroine of Mrs Nasim's stature. Even my imagination balked at the thought. Poor Mr Nasim could not make the transition from two-dimensional monochromatic to movie-style Technicolour. I wondered how a woman like Mrs Nasim, whose imagination, I feared, was much more limited than mine, tolerated her husband. She didn't seem particularly happy on the days that Mr Nasim came to pick her up, slumping into the front seat as he lunged at her solicitously.

'Array, choro, Ferzana! Why do you always ask about him?' Mrs Nasim once snapped crossly as she painted my toenails an electric-pink. We sat in the semi-darkness of the crawl space beneath her desk. I closed my eyes till all the playground sounds, though faint, seemed magnified in my head: the hollow thud of bats and balls against asphalt, the shrill protest of girls being taunted, a howl of injury from someone who had, perhaps, fallen and scraped her knee. It wasn't fair. I crawled out from under the desk and stood up to look at the playground through the window. My eyes slowly focused on a group of girls in the foreground; there was Raabia, the one who sat next to me in class and who once shared a sandwich with me when I had forgotten my lunch. 'Miss, I want to go outside,' I said as I hastily pulled on my socks and PT shoes. I ran out of the classroom before Mrs Nasim emerged, jewellery tinkling, from beneath the desk, her face, as I glanced back, chalky and panic-stricken.

Once outside, I joined the group of girls I had seen through the window. A few of them looked up in surprise. It was Raabia who spoke first: 'So, teacher's pet finally decided to come outside? Did Mrs Nasim get bored of you? I knew,' she continued, looking meaningfully at the others, 'that it couldn't last. Aside from her funny accent, she's really not that interesting.' Then, within seconds, the recess bell rang and everyone lined up to go back inside. I remained where I was, staring at the tangled laces of my PT shoes until the supervising teacher sharply called me to attention. I should have realized, of course, that my closeness with Mrs Nasim would affect how my classmates treated me. Still, the temptation of privilege and the conspiratorial nature of our gossip sessions pleased my instinct for subterfuge. Within a day or two, Mrs Nasim had plied me with enough toffees to make me forget the injustice of having to divulge details of my family life while she remained reticent about hers. After all, as she explained to me, she was a grown up and my teacher. That gave her rights over me which I couldn't possibly hope to have reciprocated.

The only person with whom I could discuss this puzzling state of affairs was Shahnaz. I had smuggled her into our dark little sanctuary. The light that entered the crawl space in shafts from between the stairs fell, zebra-like, across the opposite wall, intermittently illuminating the grotesque drawings Jamila and I had pasted on to it, artistic renditions of our alter egos in various poses of sweeping retribution, haughty indifference, or play. There was Lady M, arms raised over a blazing fire of orange, red, and yellow Crayola swirls, Dag, green eyes flashing, surveying the city of Karachi at night, its stunted cement buildings rising like corpses from a swamp of watery grey. Another series of drawings depicted Timmer and Little Furry performing a maniacal dance in a fantastic garden of gargantuan tropical blossoms. Shahnaz was speechless. Then, in an unexpected burst of enthusiasm, she slapped my back with gusto and exclaimed, 'Waah!'

Pleased, I sat down opposite her on the dhurrie and then proceeded to outline my troubles with Mrs Nasim. She listened to me thoughtfully. Then, when I had finished my (slightly) exaggerated account, she only had one question to ask of me. Leaning back against a drawing of Little Furry capturing the Sloth, she asked, 'So, what kind of toffee does she keep under her desk? Because,' she continued ruminatively, 'my favourite is the one in the purple and gold wrapper.'

'Shahnaz!' I hissed. 'You're supposed to help me.'

'No, I'm serious,' she replied. 'In my mind, it's pretty straightforward, Ferzana. Unless the toffee is really good – and I'm talking the purple-and-gold kind or the imported ones – I'd ditch the teacher and go and play outside. It's more fun, and your class fellows won't hate you for being singled out. If she has notes to give Raza Bhai, why can't she just do it herself? It's only homework, right?'

'I'm not so sure,' I replied slowly, thinking back to the day Raza tore up Mrs Nasim's note but didn't allow any of us to read it.

Shahnaz suddenly sat up, a wicked smile on her face. 'Accha,' she said meaningfully, 'So that's it, is it?'

'What?' I asked blankly. I could see a disembodied pair of round eyes, a ghoulish mouthful of glinting teeth, and little else.

Oh.

'Oh no,' I responded, shocked. 'But she's married!' An image of poor besotted Mr Nasim with his schoolboy earnestness rose to my mind's eye next to an equally persistent image of my brother, his hulking frame and roguish good looks, I suddenly realized with shock, persuasive enough to supplant his timid though lawfully-wedded rival. Shahnaz's theory made perfect sense. It also explained why Mrs Nasim always wanted to talk about our family. I recalled our last conversation, a puzzling, circuitous analysis of Raza's favourite foods, his previous girlfriends, his taste in music. I thought back to earlier conversations and most of them, after a nominal discussion about me or my family, led back to one individual: my brother, of course.

I shuddered.

'What?' Shahnaz asked.

'I feel sick,' I said, as I crawled out from under the stairs and stood up, leaning against the wall for support. My skin burned. I could imagine it turning scarlet.

'Honestly, you should have been one of those drama actors on TV,' Shahnaz grunted as she pulled herself out and stood beside me. 'What? You haven't been used before? I mean, are you serious?' She shook her head in disbelief.

Used. A short, hideous, stunted word, but so expressive of my relationship with Mrs Nasim over the last six months, which was anything but the wholesome friendship I had imagined. I had thought of her as my special grown-up confidant, someone whom I could rely on and who would protect me from bullying classmates. How despicable of her to use me like that. But there was another person who made me angrier still. I knew my sisters would join me in condemning that selfish brute. My rage, which began with a mixture of embarrassment and self-hate, ballooned and pulsated, its target, my brother. But, I realized, it would not do to confront him just yet.

And then, a voice from across the courtyard startled us: 'Ferzana! Come here! That silly girl is with the driver's daughter again! Ferzana!'

Sighing resignedly, I slumped against the wall. All of a sudden, I was an eleven-year-old child again, obeying my grandmother's summons.

'Ayee, Dadi,' I shouted.

Shahnaz turned to look back at me as she slipped out of the door and into the mosquito-and-cricket-hum of our garden at sunset.

CHAPTER 14

'Before the completion of the sacrificial phase, we have to obtain our pound of flesh,' Lady M reflected, referring to the fact that Baba's recovery meant an end to Dadi's weekly qurbani. 'It is clear that these local customs have effected a change in him,' she continued, 'and may be of help to us in our mission to get home, too.' For three or four months now, the crows of C44, battening on the generosity of Dadi's religious convictions, had grown to disturbing size, till now, swollen like black balloons, they floated languorously over the roof in anticipation of another free meal.

We were hiding behind a cluster of coconut palms in the courtyard, facing the main unit, where at around eleven on a Thursday morning Dadi was known to climb the winding cement staircase to the roof, scattering goat flesh across its flat, sun-bleached expanse as hundreds of black, beady-eyed creatures watched from the branches of the surrounding palms.

'Yes, Lady M,' I nodded obediently, my eyes fixed, through my binoculars, on the brass handle of the door, which was just about all I could see. (The fact was this visual aid was completely unnecessary at such close quarters, more a matter of style than necessity.) Suddenly, the handle shifted, blurring my view, and Lady M whispered urgently, 'Little Furry, look! Here she comes.'

As expected, Dadi emerged through the screen door with a small plastic bag that sloshed this way and that as she lumbered up the cement staircase to the right of the unit. We waited till she had made her way down again and had disappeared through the kitchen door, the bloody bag now empty, flapping in the breeze like the pelt of a butchered animal. Lady M and I darted across the courtyard, then wound our way up the cement staircase, twisted like a bakery cheese straw and pressed, like an afterthought, against the side of the house. Still dizzy from the climb, our heads rose above ground level. We balked at what we saw:

Within seconds of our arrival at the top, we were surrounded. I rubbed my eyes in disbelief, casting a glance at the sun for reassurance, although it was obscured, eerily, by wings of black, hundreds of them, with beaks and talons and glossy chests silhouetted against the light. They were less like birds and more like the vengeful harpies I had read about in my book of Greek mythology. There was a cacophony of grating protest as two or three dozen of these aggressive little beings, motivated by their instinct for self-preservation, fought for the meat. We stood by and watched this display of avian hysteria. For a moment, lost in thought, I wondered at these creatures, whom I hardly noticed but for their early morning cawing, and at the singleminded tenacity that drove them.

Finally, Lady M said a little desperately, 'Little Furry, we've got to grab at least one piece before these pesky birds fly away with them all!'

I knew then that it was up to me. I scanned the rooftop with my binoculars and found a relatively obscure morsel of meat, which had rolled under a discarded bridge table, part of a significant number of abandoned objects near the water tank which I had already rifled through before. Bracing myself against potential attack, I placed my arms criss-cross over my head, looked down at my feet, pathetically inadequate against my rivals' talons, and barrelled my way through the birds, imagining all the while that I had been shot out of a torpedo gun. Eyes still closed, I fell to my knees and groped the floor in search of something wet and spongy, my fingers coming up against nothing but the sharp edge of rusting metal, the hard lines of tin trunks, tables, and disused chairs. Then, within seconds, there was a sudden change, as of a drop in temperature; dozens of wings began flapping frantically, the cawing rising in pitch till I suddenly recognized it for what it was – a cry to battle. Within that instant, I felt the hail stones, gentle pinpricks at first, followed by a series of sharp digs into my head and shoulders, as if large chunks of ice were being pelted at me. My hands went instinctively to my scalp and came back wet. I opened my eyes and saw my palms covered in blood.

'Little Furry, abort mission! Abort mission!' came Lady M's stricken voice from a distance, then indistinguishable noise, shouting, cawing, and the ringing in my ears from the sight of blood. I scrambled into the foetal position and tried to remain as still as I could. Seconds later, I heard adult voices, and then felt myself being swooped up, carried down, brought inside to safety. Suddenly, it was cool and dark.

By this time, I was unabashedly weeping, the wounds on my head and neck stinging with pain. I recognized Baba's aftershave as my face pressed into his shirt sleeve and immediately relaxed, going limp in his arms as he sat me down beneath the fan, gently wiping the blood away from my skin with a wet cloth. Suddenly, from the bustle and activity came the sound of an unfamiliar voice directed at me in loud and simple English, asking me all sorts of questions about where, how, and most of all, why. I had no answers. At least none that I could share with everyone, for by now the entire family had gathered in Dadi's living room, all eyes on my back, which I couldn't see but imagined a pickled mango, for it burned as if someone had spread crushed chillies on it. When the wounds had been disinfected and bandaged, I was finally made to sit up, Baba and Raza restraining me as the doctor gave me a tetanus shot amid my howls of protest.

The doctor left soon after I had been put to bed. Baba, Fatima, Raza, and Jamila sat around me, no one venturing to speak for several minutes as I continued to moan, lying on my stomach with my face towards the window, where I could only see the sky, now flush from the sun's rapid decline.

'Chhoti, I'm not even going to begin –' started Raza, his voice rising in anticipated sarcasm as he postured as an irate parent. Before he could go any further, however, Baba intervened and in a voice calmer and more level, placed a gentle hand on my injured back, and said, 'Ferzana, what were you thinking? You know you're not allowed on the roof. You could have gotten yourself killed.'

'It's those nasty crows,' I mumbled, burying my face in my arms.

'Those birds don't attack unless you give them cause.'

I knew I couldn't admit it was all Lady M's fault. The whole crow-scheme was her idea. The penalty for betraying a member of our parallel universe was brutal, namely permanent exile. Although I couldn't see her, I sensed Jamila was agitated, her body pressing into my feet, and her arms and legs busy with movement. A few seconds later, she attempted to speak, but instead of a coherent sentence, she came out with a few disjointed words that no one except myself could understand. It was apology enough. Wincing, I sat up and turned to face my family, one hand surreptitiously slipping into my pocket, where my fingers felt the spongy texture of raw flesh, now slightly slimy and well on its way to decomposition.

'Jamila, what's the matter, beta? Slowly,' Baba coaxed, his voice gentle, as it always was when he spoke to her. 'I can't understand what you're saying. Qurbani, mission? Meat? What's going on?' He looked up questioningly at Fatima and Raza, who had exchanged glances at the word 'mission' but now shrugged as if they had no idea what Jamila was saying. A second later, Raza, staring directly at me, raised a hostile eyebrow and scowled meaningfully.

'Baba,' I wailed, my voice plaintive, 'I hurt all over! I want to sleep.'

'Quite right, beta,' said Baba as he swiftly turned me over on my stomach, arranged my arms at my sides, and wrapped me in sheets with the deftness of a pharaonic embalmer. 'Come on, kids. Let her rest for an hour or two.'

I waited a few seconds after the door had closed, then raised myself an inch off the bed so that my fingers could slip beneath my pelvis and into my pocket, now almost sealed shut from the globular slime my prize was fast secreting. Wincing at the movement but determined to go on, I pushed my fingers through the opening, pulled out the meat and, wrapping it in my fist, proceeded to prise it out from under me. Then, raising my fist to the light, now blazing orange through the trees, I reluctantly uncurled my digits one by one to reveal – O wonder – a perfect roll-shaped boti, a jelly bean of flesh, a fine, delectable morsel of goat, one that any self-respecting crow would have sold his right claw – nay, both claws – to acquire. I smiled triumphantly. Opening my bedside drawer, I dropped the sticky qurbani into a bejewelled trinket box that I usually reserved for my most precious objects. This was our little piece of the sacrifice now. Maybe, just maybe, it would help us get home to Chicago.

'Chhoti,' Uncle Raff whispered into my ear, 'what made you do it?'

I felt his bony hand, weightless like a sparrow's frame, brush against my back, pausing frequently to trace the patchy outline of my bandages through the thin cotton of my shirt. My head rested against his chest, just beneath his chin, from where I could hear his heart beating, the slight rasp of his breath as he laboured, I suddenly realized, to support my weight. I removed my arms from around his neck and slipped into the space between him and the armrest. Across the patio, Dada glowered at us over his tea cup like a wary sniper his target.

Leaning over, I whispered back, 'Secret Mission, Uncle Raff.'

'But you don't mess with those black aviators, Ferzana! You're army, they're air force. The lines of separation are clearly demarcated.' Then, a few seconds later, I saw him close his eyes and fall back against his seat as if exhausted by this short exchange. All of a sudden, raising an agitated hand into the air like he was fending off a swarm of wasps, he questioned irritably, 'What are you fighting anyway?'

'Ferzana,' Dada called sharply from across the table, 'leave Uncle Raff alone.'

Since my encounter with the crows, Dada had become even more distant. Perhaps it had only convinced him of the view he already held – that we Amriki were paagal. Nestling closer to Uncle Raff, I looked away, suddenly fascinated with the tipsy movement of a stray cat, its flea-bitten pelt hanging loosely on a sleek frame of bone as it negotiated its way across our glass-encrusted boundary. A minute later, the cat, the wall, the sky above it, the entire focus of my gaze melted into a dreary slate-coloured grey, a nondescript murky darkness like the swirl of the Arabian Sea, pulling at my feet with its powerful drag, the ground underneath me slipping. It was impossible to resist this fantasy of escape. Even plunging into an imaginary ocean was preferable to interacting with my grandfather.

'Ferzana.'

Dada's voice again. I ignored it, finally allowing myself to fall away and down, the grainy sand treacherous beneath my feet, the rest of my body, first buoyed upwards by the waves, then sinking, fathoms deep, my hair floating around me like a mermaid's, my silvery fish-tail tingling like a newly-discovered muscle ready to be flexed.

'Ferzana, beta, come here.'

Watery but persistent, the voice followed me even as I dove deeper into the darkness. Periodic swirls of eerie blue light electrified the deep, exposing the gigantic gaping maw of a fanfin seadevil or, lower still, the seemingly disfigured head of a big-eared dumbo octopus. It was quiet here, and dark, too, and the water was warm enough to feel like a nurturing bath. I somersaulted slowly, eventually pulling my tail up to my chin, rolling like a buoyant beach ball through the deep. The voice, still audible, persisted:

'Ferzana!'

I opened my eyes and discovered, with a start, that it was Baba's voice, not Dada's, that had pulled me out of the sea and left me gasping, his vocal cords, like a fisherman's net, catching me unawares. I could see my father sitting in the chair opposite, where Uncle Shahnawaz had lifted himself out of his layers to sit up like an alert sea turtle, his hands on his knees and his pebble-like eyes protruding short-sightedly as he looked from me to Baba, and then back again. Baba, Dada, Dada, Baba – the only difference between them a pair of identical consonants separated by the same vowel sound. It had never occurred to me that there would be other elements of commonality between them, that like other fathers and sons the world over, Dada and Baba shared characteristics, some immediately obvious like the sound of their voices, others encoded in their genes, appearing in fits and starts at different times in their lives – a swagger in their youth, an absent-minded gesture repeated, the pucker of their downturned lips while concentrating on a difficult task, perhaps (I shuddered) even an as-yet-unmanifested tendency in Baba to age cantankerously like his father, retreat into cranky isolation, and ultimately succumb to genetic predisposition by lambasting his future grandchildren.

'Ferzana,' Baba said, using his thumbs to dry my eyes, 'are you okay?' He lifted my kurta to check if my bandages were in place, then pulled me onto his lap. I pushed my head into the space between his shoulder and forearm and whined unintelligibly. The beauty of Baba was that he always understood.

'Dada doesn't mean to sound gruff. He's just worried about Uncle Raff. He had dialysis yesterday. You know Uncle Raff doesn't keep well.'

'But Uncle Raff loves it when I sit with him!'

'I'm sure he does.' Baba shifted so that my head was no longer sheltered in the crook of his arm. 'Sit up now. You have no idea how much your dada loves you, too.'

I sat up, mouth open, and turned to stare at my grandfather, who was pretending to be busy with a bottle of chilli sauce, raising it to the light and attempting, somewhat theatrically (glasses adjusted, eyes closed to slits in squint), to read the label. I couldn't believe that he loved me. There was a space between us. It was easier for me to imagine being loved by a doorknob, a bath tub, or even a swiftly decaying morsel of goat meat. Inanimate objects held more warmth for me, I decided, staring at my grandfather as if at a stranger, no love in me as I coolly compared him to his friends, even envying him his robust health when I noticed sadly the outline of Uncle Raff's calves through his trousers, the sunlight x-raying the limbs that several years' of illness had whittled down to the bone.

Baba frowned almost as if he knew what I was thinking. He whispered, 'Go and give your dada a hug.'

'Why?'

'I think he needs one.'

'He does not!' I protested, knowing full well that a hug from me would make the old man cringe. Sometimes blood was not enough. But even as I had this thought and was congratulating myself on its profundity, the bottle fell out of Dada's hand and onto the table, where it broke with a tremendous crash, a spray of glass and gelatinous chilli sauce rising into the air then splattering onto Dada's knees, the tea table, even as far as Uncle Raff's sandalled foot. Both of my grandfather's friends sat up, startled, Uncle Raff almost rising to his feet in consternation when he mistook the red sauce for blood. I turned to survey the mess, smiling smugly to myself as I thought, 'The culprit needs court-martialling', cocking my head to one side in imitation of my grandfather at his most military and irate.

Within seconds, poor Baba was already on his knees, calling to the kitchen for help as he pushed the glass to one side with a cloth napkin. 'All of you old boys are sockless and sandaled,' he said jocularly to Dada and his friends. 'I don't want anyone to get glass in their feet.'

'Baba?'

'Ferzana, please stay on that side. You're wearing chappals, too.'

'Baba, if you get glass in your foot, does it travel through your blood stream and cut you up inside?'

'Haven't a clue, but you have enough to worry about with your pockmarked back!'

I heard Uncle Raff chuckle and thought of how moody he had become of late. It was impossible to rely on a friend whose temperament was so unpredictable. At least Dada could be counted on for being the same all the time – grumpy. I looked over and was surprised to see the old man less than collected: he stared at his son's bent head in complete bewilderment, his eyes milky and unfocused, his right hand trembling as he distractedly pulled at his trouser leg. Fascinated, I kept staring. I had never seen him like this before; he resembled a lost boy in the hands of strangers. Frail was the word. Almost as helpless as Uncle Raff in his decline.

Embarrassed for him, I looked away.

CHAPTER 15

'Look at her.' Said with a sneer.

'How long has this been going on?'

Scowling into my chador, I bent my body to the ground, using my hands to block out their voices as I placed my forehead on the prayer mat. It was difficult enough to concentrate. The words of the prayer were still alien on my tongue, my wayward accent refusing to mould itself to the inflections of a language more perplexing to me than Urdu. Sometimes, these strung-together verses, like ropes of oyster sea-pearls, took on a life of their own, carrying me through the motions of the prayer while my untethered mind wandered, a mathematical problem at school or a conversation with Shahnaz distracting me from the moment. I was petrified of losing my place in the long sequence of verses. Aslam had warned me that any lapse in concentration heralded the arrival of someone whom he referred to as 'Shaytaan', the good angel gone bad, and that Shaytaan was the one who prompted me to do evil things. While the thought of Shaytaan terrified me for the most part, it was strangely comforting to know that I could blame my bad deeds on someone else. Unfortunately, this comfort was short-lived. When I double-checked with Baba, he replied cryptically, 'It's more complicated than that.' But he was no help in these matters anyway. Whenever I questioned him on theological issues, he always shrugged apologetically as if to say, 'Go ask someone who knows'. And now I was surrounded by people who 'knew' and who took religion like I did my fairytales, sometimes quite literally.

'Does Baba have any idea...?' Fatima's voice trailed off as I stood up, folded my prayer mat with deliberation, and then proceeded to disentangle myself from Dadi's chador, whose copiousness often led me to curse my height which, at just a little under four feet, made it ankle-length on me and therefore embarrassingly close to a burka.

'You look,' Raza sneered, 'like a dwarf-nun. What on earth do you think you're doing?'

Truth be told, I wasn't sure myself. Was it my afternoon siestas in Dadi's lap, a symbiotic transfer of religiosity through the warmth of her blood, bones, and skin, through the sheltering comfort of her sagging breasts? Sometimes it seemed as if the very walls of C44, from the treacherous glass-topped boundary that sheltered us from the chaotic market place to the pastel-coloured ones within constructed by my grandfather decades ago, emanated a hypnotic piety. In the evenings, the sky flush, sound and light became one with the muezzin's call, the rhythm of the ritual calling to me, too, to break from play or homework, retreat into the bedroom, and participate. So far, I had managed to keep this a secret from my siblings, who often spent that time in the main house, watching the hour of television allotted to us by Dada. I knew that they would not view this development with the same enthusiasm as the rest of the Mahmud clan. Guilt, I believed, the main cause.

'When did this start?' Fatima demanded.

I thought back to the day, a few weeks ago, that Shahnaz and I sat on the front steps of Shahbaz Chacha's unit, pausing from the sweaty pursuit of a stray cat to a quieter pastime. This involved using our thumbs and forefingers to pluck apart bunches of bougainvillea blossoms for a craft project of mine, which required cardboard, glue, and the paper-thin leaves of this prolific creeper.

'Do we have to count the leaves as we collect them?' Shahnaz asked irritably, the mound of fuchsia in her lap considerably smaller than mine. I could see she was not as enthusiastic about this project as I was, preferring instead to pant around the garden (like a dog, I told myself, irked) in the chase of small animals.

'Yes,' I snapped, 'counting is a must. I need exactly' – here a moment of hesitation for a number grand enough – 'a thousand.'

'What for?'

I glared at her. 'I'm making something special for my sister, Fatima.' She had been so upset lately that I thought a giant heart, crafted of pink bougainvillea leaves, was exactly what was needed to cheer her up.

'Fatima,' Shahnaz repeated thoughtfully, as if trying to remember which one was which, although the difference between my sisters was, to me, so self-evident that it came as a surprise that anyone should find it otherwise. Suddenly brightening, she exclaimed, 'Oh, you mean the normal one!'

Now, counting bougainvillea leaves is no easy task. Known as 'paper flowers', their veined leaves are so airy and light that to manipulate them with fingers like mine, sticky from the sap of dozens of tiny dismembered flowers, was complicated enough. And then, of course, to have to use those same sticky fingers as counting aids, my whispered eighty-four, eighty-five, eighty-six so large in my thoughts, completely engrossed, eighty-seven, eighty-eight, eighty-nine, Shahnaz's words pushing to rise to the surface of my thoughts… Suddenly, I stood up, a cascade of pink as the leaves fell to the ground. Who cared about this anyway? What?

'Shahnaz, what did you say?'

From where I stood, all I could see was her face, round as a plate, her eyes larger than usual, mouth open so that her front teeth, the third from the left missing, were all visible, even down to, way back, her molars.

'What "what"?' she asked defiantly, standing up, too, the painstaking work of an hour landing in an unceremonious heap on the floor, the entire porch pink as if a flock of one-legged flamingos had come to roost.

'What you said about Jamila – '

'Wait a minute,' she snapped back. 'I didn't say anything about Jamila!'

Confused, I began again: 'Okay, but what was it that you meant about my sisters?'

'Listen, Ferzana,' Shahnaz replied, her voice slightly raised, 'don't tell me you don't know. Jamila isn't like you or me. She talks funny, like her voice is stretched out, she limps, her movements are slow. Even her face—' She stopped abruptly. 'You really don't know, do you?' she asked, astonished. Then, mumbling to herself, words that sounded to my confused ears like 'these crazy Amriki', she leapt over the stairs and disappeared after the mangy stray cat, whose misfortune it was to reappear at this strategic juncture in our conversation.

Once she had left, I sat down again, this time in a pile of bougainvillea leaves, stunned. I couldn't stop crying. One obvious truth: our mother was dead. Another obvious truth (to the world, it seemed, but not to me): Jamila was … different. I wondered why this had never struck me before. Suddenly, hundreds of instances pointing to the evidence of disability came at me from all sides, as if the shadows of the garden had risen to collect around my hunched figure. I didn't want to lose the image I had of my sister as someone whole. To me, Jamila's shortcomings were like Fatima's sulky rages or Raza's cruel streak – flaws to be tolerated because of her innumerable other qualities. I sat there for close to an hour, the sun's light now casting dark shadows across the courtyard as it prepared for its daily disappearance in a cloudless sky of raw pink. From where I sat, I could see Shahnaz make a few furtive attempts to re-join me on the porch, her lithe body darting like one of the sun's cast-shadows, across the courtyard, behind the rusty swing and the garden chair, in between two slender tree trunks. At last, put off, perhaps, by my lack of interest, she disappeared from view, retreating to her quarters behind the house, where the reassuring monotony of her mother's scoldings put an end to her day of play as she undoubtedly ate, washed and crawled into bed.

Just as I was preparing to leave, I noticed movement near the entrance to Jamshaid Chacha's unit. Shahana Chachi and Parveen emerged amid several dozen yards of cloth, this time stripes and checks the predominant motifs. Despite my efforts to blend in with my surroundings, being a little girl and not a chameleon, I was, of course, immediately discovered and, before I could protest, found myself tangled up in a persuasive blend of expensive cotton and ittar. A few seconds later, I was perched on Shahana Chachi's lap, my hair tied back and bonneted, for want of a better word, in a pink headscarf, being transported in a cloud of fumes to the other side of the city, where the new houses gleamed of wealth and a fancy lady with painted nails opened up her drawing room for the edification of the pious begums of Karachi.

'The rest, of course,' I told Fatima in answer to her question about my new-found religiosity, 'is history.'

'They took you to one of their dars?' Raza asked incredulously. Then, looking at Fatima, he continued grimly, 'Wait till Baba hears about this.'

'Then what happened?' Fatima pressed.

I wasn't sure, at least to begin with. I spent the first half-hour staring at my surroundings, the high-ceilinged drawing room full of treasures to a little girl's eye, the bejewelled chandelier heavy in the centre of the room attracting me to it with its pendulous cluster of cut glass and its shimmer of royal glamour. Tables, of which there were many, were cluttered with resplendent objects in gold, silver, and fine bone china, the richly carpeted floor covered with sheets and decorative cushions. The entire house was centrally air-conditioned, uniformed servants stiffly offering sherbat on silver trays to ladies who sat cross-legged on the floor. A few women nearby smiled in my direction and there was one, at least, whom I recognized all too well – Rizwana Hameed – although it was not immediately clear whether she knew who I was. When I was offered a frosty drink, I suddenly realized that while I had been absorbed in my surroundings, the lady in front had already been speaking for more than fifteen minutes, the topic: Islam and renouncing materialism.

The speaker, who had spent the last eight years at Al-Azhar in Cairo, was surprisingly young, her kindly face beaming from within the folds of her head covering, her clothes, of fine embroidered cotton, falling in stiff gathers around her slight figure. The audience, comprising mostly of middle-aged women, sat in earnest rapture, some with notebooks and pens in hand, a few with brows furrowed in concentration. There were also several girls of Fatima's age and even a few whom I recognized from her class. Of course, there wasn't much that I could understand of the lady's speech, consisting of lengthy quotations and a string of polysyllabic words but, when I finally focused on her voice, gentle and persuasive, instead of on a crimson decanter, I realized that she was speaking in English. I sat up, the events of that evening making me more receptive to her closing words. She spoke directly to me, as if she knew I was lonely and lost and missed my dead mother.

Later, once the lecture and discussion were over, Shahana Chachi grabbed my sweaty hand and led Parveen and I to the rapidly growing crowd around Rizwana Hameed. I noted, with surprise, that some women were asking for her autograph, to which she obliged with a flourish of the ringed fingers of her left hand, large, emphatic swirls of illegible colour. After several minutes of standing deferentially to one side, Shahana Chachi pushed me towards her.

'Beta, say salam to Rizwana Aunty.'

Rizwana Hameed looked up in displeasure. 'Janoo, I'm no one's "aunty". I can't abide that form of address.'

Parveen immediately left for the refreshments table. From the corner of my eye I could see her nervously bite into a sandwich. A few of the ladies who had overheard this comment tittered. Only one pure soul, a friend of my aunt's, turned away in solidarity, suddenly moving to one side and fussing with the rhinestone brooch that held together her hijab.

'I'm so sorry. I just thought — this is Ferzana, Aftab Mahmud's daughter…'

Rizwana Hameed paused only an instant before I found myself gasping for air amid the suffocating folds of her drapery. When I finally emerged from her embrace reeking of jasmine, she drew us aside and began speaking to Shahana Chachi of college days. I, pressed between their stomachs, suddenly ducked and escaped to the refreshments table to join Parveen.

'Well, what happened, Ferzana?' Fatima repeated.

'Nothing happened. I sat there with Shahana Chachi and Parveen, listened to the speech, ate a chicken patty – the cute cocktail-sized ones – and came home.'

'But what did the speaker say?' Fatima insisted.

'Nothing. Just some religious stuff,' I mumbled vaguely.

'She probably didn't get any of it, Fatima,' Raza said. 'Just as well. According to them we're kaafirs anyway.'

I kept quiet. It was obvious that they would never understand. In the meantime, it would be useful to know what the word 'kaafir' meant, as I had heard it on more than one occasion.

'Well, keep it up,' Raza called as he left the room with Fatima. 'People who are attacked by crows need all the help they can get.'

Thankfully my bandages had been removed within a few days of that wretched incident, and the second tetanus shot administered that morning. I peeled back the sticky tape on my arm and looked closely at my skin, where the tiniest of dots indicated the point of penetration. Then, in what had become a daily ritual of sorts since my encounter with the crows, I blocked my nose with one hand and with the other pulled open my bedside table drawer. There it was, the bejewelled trinket box, hidden beneath my tattered diary and a tangled mess of ribbons, hair bands, and barrettes. Pausing for air before I clamped my nostrils again, I struggled to open the lid, accidentally knocking the box over so that a trickle of decomposed slime fell onto my white 'ABC' bedspread, an obscenely dark stain spreading rapidly through its absorbent fabric while I stood by, helpless.

'Little Furry,' a voice called from the doorway, the metallic edge to it indicative of extreme displeasure.

There stood Lady M, leaning slightly to one side so that she looked, in the shadows cast by the light behind her, as if she were walking directly out of a wall.

'You scared me!' I whispered.

'That was my intention. What have you done to our sacrifice?'

'I apologize, Lady M, I was— '

'Did I not tell you that it was foolish to keep opening the box?'

She swept over to the bed with a fistful of tissues and, within seconds, the solid remnants of our sacrifice had disappeared, leaving a dark brown stain in the shape of, strangely enough, a bird, a bird, some would even say, closely resembling the crow.

'This,' she said as she raised her fist over her head, 'will be buried in the garden tonight.'

I nodded solemnly in acquiescence.

'Baba, what are "kaafirs"?'

'You and me, Chhoti.' I saw his Adam's apple turn somersaults as his raspy laugh echoed in the high-ceilinged bedroom where he lay, still in his pyjamas, on a tepid Sunday morning, the overworked air conditioner now knocking in protest as it pumped cold musty air into our faces.

I raised myself up on one elbow and looked closely at him. 'Baba,' I asked, 'are you joking with me?'

'Chhoti, what genius introduced you to this word?'

'I keep hearing it … all over the place,' I replied vaguely.

'Well, in the strict sense it means non-believer. Someone who doesn't believe in Islamic teachings.'

'So why would someone think we're not Muslims? I mean, we are, aren't we?'

'Ferzana, there are some people in this world who think it their business to interfere with other people's religious beliefs. Just ignore them.'

I must have looked confused because Baba continued, 'You are what you believe in, and what you believe in is between you and your God.'

'But,' I began slowly, 'I'm starting to get the feeling that it isn't all that simple."

I was surprised to hear Baba groan from deep within the tangled sheets he had pulled over his face. For a few minutes we lay like that, I on my side, legs pulled up, kidney-shaped, my father straight and rigid as a yardstick, still sheathed in white. At last, he threw off the bedsheets and sat up, his face buried in his hands. 'I'm sorry you've had to learn this so soon,' he mumbled.

'But Baba,' I corrected him, 'I've known for a long time. Don't you remember what happened in Chicago last year? In gym class?' The incident I referred to marked the loss of my religious innocence, my introduction, as it were, to the fractured world of religious schism. Ironically, it was nine-year-old American-born Uzma who had first asked me whether I was Shia or Sunni. At the time, I had no idea what that meant. Later, I found out she was neither, being a follower of the Aga Khan, and therefore Ismaili.

'Hmmm,' Baba grunted.

'It's not just that,' I protested suddenly. 'It's more. There's a problem here,' I waved my hands all around me, 'in this house.'

Baba raised an eyebrow.

Then, even before I could make a conscious decision, the questions that had been foremost in my mind for months were out there in that high-ceilinged room, floating above us like so many inflatable question marks:

Why was there opposition?

Why did you elope?

And then, although this should have been first, How did you and Amma meet?

CHAPTER 16

'It may have looked like I was sleeping but in fact I was gathering information essential to our mission!' I reported excitedly as I turned to face a mostly deadpan audience, my circle of co-conspirators looking anything but impressed as they slouched over the photograph of Shahbaz Chacha as an infant that Lady M and I had secreted from the family albums.

'Little Furry,' Lady M spoke, clearing her throat for emphasis, 'we need results. It's difficult to believe you weren't sleeping when I actually heard you snoring.'

I scowled at the rowdy laughter this comment generated. 'Well, I don't see any of you doing anything!' I retaliated.

'I think we'll have to be more involved from now on, though,' Timmer replied, looking at Dag. 'After that silly crow incident – what were you two thinking? – we're being watched more closely.'

'Always the crows!' I wailed in exasperation. 'It's as if I can never do anything right again!' Then, in a calmer voice, I began to explain what I had learned the day before as I feigned sleep, my eyes half-closed against the light, my head firmly tucked under one of Dadi's layers, a position eminently suited, I had recently discovered, to my afternoon rest.

'Durri,' Dadi began, her fingers still tangled in my hair, which she had been stroking softly for the better part of an hour, 'do you remember anything of the year we lost?'

'Ma, why do you always refer to it as "lost"?'

'Well, we weren't together – as a family, I mean.'

'I remember it quite clearly. Bhai Jan was fourteen, Jamshaid Bhai twelve, and I was about six, wasn't I?'

'I keep thinking,' Dadi continued, 'of those children. My own grandchildren. This is their lost year – but so much worse. In their case, the separation with their mother is permanent, lifelong.'

'Yes, Ma. I know,' Durdana Phupo said softly.

My hand, tucked under Dadi's stomach, flew to my face, a gesture recently adopted to comfort myself in times of crisis, the feel of my nose in between the curve of my thumb and forefinger a reminder of how much I resembled my mother.

'The year we spent without your father, and under those circumstances –' For a few seconds, Dadi couldn't speak. Finally, she continued more calmly, 'If it weren't for Rafiq Bhai's family here in Karachi, his sisters in particular, I don't know what we would have done. All alone like that, with four children, and Shahbaz only a few months old...'

'I know, Ammi. There's no question about it. Uncle Raff has been a wonderful friend to us all.'

'Yes, Durri, and now ... I'm scared for him.'

'I know, Ma, I know. Think how Abba feels. His best friend, after all – over fifty years of association. Abba just hasn't been himself lately, and I think it's because he's worried over Uncle Raff's condition. I wish we could explain this to the children. Maybe they might be more considerate of his feelings.'

'Durri,' Dadi's voice was strange, 'I, too, find it painful to see Rafiq like this.'

'Well, of course, Ammi—why, you're crying!' Durdana Phupo suddenly exclaimed, shocked. For a few seconds, there was an uneasy silence. I gingerly edged my way out from under the hem of Dadi's chador to better observe them but only managed, after all the subtle manoeuvering (it wouldn't do, after all, for them to discover that I was awake), to catch a glimpse of Dadi's face, the soft folds of her plump, wrinkled flesh wet before she grabbed the very hem I was hiding behind to use as a handkerchief. I lay as still as I could, eyes closed.

'Ammi,' Durdana Phupo whispered, 'what's going on?'

'Nothing, Durri. Nothing,' Dadi moaned. She made as if to rise, then settled back into the cushions with a start when my heavy head, still on her lap, reminded her I was in the room. 'I hope Chhoti hasn't overheard any of this,' she whispered, as she resumed caressing my head, peering over the folds of her chador to make sure that my eyes were closed, my breathing rhythmic.

'Ammi,' Durdana Phupo's voice rose hysterically on the second syllable, 'are you hiding something from me?'

'Durdana,' Dadi replied, suddenly firm, 'let me speak.'

Noteworthy among Dadi's features was her voice, with its refined Urdu lilt, characteristic, she never tired of reminding

me, of her genteel origins in a city steeped in culture called
Lucknow, now (she would sigh nostalgically), on the far
side of the border in neighbouring India. As I lay there, eyes
half-closed, waiting for her to speak, I looked forward to the
faint musicality which made so much of her conversation,
particularly on sleepy afternoons such as these, my lullaby.
In a ludicrous pattern of association, perhaps to do with my
English literalization of 'Lucknow' as a place of luck, my
mind jumped from her to a leprechaun, the famous television
leprechaun of frosted cereals, his jaunty Irish accent so, I
realized with a start, like Dadi's. When she finally spoke,
however, it was in a monotone, wholly devoid of cadence,
just about as musical as the kut-kut-kut of a door repeatedly
falling back on its hinge. But where she lacked in expression,
my imagination compensated till, eyes now fully closed, I
saw the images of her narrative against my lids.

I lay still, my lids closed against the sunshine, my lashes
brushing the pale yellow of Dadi's starched chador, through
which, when I chose, I could look at her face, not as she
was now, her features soft in their bed of loose flesh, but as
she was in the photograph I found in the picture library, her
pale round face regal in sepia, her hair swept up in bunches
of white motia flowers, her sari a-swirl with the vibrance
of citrus. In the garden, in the barracks. The tropical mist
of early mornings, the gnarled trunks of ancient trees with
wide arms and their cluster of dusty foliage overhanging
tin-metal roofs and sandstone structures, officers, their
uniforms crisp, walking briskly down dusty tracks. Who
knew where these images, of a past I couldn't have known,

had come from. Was it from the hundreds of photographs I had surreptitiously looked through, the topsy-turvy early albums, their dark pages covered with tiny squares of black-and-white, some crooked, some unstuck from the dusty tape of decades ago? Flashes of a life lived, preserved, now over, that I had somehow internalized, the memories of my family *my* memories, part of my consciousness, too. Later, when I thought of the extraordinary affinity I felt to my grandmother's past, I realized that there was more to it, that with the gradual closeness I felt for her, my imaginative empathy with her history grew till I could relate to her stories almost as much as if I had lived through them, just as I often found myself quite literally walking into Amma and Baba's past.

'Durri,' Dadi began, 'the year leading up to the '71 war was a lonely one for me. Your Abba was away for much of 1970, first in the US for additional training, then later on temporary assignment in West Pakistan with the cadets. There was great unrest in Dhaka, and I remember wishing he were with us even though life in the cantonment was relatively peaceful. We were fortunate to be surrounded by friends – remember Nasreen Aunty, Brigadier Elahi's wife? You and Jamshaid used to play with her daughters, and the younger one, Salma, was your class fellow at the Army school. But by nightfall, when families generally sat down to dinner, it was just the four of us – you three with your little problems from school (Jamshaid and his schoolyard brawls!) and I the only adult to solve them. I was so depressed, I had no interest in taking care of the house or cooking. I left everything to the orderly, and we used to eat the bland food he served us day in and day out.

'It was during that time that Rafiq began visiting us. I'm sure you remember because he used to bring you pocketfuls of toffee and often played cricket with your brothers on the back lawn. Abba and Rafiq had been together since their cadet days, but my interaction with him had been limited to a few brief meetings until we were all posted to Dhaka. He was still a bachelor and perhaps missed the comfort of family life because he began visiting us frequently, spending the early evenings playing with you, the after-dinner hours with me. My interest in cooking returned. How he enjoyed my meals! We talked with the ease of old friends, and he meant a lot to me during those trying times. I think,' Dadi faltered, 'I think I proved to be a good friend to him, too. After a while, he began confiding in me. Like us all,' she paused, 'he had a secret which, given the fact that we were on the brink of civil war, would have cost him dearly to disclose – loss of reputation, perhaps even career. It was something he felt he could not even share with your father.'

'But why you?' Durdana Phupo asked.

'I don't know, Durri,' Dadi replied softly. 'Sometimes people form attachments – unusual attachments – when they are thrown together like we were that year. It wasn't easy. There was even talk – you know the rubbish people come up with – that we, Rafiq and I... And it was awkward for me to broach the subject with him. I didn't want to stop him from visiting because we were the only family he had, but at the same time – ! What, after all, is a military cantonment without gossip and intrigue? I must confess I was terrified word would get back to your father.'

'But, Ammi, you had nothing to hide, right?'

'And then,' Dadi continued, still caught up in her narrative, 'your father returned for a couple of weeks, only to be called back suddenly, our farewells hasty and brief the night before he left. Shortly after, the dizzy spells began, followed by doctor's visits. You can imagine my reaction to the news that I was pregnant again at thirty-eight. In those days, women in their late thirties were grandmothers. With the three of you all grown up and independent, I had thought, with some relief, that my childbearing days were over. I was distraught, but your father, in a letter he later wrote to me from Kakul, insisted that all would be well.

'It was a difficult pregnancy. The months seemed to drag. In the early days, I had horrible bouts of nausea. I still remember how much it frightened you to see me in that state. I would wake up in the middle of the night heaving into the bucket beside my bed, you trembling next to me under the sheets. I cursed myself for my carelessness. A fourth child and the times so uncertain! People had begun speaking of civil war. It was all I could do to protect myself and the three of you.

'What was worse was not being able to confide in anyone. I was too embarrassed. Even Nasreen Apa, who was like an older sister to me, didn't know till I was in my seventh month. I kept to myself most of the time, pretending that your activities left me little time for socializing. And as for family – well, my parents and brothers were far away in distant Lucknow, the means of communication slow and cumbersome, telephone lines unreliable. And in the midst of all of this, there was that life inside me, that poor unwanted life that kicked the insides of my belly till I was sore. I still remember those long hot nights, sleepless under the grating fan, my legs aching, your thin body pressed against my side...' For several minutes, no one spoke.

My eyes closed, I dreamt of that tiny unwanted life, imagining him inside my grandmother's stomach, rolling around and around endlessly, his arms and legs sinewy with pushing against her insides, his fingers curled into fists, the arches of his feet flexed for attack. My images of babies in utero were limited to two ultrasounds I had accidentally seen, one of my friend's baby sister at eight weeks, a grayish bean in a sea of black, and another of the same baby at eight months, a three-dimensional image of her face pushed up against the probe, her features bulbous and swollen, like pulverized onions. These accidental sightings captured my imagination for several months of my sixth year, prompting my parents to ban all talk [even remotely connected] to reproduction in front of me.

'You were a great help to me during that time, Durri. Do you remember?'

'I remember, Ammi,' was the terse reply.

'Of course, one other person knew, too, almost from the moment I found out myself.'

'Uncle Rafiq!' The fierceness with which this was uttered startled me.

'Yes, Durri. How could he not guess, being such a frequent visitor? It was apparent to him from the very beginning. In his own clumsy way, he did all he could to help, bringing me basketfuls of kamranga and leechi that summer. There was very little else that I could eat in the early months.'

'And Abba?' Durdana Phupo asked.

'He came once before the war broke out, in October. He found me much altered with bloating and sickness, and the three of you grown beyond recognition, your frocks falling above your knees and your brothers' gangly arms and legs inches out of their shirt sleeves and trouser cuffs. And such serious little people! I sometimes thought it was the separation that did that, later the war. You all grew up that year, especially poor Aftab, who tried to compensate for your Abba's absence.'

'I have this memory,' Durdana Phupo began uncertainly, 'this strange memory of an afternoon in late summer, and it was raining, the water falling at such great pressure that it seemed to crack the earth open, huge ugly gashes bubbling with mud and water. On my way home from Salma's, I tripped over a rock and fell head-first into one of these khaddas. As I struggled to get up, covered in mud, my hair falling in streaks down my back and over my face, I saw a man in the distance. He looked like Abba. The same gait, the same stance, his shoulders wide over stocky legs, lumbering forward against the rain. I thought he saw me, too, because his pace quickened and he moved towards me in stages, like the shifting images of a child's flip book. I ran to him against the rain. When I finally reached him, I wrapped my arms around his waist. I looked up. I saw his eyes, which were not brown like Abba's, but golden like a lion's, a stranger's

eyes. It wasn't Abba at all. Frightened, I ran away from him.
I thought he was following me, so I scrambled through the
waterlogged grass towards our house. Your face was at the
window. When I neared, you ran out to meet me.'

'I remember, Durri,' Dadi said softly. Her fingers had
begun spinning again, deftly threading strands of my hair in
and out, the gentle tug of the pressure soothing on my scalp,
her fingertips light as a child's. I was confused, the beginnings
of a headache creeping its way upwards from the base of my
skull. Dadi's half-told tale merged with Durdana Phupo's.
What did the two have in common, I kept wondering … if
anything at all? My eyes felt heavy as I imagined Durdana
Phupo as a little girl in the rain, her hair, like twisted rope,
falling darkly over her shoulders, the thin cotton of her dress,
now transparent, sticking to her bony frame.

Then there was the 'unwanted life', complex as he grew
inside my grandmother. He was the product of many unions
– my grandparents' love, Uncle Raff's friendship, the taste of
leechi and kamranga – and yet he was created in uncertain
times, when the unity of the state was threatened by civil war.
Images of officers and their wives, school children in neat
rows, prize-giving ceremonies, medals bestowed on men in
uniform by men in power – images I had gathered into my
memory from the albums I had looked through wove in and
out of my dreams. I slept.

When I finally awoke, it was to the sound of several
voices, the loudest Jamila's, calling out my name, then her
hands shaking me back to the present, the familiar lounge
with the glossy calendar open to the month of March and

Nanga Parbat. Dadi yawned and stretched as I stood up, then asked us each to grab a leg and massage away the stiffness, which we did willingly, for it was always enjoyable to knead that flesh, so soft from age that it hung like chapatti dough from her strong old bones. Then, calling to Jamila to assist her in the kitchen, Dadi kissed me on the forehead and disappeared amid the dusty fragrance of atta turning to ash on the blackened tawwa.

Dag and Timmer were speechless. Inwardly gloating, I looked at everyone's faces expectantly, hoping for an apology or at least a random look of remorse.

After a minute or two of round-eyed silence, Timmer said, 'My God. I think the little snoop might actually be onto something.'

'Maybe you should ask her to investigate those emails, too,' Dag suggested, turning to look at me appraisingly with those green eyes of his, which, when thoughtful, always reminded me of dragon's skin. 'How about it, Little Furry? Do you think you can unmask the identity of Colonel Bogey?'

I feigned indifference with a toss of the head: 'Show me the emails, and I'd be happy to help.'

'Friends, focus,' Lady M ordered. For a few minutes, none of us spoke as we pondered over how best to proceed.

'I could continue my afternoon spying sessions,' I offered.

'Yes, but what are the chances that they'll speak of that time again?' Lady M pointed out.

'Maybe somebody kept a diary…?' Timmer began doubtfully.

'Personally, I think Little Furry should get right to the heart of the matter and question Air Commodore Rafiq Nawaz.' Dag sat back, arms folded, eyes closed, anticipating the chorus of protest that this idea would undoubtedly generate – as it did.

'He's sick …' Lady M's voice trailed off.

'No, I don't think that's a good idea,' Timmer agreed emphatically. 'Have you seen how weak he looks these days?'

'Well, then he must be emotionally vulnerable, too,' Dag snapped. 'The question is,' he raised his green eyes speculatively to the ceiling, 'is Little Furry prepared to follow through? Can she bully an old man nearing death?'

The three of us protested at the heartlessness of this course of action.

'Hah. Little Furry doesn't have it in her,' Dag finally concluded, rising abruptly and disappearing before I had a chance to defend myself.

CHAPTER 17

'Bhai Jan, it was an incredible experience! And everyone loved her!'

Baba, expressionless, sat at his customary place at the dining table and stared with unusual intensity at a completely ordinary bowl of daal that had, seconds before, been brought from the kitchen. As Shahana Chachi elaborated on the young teacher from Al-Azhar, Baba's attention remained wholly on the daal, lowly staple of the South Asian diet, unremarkable in a household where it was served daily and about as interesting at that point in time as the fly that squatted proprietarily on the tightly-sealed jar of gurr on the sideboard.

'I thought there could be no harm in taking the child. It was a place of learning.' And after a moment's pause, she added, 'We also met an old friend of yours there.'

From my vantage point at the children's table, it was impossible to determine Baba's reaction to this news, but it was apparent, even at this distance, that his focus remained the daal. I wondered if, like I sometimes did, he was indulging in an imaginative fantasy, poised in his mind's eye on the thick glass lip of the bowl in an insulated scuba suit. He appeared miserable enough to jump if pressed.

Jamshaid Chacha murmured 'No harm done' as he brought a forkful of food to his mouth, then ventured less coherently, 'Hmm… A dose of that is always… Good. Children need it.'

Baba muttered softly, 'I do take issue if my eleven-year-old has already been introduced to the word kaafir.' Shahana Chachi ignored this comment and continued effusively, 'Bhai Jan, Rizwana Hameed was delighted to see Chhoti! Everyone was so jealous when she hugged her so warmly! She said she was anxious to meet you as well.' Here, Shahana Chachi glanced at Dada, who had paused with fork in mid-air, and whose eyes I thought resembled that of a bird of prey, a hawk no less, black irises huge in their puckered sockets. He surveyed my father for possible signs of weakness, but Baba, poor man, had turned his attention back to the lentils.

Shahbaz Chacha stared at Shahana Chachi in surprise. He appeared to be the only Mahmud who didn't know of Rizwana Hameed's connection to Baba. 'What? You know that woman?' he asked incredulously, his handsome face suddenly animated. 'Bhabi, that woman is dangerous! Have you ever seen her TV show?'

'Well, of course I have.' Shahana Chachi, flushing, adjusted the brooch on her hijab, and countered, 'I've never seen such evenhanded television.' By now, Jamshaid Chacha, Aslam, and Parveen, who sat across from me, had paused in their meal, their expressions identical and, for the most part, hostile.

'Evenhanded?' Shahbaz Chacha exclaimed. 'The woman is a sophist, for God's sakes! I don't know why she's even allowed on television. She doesn't have the credentials to conduct a programme on religious issues. Her influence is turning normal women mad everywhere!'

Here, Tania Chachi placed a hand on her husband's shoulder and bent to whisper something into his ear. For a second, he looked distracted, but he was so involved in the conversation that he brushed her away and settled more firmly into his seat in anticipation of a rebuttal. I noticed Tania Chachi put down her fork, then cross her arms tightly against her chest as she looked away from the table at a point somewhere on the opposite wall, which was so ordinary in appearance, so unadorned, that I couldn't imagine anyone finding it interesting for as long as she did. She was almost as riveted by that blank wall as Baba was with his lentils.

'Well, I think that's a little harsh—' began Shahana Chachi but before she could finish, Jamshaid Chacha, wrapping a fist around his beard, interrupted belligerently.

'Are you saying my wife is mad? Is that what he's implying?' He looked around fiercely, as if to dare the rest of us to speak.

The adults did, all at once in fact, so that we hardly knew who said what, but it was a mixture of low, conciliatory sounds that, when heard together, sounded curiously like a barnyard in uproar. Raza stifled a laugh as he bent over his plate. Fatima had stopped eating minutes earlier and stared in frank, open-eyed wonder at the turn the conversation had taken. It was odd to see our youngest, generally affable, uncle so outraged.

'I'm not implying anything about Bhabi,' began Shahbaz Chacha, 'But the evidence is everywhere. Where do you think this rigid, intolerant, unforgiving version of our faith has sprung from?'

'Certainly not from Rizwana Hameed's television show!' Jamshaid Chacha expostulated. 'What about the filth these people have brought into our country?' he demanded, his heavily bearded chin raised in challenge as he waved his arms, curiously enough, in our direction as if Raza, Fatima, Jamila and I were somehow responsible for the lascivious content of satellite television by virtue of our nationality.

'Beta, Jamshaid, Shahbaz. Please. Let's avoid this... In front of the children at least...' Dada's voice, generally of the drill-sergeant variety, had lost its military, no-nonsense authoritarianism. He raised a tentative finger in admonition then proceeded to use that same finger to scratch the bald portion of his head which was now red and beaded with perspiration.

'No, Abba, we need to have this out. My brothers think that I'm a religious fanatic just because I practise my faith.' By now, Jamshaid Chacha was standing, his demeanour combative, a warrior of olden times, like the crusading knights I had seen in history books (although I knew just enough to realize that Jamshaid Chacha would not appreciate the comparison, which happened to be deeply wrong at some level, though why I could not say). He thrust out his chest and, by default, his ample belly, then threw down his fork, which fell against his plate and splashed his neighbours. 'You all think I'm some crazed lunatic, don't you? Listen,

I've done it all, lived like you, even travelled the world more than you have. What makes you think you're better than me? Does my beard make me inherently backward? I'm sick of this belief on the part of you liberals that anyone who follows the Sunnah and tries to practise his deen is a fundamentalist or a radical.'

Shahbaz Chacha shook his head in apparent disbelief. 'I never said I was better than anyone. And I wasn't attacking you personally. I'm talking about this woman, this vile woman who has nothing to do with any of us, who's going around spreading doubt in people's minds and using her celebrity influence to make fools of us.' Then, as an afterthought, he suddenly burst out, 'You'd think the woman was part of our family the way you're defending her!'

There was an uncomfortable silence.

'What? What?' Shahbaz Chacha repeated, mystified.

All at once, my beloved Tania Chachi, a soft-spoken, sensitive, elegant import from a family of mild, beatific people with artistic leanings, stood up and screamed tearfully, 'I'm pregnant!'

I leaped out of my seat and ran to her, struggling to push through the rest of the family, who had gathered around her and Shahbaz Chacha. I watched in wonder as these three brothers, grown men now with such different ideological viewpoints, embraced one another, laughing like there had been no uncomfortable discussions. Grown men, I decided, were strange creatures who angered quickly, fought, and then forgot. Somehow I managed to find a way of crawling under and around everyone's legs, emerging eventually between Tania Chachi's newly-important stomach and Dadi's deliciously soft and saggy one. I was at just the right height to press my ear against Tania Chachi's belly, listening intently to her stomach in the hopes of hearing a baby's cry.

'Chhoti!' Dadi laughed, pulling me out from in between their embrace. 'What are you doing, silly one?'

'Nothing,' I said, but I had already had several seconds to whisper an urgent message to my cousin who, though quite earless at this stage, was informed in no uncertain terms that he or she, once born, would inherit that despicable appellation which had been imposed on me by my family and which I felt diminished my stature as a person. After all, would any self-respecting human being be taken seriously if known to the world as 'the littlest'?

I think not.

Curiously, the mention of Rizwana Hameed made me think, once again, of a topic of endless fascination to me – Amma and Baba's courtship. I remembered the beginnings of a conversation several months ago in Baba's room which ended, like most of our exchanges, in tickles, hysterical giggling and, eventually, me fast asleep in the crook of his arm, pressed against his side like a contented bean seed. After the meal was over, I followed Baba through the garden and into our unit, then upstairs to his bedroom, where I threw myself helter-skelter on his bed before arranging myself comfortably on a stack of pillows. 'Baba,' I asked, 'why on earth were you staring at that bowl of daal? Was there a fly in it?'

Baba laughed. 'So I was being observed from the children's table, was I?'

A knock at the door, and then Jamila entered, smiling like our mother, her face, generally so misunderstood because of its supposed asymmetry, suddenly radiant. She fell face first onto the bed and then settled herself next to me, her head on Baba's lap. Within seconds, Baba's slender fingers were stroking her hair, an unconscious habit I now knew he had inherited from Dadi. Another minute passed, and then there was a second knock, then Fatima and Raza joined us on the bed, already straining under the weight but so solidly constructed of cane that it shifted magnanimously to accommodate us. This was rare; all five of us together in one room where we could speak without inhibition. I knew this opportunity would not come again.

'Baba, did you and Amma fall in love?'

'Honestly, Chhoti, what's your fascination with all of this?' Baba looked embarrassed, even irritable, as he leaned back against the headboard and closed his eyes. His actions indicated that this conversation bored him.

'Well, for one thing,' Fatima spoke up, 'you eloped.'

'I'd say that was interesting,' Raza smirked.

That had the desired effect. Baba sat up and looked at each one of us in turn. 'Who told you that?' he asked sternly. 'Your grandmother?' Then, as if to himself, he muttered, 'Trust her.'

'No, Baba. Dadi didn't tell us.' Over the months, I had become better acquainted with my grandmother and knew that this much loyalty in the face of wrongful accusation was expected of me. 'It wasn't … her, but…' and here I wondered if I could reveal that we had secretly met Amma's brothers, but was abruptly silenced by a murderous look from Fatima, who had been observing me like a sniper.

'Well, who else…?' Baba raised his eyes to the ceiling and, throwing his hands up in mock prayer, declaimed, 'Lord, please save me from these children!' Then he ran a weary hand through his graying curls, finishing off with an agitated pull that nearly tore a fistful of strands out of his scalp.

This little theatrical demonstration indicated that Baba was more exasperated than angry. Suddenly emboldened, I pressed on, convinced that love affairs, too, had paper trails like other nefarious crimes. Twisting over onto my stomach to better examine his face, I casually asked, 'So, Baba, were there any love letters?' This question, like most of my weighty and philosophical contributions, was greeted by laughter of a kind I didn't appreciate: it was the hilarity of grown ups amused at a child's expense. If it weren't for Raza pinning me down on the bed, I had every intention of running out of the room and throwing myself down the stairs where, later found by Dada and bleeding gruesomely, I would be carried out on a stretcher to the hospital.

'Chhoti, Chhoti,' Baba coaxed, as he saw the tears coming, 'I understand your curiosity about our past. It's only natural. Things were very different in our times. We weren't crazy like the lot of you.' Here, Baba punched Raza on the shoulder and helped me out of his athletic stranglehold. I took a moment to glare at my brother. Then, Baba pulled me onto his lap and cradled me like an infant, his body rocking as he smiled down on me for several seconds without speaking. I could not decide whether he was happy or sad.

'I never wrote any love letters to your mother,' he said simply.

'But, Baba –' I began.

'It just never happened, Ferzana. And sometimes, you know – ' he paused, as if he had no words at his disposal, 'sometimes after all this,' and he looked around in disbelief, 'I wonder if, perhaps, I should have. For the last half-year, I haven't felt anything. I was bewildered, depressed – ' then, realizing that he was addressing an eleven-year-old, quickly corrected himself: 'I guess I missed your mother but tried not to think about her, or anything, for many months, just so that I could get past the shock.'

Raza placed a tentative hand on Baba's shoulder before saying in an uncharacteristically gentle voice, 'Really, Baba. You don't have to do this you know. We understand.'

'No, no. This needs to be done, as much for myself as for all of you. It wasn't fair of your mother and me to keep this part of our early life together a secret. And now that she's gone, it remains for me to tell you what happened. So,' he paused briefly, smiling ruefully to himself, 'if I were to write a love letter to your mother now, it would probably start something like: Dear Najma, I love you...'

I sat up.

'...But did you have to leave me at the mercy of these brats?'

'Baba!' I squealed. 'Be serious.'

'Okay, okay.' He laughed.

O, the anticipation! The joy! The skin around each individual hair on my body suddenly erupted into gazillions of perfectly round goose-pimples as I shivered in delight at the prospect of sharing a grown-up secret, a long-ago secret, a secret that – most thrilling of all – actually concerned me and my parents. As I leaned back and closed my eyes, I felt the same way I always felt when beginning a new storybook, my mind receptive to its suggestiveness, to the mesmerizing draw of its plot line and the three-dimensionality of its cast of characters. Surrendering to self-forgetfulness, I imagined my role in Amma and Baba's story, a spot in the sky looking down, the as-yet-unborn daughter of a young man and a young woman who first met two decades ago in the southern sea port of Karachi.

CHAPTER 18

My dearest Najma,

The necessity of writing to you now, when all is done, when your very existence has ceased in the way that we knew it, is an ironic testimony to the inventiveness of your children! For though your cat's eyes, your once prominent cheekbones softened with age (yes, you would say you had grown fat, but I always disagreed), the tangible reality of you is no more, you have left behind four individuals with an insatiable curiosity about our past life together.

Though — here I falter at the wonder and audacity of it — we have created these human beings, these combinations, reflections, fantastic transmutations of ourselves through our union, they have grown past and beyond us in the months since your absence. So, although I cannot hold you in my arms and keep you from leaving, this is my way of remembering you. I want our children to finally understand what we have between us.

Cynics would say that my attempt at a love letter after the fact (and can the fact ever be over if I continue to love you?) is a pitiable widower's indulgence. I regret not having written to you earlier. How many times have we told ourselves 'We must do this or that', then don't, and then later lament over it when it's too late? Even in the early days of our courtship, when young people have the boldness to make wild promises and commit them to paper, I never wrote. As we often discussed in later years, I grew up in a household where there was a stranglehold on emotion. A by-product of being an army man's son, perhaps. Our upbringing was strict and uncompromising, particularly in matters of the heart. Our father was hard on us boys; Durdana got away with more, being a girl and our mother's companion. I don't blame Abbaji; I remember him being lighter, more open, as a young man. As little boys he'd lift us up to the fruit trees in Quetta where we would grasp gigantic peaches, pears, fistfuls of grapes. But he became progressively sterner. I think '71 and his time as a POW hardened him. He came back thoughtful, inward-looking. He'd spend hours on his prayer mat, visit the local mosque, took to wearing a prayer cap. All out of character for him and certainly unusual for the time.

The point is, if I hadn't met your brothers, and by extension you, on that fateful day at the student rally on campus, I would have been a very different person. My friendship with Salaar and Alamdar, notwithstanding a few rough years (running off with their only sister would do that!), is all the more valuable to me for the way it changed me, made me more receptive to feeling and nuance. I remember the first majlis I attended with your brothers startled me into an awakening – that grown men could cry for an event, though tragic, that happened centuries ago was remarkable. It was alien to me; I must confess, I felt a little disgusted with the effusion of emotion, the wild beating of chests, the extremity. Later, I came to admire your brothers for their passion, for their support of, let's face it, sometimes ridiculous causes (remember the proposed museum for your poet-ancestor?), and for their political activism, which, if one is to believe them, was inspired by the example of their great Imam or leader, Hussain. Though not as emotionally uninhibited as Alamdar (not many men are, even among the Shias!), I learned through time that this release is cathartic, even necessary.

When I first saw Salaar and Alamdar, they were involved in a heated debate with a group of students from a rival political party. I happened to be passing through on my way to class and got caught up in this violent exchange, more as a spectator than a participant, fascinated at the bravery of these young men who had the nerve to challenge a much larger group. I remember Alamdar, by the sheer strength of his brawn, managed to put away at least half a dozen of his measly, thin-chested opponents. Drunken with success, he taunted the group. A few men pulled out firearms, and it was then that I realized that something had to be done before we were all implicated in murder. It took all my and Salaar's strength to hold back Alamdar, who was wild by this time, but we managed to drag him several feet away, then calmed him as best we could before we heard shouts that the rangers had arrived. Everyone vanished, including us, but not before exchanging names and classes. After that, the three of us were inseparable, but it was months before I knew that these friends of mine had a sister, and that she, too, was a fellow student at the University.

For that, I had to wait till the winter of 1978, when a group of business students, including myself, went to the university library to prepare for our examinations. I sat with my open textbook, while the others laughed and jeered at my apparent studiousness, which, mind you, was just a façade because while the book was open and the words and diagrams very much there, they only appeared in front of my blurry eyes like so many floating boxes. I had spent the previous night watching a much-coveted copy of Amitabh Bachchan's *Muqaddar ka Sikander* on our newly-acquired VCR, a fairly recent technology that was all the rage in our neighbourhood and which, much to Abbaji's chagrin, had drawn a large and boisterous crowd to our house. The last of my neighbourhood friends was booted out around fajr, when Abbaji, rising for his early morning prayers, caught us still drinking Cokes out of paper straws and playing Karom. I suppose the point I'm trying to make is that my mind was filled with images of the beautiful Rekha, who played one of the central roles in the film and whose face, dare I say, resembled yours, Najma.

Rashid, a fellow business student, was the first to see you in that kurta and churidar pyjama that I remember so well, the cool sea-green of it against your skin, the Multani embroidery around the neck in violet making your beautiful collar bone stand out as you stretched to reach a volume on a shelf higher than your petite 5'2". He ran over to help you before I could shift my focus from my garbled text to the supra-clarity of your vision, as you stood there nervously, the volume now in your slender hands (was it Hemingway or Ghalib, Shakespeare, or Manto, who knows?), uncertain where to look as all five of us boys stared at you with unabashed interest. I think, if I were an observer watching this scene unfold, the elderly librarian, perhaps, I would have smiled with bemusement as my friends vied for your attention, Rashid thrusting out his bony chest and straightening his stoop, Asif cracking an awkward joke about your height, Faisal grinning sheepishly under his stringy moustache (let's face it, we weren't a good-looking lot, were we?) and I, still transfixed, hardly breathing, my neglected textbook still open to the same page as I struggled through sleep and enchantment to fight off the illusion that I was beholding a cut-out still from the film I had just seen. Before I could even attempt to impress you like the others had, you spoke, thanking Rashid for his gallantry and disappearing down the rows of dusty shelves that stretched towards the long narrow windows at the far end, the only thing visible before you completely vanished the tail-end of your lace-edged dupatta.

Crushed, I slammed my textbook shut and stood up abruptly, irritated with my boisterous friends, exhausted and over-caffeinated. I was just cursing myself for not having the presence of mind to at least ask your name, when my own was called out so loudly that there were several murmurs for quiet and a sharp reprimand from the librarian. There was your brother, Alamdar, in all his muscular greatness, walking towards me with a grin and a swagger, a thin book, no more than a pamphlet, wedged between thumb and forefinger, which he was waving at me excitedly. 'This,' he began grandly, 'is the solution to all our problems!' He pushed the booklet into my hands and gave me a moment to examine it. It was a simple, light-blue publication that seemed to have been printed a few decades ago, its edges worn, its binding coming loose at the seams, even some of the words of the title faded. It was called 'The Heart's Discourse —', followed by something illegible from over-handling, and the poet's name a mystery, too, because of the tear on the cover. Least interested in that moment of time in poetry or life's problems, I quickly rifled through the pamphlet from beginning to end like a child's flip book. I could see the blur of couplets and stanzas, together forming poems of varying lengths in Urdu, a few in Farsi, even one or two in English towards the end, with grand, 19th century anglophilic titles like 'Merry England's Call' and 'From the Hills of Bangalore to Britannia'. I said nothing as I handed the book back to him.

'Don't you see, Aftab? This is fantastic stuff. The best part is, this man, the poet, he was related to us! A cousin of our Nana's, no – a second cousin of our Dada's uncle – well, whatever! I know he's one of us. Just think: our family is famous!'

'Bubbly, come on. When are you taking me home?'

The voice came from behind him. I looked down and from in between the hefty trunks that formed Alamdar's legs noticed a pair of slender feet, toenails painted, in brown kohlapuris, the 'churis' of a sea-green pyjama gathering at the ankles. Her, I thought to myself, suddenly excited. Then, after a second's reflection, my excitement turned to despair. 'Bubbly?' It took a while for me to come to terms with a man of Alamdar's personality and stature being referred to by this grossly inappropriate nickname, and that, too, by the very girl whom I had set my sights on. I thought for sure that only a girlfriend could see the 'Bubbly' in Alamdar who, though emotional to an extreme, could hardly qualify as light-hearted. As I had learned over the months, tragedy was more his thing.

'Ah, Aftab, my dear friend,' Alamdar exclaimed, moving to one side so that you were clearly visible, your dupatta casually thrown over your head as you frowned from underneath it, one foot now tapping the carpeted floor in obvious impatience. You tugged at Alamdar's arm and raised an eyebrow when you noticed the light-blue pamphlet in his hand.

'You'll have to excuse him,' you said sharply to me. 'He's a little obsessed with this book. Its merit is ridiculously exaggerated. In my opinion, there is nothing revolutionary about this poet, and I am the literature student around here.'

'Ah, Najma, how wrong you are!' Alamdar waved the book frantically over his head, using his other hand to clutch his heart. (Quite literally; he had managed to grab an entire breast.) 'How harsh you are!'

I stood there in marked silence, somewhat uncomfortable with the ease with which you and Alamdar were conversing, your banter so familiar that I assumed, with bitter disappointment, that you were together. I murmured something about another class, and was about to turn around and walk away when Alamdar said, 'Yaar, what kind of a friend are you? Have you no manners? There's a lady here I want to introduce you to. Najma, meet Aftab. Aftab – Najma.'

You smiled, and I nodded politely.

'Array, yaar!' Alamdar bellowed, amid protests from all sides as the more studious amongst us vented their frustration at his consistent loudness. You pushed him towards the exit, and I accompanied you reluctantly, dreading the introductions and forced pleasantries that would follow. Once safely out of the library and into the warm sunshine of that crisp winter day, Alamdar turned to me and laughed. 'Can you imagine living with someone as bossy as her?'

Live with? So things had reached that level of seriousness, I thought with disgust. I couldn't imagine why Alamdar would have kept his marriage a secret from me.

'Your friend appears to have lost his voice.' You were smiling at me, your eyes now looking directly into mine, the bashfulness completely gone as you surveyed me frankly, maybe even liked what you saw. I looked from Alamdar to you, then from you to Alamdar, once, twice, a third time before I registered that you shared certain characteristics – the shape of your eyes, your prominent jawlines, the texture of your voluminous hair – just as we Mahmuds did, that indicated a shared ancestry, even common blood. Before I knew what I was doing, I burst out, 'Of course, you're Alamdar and Salaar's sister!'

I clapped a hand to my mouth. Had I said that aloud?

Alamdar turned to me with a befuddled expression. 'Well, of course. What else did you think?' Then, with his usual impatience for detail, he moved on, opening the blue pamphlet and declaiming from 'An Indian in South London' in heavily-accented English as if to an audience of thousands as you laughed and jeered at him, all the while (don't think I didn't notice) looking at me out of the corner of your eye. Within seconds, I was laughing, too, and that, Najma, was just the beginning...

We weren't ideally matched, you and I. Our personalities, for one, were very different. You were the artsy type, bold in your opinions, confident without being labelled 'fast' by your traditional aunties. I, on the other hand, was the polar opposite; reserved to a fault, emotionally emasculated, conservative in dress and behaviour, boringly conventional. I was incredibly naïve and inexperienced when it came to dealing with women. I hardly cut a dashing figure in my staid shirts and nondescript trousers, particularly when standing next to the daring young intellectuals who frequented your house, some of them jauntily dressed in berets or stylish scarves as they argued vociferously over cups of tea.

After that first, all-too-brief meeting, we began to contrive ways of spending time together without arousing suspicion. I became a frequent visitor to your house, joining the dozens of other men, young and old, who gathered there weekly to discuss books and politics with your father. I was usually the quiet one in the corner, listening with feigned interest to the socialist thought of the time, all the while admiring you as you sat among the men and offered your views on politics, religion, or feminist theory. The discussion of these topics was new to me. I had spent the first two decades of my life within the rigid confines of cantonments and cadet colleges, where drills and regimentation were de rigueur and free thinking frowned upon. Unfortunately (or fortunately), I wasn't bloodthirsty enough to follow through on my early military education for a career in the armed forces and disappointed Abbaji by opting for a degree in Business, coming to the University late, too late, in fact, to have developed opinions on what most interested my peers. At those weekly sessions with your father and his admirers, I watched with fascination and envy the absoluteness with which men, barely in their twenties, expressed convictions. I felt certain of nothing.

Perhaps that's what attracted me to you. You seemed very clear about what you wanted, even at twenty-two. You searched for something beyond the limited confines of the world you inhabited. Your mother, you told me in our first or second meeting, had died only a few days after you were born. You were raised by your father and then, more intimately, by your brothers Salaar and Alamdar. That may have accounted for what I always thought was your ability to switch thought-process, to step back from feelings natural to you in a given situation and see it from another (and generally, male) perspective. You dealt with your father and brothers with supreme tact, caring for them, loving them, but often guiding their individual wilfulness towards cohesion. I sometimes wondered where I would fit in. The last thing I wanted, of course, was to break up your family.

By the summer of 1978, we had become quite serious about each other. We had just completed our degrees. Many of our contemporaries were leaving for the United States and Canada for better educational prospects and securer futures. I had applied to various colleges and was hopeful of getting a scholarship. Predictably, Abbaji and Ammi were against my leaving but finally agreed on the age-old condition that I marry first. Ammi in particular was certain that a single Pakistani male like myself would be in extreme danger in the United States, the unsuspecting target of rapacious blondes after me for my wholesome sense of commitment and my 'dark' good looks. I rejoiced – until I found out that they had pre-selected a candidate, a third-cousin from Ammi's side who lived in San Francisco and whose existence I vaguely remembered from a fleeting glimpse of spectacles and braces (that's all I could recall of her) in a photograph dated 1967.

We arranged to meet at the library that day. I told you about their plans, and I still remember your composure as you said matter-of-factly, 'Fine. It wouldn't have worked anyway.' Then, you went on to say that, though progressive, your father would balk at your marrying outside your sect, that your brothers would never countenance it.

'So, that's it?' I asked. 'You're willing to give up that easily?'

'Go and see,' you challenged. 'Ask your parents. Do you honestly think they'll say yes?'

I had never thought about it. That evening, I sat them down and told them about you. Of course, I had anticipated a reaction – it would have been naïve not to. There was the

customary wailing on Ammi's part at not having her way,
the pulling of hair at the shame this would bring upon us,
the beating of breast at the guarantees she had given the
girl's mother, the vulgarity of it all. Within half an hour, the
passion spent, she sat skulking at the far end of the sofa. I
thought Abbaji would be the rational one. After all, what
would he care whether I married Ammi's distant relative or
the charming girl I had met at university? When he finally
spoke, it was with a frosty sternness and a newly acquired
formality of tone that necessitated the repeated use of 'Sir'
before every sentence he addressed to me.

'So, Sir, you will disregard our feelings in this matter?'

'At least meet her, Abbaji!'

'Sir, as far as I am concerned, I will have nothing to do
with you if you take this step.'

I couldn't believe what I was hearing. 'But, Abbaji—'

'Sir, no one in our family – trace it back centuries – has
ever married a Shia.'

'Manhoos Rafzi! They're not even Muslim!' Ammi wailed
from her corner.

I had underestimated Abbaji's prejudice. While I
understood that he had become progressively more
conservative over the years, a practising rather than nominal
Muslim, I had no idea that a western-educated army man
could do such an about-turn. This was a narrowness that I
had not expected of him. I lost my temper. I began yelling,
raged, said many things I shouldn't have, all the while
acknowledging somewhere at the back of my mind that
these words – most of them disrespectful and mean-spirited

– could not be taken back. I had never spoken to my father like that before. I realized, with the prescience of someone taking a momentous decision, that you, Najma, were worth even an irreconcilable break with my family. I left the house with only one thought, to find you, marry you, and take you with me. It felt amazing to be certain about something for once.

An hour later, we sat at our customary table at the library. I was agitated, explaining what had happened in a rush of words – mostly expletives – as you sat there calmly, staring at your hands splayed on the table as if, of all things, contemplating a manicure. I paused in mid-sentence and frowned. 'Najma!' I whispered urgently. 'What on earth are you thinking?'

'I'm thinking,' you said with a smile, 'that it's about time you felt strongly about something. I've never seen you look so determined.'

'So,' I asked, 'does that mean…?'

'Of course!' you laughed, slipping your hand under the table to grab mine.

CHAPTER 19

Now, if asked what my mother was like, I would have to think back to a time before her illness, but that time is already remote in my mind, like a distant holiday looked at decades later in photographs, snatches of smiles and faces pressed together in perfect white-bordered squares, contained and unapproachable, the captions illegible so that the once-memorable landmarks, the parks visited, the tangled paths of forests explored are all untraceable, only the essence distilled; then I wonder, did it really happen, or were these images just a cruel photographic illusion? What I most remember of her was of the days when she wasn't quite herself anymore, just a body in a printed hospital gown, the gown dotted, like a field, with pale blue flowers, surely a laughable strategy on the part of palliative care to prettify the institutionalized near non-existence of its sickest patients. It was to palliative care that Amma was moved in her last days. I was too frightened to ask what that meant – we all were. One afternoon, quite by accident, Fatima happened to see the word, side-by-side with its definition in the TV Guide, its meaning unequivocal in the title of a forthcoming documentary: *Palliative Care: The Last Days of Living*.

But even then, it didn't seem real to us. As children, we couldn't accept a life without Amma. We kept pestering our harried Baba for a holiday when it was all over, some surreal island off the coast of Africa to which we would journey by plane and by boat after all this, the hospitals, CAT scans, surgeries, were over, when, at last, this year of hardship was safely behind us. There, on the shimmering silver sand of an untouched shore, Amma would be whole again, fully restored, sinewy even, running with her hair streaming and limbs free, the diseased parts of her falling away, a butterfly emerging out of a chrysalis... If only it could be: the six of us in the sun, natural in the companionship that nothing but family life can bring, the daily waking, eating, sleeping of normal existence, the intimacy of kinship. This dream was just another form of escapism from the incomprehensible. That tropical paradise now only existed in our minds, and we returned to it, again and again, like our games.

I remember vanilla on her breath as I was lifted high up to the hospital bed to kiss her goodbye, her eyes open but distracted as her fingers absent-mindedly tugged at the sheets that imprisoned her. Her face looked smaller, intensely pure, as if she had left many things behind, which, in fact, she had, her mind floating from consciousness to places beyond, where normal human concerns didn't matter anymore, like a breast bared in front of strangers as a hospital gown unravelled. There, even love didn't matter, husband and child forgotten in a battle with self, with the minute cells of the body, reproducing in places unknown, secret cankers beneath the skin that crept stealthily, like predatory animals, over the ground they consumed. An epic battle, life and death, where skirmishes were fought at a molecular level, and body and soul wrestled half-heartedly for supremacy.

Sometimes, just before drifting off to sleep in the warm wet darkness of a Karachi night, I would suddenly feel cold again, like I did in Chicago, the skin beneath my cotton pyjamas tingling like it did that day in February, almost a year ago, when I awoke paralyzed, my body under the sheets stiff with a kind of internal tautness of the nerves. It was the 23rd, and so bitterly cold that my imagination transported me to the grocery's deep freezer, that petrifying room-sized box lined with sacks of pulverized vegetables where the worst of winter is preserved in an eternal frost. Shivering, I pulled myself up till I was leaning on my bare elbows, then looked out through the window onto our sloping front yard, the tufted snow peaking into hillocks that rose and fell, rose and fell, falling away, finally, to the roadside mounds the snow ploughs had left behind. The windowpanes were covered in frost, the shadow-souls of summer's leaves pressed against the glass in feathered patterns of longing, so that the scene outside appeared twice-removed, or faded, as in a weathered photograph.

The world was waking up to another day, another day, only my mother would no longer be a part of it.

'Little Furry!'

Startled, I nearly knocked down the slender candle that Lady M had precariously balanced on a chipped china saucer from the kitchen and placed at the center of our circle. For several minutes now I had been staring at the pearly beads of wax that slowly dripped down its sides and fell in clumps to the bottom, where a creamy pool of white threatened to overflow onto our precious rug. A cheap candle, no doubt. One that melted within minutes and cast only a faltering light on the walls of our hideout, making the characters in the drawings step down into three-dimensionality and stand behind us, their fantastic, gargoylesque faces pressed heavily against our backs. Burdensome, they breathed into the hot, stale air.

'Little Furry,' Dag snapped, 'haven't you heard anything we've talked about? We're waiting for your report. What happened when you questioned Air Commodore Rafiq Nawaz on Shahbaz? Is there a connection or not?'

Timmer, the mildest of the three, spoke up gently, 'Don't pester her. She'll speak when she wants to. I'm sure it wasn't easy for her...' She raised her arms above her head and stretched, the feline movement rising in silhouette above our heads and onto the jagged cement of the staircase that sheltered us from discovery. It was past midnight, the doors were locked, and Baba's snores could be heard accompanying the drone of the air conditioner. Before I could stop myself, I yawned. As soon as I realized what I had done, I looked up at Lady M. Her expression was inscrutable. When she spoke, her voice was cold and clear: 'Little Furry, we entrusted you with a task and expected you to follow through.'

How could I tell her that instead of seeing Uncle Raff on the customary Tuesday, I suddenly came upon a slightly bewildered Dada sitting alone in the garden, his movements slow and hesitant as he raised a tea cup with both hands to his lips? There was no Uncle Shahnawaz, no Uncle Raff even, just a couple of gluttonous crows perched a few yards away on the rusty swing, awaiting the chance to swoop down at the crumbs that had fallen from the plate of biscuits on the table. Dadi was asleep in the lounge, and Durdana Phupo was at the office, helping her boss prepare for a conference in Jakarta. Suddenly, I realized the old man was alone and, afraid of being discovered, began edging away from his line of vision, preparing, ultimately, for a marathon sprint across the garden to Shahnaz's quarters. I had reached the first coconut palm when a querulous voice called out uncertainly, 'Ferzana…?'

Resigned, I said in a monotone, 'Yes, Dada?' What now? More pakoras from the kitchen? The tea wasn't hot enough? Fetch the nail clippers? For Dada, any woman (even one of my size) was merely a means of conveyance, a two-legged, upright pack animal. Being the only such creature around, I turned back reluctantly and stood before him, my hands clasped in front of me so that I would avoid the obvious, a military salute, the only gesture, it seemed, regimented enough for this crusty old man.

I noticed him carefully put down his cup before placing a hand on the sofa as if to suggest, of all things, that I come and join him. I remained where I was, too shocked at this unexpected invitation to move, but then, there it was, the command, belted out from revived vocal cords with no-nonsense authority. I jumped to obey him and within seconds, found myself sitting next to him, his wrinkled old hand resting gingerly on my right knee, the fingers splayed like a crab's legs. I stared at his hand, uncertain what to do next.

He offered me the biscuit plate, and I took one. It was from his stash of imported shortbread from England, which Jamshaid Chacha kept adequately replenished from his regular trips abroad and which were stored, along with boxes of Turkish Delight, Swiss chocolates and Devonshire toffees, in a small padlocked fridge in his bathroom. I bit into the powdery biscuit and felt it explode on my tongue, magically turning into sweet butter in my mouth. I couldn't believe I had been asked to partake of this precious hoard. Suddenly smiling, I looked up at my grandfather and asked, 'Dada, where are your friends? And Uncle Raff?'

Dada's hand flew off my knee and landed, with a smack, on his own thigh. Startled, I turned to look at him and noticed with growing unease that his face, the austere lines around eyes and mouth from a lifetime of unsmiling rigidity (that's what I naturally put it down to), the sacs of soft skin that drooped on either side of his face, the furrowed brow were all in motion, an unusual kind of frenetic animation that, distressingly, looked almost as if he were about to cry. Mesmerized, I put the last piece of biscuit into my mouth and let it lie there on my tongue, its sweetness intoxicating as I watched this generally unemotional man struggling to contain his feelings.

'What is it, Dada?' I asked, genuinely concerned when, to my surprise, he covered his face with both hands. It wasn't funny anymore and suddenly I was scared. At their age, anything could happen. Had someone died?

'Ferzana,' Dada began, 'I was going to speak to you earlier. Shahnawaz is fine. He's gone to England to visit friends.'

Thank goodness, I thought. A temporary absence was acceptable.

'It's Raff...' Dada continued nervously. 'Well, you know how fond he is of you.'

'I love him, too,' I said simply. Inside, I felt sick.

Dada was silent at this admission, then nodded in magnanimous agreement, stating after a lengthy pause, 'He is in kidney failure.'

Kidney failure? I knew only too well that the body could fail, fail abysmally, that it was subject to the most terrifying tests, to intimate examinations with uncertain outcomes, and that the incorrect answers it gave when it buckled under pressure – mottled x-rays and CT-scans, garbled blood counts – were indications of its lacklustre performance. But I was puzzled by the kidney, only having a vague understanding of its function in the human body. I knew there were two. Surely one could tutor the other through its failure?

To Dada I merely said 'That can't be serious' but thought back uneasily to the day that I had noticed Uncle Raff's legs, almost as slender as my own, more bone than muscle, in fact, and virtually translucent in the sun. I remembered his laborious walk to the car with the assistance of his faithful driver, Habib, the painful shuffle of his feet over the dusty asphalt, and the number of times he attempted to pull his left leg up into the car, finally relinquishing control and allowing Habib to gently lift it inside and place it, like something outside of himself, next to his other leg.

'Well, Ferzana,' Dada replied slowly, 'it can actually be quite serious. He's in the hospital. Has been for the last few days. I went to see him yesterday.'

When I didn't say anything, Dada added, 'He – well, he wanted to see you.'

'When is he coming home?' I asked quietly.

'The only way to see him at the moment is at the hospital,' Dada said, shaking his head regretfully. 'Think about it, Ferzana. Talk to your Baba if you like. I know,' he looked directly at me, 'it can't be easy after everything you've all been through.'

'What do you mean, Dada?' I half-knew I was throwing down a challenge. Looking down, I squeezed my eyes shut while I waited for an answer. Much would be decided between us, once and for all, based on how he framed his response. Could it be true – had he really changed over the handful of months that I had known him?

'Well, child…' he fumbled, suddenly looking confused, then passing me yet another biscuit from his prized collection while he paused to reflect over what he was going to say, almost as if he, too, realized that the way he framed his answer would have repercussions. 'Well, your mother, Najma, and all that she went through, and so bravely – but it's not fair to expect you to be as brave, or to want to visit Raff in the hospital.' He raised his hands, pressing both palms together, resting his chin on the frail tips of his fingers as he looked out across the lawn to where Shahbaz Chacha and Tania Chachi, just returned from work, were walking slowly, arm in arm, towards us.

An old pelican, I thought to myself, the tufts of hair on either side of his bald scalp disheveled like a bird in flight. Or better still, an eagle. I recalled what Dadi had said about his army service and the period he had spent as a POW across the border in neighbouring India. This man had an entire history that preceded my arrival on the planet. It was unimaginable to me that he could have lived through experiences similar to mine, could have learned the 12-times table in the third grade, could have fought with his three siblings (all dead now), or spied, quite by accident, the cook pulling the massi into a darkened closet. In the supremely egocentric mould of a preteen, all events revolved around me, of course, and my relationship to others. For the first time, I wanted to know everything about this man.

Made uncomfortable by my silence, perhaps, Dada felt compelled to admit, 'The fact is, Ferzana, even an old fellow like myself gets scared sometimes.' Shocked, I turned to look at him. A rare sight, the grim line that usually parted his face in two turned upwards in what appeared to be – no was – an embarrassed smile, an almost foolish, self-deprecating acknowledgement of his own ridiculousness. A seventy-eight-year-old army man afraid of infirmity, mortality, the end? I inched towards him on the sofa, then buried my mouth, sticky with crumbs, into his arm. He remained still, venturing after a second to pat my head, running his unsteady fingers through my hair.

'Good job, Dada. Good job,' I thought to myself in excitement; after nine months of living virtually under one roof, he had said my mother's name.

'Lady M,' I spoke, 'I'm afraid Air Commodore Rafiq Nawaz is in the hospital in serious condition. The only way I can interview him is if I' – here I faltered – 'visit him in the hospital.'

Lady M was quiet, as were the rest of them. Here was an obstacle no one could have foreseen. In our minds, a hospital was a place of unhappiness, a place to be feared for its steel-edged machines emitting inhuman sounds, its endless corridors fanged with doors that led to dark rooms of suffering. I could see Lady M, generally icy and controlled, struggle with herself before turning uncharacteristically to Timmer for assistance.

'Of course there is no question of us expecting you to go to such lengths, Little Furry,' Timmer reassured me, and the others quickly nodded in agreement. Frightened, I looked at Dag but was surprised to find that his penetrating eyes, instead of glaring at me, were focused on the candle, which now flickered madly, its brief struggle with itself coming to an abrupt end, and darkness. I reached out for the nearest hand and felt the rough warmth of a man's grasp, large fingers wrapped tightly around mine.

'Oh, there's one more thing,' I suddenly spoke, my voice high-pitched and unfamiliar in the darkness. The others, then rising for bed, were startled; I heard a sharp intake of breath from Timmer. Unperturbed, I continued, 'I did overhear Brigadier Mahmud inform Shahbaz that Air Commodore Rafiq Nawaz was extremely anxious to see him in the hospital, too. They were both puzzled by this because Shahbaz isn't close to Air Commodore Rafiq Nawaz and has never spent that much time with him.'

'This is interesting,' said Lady M. 'Well done, Little Furry. Could this be the proof we need to establish that Shahbaz is Air Commodore Nawaz's love child?'

'The only way to determine that is to be present at the meeting,' Dag pointed out.

'But we will not put Little Furry through that. Agreed?' Lady M said authoritatively.

'Agreed,' Timmer and Dag replied in unison.

Half an hour later, while the rest of the family was asleep, I sat perched on the window sill, my nightie hitched up to my thighs. I sighed as the blast from the air conditioner cooled me from underneath, bringing some relief to my unfortunate posterior, a victim of prickly heat. The garden was lit in parts by the intermittent appearance of a moon in the clouds. I imagined, through the closed window, the overpowering scent of its masses of tropical flowers, which grew unattended, almost wild, on the trees and bushes that lined the boundary walls. My favourite was the waxy champa, its white petals opening buoyantly to a yolky centre, its pale stem pliant when strung with needle and thread into garlands.

I remembered Dada's request. The thought of entering a hospital after our recent experiences terrified me. It wasn't so very long ago that we had made our own dreary way to the grey-bricked building where Amma had spent her last days. As I looked out at the garden, my eyes focused through the dim light on Tea Central, at this time of night a cluster of disused and ramshackle cane, Dada's sofa slightly warped where his weight, over the years, had caused the dusty structure to sink. Suddenly, it occurred to me that I wasn't required to enter that hospital as the supremely confident Little Furry. I could also go as just me, eleven-year-old, normal, everyday Ferzana Mahmud. Somehow that made it easier to believe that I could survive the long stomach-cramping drive, the unavoidable entrance into that Phenyled environment through the wide-swinging teak doors, the weak-kneed walk through those interminable corridors, some burrowing deep into the entrails of the building, others open to the sky – and, finally, see the old man whom I loved. I wouldn't do it for the sake of a game, even a game as important as ours.

I would do it for Uncle Raff. And for my Dada.

CHAPTER 20

Shahnaz and I stood before the full-length mirror in the bedroom that I shared with my sisters, triumphant. She had never been upstairs, in the so-called 'private' or family areas of our compound, her presence here a miracle of subterfuge and ingenuity, the result of several weeks of reconnoitring on our part to determine the most efficacious time to slip her, unnoticed, through our front door, up the stairs, and into the room where we now stood, flushed with victory, in front of the mirror. I looked appraisingly at our reflections: roughly the same age and height, we wore shalwar-kameezes pulled randomly from my overflowing chest of drawers, both of us prim in the floral prints and matching lace that Dadi, my dress designer, was so fond of, faces washed, hair pulled back, and hands locked together.

'I almost' – Shahnaz stammered – 'I almost look like a girl!'

More than that, I thought to myself enviously, more-than-girl, she looked womanly, even grown-up with her puffy chest exploding out of my pathetically childish, too-narrow kurta, her clear sunkissed complexion peachy beneath her golden, short-cropped hair, eyes green as the sea under a wave of thick lashes as she squinted at herself and laughed, the laugh, husky like a back-street goonda, but somehow adding to her attractiveness, making her slightly dangerous but bewitching, too. I had never seen her like this before – the tomboy turned beauty queen. I looked at myself in the mirror, at my tangled black hair and sallow complexion. I made a half-hearted concession to friendship by smiling self-consciously into the mirror, my eyes focusing, unfortunately, on the conspicuous bulge below her neck, wondering whether that extra flesh was a desirable appendage or not, when it became so, and how ladies managed to rein theirs in with undergarments. Until now I had thought of it as an irritating encumbrance which, thankfully, I was free of. I folded my arms across my bony chest, feeling a little sorry for myself.

'What do you think?' Shahnaz asked, twirling girlishly on one foot, both arms raised over her head so that the kurta rose ever higher up her shapely hips. Then, without any warning at all – after all, friends should warn each other before bursting into song and dance – she began moving, and moving fast, shaking in ways not humanly possible, I thought, her hips swinging back and forth, arms curving gracefully in-and-out, in-and-out, while she hummed a lively tune that was always on the radio, a medley of songs from a recent Indian film that could often be heard in snatches as we drove with our windows down through Saddar.

'Try it!' Shahnaz said, and lifted one of my limp arms up into the air in encouragement. Stiffly, almost robotically, I shifted my arms and legs in pale imitation of her expert moves, finally standing back and observing, first with envy then with awe this friend of mine who had, for months, concealed these very womanly talents from me beneath her boyish attire and straightforward bluntness. I found myself blushing, uncomfortable with the way her movements made me feel, the freedom of her body in motion so different from our gangly races, our climbing of stairs two-at-a-time, our flying jumps over objects small and large in the garden. I was so absorbed in watching her performance that for several seconds I was unaware that we, too, were being observed. It was not until Shahnaz grabbed me by the waist and lifted me up, twirling my stiff, reluctant body round and round that I caught a glimpse, in the dizzying whirl of the moment, of my brother's astonished face at the door.

Struggling out of her grasp, I pushed her roughly to the ground, for all her womanly curves now just an irate little girl spurned by her friend, arms and legs sprawled out, completely unladylike, with her shalwar's nafaa forming a tuft of unwieldy cloth between her thighs.

'What do you want?' I asked Raza, hoping my confidence would deflect the seriousness of our transgression. Although there had been no confrontation yet, I was angry at him for his suspected involvement with my teacher and couldn't care less what he thought of me and my friend.

'Just admiring your performance,' Raza answered coolly, his eyes still on Shahnaz, who quickly stood up and pulled her kurta down, only serving to accentuate its tightness around her chest and hips. Hastily, she tugged at the dupatta which lay coiled, snakelike, at her feet, tossing it first around her neck then, suddenly conscious, stretching it out over her chest. 'And you are…?' Raza continued, still staring at her.

Before the surprised Shahnaz could speak, I mumbled under my breath, 'She's a friend from next door.' (Which, after all, was true.)

'Oh,' Raza replied, then walked away.

Shahnaz and I looked at one another. She was first, her full lips and wide mouth suddenly opening to reveal not just her teeth, but her very tonsils, guffawing hysterically (there really was no other word for the sound, and it was *not* ladylike) as she held her stomach with one hand and used the other to slap her knee in mirth. I wrapped my arms around her, my knees buckling, and we both fell to the floor, shamelessly delighted with the success of our venture, our laughter now bold, loud, and untamable. It took us several minutes to calm ourselves down, but when we managed to look at each other again, suddenly stony faced – an art, mind you, that we had almost perfected – I realized something quite profound. I watched Shahnaz fuss over my clothes on her body, pulling at a lace here, straightening the edge of a sleeve there, at one point even transfixed by the crisp fold of the starched shalwar, which refused to budge even as she rolled her legs left and right experimentally. Over the months that we had known each other, she had grown, not just in the way children do, but up, as they say, figuratively 'up' like a grown adult, and I hadn't. It wouldn't be fair to hold that against her. After all, it wasn't in her control any more than the lack of 'up' to my growth was mine. I could only record a measly inch-and-a-half in height, half a pound in weight, and no movement whatsoever in the chest area which remained, like uncooked chappati, stuck to my ribcage.

'Where did you learn to dance like that?' I asked with unabashed admiration.

'Here and there...' she mumbled vaguely. 'I mean, don't you people watch TV? Oops, I forgot. That's right. You don't. Well, with Dish, we can watch just about anything. Ammi usually puts on the Indian song channels. When she's not in, I watch the English music channels.' Giggling, she ended with, 'Naughty, right?'

'Hold on, hold on' – I tried to conceal my excitement – 'you mean all this time you've had a TV in your quarters?'

'Of course. Babaa' (she always stretched the last vowel sound in her version of the fatherly appellation) 'bought it off Jamal when we moved here. It's small but it works. We just borrow the Dish connection off of yours – I mean, off your Dada's. Don't tell, okay?'

'I won't.' There was enterprise for you. In all the time we were here, I wondered, why hadn't we thought of that? Despite all the hoopla about our being 'chaloo Amriki', we were really quite simple, and in this particular, I realized with dismay, downright stupid.

'What next?' Shahnaz asked, as she slowly rose to her feet while keeping one eye on her profile within the carved framework of the full-length mirror, so that as the late afternoon sun streamed in through the windows her chest, wondrously illuminated from behind, seemed to radiate sunlight. I tried to ignore this vainglorious display, turning my back to the mirror and choosing instead to arrange a stack of type-written sheets in chronological order on my bed. I scanned the headings of the emails, all purportedly from someone named 'Colonel Bogey' and addressed to Fatima, sent sporadically over a period of nine months, which was roughly a few weeks after our arrival in Pakistan.

'What is all that?' Shahnaz asked, joining me at the bed.

'Some of Fatima's emails. She's upset over them.'

'How did you get them?'

I turned to Shahnaz in displeasure. 'I just took them from her drawer, okay?' I retorted hostilely. 'Besides, Raza once told me I was the only one who could figure out who's sending them.'

'You mean this person still sends her letters?'

'She just got one last week. I heard her crying over it in the bathroom.'

Shahnaz gingerly sat on the edge of my bed, then looked up at me as if to ask if that were acceptable within the fluid bounds of this curious new relationship we had concocted with a simple change of clothes. 'Go ahead,' I said, surprised, never having had any of the class or economic prejudices that marked my grandparents' interaction with those whom they disdainfully referred to as 'the servants', their tone slightly accusatory as if anticipating betrayal. Even after months of living in Karachi it struck me as odd that people were not always seen as individuals but as products of several abstractions which, when combined, typecast them as surely as if they were mediocre actors in a third-rate comedy. Whether it was ethnicity, religious affiliation, lineage, economics, class, or that most divisive of factors, point of origin (Were we, I once asked Baba, Punjabis or Mohajirs, or Sindhi like Momal, who arrived at school in a land cruiser with armed guards and was whisked away to her village in the interior during breaks?). The point of origin, or one's roots, was particularly important to Dadi, whose stories of Lucknow had already filled my afternoons for several months now and whose nostalgia for its courtly culture, preserved in time-warped memory, made me think of the only equivalent an eleven-year-old North American child could relate to. 'Disney Varld? Disney Varld?' Dadi had gasped when I asked her if there were any similarities, pulling at her ears and muttering 'Tobah', herself succumbing to the stereotype of the traditional Mohajir grandmother.

Dadi, in fact, was an expert at racial profiling. Baba sometimes joked that she could have worked for Homeland Security – if she had ever bothered to acquire an American passport, that is. Despite never having had any formal education beyond grade school, she sometimes startled with her pithy insights into a range of subjects, from her forte, the delicate and fragrant cuisine of the U.P. (not something rude, as I initially suspected, but the short-form of Uttar Pradesh, the Indian state where her beloved Lucknow was the capital), to glamorous fashion, local ethnic rivalries and fractious national politics, Urdu poetry and literature, regional history. I had even heard it said that she knew a thing or two about military strategy – courtesy of Dada, of course.

It was, however, as a diviner of people's backgrounds that she was at her best. I remember accompanying her to the fruitwallah one day and challenging her to describe everything she could about a young man with a stringy moustache who stood leaning against his motor bike while his burka-clad wife haggled with the vendor. Within seconds she had ascertained his ethnicity, a second-generation Mohajir from Bihar, his religious affiliation from the aqeeq on his right hand, the fact that he prayed five times a day and that he lived a lower-middle-class life making tea and running errands for the upper echelons of a large multinational. At that point, the man whipped a scrawny trouserleg over his motorcycle as he was joined by his wife, who hoisted herself behind him with one hand while using the other to raise a fist at the fruitwallah for his exorbitant prices. They sped away in a cloud of dust and curses. Just a few minutes more and I felt certain that Dadi would have traced back his ancestry to the time of the Prophet. As she lumbered out of our car and waved at the fruitwallah (Pathan, one of six children, originally from Charsadda), Dadi added as an afterthought, 'Oh yes, Chhoti. That man was also henpecked.' I now knew whose sleuthing genes I had inherited.

'Well, what does it say?' Shahnaz asked, waving an arm over the sheets I had arranged on the bed.

'I can't read it all to you. I don't even know' – between startled gasps – 'half these words are in Urdu.' Finally, I looked at her and said, 'It's all a bit rude.' Urdu or English, I had no idea what some of the words meant, the coarseness of the letter sounds coupled with their abrupt mutilated endings making me turn away in shame. Words like these, it seemed, not only had character but reputation, too, jumping out from in between the normal words and proclaiming their seedy nature by the flamboyance of their construction.

'Try me,' Shahnaz demanded.

'Well, what's this one? I think it's Urdu. Choo-teee-ya. Chootiya. Is that a braid?' I pulled at the one that neatly scraped my hair in place, falling behind me like a horse's stunted tail.

Shahnaz snorted, shoving her fist into her mouth in an unsuccessful attempt to stifle a throaty giggle. I stood by, dignified and nonplussed, as she fell off the bed and rolled – in my white shalwar – all over the dusty floor in barely stifled hysterics. I turned away from her and surveyed the bed again, scanning the emails in progression, noticing that the early ones at least were cloying love letters of the most embarrassing, most shamelessly mawkish kind, comparing my sister's various body parts to the universe and stars, her voice to a bulbul's, her smile to the radiant dawn, her gait to a gazelle's. Then, the letters became more ambitious still, as the author turned to amateur verse, line upon line travelling its drunken way across and down the page in phrases that barely made sense but lamely concluded with the simplistic end-rhymes of a child's song. Pathetic and disgusting at the same time, I wondered at the mind that could have produced this quantity of drivel and imagined my sister, her pale face framed by the dark curls that we as sisters shared, first laughing in scorn, the intellectual snob in her merciless in the critique of language and construction, then frightened as the tone of the emails abruptly swerved, delving into nightmare, the words jumping out like fists, the intensity of the sexual jealousy they represented incomprehensible to me at the time except as an unspecified threat, a sheathed but deadly weapon. I shuddered. No wonder Fatima had been so unhappy since our arrival.

Shahnaz had quickly bored of my struggle to make sense of the emails and had spent the last five minutes examining our room. With a tentative finger, she wiped the dust off the spines of Fatima's books, which were arranged in alphabetical order on an old shelf that Baba had inherited from a friend when he and Amma first arrived in Chicago. I noticed her pause to look at the tiny pictures on the spines, blushing English roses with creamy skin and wide blue eyes, fields of daffodils or daisies, the rustic landscapes of nineteenth century Europe as captured by its painters and then described by its writers in thick small-print tomes that my sister ravenously consumed. She had inherited her love of literature from Amma, whose early career at the University was suspended when she chose to marry Baba, uproot herself and move to another country where, at least in the early years, her focus was on adjusting. During long and lonely Chicago days, waiting for Baba to return from work so that he could drive her to the nearest grocery store, we must have kept her busy and, as we grew, generated the topics necessary for conversations with the wider community on cloth versus store-bought diapers, homemade baby food, laundry detergents. Impossible. She had to have aspired to more. But – and here I stopped, uncertain whether there was in fact a connection – then the third baby came and much of Amma's time was devoted to her special care.

Suddenly, I was furious at myself. There is no point, I thought, wiping my eyes roughly with the starched sleeve of my kurta, in thinking of the past. The emails on the bed merged and blended till I could only see white, the letters unfettered, floating, free-falling, rearranging themselves into words of love and words of hate. For an instant, I had allowed myself to see Amma not as my mother but as a woman whose life has been cut short, whose own ambitions had been set aside for us. When the time came for her to reclaim herself, she fell ill. All that squandered possibility was more real to me now that I knew what she had been capable of, Baba's description of her youthful spirit difficult to reconcile with the placid mother she had always been to us.

'What's wrong?' I felt an arm around my shoulder and turned to see Shahnaz, her face close to mine, her look of concern drawing me closer still, then the warmth of her arms as she wrapped them tightly around me. Several seconds passed before I could answer, 'I miss my mother.'

Instead of consoling me, she immediately turned to the bed. 'Someone is hurting your sister. We have to find out who it is and punish him. That's the fun part,' she grinned. 'Thinking of ways to punish him!'

Grateful, I allowed myself to become absorbed in the investigation again. Shahnaz and I spent several minutes discussing the emails before I gathered them together and carefully put them back into Fatima's desk drawer. We slipped downstairs and out through the courtyard but not before the voice I had been dreading called out to me from the main house, sharp and insistent, my name whipping through the static air heavy with mid-afternoon sun: 'Ferzana!' The voice seemed to gather strength from deep within the speaker's bowels, for the next call was commanding and distinctly un-ignorable: 'Ferzana! I can see you – and your friend. Come inside please. Both of you.'

Shahnaz and I looked at one another. I could see the perspiration seeping through the cloth under her armpits, the wetness around her hairline, feel the warm damp of her palm as she wrapped it around mine. 'Don't worry,' I whispered. 'Just be confident.' Hand in hand, we entered the cool interior of the marble-tiled foyer, removing our slippers and entering the lounge barefoot like Baghdadian thieves expecting a dire retribution. There was Dadi ensconced on the sofa, a ladies' digest splayed on her knees as she used the edge of her dupatta to wipe the dust off her glasses. A few seconds more of studious cleaning, and she had readjusted them on her nose – a fine nose, and the reason for her youthful reputation as a beauty (the whole of Lucknow raved and raved, she said), but at present wrinkled disdainfully in our direction, her thin lips pursed in anticipation of a confrontation. The interplay of sun and shadow had changed the constitution of the room, so that its contents looked like pulled taffy, parts striped, elongated and stretched, the back of a lounge chair taller in the half-light and therefore providing Shahnaz and me the partial concealment that we desired.

'Yahan ao,' Dadi ordered, her eyes magnified through her bifocals, round and seemingly multifaceted like a fly's. Reluctantly we pulled ourselves away from the shadows and into the pool of sunshine that came streaming in from the crack of the partially lowered chik. I noticed Jamila sitting across from her, legs pulled up on a chair, a bored and vacant look about her. As we stepped into the sunlight, she suddenly sat up and stared.

'Who is this?' Dadi demanded to know. She turned to Jamila as if expecting her to respond, but my wise sister merely shrugged and continued to gaze at us, the faintest change in expression indicating she had recognized Shahnaz.

'Ferzana, who is this?' Dadi repeated sharply. 'That girl, the driver's daughter...?' And here she fumbled with her glasses again, straining to see through the bright shaft of light that neatly sliced the room in half and in which we stood, exposed.

With the boldness of a seasoned liar, I answered a second time, 'A friend from next door.'

'Beta, come here,' Dadi coaxed, her arms stretched out before her as she continued to squint shortsightedly in our direction. I walked straight into her embrace, taking Shahnaz with me. I looked down at Dadi who, seated below, was a mound of flesh and crisp cotton, her pink scalp partially visible through the stringy grey locks of her trademark hairstyle, which like the Chinese queue, consisted of a thinning braid that I sometimes used in play as a mustache, sometimes a tail. She scrutinized my friend, taking in everything, from her short-cropped golden locks to her flushed cheeks and fine features, then examined her clothes, which she was sure to recognize, I thought, having spent forty-five minutes haggling over the material with the shopkeeper at Ameeruddin's.

'As-salaam alaikum, Dadi,' Shahnaz said primly when, at last, the survey was complete and their eyes met.

'Jeeti raho, beta,' she replied grudgingly. 'Theek hai, go and play. And take this poor sister of yours, too,' she added to me, pointing to Jamila, who leaped at the suggestion and eagerly followed us outside. We heard Dadi in a voice half-dreaming mutter, 'What a pretty little girl! I wonder who her mother is?'

Once outside, I put my arms around Shahnaz, the mid-afternoon sun burning through the thin fabric of our clothes, its radiating heat warming my skin and hers as we stood in the light, intoxicated by the completeness of our victory.

CHAPTER 21

'So, when did all this start?' Baba asked Shahbaz Chacha, waving an arm in the direction of the Jamshaids, who were leaving for prayers amid the rustle of starched cotton, the potent fragrance of their ittaar disturbing the delicate equilibrium of the nighttime garden and its bouquet of tropical blooms.

'Slow progression,' Shahbaz Chacha answered, twirling his keychain around his index finger, the flash of light on metal striking my sleepy eyes as I sat with my head on Tania Chachi's burgeoning lap.

'Oh, so you mean it wasn't like Abba. Suddenly sewing prayer caps and all the rest of it?'

'Was that how it happened with Abba?'

'I exaggerate, of course, but more or less. He came back from India a "changed man". You know, in the melodramatic sense of books and movies – and I'm not joking.'

'I wonder what happened to him there.'

'I'm not sure if it was what happened to him there or whether it was the war in general. He never spoke of it to us. I'm just happy I also knew him before he changed.' Baba paused to slap his right arm, a small cry of victory as he flicked a bloody mosquito into the dark grass.

'I know. I wish I had been a little older so that I could've seen those happier times, too.' In the half-light, Shahbaz Chacha's expression altered, suddenly thoughtful, and I was reminded of the single photograph we had discovered of him in the family albums, that small square of bloodless celluloid the only commemoration of his infancy.

For a few seconds, no one spoke. The sounds of the garden, amplified, resonating, filled the vacuum of silence. A cacophony of song, whirring mosquitoes, an orchestra of crickets buried deep in the grass, the click-click-clacking of excitable chhipkalis answering to a high-pitched chuchundar across the boundary wall. And through it all, the sea breeze, which brushed against my skin as it flew through the leaves and flowers of the garden, the sound of it like a tremendous wave lapping against the grey sand of Clifton Beach.

'I'm worried about Jamshaid, though. This isn't like his teenage craze for the air force or his obsession with pirs in the eighties, is it?'

Shahbaz Chacha's laughter filled the garden. Warm and mellow, I imagined him walking, loose-limbed, along a stretch of beach at sunset. 'No, I don't think so, Bhai Jan. The influence is all-pervasive. Even Bhabi and the kids are into it. It doesn't end there. People across the board, from all walks of life, have become more – for lack of a better word – practising. Which isn't, of course, necessarily a bad thing. It just seems as if some of them have lost sight of the essence, or spirit, of the faith in the process.'

'So, what you're saying is that we've got to live with Mullah Jamshaid for the rest of our lives? I just can't ... ' Baba paused in pure bafflement, 'I honestly can't reconcile him with the Jamshaid I knew. He was crazy in his teens, a wild man.'

I giggled, then clapped my hands to my mouth, aware that my presence often changed the tone of adult conversation. Jamshaid Chacha a 'wild man'...? I immediately imagined him scantily clad in animal pelts, his huge hairy stomach hanging over a loin cloth, his trailing beard merging with his long locks as he grunted up a tree. Then, when it dawned on me that there was something vaguely disrespectful about this picture, I desperately tried to focus on white, like the pure white of the massive dry-erase board in our fourth-grade classroom in Chicago, suddenly fearing that the outlandish image would leave an indelible mark on my impressionable mind.

'Hey, badmaash. What're you doing awake? It's way past your bedtime.' Baba leaned over and scooped me up and into his arms before he sat down again. I could feel his warm fingers running through my hair. I closed my eyes and pretended to sleep, an eavesdropping tactic that my siblings found hilarious, second only to my standing, extremely still, with my back to the conversation. 'Now,' Baba continued, 'all he ever does is sermonize. No matter what the topic.'

'It's kind of the way things have "progressed" here in your absence,' Shahbaz Chacha replied drily. 'Us artist types have remained on the fringe and go about our work quietly. We also' – here he winked at Tania Chachi – 'multiply.'

'I suppose that's all you can do,' Baba agreed smiling, his tone suggesting he wasn't finished. After a few minutes of silence, he said reflectively, 'You know, it's every middle-aged Pakistani American's dream to return to their own "personal homeland", the Pakistan they left behind in the year that they immigrated. With me, for instance, it's the Karachi I remember in the late 1970s, around the time I met Najma. It's ridiculous to think that things wouldn't change, but I have to admit I felt let down when I landed here and saw Karachi. It's just so different! Cell phones, malls, megaplex cinemas! But it's not the outward that disturbs me. I can't recognize the people. There's no sense of direction. I'm convinced Pakistanis are talented, but where are our leaders?'

'Well, most of the talented ones are in the United States, making big money.'

'I'm a student of business, remember? I don't have a problem with people making money to better their lives, but it's not always that simple. There are other reasons for staying on. And the longer you stay there, the harder it is to pull away. Then, the children – they're Americans. Why shouldn't they want to live in their own country?'

'As long as the dollar isn't a means to an end. The stories my friends have told me about the doctors in America!'

'Ah, they are a species unto themselves,' Baba agreed, chuckling.

'What does all this matter now that we're blacklisted anyway? With or without a turban, we're hauled away at immigration, then mauled and branded like cattle in the smaller back rooms. God forbid that anyone should be named Muhammad! They'll never accept us.'

'It depends. You can isolate yourself if you want to. Ethnic politics, mosque-building, desi-only gatherings... Then, yes, of course, it'll be harder to win acceptance. Najma and I tried to avoid that. I remember her telling me how many of her Pakistani friends, all educated women of the world, balked at meeting "goras", claiming that they were so difficult to talk to. Ridiculous, really, when you think you're living in their country!'

'Oh, by the way,' Shahbaz Chacha said as he stood up to leave, 'Uncle Raff wants to see me. Ammi and I are going to the hospital day after tomorrow. I wonder why the old man asked for me, of all people.'

'That is strange,' Baba agreed, then lowering his voice, he whispered, 'He's also asked for this one. I know how close they are, but I wonder if it would be good for her to visit a hospital so soon after Najma. I think it's a little too much pressure for a child so young.'

'I agree.'

I opened my eyes and sat up. 'Baba, please. I want to go.' I put my skinny arms around his neck and hung there, hoping my doleful expression would convince him to agree.

'We'll see, Chhoti. Perhaps you can accompany Shahbaz Chacha and Dadi. I'm not promising anything yet. Let me think about it.'

I nodded, satisfied with his reply, the prospect of meeting Uncle Raff accompanied by my grandmother and uncle reassuring, of course, but also the perfect opportunity to confirm all of our suspicions.

*

As I rinsed my hands in the bathroom I shared with my sisters, I paused in front of the mirror over the sink and, suddenly curious, took a few moments to stare – really stare – at my face. I watched my features emerge, cataract-like, from the mirror's rusty, partially cracked surface. My reflection glared back at me, the cracks in the glass creating ugly breaks in my face, tectonic plates shifting as I tried on a variety of expressions, some whimsical, some melancholy.

It was obvious that there had been no miraculous overnight changes. My tearful moaning on the prayer mat the day before had won me nothing: my stubby eyelashes were still the same miserable length, lacking all curl, and were about as visible on my face as the faint mole on my right cheek, hidden behind an errant sideburn. Dark and tangled, my hair hung around my shoulders in dry bunches, the curls fraying where the sun's midday rays had scorched out their shine. Looking down, my uniform shalwar still fell sedately around my ankles, meaning that even if I had grown, it was only by a fraction of an inch, and no more, the tan line that ringed each foot further proof that my upwards-growth was nominal. Yes, I thought despondently as I stared into the mirror, I was still the same Ferzana of 'Chhoti' notoriety and would probably never look like Shahnaz did, grown-up overnight, a spectacular pubescent sensation, her new curves setting her apart – even elevating her – to the realm of adults-only. I frowned fiercely into the cracked mirror, my eyebrows forming one jagged streak of black across my forehead. Chhoti I was and chhoti I would remain until, that is, Tania Chachi's belly produced a creature even smaller than me.

But, I thought, brightening a little, there was *some* change. While I may not have erupted in pimples or acquired a bra (now a coveted article of clothing), I had done another kind of growing up, not visible to the others but as real to me as the sudden and unaccountable growth of body parts. It was difficult to say exactly when the shift in perspective took place. Amma's death and its aftermath had triggered a kind of hot-house version of emotional growth in me so that I was old beyond my years. Even then, I knew that I no longer felt like the little girl I resembled.

And while I was growing internally, the exact opposite was true of my favorite sibling, Jamila. Physically, she was as womanly as Fatima or the ever-evolving Shahnaz. But her behaviour remained the same, her reactions even more childlike and simplistic after our mother's passing. As a concept, death completely eluded her. She still conversed with our mother, spoke as if she had just seen her in the garden or at the bazaar and insisted that she would join us at bedtime for stories – something Amma had not done since I was old enough to read. Jamila couldn't fully express herself, but if I ever glanced at her in one of her quieter moments, I often saw her face go blank as if the enormity of what had happened had just struck her. It was in those instances that I allowed myself – however briefly – to feel sorry for her.

One of Jamila's new grown-up habits puzzled me. Around the fifth of every month, there were days when I would find strange items by the toilet and soiled wads of cotton on the floor. My trips to the toilet were always flying visits, in-and-out with a splash of water and a wipe, before it was back to the more exciting activities of my eleven-year-old life. It took me a while to register this change but, once I did, I began asking questions. After a few days spent digging into the bathroom cabinets of all the female members of the Mahmud clan, I realized that the problem was much more serious and widespread than I had thought. Eventually, Fatima had to tell me what it was all about when she spied me using those wads of cotton as mattresses for my weary Barbies. Like many of my investigations, once I had found out about 'menses' as the ladies called it here (although 'womanses' would have been a more accurate name, I thought), I wished I hadn't. I could only pity Fatima and Jamila for their affliction.

It was all Shahnaz's fault. She was the one who first pointed out that Jamila was 'different'. Our laps were full of bougainvillea petals as we sat on the porch, the sun's light bathing the entire compound with a nectarine-like glow, the fuchsia of the flowers leaping out at us in incandescent bursts of colour. She ruined that beautiful evening with her odd bluntness, the way she had of presenting her view as indisputable fact, her total disregard for nuance or subtlety. I resented her gauche intrusion into the comfortable understanding I had come to of my family's dynamics without Amma, the interplay of personalities amongst the four of us harmoniously moderated by the calming influence of Baba. After all, being born into a desi family – or any family, for that matter – presupposed an acceptance of each individual member's handicaps. In Jamila's case, her handicap was not emotional or psychological but the result of a chromosomal imbalance. Before Shahnaz, I had accepted my sister as she was, just another variation on 'normal' just as Fatima and Raza were, their personality flaws making them who they were. In fact, till then it was almost as if I believed that every family had a child like Jamila, different, certainly, but unique, too. At least that is how our parents had always made it seem.

Once Shahnaz had pointed it out, I began seeing it, too – the slow deliberate movements and halting speech, the frequent irritation over simple tasks, the difficulty in comprehending instructions. When we went to the market, it was obvious that passersby as well as shopkeepers found Jamila curious enough to stare at without apology while the rest of us flocked around to protect her from their glare. The street urchins and beggars gathered in front of our car as Jamila, dragging her bad leg, got in, asking for money in return for praying for the 'bibi possessed by djinns'.

'Don't mind it,' Baba would reason with Fatima. 'They're just uneducated people who don't understand Jamila's condition.'

But soon after, Dadi embarked on a clandestine operation. After a few furtive telephone enquiries to Nasim Bhai's cousin's best friend's youngest daughter's teacher, who once suffered epileptic fits but was now completely cured, she procured the address of a healer in a remote corner of the city who specialized in all manner of conditions but especially possession by djinns. As I drifted in and out of sleep, I heard Dadi making these afternoon calls, her reading glasses perched on the tip of the nose of which she was so proud (the shapeliest in her family, she claimed), as she haan-ed and hoon-ed deafly into the mouthpiece, her voice rising in excitement as her findings were confirmed. Once or twice Durdana Phupo's soft but insistent voice could be heard discouraging her in pleading tones, 'At least ask Bhai Jan first, Ammi!' But she brooked no opposition: 'Pugli!' she cried. 'Is he my son or am I his daughter? Why should I ask Aftab? He's in no condition to think straight anyway. Maybe' – speculatively – '...maybe I should take him as well...?' Here, Durdana Phupo threw up her hands in exasperation, distancing herself from Dadi's plans by retreating into her little-girl room to read well-thumbed copies of her favourite *Mills & Boons*, a less damning pastime on broiling afternoons.

Once the appointment was made after weeks of secret negotiations, I was surprised to find myself in the car, tucked into the back seat between Dadi and Jamila as we wove laboriously through a chaotic thoroughfare where four major arteries met. Although it was a school day, I had woken up that morning with stomach cramps and was kept at home. Just as Dadi and Jamila were settling into the car, Khyber saw my forlorn figure by the rusty swing, and called out to me, followed more reluctantly by Dadi, who lifted me over her lap and into the middle of the backseat. Jamila remained quiet but slipped her hand into mine. For the first half hour, I pestered Dadi with questions about where we were going. Somewhere, however, between the beginning of our descent into the hell of that traffic vortex and the moment the car finally emerged like a wounded animal from amid the flames, I fell asleep. When I next awoke, we were moving forward at high speed, the area through which Khyber was driving unfamiliar and oddly spacious, the wide roads lined by dusty, pastel-coloured houses interspersed with faded storefronts or schools with names like 'Little Childs Montessori' or 'Harvard School of Matriculation'. Suddenly, my eye was caught by a massive red billboard, crawling with black letters, no uniformity in size or style but attractive enough to tempt a beginner into practising her newly-honed Urdu skills. After several halting attempts at joining together the letters from right to left, I proudly began to intone, 'Ba-ba-bawa...' then, in a moment of supreme triumph, 'Bawaseeeeer!'

Haemorrhoids, apparently.

'Chup, pagli!' Dadi scolded, glancing over at Khyber's expression in the rear view mirror. As usual, Khyber remained imperturbed, squinting as he, too, searched for the house, which eventually emerged half a mile later, a dusty squat-looking box with two wide windows on either side of a gaping doorway. The structure resembled its owner, Altaf Sahib, or 'Doctor Sahib' as Dadi insisted on calling him, who was dwarf-like in stature, his eyes magnified like a fish's behind his thick-rimmed spectacles as his toothless mouth opened and closed for no apparent reason. Thus he stood before Jamila, who cowered in her chair, peering at her face, his mouth still opening and closing as if he were swallowing an imaginary school of fish. Then, with slow deliberation, he raised his hands, a sign that Jamila should stand and walk, which she did, across the room and through the door, then out into the wilting garden towards the car.

'Jamila, beta! Beta!' Dadi cried in desperation. 'Come back! Doctor Sahib needs to examine you!' She threw open the screen door and flapped her chador-covered arms in an effort to attract Jamila's attention. But my sister, thankfully, had her own methods of resistance. Pretending she could not hear, or could not understand even if she had heard, she folded her arms resolutely and stared straight ahead, where Khyber's ornate seat covering seemed to supply her with all the entertainment she required.

Dadi, whose displeasure was evident, lumbered towards the car, followed by the pygmy-healer, whose own concern manifested itself in the rapid movement of the tasbee he clutched in his white-knuckled fist. Murmuring to himself, he peered shortsightedly through the half-open car window and made a reasoned assessment. Then, as Dadi stood by, arms folded across her ample chest in silent rage, he scuttled back into the house and returned, minutes later, with a tiny piece of paper.

'This,' he said, his voice cracking from disuse, 'should be read by you after every namaaz. And this,' here he produced a small packet from within the folds of his shirt, 'is for the bibi to wear around her neck at all times. You will see. This will cure her Inshallah. And if neither of these work,' he added mysteriously, one finger raised towards the heavens, 'there is always the healing stick.'

As usual, no one noticed me, standing in between them, my eyes focused on the tiny leather pouch that was suspended over my head as Altaf Sahib solemnly passed it over to Dadi and she secreted it, without a moment's delay, into her oversized handbag.

Dadi, Jamila, and I drove home in silence, each of us disappointed – for different reasons – with the way the day had turned out.

My poor sister Jamila. This was only the first in a series of humiliations. Dadi was not one to give up so easily. After this foray into the occult, she took Jamila to the shrine of a Sufi saint, sacrificed a goat and two chicken, fed the poor weekly for six months (at least someone was benefiting from that experiment) and took her to at least three more 'doctors' in remote and far-flung parts of the city. Somehow she managed to accomplish most of this without the knowledge (or consent) of Baba. One afternoon, as she sat thumbing through her telephone directory, mumbling unintelligibly about another healer whose power was purportedly derived from a dead tree trunk, I suddenly sat up, turned around, and cupped her soft, sagging cheeks in both hands. 'Dadi,' I said firmly, 'this is the way she is, and this is the way she will remain. And we love her this way.' She put the book down and nodded slowly before acknowledging in a barely audible whisper, 'I know, beta. I know.'

I looked again at my face in the cracked mirror of the bathroom that I shared with my sisters, imagining what I would look like ten, maybe fifteen, years from now. The changes I foresaw would not be dramatic, I knew: the hair and eyes, the nose, so like my mother's, my receding chin, all unaltered. The transformation would involve the subtler changes, the refining of bones, the stretching of limbs, the roundness of features sharpening, that combination of mind and body that signifies maturity or the very peak of growing up: adulthood. When I finally came to accept it, I had to understand that my sister Jamila would never grow up in the same manner as Fatima, Raza, and I would and that eventually we would go our separate ways and leave her behind, a thought so terrible to contemplate that it always ended in a retreat into our make-believe world.

Lady M was our leader, and in Lady M lay Jamila's redemption.

CHAPTER 22

Although the riddle of Mrs Nasim and Raza's relationship (and of my unwitting involvement in it) had been partially solved by my friend Shahnaz, there were many aspects of it which I grappled with in the weeks to come. My brother, handsome though he was, had no business, I thought, of forming any kind of relationship with my fifth-grade teacher. Mrs Nasim was a grown-up person of responsibility (despite her fluorescent nails) and was already committed by virtue of her polyester wardrobe and jangly jewellery to that poor man, Mr Nasim. Weren't there enough willing teenage girls in Karachi to satisfy my brother? And what about that stringy-haired long-distance Clarice? None of it made any sense. I spent several afternoons sprawled on my bed, marker and paper in hand, scribbling notes or drawing diagrams in an attempt to break it all down in the manner of a professional sleuth. But no matter how many ways I looked at it, there was something terribly wrong. My brother's association with my teacher was an obnoxious, potentially dangerous, intrusion. Like the Venn diagrams Mrs Thorndike introduced us to last year, Raza and Mrs Nasim were two circles that should never overlap.

One afternoon, as I lay on my bed, surrounded by the messy results of my research, fingers and face stained with permanent marker, I remembered that I still had one clue – a small scrap from the letter I had once delivered to Raza from Mrs Nasim. There it was, the writing so much 'curlier' and 'dottier' than her brutal penmanship in blood-red across the misspelled words of my English register. It reminded me of an image I had seen as a child back in Chicago, an absurd Picasso-like half-face, the one eye beautifully formed but stark, the half-nose, half-lip of a woman mutilated by the sharp edge of a folded newspaper. The image came back to me clearly as I saw it lie, there near a pool of spilled milk, on our kitchen table. Not at all interested in the contents of the article, I remember dropping my doll and running over to watch the liquid make contact with the newsprint and begin staining, like a burn mark, the woman's cheek. Curious to see what was happening underneath, I unfolded the newspaper so that the woman's entire face was visible. I barely noticed the heading above it, 'Sexual Predator', or the caption below which explained the photograph was of 'Middle School teacher Barbara Riley Anderson convicted on six counts of sexual assault on a minor after claiming that she and one of her students were "in love".' Now, older and wiser, I wondered if my glamorous Mrs Nasim might not find herself photographed thus and in the local newspapers before week's end, sandwiched unglamorously between a public tender and an article on the latest anti-corruption moot.

Just as this thought crossed my mind and I wondered how I felt about it, partially gleeful that Mrs Nasim would be punished for her betrayal of my trust but sorry for her, too, as jail-time would mean an abrupt end to her beloved bangles and shiny clothes, I heard the wail of the front gate, its metallic scrape resonating in the quiet stillness of that warm afternoon. I ran to the window just in time to see a figure slip through the pedestrian gate and into a waiting vehicle, engine running, the silver sheen of an older Corolla vaguely familiar as I strained to get a closer look. Opening the window screen, I pushed my face out and into the latticed metal grill, my nose and cheeks spilling out of one of the diamond-shaped crevices. From where I stood, the car was only partially visible now and, within seconds, was already pulling away before I could make a note of the license plate number. Just as I was about to give up, I remembered seeing a flash of red through the rear window of the car. I closed my eyes and thought back to the silver Corolla till I could picture it clearly in my mind's eye: yes, there at the back – without a doubt – was a teddy bear holding a red rose, the exact same one my teacher had scornfully described to me, a Valentine's Day gift from her disarmingly boyish husband.

Within seconds, I was standing in the doorway of my brother's bedroom, everything about its contents sending off alarms: a tangle of clothes on the floor, an open laptop, the air suffuse with the designer cologne he reserved for 'hot dates' (his words). I could also smell the damp fragrance of soap and shampoo and nearly tripped over a pair of dirty boxer shorts. Wrinkling my nose in disgust, the sister in me momentarily overcoming the sleuth, I wondered why Raza would feel the need to take a shower in the middle of the day *and* change his underpants. These basic tenets of hygiene were usually 'either/or' for him. I had no doubt that a woman was involved and that woman, I dreaded to think, was at this very moment speeding off with him in a silver car to some unknown destination for goodness-knows-what, while poor Mr Nasim, clueless and glassy-eyed like the stuffed teddy bear, was at home nursing a wilting rose.

An intervention was required. I casually walked up to the open laptop and glanced at the inbox. I was old enough to know that this was wrong. To ease my conscience, I stood at an awkward angle to the computer and squinted at the list, scanning it in a few brief seconds and then stepping away, as if from a fire. My brother was in immediate danger... or was he the danger himself? Not quite sure, I decided to consult someone else whose greater years of experience with him made her eminently qualified.

As I barrelled out of Raza's bedroom and into the hall, I collided into Fatima, Jamila trailing behind her with her arms full of starched dhobi clothes.

'Chhoti, what on earth...?' Fatima began, her voice rising in irritation as she pushed me away. 'Be careful! We could've dropped this.' She pointed to the tower of clothes that Jamila had expertly balanced and was now gently lowering onto the bed.

I looked at my sisters with what I hoped was my most persuasive of faces, the widening of eyes and raising of brows my version of extreme panic. 'Fatima, listen to me. I think Raza just left the house in Mrs Nasim's car!'

'What?' Fatima screamed, her reaction surprising even to me, self-avowed lover of high drama. 'I knew he'd do something crazy like this. Why doesn't he ever listen?' I watched silently as she spent several seconds tearfully wringing her hands.

'You – you knew about this? I mean that they...?' I stuttered, turning to Jamila, who had also paused in her work, and was staring at us curiously.

'Chhoti,' Fatima whispered, grabbing me by the shoulders and bending so that we saw eye to eye, 'what do you know about all this?'

'Nothing, nothing,' I muttered, suddenly scared. After a pause, I whined, 'But it doesn't make sense, does it? I mean, she's my teacher not his!' I was momentarily captivated by the image of me sitting next to Mrs Nasim in that silver car, the two of us laughing at some private joke not relating to Raza, our polyester dupattas flying in the wind as we raced down Sharae Faisal.

Fatima ignored me. She ran to Raza's room just as I had moments earlier.

'It's no use. There's nothing there,' I called after her.

'What are we going to do? Baba isn't even at home!' Fatima wailed as she threw herself on the bed. 'I just hope Raza doesn't do anything stupid.'

Her emphasis on 'stupid' made me wonder what she meant. In Raza's case, it could be any number of lapses in good judgement, starting with the very first: leaving C44 in the silver car belonging to my teacher. I could only imagine what else he might do. I was convinced that he and Mrs

Nasim were, at this very moment, laughing at me as they gleefully leaped over mounds of grey sand, overjoyed at having bypassed a foolish girl in the fulfilment of their devilish wishes.

'Let's follow them!' I blurted.

'Follow them where? We have no idea where they went.' Fatima had buried her head in the pillows and appeared to be contemplating death by suffocation.

'How about checking his emails?' I offered tentatively, not sure how this devious plan would be received by the morally upright Fatima.

Minutes later, the three of us were in the back seat with a grumpy Khyber, whose interrupted siesta was apparently being resumed at the wheel as he lurched drunkenly down the narrow alley in front of our house and then headlong into the maddening traffic that bridged our part of town to the rest of the city.

'I thought Karachi slept between the hours of three and five,' Fatima commented drily as we came to a halt behind the heavily adorned rear of a massive tanker, a white she-horse daintily prancing against a backdrop of peaked hillocks right up against our windshield.

We heard Khyber grunt at the mention of sleep, confirming what we had long-suspected – his knowledge of the English language was far more extensive than we gave him credit for.

It was hardly the high-speed car chase I had imagined. We crawled forth on all four wheels behind the put-put-putter of a three-wheeled rickshaw. The streets of Karachi, with their dust and motor traffic, weaving bicycles and pedestrians, donkey carts and camels, the frequent abutment of thelas with hawkers crying out their wares, were not conducive to such sensational filmi chases. Our hair, instead of flying in the wind, lay plastered to our scalps as another coat of soot and fumes greased our locks. I had to admit that the four of us, including the somnolent Khyber, were in our 'afternoon look', when the drowsy heat of mid-afternoon causes everything to wilt, bodies, minds, even clothes, the crisp starched freshness of morning gone along with all its beauty. Thankfully we had not come as our alter egos. I thought with a shudder of how furious Lady M would have been at this turn of events – no speed, no glamour. As it was, poor Jamila's excitement had waned at the sight of the first roundabout, which took us fifteen minutes to negotiate, and now lay with her head on my shoulder, fast asleep. Fatima, for the most part, continued to glare out of the window, occasionally darting a deadly look in my direction as if to suggest, of all things, that Raza's disappearance was my fault.

I drifted in and out of sleep as the feel of the car's engine, and beneath it, the uneven road, lulled me into momentary forgetfulness. When I next opened my eyes it was to the sight of a red Suzuki, its rear within a few feet of us, where three of the largest men I had ever seen in Karachi – a trio of sumo-wrestler proportions – sat in deep thought, surveying the road majestically from atop a mountain of flesh. I rubbed my eyes in disbelief. When I opened them again, the Suzuki and the philosophical pehlwans had disappeared, leaving the wide open road virtually clear, the horizon a grey blur where sand and sky were subsumed into watery sunshine.

I suddenly sat up in my seat and shook Jamila awake. Both of us leaned forward to look out of Fatima's window, which afforded the best view of the distant beach, its grey alive on a Sunday with the startling colours of holiday-makers, fabrics fluttering like the wings of birds, gaily bedecked camels laden with delighted children rocking back and forth as they lumbered past the tossing waves. I was instantly buoyed. Forgetting about my brother, I thought only of shedding the grime of the city and running with naked limbs into the sea. I knew Jamila felt exactly as I did. She squeezed my hand.

'Kahan, Bibi?' Khyber asked disinterestedly, as our vehicle slowed down next to a gol-guppa vendor, his fragile glass cart lit by a single bulb as he ladled the spicy water into chipped ceramic bowls for a crowd of impatient youngsters. Fatima scanned the beach anxiously. Finally she said, 'Anywhere, Khyber. This is as good a spot as any.' She had realized as I had that finding Raza and Mrs Nasim in this crowd was going to be quite a task. The beach extended for several miles on both sides. Like a piece of taffy pulled apart, the further reaches blurred and thinned, distance, dampness and city smog making the figures on the sand mere streaks in the sun. I braced myself for what was surely coming next: Fatima's scathing denunciation of me and my 'great ideas'. Jamila and I followed her out of the car and stood stretching in the clear sunlight. The ocean breeze, heavily infused with the dank smell of fish, invaded the open spaces of our cotton shalwar-kameezes, our shirts billowing like sails. Holding hands, we stared at the horizon as if bewitched.

'Girls!' Fatima snapped. 'Pay attention. Let's walk down this way first.'

She led us away from the gol-guppa vendor and other thelas to the west, where a dazzling stretch of sand glistened in the wet sunshine. In the distance, a few fishermen were unravelling their nets, their heavy jute baskets like beached whales by their sides. A group of adventurous holiday-makers were threading a meandering path along the water, laughing as they went. We made our way down the uneven steps and onto the beach, eventually finding it easier to walk barefoot, the packed sand beneath our toes like industrial cement, dark grey and dense. Pausing, I pushed my foot into a pool of seawater, watching the creamy sand swirl around my toes and ooze out of the spaces in between. I turned back and saw our footprints, in and out, overlapping, blending, at times looping as the three of us cut an uneven path, Jamila's bad leg dragging and I making frequent stops to collect shells or run after the tiny black crabs that littered the beach.

Fatima marched soldier-like ahead.

Ten minutes, and we had passed both the holiday-makers and the fishermen, who paused in their activities to turn and stare at us. I ran ahead and caught up with Jamila, shielding her from view. It was not until I had turned back that I realized that their eyes were not on her but on Fatima. There she was, curls flying in the sea breeze, ten feet ahead of us, her steely determination evident in her militaristic gait (must run in the family, I thought), her chest thrust out, arms swinging. I quickened my pace and dragged Jamila along, alternately running or skipping until we were within a few paces of her. It was then that I noticed that she was shouting into the wind, her voice whipped about by the crashing waves, so that what she said was lost even to me. Now I knew why everyone was staring: she looked like a crazed lunatic. I tore away from Jamila and ran the last few steps to Fatima, putting my arms around her waist to hold her back.

'Chhoti! Chhoti, leave me alone!' she shouted into my ear. I could see she was upset. She pulled away from me and resumed her march, this time her words audible above the wind: 'Raza! Raza! Stop!'

Startled, I looked ahead, shielding my eyes from the glare. The stretch of beach before me sparkled as if strewn with shards of glass, the grains of sand locked magnificently in a blinding union of light and water. This part of the promenade was an open expanse bereft of the colourful, frenetic activity of the other side, where hawkers and restaurants drew most of the holiday crowds. No camels, no pom-pommed horses and, as a consequence, no boisterous groups of children awaiting rides. Across the road and in the distance loomed the low structures of an exclusive club and beyond that the dwarfed towers of seaside apartment buildings. At this time of day, the scene was whitewashed, the brightness of its original colours swept away, wide brushstrokes obliterating all definition, sharpness. Even the handful of figures walking on the beach or splashing in the water were dark smudges against the light.

Suddenly, Fatima swerved, an abrupt movement that nearly caused Jamila and I to fall over each other. She began running towards the water. Two figures, a man and a woman, were standing ankle-deep in the sea, the force of the waves so powerful, it seemed, that they had to lean against each other for support, their silhouettes like the yolk and the white, viscous and clingy in their unwillingness to separate. The man was about Raza's height, his clothes – Bermuda shorts and t-shirt – like Raza's, well-filled out, his legs shapely and muscular. The woman wore her hair open, her black shoulder-length locks whipped about by the strong sea breeze, but the man – and this is what most convinced me he was my brother – had a head of gold. I could hear their laughter, even from where I stood, almost a dozen feet away. I was rooted to the ground. Despite my interest in the outcome of this confrontation, I could not bring myself to run after Fatima. I had grasped the seriousness of what was happening. I had to admit I was afraid.

What passed between this man and woman was private. I understood it now. Even as I stood there watching them, my tongue was acrid to the taste, the way it felt when I bit into a grapefruit, the bitterness paralyzing. I was too young to know what it was called, this act of observation that went beyond espionage in its audacity, but everything about it, the guilt and the unbearable suspense, disgusted me. Jamila remained behind me, her arms wrapped around my waist. She, too, held back. I realized that these two people could have been anyone, were representative, in fact, in the same way that black-and-white symbols held meanings beyond their starkness, that they were not just my once-beloved Mrs Nasim and my brother, Raza, that they were more, they were Amma and Baba, too, in a love that preexisted us, an embattled love that had to be wrested and won.

Was it really wrong to love like this?

This question remained unanswered as I braced myself for the inevitable confrontation. The couple was oblivious to what was coming: Fatima, like a woman possessed, hurtling towards them at astonishing speed. Just at the moment that she was about to step in between them or push them apart or do whatever it was her crazed mind dictated, I heard a voice, and it was distinctly Raza's, saying, 'What are you idiots doing here?'

But the voice did not come from the man near the water. Panicking, I turned around and saw Raza standing there in his khaki shorts and t-shirt, his face inscrutable as he surveyed the scene, the shock of finding us here no doubt overshadowed by what was unfolding. He was alone.

Suddenly, my body was in motion. Running as fast as my bare feet would allow, I shouted, 'Fatima, stop! Stop!'

I caught her just in time to prevent physical contact, although the lovers had already turned in surprise, my wild cries reaching them over the wind and the waves, their faces suddenly tense as if they expected their parents (for they were teenagers, it now appeared) or a platoon of police demanding a nikanamah. As it turned out, the boy was nothing like Raza, his hair a darker shade of brown, his physique at least twenty pounds lighter, his narrow shoulders slightly stooped as if he spent his days hunched over a computer. With my penchant for facial hair, I noted with surprise that he sported a straggly goatee. We could not have been more wrong.

Breathless, I managed to drag Fatima back. She was still muttering her apologies even as the couple, mildly irritated but relieved that they had not been discovered by the people that mattered most, turned away with hauteur and continued to stare out at sea.

'What are you people doing here?' Raza demanded.

'Where's Mrs Nasim?' Fatima retorted, one hand on her hip as she gave him her knowing look, one which even on the best of days drove him insane.

Jamila and I cowered where we stood in anticipation of the altercation ahead.

CHAPTER 23

'So, Chhoti,' Tania Chachi whispered as I lay with my face pressed against her belly, 'what do you think of It?'

We were lying on the sofa in her extraordinary drawing room. Three months ago, there I sat – or lay, unladylike – on that brocade-covered takht during my first meeting with my mother's brothers, Salaar and Alamdar, an introduction still associated (in my mind at least) with a pair of detestable underpants. I nestled closer to Tania Chachi, drawn to her by the warmth of her body combined with the hypnotic pull of the fascinating sounds it emitted, my tiny cousin's gestation a continuous source of wonder and excitement. My fingers splayed against her taut belly, I imagined It no bigger than the palm of my hand, floating in a warm bath of salt water, a minuscule barely-formed sea creature, a tiny merperson of as yet indeterminate gender.

'I love It,' I responded promptly. Yes, strangely enough, I loved even this – this diaphanous mass of rapidly evolving cells and tissue, this unformed being-in-the-making. Would that change, I wondered, if we proved It was not a Mahmud? Suddenly guilty, I turned away from Tania Chachi and her belly. Relationships were complicated. I had noticed that as I grew my feelings for people could not be satisfactorily divided into the 'love' and 'hate' categories. Moving to Pakistan didn't help. We were suddenly surrounded by people related to us by blood (some more, some less) whom we were expected to love, no matter how challenging they sometimes made it.

Then, on the other hand, there was that immediate sense of kinship I felt for my mother's brothers, as if years of distance meant nothing when compared to the tenacious hold of blood to blood. I was drawn to them as if miles of tangled umbilical cord bound us together, victims, not victors, of our own genetic code, predisposing us as much for infamy and ill health as for the occasional streaks of greatness. For we could never forget that the same mutant gene responsible for Amma's cancer was embedded in all four of us, holding us ransom until – and the thought was terrifying – it emerged, two-headed, out of the secret intimacy of our cells.

'Chhoti,' Tania Chachi whispered, running her slender fingers across my forehead, 'don't think so much. Be what you are. Be a child.'

I wanted to tell her that I had ceased being a child the day my mother was taken away from me. Instead, I focused on her use of the word 'Chhoti' and desperately wished that everyone would stop calling me that.

'So, the common wisdom is that the only good time to be hospitalized is when you're having a baby, right?'

The laugh that came out of Shahbaz Chacha's throat seemed pulled out of him, like a magician pulls out a series of coloured scarves from his mouth, only there was no mirth and no lightness, not even, surprisingly, about the eyes, which often expressed more emotion than his handsome features did.

'What on earth did he have to be nervous about?' I wondered irritably. It wasn't as if he had recently lost his mother. I glanced over at Dadi in impeccable profile, her white-knuckled hands wrapped solidly around the stubby straps of her old-lady purse. A real beauty, I suddenly realized, even at this age, her aquiline Lucknavi nose a little more erect than usual, the upwards tilt suggesting that she (along with her nose) was about to face an unusual challenge. Overall, she looked singularly determined, as formidable as a bullet-proof tank preparing to roll through enemy territory.

We were all acting strange, I noted, even for an excursion to a dear old friend's sickbed. The only sane individual amongst us was Khyber. As he drove us towards the gated entrance to the red-bricked hospital, I thought of his daughter, Shahnaz. For all her 'blossoming' womanhood, she had instantly reverted to herself again when I told her about Raza and Mrs Nasim and what had happened at the beach. 'Quick! And...? And after that?' she panted, hopping on one foot, then the other, as I shamelessly dangled my story in fragments before her, revealing the sequence of events with painstaking deliberation to lengthen the period of my own importance.

But the story was a sensational one. I imagined the scandalous headlines across the front page of Karachi's equivalent of a tabloid: 'Caught: Teacher and Handsome Student in Beach Love Tryst'. Realistically, though, the headline ought to have read: 'Brother Mauls Three Sisters to Death'. There we stood, Fatima, Jamila, and I, bracing ourselves for the worst. For a full moment, no one spoke. Battling the sound of the waves with our frail human voices seemed an unnecessary waste of energy given what lay ahead. I, at least, had to conserve my strength. I knew Fatima would blame everything on me. Whenever more than one sibling was involved, I was usually put forward as the prime suspect. It had become so much a part of routine that I had accepted the position by default, priding myself on being the evil 'child-genius' behind a number of devious schemes. This time, however, was different – there was no Amma or Baba to mollify. My brother's rage was unpredictable, volcanic in spurts, but for the most part subterranean: he was a formidable opponent.

Speaking first, I ventured weakly, 'We were worried about you…'

'Well, look, Raza – it's just not right!' There. An outburst from Fatima. Just what we needed; the chemistry between my two eldest siblings was in flammability what matches are to gasoline.

Raza did not speak, but the movement of his green eyes, a lizard's flicker, indicated that he was not pleased.

Jamila and I understood the urgency of the situation. She grabbed Fatima's arm and began pulling her towards the water, while I stood my ground, folded my arms across my chest, and demanded, 'What were you doing in a car with my teacher?' Mrs Nasim was not the only one who had betrayed my trust; my own brother had deceived me, too. And then there was poor, long-suffering Mr Nasim to think about. Someone had to stand up for him. It was obvious from his schoolboy looks and textbook hairstyle that he could no more protect what was his than a paper doll.

Raza maintained his silence.

'Well?' I challenged him again. I thrust my stomach out in a gesture of intimidation.

In three large strides, he was directly in front of me. Then, before I knew what was happening, I was seven feet up in the air, so high, it seemed, that the heavy grey of the sky came bearing down on me. Arms and legs flailing, I watched in panic as the sky, the sand, and the beach went over and under me.

'Stop! Stop! I'm dizzy!' I yelled desperately as I was thrown upwards for a second time. Three more heaves and I found myself face down in the sand.

'Serves you right, Chhoti. I'm sure you were the mastermind behind this chase. What I do is my business, not yours. And, by the way, your Mrs Nasim is a grown woman, too, not a fifth-grader.'

I stood up, brushing the sand off my clothes. 'And what about Poor Mr Nasim? She's married, you know.'

'Not for long,' Raza muttered under his breath.

'What?' I gasped.

'Don't worry. Not because of me, stupid.'

By now Fatima had struggled out of Jamila's grasp and was standing next to us. Straining to look behind her, I noticed that Jamila had begun digging for seashells in the littered sand. So, I was the sole mediator now. I looked up at Raza and Fatima and wondered how it would all end, inwardly relieved that Fatima was too heavy to be thrown into the air like me.

Raza turned to face her. He snarled, 'Yes, Fatima. It's exactly as you suspected. I'm having an affair. I'm having an affair with Nasreen, her husband found out, and now they're getting a divorce. In fact, I'm dropping out of school so that we can elope and live on her earnings as a lousy fifth-grade teacher...'

There was that word again, 'affair'. I had a vague recollection of having heard it before. However, what really intrigued me was Raza's familiarity with my teacher, *my* teacher – and I boldly whispered the entire name, trying it out for the first time – *Nasreen Nasim*. After all, who could have guessed her name was so full of melodic potential, so like a poem when juxtaposed with Poor Mr Nasim's Nasim? *Nasreen Nasim*. And then it suddenly struck me – 'Elope?' I panicked. 'Like Amma and Baba?' My mind's eye telescoped into the future, and I imagined Raza and the ex-Mrs Nasim's children standing before a wedding album bereft of photographs. 'Oh, please don't do that!' I begged.

'He's being sarcastic, Chhoti. Come on, we have to go otherwise there'll be a crisis at home when they find out we're missing.' Fatima grabbed my hand and Jamila's and began dragging us towards the car. As we were about to take our seats, Fatima could not resist the temptation of one final remark. With a smirk, she asked casually, 'Are you riding with us or with your date?'

I cringed. Would this be enough to set off a volcanic eruption?

'Very funny,' Raza replied drily, shoving Fatima into the back before climbing in next to Khyber.

But Shahnaz had not been satisfied with this recounting of events and had insisted that there had to have been more drama. 'He didn't explain what he was doing with her in the first place!' she had pointed out.

True enough, but to expect a man like my brother to justify his actions, particularly where a woman was concerned, was ridiculous. As with all things, Raza's motivation remained a mystery. For me, Mrs Nasim held all the world's glamour within the silken folds and ching-ching of her postnuptial glory, but even I could see that she was hardly the type of girl Raza usually preyed upon. Fatima suspected it had something to do with Mrs Nasim being more 'experienced', which was silly, of course, because as we all knew she had only been teaching for a few months. Whatever Raza's reasons, the story ended tragically – at least for me. When Mrs Nasim decided to withdraw in the middle of the school year, I lost both a teacher and a friend. Alas, her substitutes were never as glamorous. As the days progressed, my understanding of Islamiyat, Pakistan Studies and Maths grew exponentially almost in direct relation to the disappearance from my life of Nasreen Nasim and her beleaguered husband. I sometimes wondered what became of them, whether they divorced as Raza had predicted, or whether Mrs Nasim had truly transformed into the perfect counterpart to Poor Mr Nasim: Poor Mrs Nasim, the loving and obedient wife.

As for my brother Raza, it was only too obvious that he would never look back.

'Chhoti!' I straightened up, startled. The window to the right of me brought the main entrance of the hospital in full view. There it was, a massive arch, like the dank and odious maw of a fanged, multi-organed monster. I imagined all the twisting that went on inside it, the convoluted guts and the pulsating, interconnected sacs of flesh. Suddenly, I felt my stomach lurch, its contents gassy and noxious.

'Dadi,' I moaned weakly, waiting impatiently as she took almost a minute to edge her bulk out of the low car seat, one hand resting heavily on Shahbaz Chacha.

'Out you go, Ferzana!' Shahbaz Chacha sang out gaily, for he seemed unusually cheerful as he scooped me up and into his arms, throwing my upper half across his shoulder so that my stomach pressed against his chest. Feeling worse, I watched with half-closed eyes the restless passage of hundreds, thousands, of feet across that great expansive courtyard partially open to the sky, reluctantly carrying their owners down corridors that led to wards spiked with the odious scent of Phenyl. Then, I imagined giant yellow bins marked with ominous signs, 'Biohazards', tangled entrails and tumors removed in surgery in a stew of blood and gore.

'Shahbaz Chacha, I feel sick...' I mumbled.

But we were already in the spacious elevator, wedged in between a nurse and a gurney, a young woman in a wheelchair, and two other adults sheathed in chadors. I peered over Shahbaz Chacha's shoulder at the man lying on the gurney, his gaunt body the longest I had ever seen, his bones visible, x-ray-like, through the thin gray sheet he was wound in.

'Chhoti, don't look!' Dadi snapped. But my eyes continued to travel down, from his narrow face to his chest, down, down, to where there was a mysterious bulge at the point where his legs parted. I stared. Although not entirely visible through the sheet, it appeared as if a plaster cast had been fitted to an awkward area of his anatomy perpendicular to the rest of him.

'What's wrong with his peepee?' I whispered.

At that very moment, the elevator came to a shaky halt, the doors opened and the nurse elbowed her way forward as she pushed the gurney out into the corridor. I heard the man groan and place a wizened hand on his crotch.

'Ferzana,' Shahbaz Chacha responded at last, 'must you notice everything?'

We walked down the breezy, sun-speckled corridor that ran alongside one wing of the hospital, concrete benches full of exhausted care-givers in sprawled sleep or vacant trance, some dipping into small tiffins of fragrant lunch with naan or roti. The sight of food and the fresh air suddenly re-energized me. By the time we reached the door at the end of the corridor, I tugged on Shahbaz Chacha's ear and motioned for him to put me down. I walked the last few steps to the door of Uncle Raff's hospital room entirely on my own, without even the moral support of a grown-up hand. Summoning the courage of Little Furry, I knocked on the door then pushed it open with my shoulder.

A rush of stale dark air escaped into the corridor. For an instant, I thought I had entered the wrong room, for on the bed, higher than the ones we slept on, lay a woman, her head wrapped in a floral scarf, her small hands folded on her breast, one on top of the other, in a gesture of peace, folded like the wings of a sleeping sparrow. Her eyes were closed. The light that fell from the partially drawn curtains sliced her body in half with surgical precision, the upper portion painfully bright, illuminated with all the concentrated strength of the midday sun, the lower in shaded darkness. Entranced, I moved forward as if in a dream. Then, I was standing beside her. There were no drips, no machines, no restraints. I pulled myself up, using the cold metal guard rails as a ladder. Peering closely at her, I felt her breath, fragrant with vanilla, on my face. The woman smiled in her sleep. Then, even as I watched, her lids flew open, her brown eyes, her smooth brow, the dip between nose and cheek, all so familiar, so right, and before I knew what I was doing, my own, our faces touching, mine resting perfectly, like the answer to her puzzle, in the dip between her nose and cheek.

'Amma,' I whispered.

'Ferzana, beta, please,' Shahbaz Chacha admonished. 'Step away from Uncle Raff's bed. Give him some space.'

My eyes refocused and there he was, my dear Uncle Raff, his frail body tangled in a mess of sheets and tubes, looking so remote high up on that narrow bed where, seconds earlier, I had been. He was my friend, and he needed me. I clasped his frail hand and said, 'Uncle Raff, it's Ferzana. Can you hear me?'

A swarthy nurse in white uniform called briskly, 'Drip change karna hai' and, with a few swift movements of her thick-fingered hands, replaced the bag of clear fluid that was being pumped into his system.

'Aaah, Ferzana!' he responded, squeezing my hand and attempting to turn towards me. It was then that I noticed he had a piece of yellow plastic protruding out of his neck, the skin around it blotchy and purple. 'Don't worry, my girl,' he chuckled, 'that's just my lifeline. I haven't been bitten by a vampire.'

'It's okay,' Shahbaz Chacha whispered to me. And it was, at least for the next ten minutes. Although Uncle Raff did not speak much, I entertained him with as many stories – both real and imagined – that I could think of. In some, I cast Dada as the nasty villain, not because I still thought of him that way but because I knew that Uncle Raff always derived a mischievous pleasure from such lurid portrayals. Today, however, he smiled little, his unshaven face narrow and strained, his eyes often closing even at the parts that I deliberately embellished for his benefit. I felt as if he were already far away, the things that were once important to him, like me for instance, receding into the distance. And then, as if on cue, Uncle Raff raised a frail hand to silence me, asking for a kiss before he said, 'Ferzana, you be a good girl. Take care of your Dada. He loves you and your brother and sisters very much.'

I nodded mutely. His cheek felt rough as a corn husk against my lips.

'Now, my dear girl, do me a favour. Could you step out for a few minutes while I speak to your Chacha and Dadi?' Step out? I was to be excluded from this all-important meeting – I, Little Furry, the intelligence-gatherer?

Dadi faltered as she rose heavily to her feet. Her earlier determination had all but disappeared. 'Jao, beta. Jao,' she urged, as if suddenly exhausted.

I frowned. This couldn't be happening. 'Please, Dadi, let me stay over there –' I pointed to the far end of the room. 'I promise I won't listen.'

'Ferzana!' Shahbaz Chacha said sharply. I could tell something was wrong. He never spoke like this to anyone.

And then, Uncle Raff's own voice, from across the room, distant and pleading, 'Ferzana, my dear...'

It was enough. Without further protest, I left the room, closing the door behind me. I made sure, however, that I did not go far. With an ear pressed against the door, I watched with increasing panic as all manner of steel carts laden with medical apparatus or containers of refuse were pushed back and forth by white-clad nurses and orderlies, followed, every few minutes, by a jharoo-wielding massi who swept away the debris. Straining against all of these sounds, the grating screech of un-oiled cart wheels, the beeping of monitors, the raspy chatter of less industrious nurses, I pressed my ear against the door but still heard nothing except the undifferentiated hum of human voices. I must have stood there for at least fifteen minutes before the door finally opened and Dadi and Shahbaz Chacha stepped out, both visibly upset. I tried to peer into the darkened room, but Shahbaz Chacha barred my way, saying tersely, 'He's asleep. Let him sleep.'

In the car, relations deteriorated further. My two grown ups did not speak until we were safely out of the hospital grounds. I sat in between them wondering what had happened until Dadi cleared her throat: 'Shahbaz, beta, you understand why we kept it from your father, don't you?' She stretched over me and placed her hand, white as porcelain, on his knee.

'Ammi...' There was a pause as Shahbaz Chacha smiled bitterly, his handsome features briefly contorted. 'Please. I don't want to talk about it.'

Two days later, we were informed that Uncle Raff had passed away.

CHAPTER 24

Durdana Phupo, draped in pink lace, was fussing over Dada who had fallen asleep over his newspaper. Tenderly unhooking his reading glasses from around his ears, she shook her head with a 'tch, tch' as she stepped back and sadly surveyed her father.

'Look at him,' she muttered. 'Poor Abbaji. Losing all his friends, one by one.' I knew what she was thinking, of course: just as he had lost his friends, one day we, too, would lose him. All of a sudden, this struck me as a terrible thought. What was worse: experience had shown that it was not always the oldest among us who was the first to go.

Naturally, Dada, Dadi, and I were deeply affected by Uncle Raff's death. The day he was buried, I spent hours sitting on his chair at Tea Central and had to be carried up to bed, still dreaming that I was on his lap, the arms of the cane chair wrapped around me like his once used to be. Strangely enough, however, the most noticeable change was in Shahbaz Chacha, who had cast off his carefree ways and now spent most of his spare time in the privacy of his own unit. In order to see him these days, you had to seek him out with a certain degree of determination, through his fantastic drawing room, which always proved a distraction, up the dark staircase and to the bedroom at the far end, where his supine form could be found on the bed, his once witty conversation reduced to unintelligible grunts. I missed my old uncle, who delighted in tales, the more far-fetched the better, encouraging me with a laugh to exaggerate to my heart's content. Now when I visited, he was indifferent to my stories. Our trip to the hospital had broken him up inside, so that I was reminded of Baba after Amma's death. What was he mourning, I wondered? More importantly, how would he put himself back together again? Tania Chachi, wider around the belly, sat in a corner helpless in her own infirmity, her frequent retching relieved only by a certain type of despicable tamarind candy that made my tongue curl instead of the 'nutritious' foods that Dadi industriously prepared in ghee. As for what was growing in her belly, It was still in a state of evolution and could hardly be counted upon to help, consumed as It was in its own growing.

'What's wrong?' I asked finally, unable to see him like this, even resorting to 'This Little Piggy' in the hopes that it might prove to be a universal cure for depression. Uncurling his toes one by one, I sang it as gaily as I could, but he merely laughed, then commented caustically, 'Sing that a little louder and the mullahs will be after us!' I had forgotten that this nursery rhyme meant nothing to him, or to anyone else in Pakistan. In fact, unbeknownst to this generally well-liked farm animal, the pig was reviled here, its protruding snout and flushed complexion synonymous with filth. Censored out of imported textbooks, like naughty body parts or historical 'inaccuracies', the pig was just about as welcome in Pakistan as a troupe of proselytizing Hare Krishnas.

So, when even this nursery rhyme had failed, I sought Baba's help.

'Yes, Ferzana. I have noticed a change in him,' he conceded. 'Perhaps he's sad because of Uncle Raff.'

'But they were never close, were they? Shahbaz Chacha said so himself.'

'Well, death affects people in different ways…' Baba's voice trailed off as he paused a moment in reflection. 'I'll have a word with him,' he promised, then added, 'but don't expect me to share my findings with you.' Laughing devilishly, he winked at me before sauntering out of the room.

Durdana Phupo appeared just as confused as I was. I found her on the cane sofa on one of her rare sick days, her nose, unfortunately not as shapely as her mother's, the same colour as her trademark pink dupatta, a large mug of yakhni in her hand, her doleful eyes even larger in a face tightened by several days of persistent infection.

Sinking onto the sofa next to her, I moaned, 'Everyone's depressed.'

'They are, aren't they?' she agreed, suddenly turning to look at me suspiciously. 'Do you know why, Chhoti?'

'No. Thought you might be able to help.'

'I know nothing,' she snapped. 'No one tells me anything around here.'

'That's why people like us have to ferret things out,' I said.

'Is that how you survive?'

I shrugged. 'I actually enjoy the process,' I admitted as I cast an appraising eye over my maiden aunt, whose eyes were now tearing up. This did not surprise me. Like the other Mahmuds, we, too, had taken to ignoring these outbursts. Dadi explained that it had to do with chemicals released by Durdana Phupo's unused lady-parts. Though curious, I refrained from asking what that meant for fear of learning something odious about my own body, which was more than likely to grow parts like hers. In any case, I understood her need to cry. I would, too, if I were forty-one and still trapped in my little-girl room, where dusty old dolls with broken glass eyes and tattered Enid Blytons lay strewn over furniture that I had slept on since the age of six. I imagined Durdana Phupo as Alice, her arms and legs growing till she was crouching, limbs bowed, with her giant head pressed against the cracked ceiling of her minuscule compartment. It wasn't just that she was unmarried in a land where to be single was sacrilege or that her noticeable obsession with Madam Shaista caused Dadi to wake in the middle of the night in cold sweats, only a string of 'tobahs' and sleepy ear-tuggings effective in calming her; Durdana Phupo just did not function like an adult.

'It all has to do with her unloved body,' Raza once said nastily. 'Better be careful, Fatima, or you'll end up like her.'

'Oh please. Are you saying that every woman's problems are solved by marriage?' Fatima asked.

'Who said anything about marriage?' Raza replied.

After a brief hiatus, marriage seemed to be on everyone's minds. I had all but forgotten Rizwana Hameed in the aftermath of Uncle Raff's death, but it turned out that she had not forgotten us – or by 'us', I meant Baba. Our dear, sweet Baba had begun receiving mysterious calls on his cell phone from someone who only responded when he answered. When confronted, he sheepishly admitted that 'an old school friend' was trying to re-establish contact. Fatima and I gave each other knowing looks. Was his obvious embarrassment an indication of interest? Just in case, I made sure I was near his cell phone one evening and grabbed it as soon as it rang. When I heard nothing but heavy breathing, I hissed in a most threatening manner, 'I don't know who you are, but you better leave my Baba alone!' The calls became less frequent. Even so, none of us had the courage to question him about it.

'It's a funny thing,' Fatima shared with the rest of us, 'how people assume that if someone loses their spouse they're immediately in the market for another. I even heard people talking about it at Amma's janaza. They were so concerned about Baba and how he's too young to be alone, the burden of four kids...'

'I can bet the ones most concerned were spinsters or divorcees,' Raza snarled.

Of course, I knew better. I had no doubt that unmarried ladies everywhere found my Baba irresistible because there was nothing not to like about him: his gentle disposition, handsome features, and grey curls aside, his widowed state lent him a certain wistful, tragic charm, the male version of a damsel in distress, waiting patiently till the right person arrived to rescue him. However, I had overheard one too many conversations between my grandparents to know that Baba's situation would not be left to chance and that definite plans were afoot to find him a suitable wife. After all, single people could not be trusted to lead wholesome, satisfying lives on their own. They had to be 'assisted' until they were married and, therefore, 'normal' again.

Even Aslam had taken to expressing his views on marriage, announcing one day that he felt he was 'ready', having just completed a degree in his twenty-third year of life. Fatima, who happened to be in the room, rolled her eyes and stuck a finger halfway down her throat in mock revulsion. This did not deter Aslam. 'Our Prophet' (here he said a string of words in Arabic) 'advocated early marriage among his followers.' He went on to enumerate the benefits of said early marriages, but the only ones left in the room to hear his lecture was a pair of disinterested (and presumably married) chhipkalis near the ceiling fan. I, too, was already out of the door and into the garden when I realized that, having Aslam to myself, I could retrieve my 'black mask' and slip it back into Fatima's underwear drawer so that one sorry tale could finally be put to rest.

'Aslam Baee, Aslam Baee!' It took a few seconds to arrest him in mid-sentence. He paused, bewildered. It appeared he had not realized that his audience had dwindled. One of the chhipkalis darted across the ceiling, click-clucking in protest. I could tell my cousin was not pleased. 'What is it, Chhoti?' he snapped impatiently, straining to look out of the window to where Fatima, Raza, and Jamila huddled over the dusty chairs of Tea Central.

I lowered my voice to a whisper: 'I need my mask. The black one.'

'Oh really? Why should I give it back to you?'

'Well, because I gave you what you wanted! I gave you the email address!'

'Soon,' and he smiled smugly as if he had just swallowed a great secret and it felt warm and snug in his belly, 'I won't need either one.' I imagined him rubbing his hands together gleefully in the manner of TV villains.

'What's wrong with him?' I thought to myself. To his face, I merely reiterated, 'The mask. Now,' and then, as a sheepish afterthought, the reluctant 'please', through force of habit.

'Fine, fine,' he agreed at last, walking out with me into the courtyard and towards the others who, startled, jumped to their feet in hasty escape.

'Wait! Wait!' Aslam called desperately, now running, breathless with the weight of his stocky frame, his tresses (the virgin beard, of course) flowing in the wind, lending his exertion an aerodynamic edge as he flew across the lawn.

'What?' Fatima snapped, turning on him with her hands on her hips.

This was not the first time I had pitied poor Aslam, and it would not be the last. For some reason, he brought out the very worst in Fatima. Just the sight of him unleashed the demon within her, and she tore into him with the same relish I had observed in Raza when gnashing at steak. I could not understand what passed between them. It went beyond my simple grasp of human interaction to a realm beyond: one's attraction and the other's revulsion contingent upon some force which I, as an eleven-year-old, was blissfully unaware of.

Aslam's mouth opened and closed wordlessly for a few seconds before he could come out with, 'Why did you all leave? I was sharing something very important with you.'

Fatima smiled in what appeared to be an encouraging manner, but when she spoke, it was coldly: 'I have a few classmates whom I can set you up with if you're so desperate to get married.'

Aslam was rendered speechless for a second time.

'No, you don't understand – I didn't mean…'

But Fatima had already turned away from him and was walking towards our unit.

'Fatima, Fatima!' he called after her weakly, without making the slightest attempt to follow her. He knew as well as I did that such a course of action could only lead to more ugliness.

'The mask?' I reminded him, tugging at his starched white kurta. It was not the best time to annoy him, but I was determined to retrieve that fine multi-purpose article.

'I heard you the first time!' he snapped, waving an impatient hand in the direction of his house to indicate that I was to follow. As I passed their kitchen, I caught a glimpse of Shahana Chachi with Parveen, both hijab-less in the privacy of their own home, huddled in mirth over cups of tea, their features so alike in laughter, their extraordinarily large buns pinned, with identical style, to the napes of their necks. For an instant, envy prompted me to think, 'Why bother to grow all that hair if no one sees it?' And then the feeling passed, and I felt guilty as I continued up the stairs, the meanness gone but not the sense of loss, a shared moment between mother and daughter one thing that I knew I could never have.

Aslam's room, tidy in the extreme, still had a disturbing mustiness to it, the result, perhaps, of a pile of sweaty clothing near the bed destined for the dhobi. I noticed his new laptop blinking hypnotically as rainbow-coloured Arabic wove in and out, pulsating soundlessly like an Islamic screen saviour. Aslam tore into the first drawer, throwing clothes this way and that as he searched for the missing article, then moved on to his built-in floor-to-ceiling cupboards, unlocking the first door to reveal, astonishingly, a wealth of what appeared to be military paraphernalia.

'What's all of that?' I asked curiously, stepping forward.

'Nothing!' he muttered.

'Is that Dada's stuff from the army?'

'Some of it. I asked him for a few things for my collection.'

I could not imagine a more unlikely candidate for the Pakistan Army: a soft-bellied, bespectacled, bearded fanatic like my cousin. I couldn't help laughing. 'Don't tell me you're thinking of enlisting! Is that before or after your early marriage?'

'Chhoti, shut up. If you want your "mask", you better keep quiet and let me concentrate.'

As he was searching, I edged closer to the cupboard with the fascinating medals, black-and-white photographs, and dusty books with tattered covers on war theory and wondered what possible interest Aslam could have in the military. It was probably a hobby, harmless enough, a bit like the collection of Civil War memorabilia that lined the shelves of our former pediatrician's office. I gingerly opened a scrapbook and saw clippings of Air Force shaheeds, young men, their faces smooth like the pebbles I collected from the stream that once flowed through the tame wilderness that edged our suburban community. Aslam's scrapbook was, like his room, neat and meticulous, the photographs and articles forming razor-edged divisions in tidy squares across black mounting paper. Now I knew why Dada had appointed him 'Keeper of Photographs'. He certainly had an interest in history, his talent for organizing and cataloguing evident in his obsessive labeling.

'Aslam,' I asked thoughtfully, 'have you ever noticed how there's only one picture of Shahbaz Chacha as a baby in the family photo albums?'

'So?' he mumbled, without looking up. Then, straightening, he added plausibly, 'It was wartime. Did you expect an American-style portrait session at the local mall?'

He was probably right. Then why was everyone so shaken after we visited Uncle Raff at the hospital?

'I can't believe I've misplaced it…' Aslam muttered.

Neither could I. It was probably the only feminine thing in his entire room.

'What are these?' I asked, picking up what looked like a large, black donut-shaped cd in a dusty paper cover. The cover had a soldier on it, and above his head were the words 'Military Marches'. There was a stack of these discs in the same cupboard with the rest of the military paraphernalia.

'That's a record. Music was recorded on one of those before there were CDs.'

'Can we listen to it?'

'You need a gramophone or record player. I don't have one.'

Disappointed, I turned away and scanned the rest of Aslam's room, which was unremarkable in its starkness, a few mounted shelves in a corner containing paperbacks – science fiction, mostly, as I gathered from the fantastic titles – and several obscure tomes on religious theory. There were no posters or family photographs.

'Wait! Now I remember!' he burst out, turning away from the cupboard and making his way back towards the bed. Midway there, he froze, then turned around, red-faced, and asked me to leave the room. Mystified, I complied, but not without selecting a position outside the door that afforded me a view of what he was doing. To my complete horror, once alone, he calmly strode towards the bed, lifted the pillow, and pulled the black mask out from under it. 'Why on earth…?' I asked myself. Then, even though I was too young to understand why, the thought of this grown man sleeping with my sister's underpants deeply unsettled me. Scream or cry, I couldn't decide which, and then the mask was thrown at my face, the door slammed, the lock bolted.

Bewildered and upset, I made my way back down the stairs after carefully secreting the mask in my kurta pocket. What possible interest could Aslam have in this innocuous piece of three-holed cloth where trunk and limbs were inserted?

It was just a covering, after all, with no significance beyond its function. As I puzzled over this, I saw Tea Central at a distance, where, along with the dusty chairs and table, sat a hunched figure with about as much life in it as the dead cane upon which it sat. As I neared, I realized it was Dada, his customary cup of tea steaming, untouched, on the table before him, his chin resting on his bony chest. Running to him, I placed a hand on his shoulder and roughly, uncertainly, passed my other hand over the shiny gloss of his balding head.

'Ferzana...' A faint smile on his lips at the sight of me or just a squint from the brightness of the sun? His wrinkles always complicated my reading of his moods. I assumed it was with love that he looked at me and taking advantage of that warmth, found a comfortable position on his lap before asking, 'What is it, Dada? Do you miss Uncle Raff?' As soon as I had spoken, even I realized what a ridiculous question this was. Was it not obvious from the fact that it was Tuesday and that he sat outside by himself while his best friend, in the graveyard across the city, was making peace with the earth, with the maggots and the ants and the flies that swarmed around his headstone?

'Ferzana, you can't imagine what it's like to have known someone for over sixty years – and then, my God, to lose them...'

That was true. I had only known my mother ten years when I lost her. Still, her death had left a permanent absence in my life.

'You know, beta,' he continued, 'Uncle Raff was my best friend, but he was also a great friend of the Mahmuds. The year I was away – ' he faltered for an instant, 'he was the one who took care of your Dadi, your Baba, phupo, and chachas. If it weren't for Raff, I don't know what they would have done. Why – ' here he slapped his knee, suddenly animated, 'I remember now that Shahbaz was actually born while I was away!'

'But, Dada, where were you?'

'It was wartime, Ferzana. Things were bad. I became what is known as a prisoner of war and was taken to India for some time.'

'Do you think that that experience changed you?' I asked, remembering the conversation I had overheard between Baba and Shahbaz Chacha.

'That's what your Dadi thinks. Perhaps it did, or maybe the change came earlier.'

'Tell me about it, Dada,' I begged. Since Amma, since Uncle Raff, I felt unmoored, floating uncertainly in the dark oily sea that heaved its burden of debris, some natural, like brittle shells and tangled sea weed, and some the hand-crafted remnants of people's lives, on the littered shores of Kemari and Clifton Beach.

'I don't know, I don't know…' he shook his head ruefully. 'Why would you want to hear about all of that? It's boring, Ferzana.'

'Dada, please?' I pleaded, suddenly desperate. I wanted to hear my parents' story, the stories of their parents before them, first-hand. I wanted the reassurance of a familiar voice, the warmth of a lap to sit upon, the support of a shoulder to rest my head, for, in the end, wasn't that better than the arduous process of spying, ferreting, intelligence-gathering and then piecing together fragments of half-finished tales?

CHAPTER 25

Ferzana, my dear, I can't imagine why a chit of a girl like you would be interested in my stories, dry, stale, depressing, long-winded, an old boodha's reminiscences of a youth that ended in early disappointment. You are a boodhi rooh, an old spirit inside the body of a little girl, aren't you? Sorry. I'm afraid I have no fantasies, no fairytales in my repertoire, no stories of espionage and thrill. Of course, when I was your age, I was interested in much the same things as you. I watch you sometimes – there, see, you're surprised – skulking about in the champa bushes or hiding behind a door 'spying' on all of us. I had dreams, too. I wanted to be a general in the army. I wanted to lead troops into battle. At your age, I never imagined that I would fight my own people, blood for blood, in a war that tore families apart.

'Your Baba will tell you that I loved army life, its discipline, its order, the grid-like geography of cantonments, the clockwork precision of marches, the smartness of salutes … This love came from a life that began with regimentation. I was sent to boarding school at age five. By the time I joined Aligarh, I had spent the better part of my childhood with other boys at institutions, seeing my parents over the brief holidays, where the atmosphere of restraint that prevailed at home made my brothers and I seek comfort in days spent outside. My father was a district judge, an important man in the community. Unfortunately, his sense of justice permeated everything, even such simple daily activities as our evening meals, which he presided over like sessions. We were always in fear of his retributory eye. If there was any charm to coming home at all it was to see our mother. Your par-dadi was a grand lady, regal in her flowing ghararas and jewels, but to us she was our mother, and we would run to her for the comfort which our father was unable to give. I remember picnics with her outside, lying with my head on her lap and looking up at the feathered leaves of the ancient neem tree that had graced our garden from the time of my dada's dada.

'You and your siblings think I'm a stern man – don't deny it, my dear. I am, but as you see, it wasn't entirely my fault. Sometimes we appear a certain way to the world because we are afraid of being ourselves. I was always taught that it was unmanly to give in to my feelings. It was the way most of us were brought up at the time and the army only served to make me more rigid – I wore my uniform like a sheath. In 1944, at barely eighteen, I enlisted in the army, like countless others. It was the Second World War. My father wasn't entirely happy with my decision, hoping that I would take up law, but India was changing and so, imperceptibly, was he. Everyone could sense that something cataclysmic was about to happen, not only in the world at large but also in our own country.

'It was during this war (for there were others, unfortunately) that I was introduced to a young man from Delhi whose family, several generations back, had known mine, our great-great-grandfathers friends with a common interest in shair-shairee, conspiring to meet every few years over a meal, the special culinary delicacies of our hometowns proudly showcased to the other. There he was, this dashing young air force pilot (they were rare in those days, a chosen few) holding court at the party to which we had been invited, his charming smile and dark curls making him irresistible to the ladies. Yes, it was Uncle Raff, or Muhammad Rafiq Nawaz, as he was introduced to me that first time in the winter of 1943 or '44, can't remember which ... I must admit, I was jealous of this young man's ease with the ladies until I noticed that his high spirits were infectious, his generous, open nature making him a friend to everyone. Like our great-great-grandfathers, we hit it off immediately, as you young people say, and that was the start of our association. Soon after our first meeting, I went on home leave and found myself in a few confusing, delightful days married to my cousin (what a beauty!), just sixteen years old and as much in love with me as I with her. Raff may have been popular with the ladies, but I was happy with my one, my Zubaida. So, you see, your Dadi knew Uncle Raff almost as many years as I did. In fact, he was one of the few people who attended our wedding – yes! Weddings were simple affairs then, not like the bloody circus productions they are now.

'What happened then? Well, Chhoti, I'm afraid things changed for all of us – for India as a whole. I won't go into the details of Partition, except to say that India was divided in August 1947 – right, you know that already – and I and Uncle Raff opted for Pakistan, joining the newly created armed forces. We were the lucky ones, travelling by train across the border before the massacres began. Of course, my family's property in Lucknow was taken over, our belongings displaced, but others suffered far greater hardship so we were grateful, humble even, when we were given accommodation at the spacious barracks near Queen's Road. I brought my parents with me and two of my three brothers. Kamal stayed on in India and it was to be many years before we met again. In Karachi, it was like starting all over again. We were nobodies, with no links to the land we had chosen. This displacement was painful, Ferzana. Have you noticed how your Dadi still refers to Lucknow every chance she gets? A place she left as a young bride, almost a child, really. Her family stayed on in India, and I often think that's the reason why she has never been able to forget even after spending the better part of her life here in Pakistan. We slowly adjusted to our new circumstances. We were among the fortunate, the armed forces giving us, gradually, the structure and the security we needed to survive.

'Although Raff and I kept in touch, in the early years I was stationed all over Pakistan with the Ordnance, Malir, Quetta, Pindi and, eventually, Dhaka, which was East Pakistan at the time. (You have heard of Dhaka? Good.) There, Raff and I were reunited, a year before the '71 war. He was still an inveterate bachelor, his charm ever-fresh, romancing all the girls but, as usual, serious with no one. If he wanted family

life, he would come over and visit your Dadi and me and
play with your Baba, Jamshaid and Durdana.

'Did he ever marry? No, he never did, Ferzana. But – and
this is a secret – he was once in love. I, for one, was against
it from the start. Why? Well, it isn't natural to go against
one's background and marry into another culture. And even
that can be forgiven, I suppose, but to forsake one's religion?
That's where I draw the line. She was a young Bengali, a
university lecturer. I saw her with him on a few occasions – a
beautiful girl, really. Long, black hair, large eyes, slender as
a reed ... I could see why he loved her. Arti, her name was.
Still, I made it clear that I wasn't going to accept their union.
What did Raff care? He went on doing what he wanted,
despite the looks he was getting from the higher-ups. If it
weren't for the war, and its consequences, he would have
married that Hindu girl. I know, I know. You think I'm a
bigot. Yes, we are a prejudiced people, but what people is
not? If you really look deep enough into people's hearts, you
will find reluctance over something or another – religion,
skin colour, politics, class...

'Why, even with your parents... Oh, you were told...?
Yes, yes, I know – your mother was a Muslim, too, but her
version of the faith was very different from what I had come
to believe, through experience, was the right path. There are
fundamental differences between Shias and Sunnis, and it's
best, if only for convenience's sake, that they marry within
their own communities. No, Ferzana, don't turn away,
and don't be angry. Of course I regretted the rift between
your Baba and myself, the distance between us and our

grandchildren. What? Yes, your mother... Well, the poor woman is no more. Yes, I know her name. Why don't I say it? Her name was Najma, Najma – there, better? Would I behave the same way if it happened again? You are putting me on the spot now... I suppose any union of two people who could produce an extraordinary little girl like you couldn't be all bad, right?

'Anyway, I digress. Even before the war officially broke out in December of 1971, Dhaka was in a state of unrest. There were political arrests, especially of young university students and intellectuals. Uncle Raff's friend was one of them. He was beside himself with worry. Later, he told me there was a special reason he was concerned for the safety of the girl. No need to go into that because nothing came of it – no, Ferzana, you are too young to know everything, my dear. Meanwhile, all kinds of terrible things were happening all around us. We followed orders as best we could, but it was obvious that the situation was getting out of hand. As soldiers, we had no right to be conflicted; only obedience was demanded of us. Even so, most of us had consciences. Such atrocities, such bestiality – it broke me to see what humans were capable of. It was a bitter and bloody civil war, and then India got involved.

'Ferzana, the very worst thing for a soldier – the ultimate humiliation – is, of course, defeat and surrender. I can't describe how I felt on the day it happened. Over 90,000 soldiers, including myself, were taken prisoner by Indian forces and shipped across the border to various camps. I only had time to send word to Zubaida that I was alive and well and that she and the children should make their way across to West Pakistan as best they could. She was full-term with your Shahbaz Chacha, and the times were so uncertain. Raff, with his luck and ingenuity, managed to escape capture, and I was sure that he would look after everyone, as he eventually did, of course. Later, he told me that he had searched for Arti, too, but never saw her again. He didn't speak of her after that, not even in his last days. Sometimes, I, too, wonder what happened to her...

'It would be wrong to say that my experiences as a POW hardened me. The change had started much earlier than that. In our last few years in Dhaka, I had witnessed enough to make me feel like the disconnect between what we had to do and what we ought to do was far too great. As an army man, I was more conflicted than I had ever been, my blind trust in the rightness of my superiors seriously put to the test by each passing day. What pained me most was that we were fighting among ourselves. Yes, I didn't agree with the political agenda of some of my East Pakistani compatriots, but as long as we could coexist peacefully, I had no problems. Here, however, were fissures on all sides, race, ethnicity, religion, politics – there was no common thought on anything, no unity. And then the cyclone of 1970 took away the lives of thousands, as if nature itself was at war with us, too.

'Once at the camp, we slowly settled into a routine. A prisoner of war camp is regimented, too, but it's a different kind of regimentation, at least for the prisoners – a regimentation without useful purpose, where the most important thing is to somehow get through the day without giving in to despair. At times I didn't know if I would ever make it home again to my family. I often thought about my youngest, little Shahbaz, who was born while I was away, and whom I feared I would never live to see. A few desperate men attempted escape, one or two even managing to find a way out, but they were caught once outside, their fates worse than ours. Did they hurt us? No, Ferzana, not in the way you'd think. The Indians had signed an agreement called the Geneva Convention, which protected the basic rights of prisoners of war. But our fate was linked to the Indian prisoners of war in West Pakistan, and our safe return was dependent on the governments of the two countries – and the new government of Bangladesh – coming to an agreement. As you can imagine, the wait, the cycle of hope and despair, were torture enough for most of us. It was then that I started to say my namaaz again.

'Of course, as you know, we eventually made it back home. I met my new son, who was a little over a year old when I finally held him in my arms and who howled in protest at being handled by a stranger. And the other children, older, much older than I remembered, your Baba a strapping teenager now whose voice as he greeted me sounded manly and unfamiliar. Zubeida, the children – they all stared at me as if I had changed, but I think we had all changed in one way or another that year. It took me many months to readjust to life at home. It often seemed as if everyone was afraid of me – of my temper, of my moods, even of my new-found religiosity. Zubaida, who had always been my confidante, grew distant, fearful. I noticed her holding back, and it pained me, but I knew I could never be the man I was.

Shaving off the beard I had grown at the camp would have made no difference. It would have done nothing to alter how I felt.

'Sad? Yes, Ferzana, it was, but we readjusted and moved on, like people do. And then there were new worries, the education of the children, their choices in marriage, their children's children … and so it is, to this day. Now, with Raff gone, I have very few ties to that time, to that other life, to Lucknow and Dhaka, to my years in the army. But, and here I'm confiding in you, and you alone, the arrival of your Baba and the four of you has, over the months, given your grandmother and myself a new purpose to our lives…'

Long after Dada had gone inside, I sat there in the garden, my knees pulled up to my chin, staring vacantly into the growing darkness, as I thought about his story and how that story intersected, overlapped and connected to other stories, ours for example, and that of our parents, and how eventually that all came together like the pieces of an elaborate Sindhi rilly, whose dizzying geometric sequences, when looked at as a whole, formed an intricate, multi-layered pattern that told the entire story of the past.

CHAPTER 26

'Why,' Baba suddenly asked as the four of us lay in his bed, 'have we been here almost ten months without meeting your mamus, Salaar and Alamdar?'

I rolled over onto my stomach and raised myself so that I could look straight into his eyes. He was smiling innocently enough, his expression neither mischievous nor ironic. Then, as if surprised by his own question, he exclaimed, 'What was I thinking! Of course you children should meet them – they are your mother's brothers, after all!'

'And your best friends,' I added.

'Yes, so they are…' he agreed thoughtfully, closing his eyes as if to revisit the days he would walk under the dusty trees of the vast grounds of the University with Amma and her older brothers. 'My best friend,' he said quietly, 'was your mother, Ferzana.'

There was a long pause.

'We weren't sure if you were up to meeting them,' Fatima said gently as she tugged at the lacy hemline of her kurta.

'You weren't sure? You mean you people were trying to protect *me*?' Baba asked incredulously, suddenly sitting up and staring. 'Imagine that...' he said, as if to himself, but I think he was actually addressing Amma. 'And here I was trying to protect you! Knowing those two, they'd wail at the sight of you and overwhelm you with their lamentations!'

'Well, there was some of that,' Raza admitted. We couldn't help laughing, our memory of that first meeting now comical in the light of Baba's comments.

'You mean you've already met them? How did that happen without my knowledge?'

'Shahbaz Chacha helped us,' I blurted out, only realizing after I had spoken that I had further jeopardized my poor uncle's fragile happiness.

'Don't worry. I'm not angry, Ferzana – just astonished at Shahbaz's initiative,' said Baba.

Eagerly, the four of us told Baba about our mamus' first visit to Shahbaz Chacha's house, followed, soon after, by the 'tour' of the city which ended ultimately at Amma's childhood home in Nazimabad. 'There's also someone related to us who's really, really famous!' I added proudly, remembering with pleasure the portrait of our irascible poet-ancestor.

'Yes,' Baba acknowledged drily. 'The great poet-ancestor.'

I paused in surprise, registering that at some level Baba did not believe what he was saying. 'You mean,' I asked cautiously, 'he wasn't great?'

'Of course he was, Ferzana,' Baba said in a reassuring voice, patting me on the head in the manner of a trainer condescending to its pet monkey.

But the conversation had already moved on, and Raza, Fatima, and Baba began to plan a future meeting with

Salaar and Alamdar while Jamila and I lay with our arms wrapped around each other, overcome with excitement at the thought that the two halves of our family were about to reunite. Eventually, it was decided that Baba would speak to the brothers and arrange for us to meet them at a restaurant in the centre of the city, an older establishment that they used to frequent as students for kebab-paratha and where the chicken tikka was always devoured by our mother before the boys could have their share.

'Oh yes,' Baba added once the plans had been made, 'I'd appreciate it if you didn't mention this to your grandparents.' The others nodded in agreement, Raza muttering, 'Of course not! That would ruin everything!' For once, I kept quiet. Earlier, the conspiratorial nature of our family powwows had thrilled me. I gloated over the whispered conversations that took place in Baba's room as if they were top-level international spy conferences. It was always a case of 'us' versus 'them', where 'them' consisted of a demonized Dada and Dadi presiding over a gang of ruffians called the Jamshaids. It just made it easier to hate them. But today, I felt sorry for my grandparents and Dada in particular. Having spent enough time with them, I had come to realize that they were now ready to accept almost everything about us – including, I hoped, our Shia relations. I was convinced that Dada, despite his crusty prejudices, would no longer hold out on anything that would affect my happiness.

'Listen, Alamdar, Najma always hated it when you did that. Do you remember the time that you tried to teach her how to drive and she pulled your mustache half off your face for twirling it while you were demonstrating how to reverse?'

'She was always after me to shave it off, wasn't she? Funny thing. She never hated your "Shia beard" during Muharram.'

'That was different,' Salaar insisted. 'That was religious.'

'Hah!'

'Did you know that when Najma was a little girl, your ape-like mamu, Alamdar, actually made her hair before she went to school? I still remember him fiddling around with bows and clips, and using his thick fingers to braid her hair into ponytails!'

'She had the longest hair of us all, of course. It was always a tangled mess after she bathed, and she wouldn't let Amina – remember Amina Baji, that old crone? – comb it for us. It was always "Alamdar Bhai", as if I had some magic in my fingers. Who would have imagined a hulk like me' – and he pointed to his extraordinarily muscular frame – 'as a maker of little girls' hairdos?'

'We mothered Najma,' Salaar continued, suddenly thoughtful. 'She lost her mother even before you lost yours. She never knew Ammi. The three of us, Alamdar, Abba and I, were all she had. I'm glad she was blessed with you three girls to balance out all the men in her life.'

'Bhai, I can still picture her with her tongue sticking out as she sat in her blue-and-white uniform at the back of the van that took her to school each day, her ponytails flying in the dust, remember? By the time she'd come home in the afternoon, her pluck all gone, she'd be a sweaty mess, tearing up at the slightest provocation until Amina Baji had served her up some lunch. She loved her chicken!'

'Aloo gosht, don't forget!' Salaar added with a laugh.

'Funny thing. Despite her love for food, she hated cooking. Your Nana, of course, agreed with her wholeheartedly that a woman's destiny consists of more than just mixing masalas. Still, Bhai and I, we always dreamed of a house where we'd come home to meals cooked by her the way we remembered Ma cooked for us when we were little. I'd always envy my friends, whose tiffins were full of warm home-cooked treats. Amina Baji's cooking – '

'Don't remind me!' Salaar laughed, holding his belly in revulsion. 'All I can say is – and I'm sorry if this sounds cruel – but her demise over a pot of bubbling haleem on the 10th of Muharram in '72 was a blessing for all of us. For her, because she died on a holy day, and for us because in the hustle-bustle of her death no one had a chance to sample her haleem.'

'Ferzana,' Alamdar interrupted, 'when I first saw you I thought I was dreaming. You look exactly like Najma as an eleven-year-old. I have this memory of her at that age, so clear in my mind, I could draw it on a piece of paper. She came home from school unusually tired. How could I tell? Well, I had followed her into her room after lunch and saw her lying on the bed, fighting off sleep as she pulled open her maths register and proceeded to re-do a line of sums. I noticed her score: 22 correct out of 100. She usually averaged about 30 on good days, maths being her least favourite subject. (Don't be shocked, Fatima – all of us are abysmal with numbers!)

'"What's wrong, chutki?" I had asked her, concerned. Her maths grades were always a joke with us, so it was unusual to see her upset over them. After several minutes of pestering, it finally came out.

"'I hate Zeenat." Zeenat was her best friend.

"'Why?" I asked, baffled.

"'She always tricks me. She asks me my grades. I tell her she has to tell me hers first. She told me she got 15 out of a 100. I told her what I got. Then she laughed and said she was lying – that she actually got 77!'"

'Well, I never liked Zeenat myself. The little brat rarely visited. She lived in a palatial home in KDA where Najma was invited only at birthday celebrations, so that Zeenat could have a chance to show off her lacy English dresses and foreign toys, her fingers full of lemon cream from the fancy tarts her father bought her from the club. We were never good enough for her or her father, an Additional Secretary who always regarded us with suspicion because of our father's socialist views. I told Najma that I would beat up Zeenat, and she suddenly sat up in panic. She was peace-loving. "No! Please don't. Forget I said anything!" she protested, really upset. I gathered her up and put her on my lap. "You'll find better friends, Dopes," I reassured her. And she did. She found Aftab, didn't she?'

'Alamdar and I had no idea what was going on between them for the longest time. We must be the stupidest pair of brothers around. Here we thought Aftab enjoyed our company and wanted to spend time with us, but there was always an excuse to have Najma along: "She likes chicken tikkas", "She loves that film director", "She'd enjoy this or that"! Aftab was a wily one. To tell you the truth, we kind of resented it at first. We were the only men in Najma's life till Aftab came along. And then – well, it felt as if she had been stolen from us against our will when the two of them decided to run off and get married. We were worried for her. Frankly speaking, we couldn't understand why she'd want to be part of a family who didn't want her.'

'Bhai, please. Leave it.' Alamdar glanced at us anxiously.

'I'm sorry. I know this was all in the past, and we sorted it out later, but the kids have a right to know, don't they?'

'I've got tons of stories about your mother,' Alamdar intervened again, his husky laugh a little forced as he glanced at his brother. 'Did you know that as a little girl – and even up to the age of five – Najma referred to herself in the masculine? I really think she thought she was a boy. There's this funny story' – and his chuckle was genuine this time – 'where, seeing us boys relieve ourselves, Najma pulled down her pants and stood in front of a wall to pee like us! In the early days, she was a real tomboy. That's when we knew how to handle her. But at sixteen, she began dressing differently and wearing kajal, styling her hair like the movie stars... A year or two later, and she had come into her own, lording it over us, asking me to trim my moustache, pick up after myself, stop belching out loud ... In fact, she began mothering us. It was different, but we accepted it like we'd accept anything about her. We all doted on her. She could do no wrong in our eyes.'

'To Najma, I was "Bhai Sahib". Because there were five years between us, I was treated with a bit more respect than old Alamdar here. Despite the gap, she knew she could get me to do anything she wanted. I was the one who had to tell Abba about the elopement. Believe me, that was no easy task! Yes, our father was liberal, even forward-thinking on many issues, particularly women's rights, but this was a personal betrayal, and by the one person whom he thought could do no wrong. Children, it wasn't about sect for us, although there were some clowns in our extended family – a few cousins who wanted to marry Najma themselves – who were furious that she had married outside of the community. We weren't so narrowly conservative. For us, it was a stab to the heart.'

Then, Baba spoke for the first time.

'If I had to do it all over again, you know, I would have done things differently. We were young and stupid. I was upset with my father, and at the time, eloping seemed the best way out. Najma convinced me that all of you would come round – as you eventually did. She knew that your love would be enough for her, especially afterwards when my family turned us away.'

'Enough serious talk!' Alamdar interrupted. 'Even Najma's bored of this dreary conversation. Let's talk about the good times – her spirit, her determination, the legacy she left behind in these beautiful children.'

And then, as if the grand finale to an evening of conversation in honour of our mother, Alamdar Mamu recounted a curious tale, one that sounded as if it had been pulled straight out of the imagination of a wizard, for it contained dreams and magic and a certain amount of make-believe, and it was strange to hear all of these amazing things come out of the mouth of one so earthy and literal. Some of these, the belief in saints and intercessors, the pageantry of battle, the mythology of great men and brave women, were a part of that religion, a fractured piece of the whole, to which my mother and her family belonged. While religion was buried in the very cracks and crevices of C44's foundation, the insistence on prayer times, the profuse beards, and the austerity of rules made faith seem a dry and brittle thing, an unyielding bone blanched by the sun. There was something about the magic of what my mamu recounted, the element of mysticism, that immediately appealed to my imagination.

'So, children,' Alamdar Mamu began, 'when your mother was nine, we took her to her first Jaloos. I'm not sure if you know what that is, so I'll explain. On the tenth day of Muharram, or Ashura, there is a special procession that winds its way through the old city to commemorate the sacrifice that Imam Hussain and his family made at Karbala. The experience can be frightening for the uninitiated. Imagine a procession with thousands of people in mourning, some carrying pennants representing the martyrs, others beating their chests with their hands or with chains, the revered horse of Imam Hussain, Zuljanah, in full battle regalia, and the sobbing – well, it's not easy in the heat and on an empty stomach. That year, though we hadn't planned it, Najma insisted on accompanying us. We weren't comfortable with it. Salaar and I resented having to look after our little sister in that crowd when we'd much rather have been with the rest of the youth, either doing maatam or helping with the arrangements. Still, as I said, we couldn't say no to Najma, particularly when her pleading gave way to tears. Draped in a black chador, her tiny frame practically disappearing within its folds, she followed us out of the car bravely and walked with us as we joined the rest of the crowd.

'Of course, there was a lot of noise and movement. I kept her close to me, holding her sweaty little hand as tightly as I could without hurting her. I glanced down and saw that her eyes were huge, her mouth wide open like a startled fish! I began to think that bringing her along wasn't such a great idea, especially when I heard her gasp at the men in the medical tent, their bloody gashes being patched up by volunteer surgeons. "Are you okay?" I asked her, as I noticed her grip on my hand loosening. She looked up at me and nodded bravely. Her forehead was beaded with perspiration. It was blazing hot, and she was wrapped from head to toe in black fabric. I cursed myself for not bringing a bottle of water for her. Salaar had already pushed his way to the front of the procession, where he was doing maatam in rhythm with the thousands of men around him. I felt helpless on my own with Najma, wishing – and it wasn't for the first time, I can tell you – that we had an older woman in our lives who could manage this remarkable creature, full of surprise and delight for the most part but as difficult to handle for clumsy men like ourselves as a tray of fine crystal. I picked her up and felt her go limp in my arms. I paid no attention. She was tired, of course, and dehydrated from the heat. It was mid-afternoon in Karachi, the asphalt beneath our sandaled feet radiating an intense heat that rose in waves all around us. I began feeling a little lightheaded myself.

'As soon as I could, I pushed through the crowd to my right and managed to come out of the rush and into a quiet side street. "Najma, are you awake?" I asked her, shaking her a little in my arms so that she'd realize where we were. A toothless old woman peered down at us curiously from one of the windows. Ignoring her, I muttered, "I told you, silly girl, that this is no place for you!" I couldn't conceal the irritation in my voice. As a Shia youth, Ashura was the focus of my entire year and to have missed out on it because of my little sister seemed completely unfair. I flipped her over in my arms and examined her face, wet with perspiration. Now, more than ever, she looked like a fish pulled out of the sea, lifeless without the element that sustained her. Shaking her, I suddenly realized that she wasn't just asleep but that she had passed out. I glanced up to see if the old woman was watching but there was no sign of her, only a thin trail of betel juice trickling, like blood, directly beneath the window. I ran back to the crowded area, pushing through the sheer weight of human bodies, the stench of perspiration and blood nauseating as I forced my way towards the medical tent. Once there, a young doctor pulled her out of my arms and immediately began sticking needles into her. Within minutes she was lying on a makeshift stretcher, her eyes still closed. I buried my face in both hands.

'"Bhai," she said weakly, opening her eyes at last.

'Of course, I wanted to shout at her for putting me through all of this. I had spent the last hour in agony, wondering what I would tell Abba when I took her home with a potholed arm. Before I could speak, however, she suddenly smiled, the sweetest smile – I swear it lit up her face – that I had ever seen. She disarmed me completely. I sat there looking like an idiot, my chin cupped in my hands, speechless.

"'She told me you'd be angry," she laughed.

"'Who told you what?" I snapped, unnerved. 'You fainted. I bet you didn't eat anything before we left, right? I told you you're too young to do faaqa. A little kid like you needs food and water, especially out here."

"'I just fell asleep," she pouted. "And I finally met her."

"'Met who?" I shouted, the anger in me out at last.

"'Ammi jan. She was sitting beside a little girl who was about my age. At first I was jealous, but then Ammi jan told me that she was a Shehzadi, a pure soul who had befriended her and who would befriend me, too."

'I waited for her to speak again.

"'The little girl's name was Sakina."

'Now, children, perhaps you don't know the significance of this, but Bibi Sakina was the daughter of Imam Hussain. She saw her father killed on the battlefield and her whole family decimated. Najma claimed that she had seen not only her, but our mother, too. It was uncanny the way she described Ammi jan. Her mannerisms, the little details of facial expression and hair, the laughter! And remember, Najma had only seen her in pictures! The anger drained out of me. I didn't know what to feel, what to believe. Was it a dream or a vision? Were we deluding ourselves? Whatever it was, it was an amazing incident, and I'll never forget it as long as I live.'

For a few moments, we sat in complete silence, reflecting over what we had just heard. Ridiculous, self-indulgent, completely unbelievable – all of these could be said of Alamdar Mamu's story. And yet, I still wanted to marvel at it and accept its authenticity because it left open the possibility of more – more than just a permanent separation. Hearing this and other stories about our mother's life before she knew us made her personality more whole to me. I wasn't ready to give that up. It appeared my brother and sisters felt the same way because when I finally lifted my head to look around the table, I wasn't the only one crying.

Later, as we were leaving the restaurant, I thrust out my belly for the sheer joy of it, letting my stomach muscles relax in a celebration of comfortable fullness. I was elated that the meeting had gone off so well. Just as I reached the exit, the door opened and there stood a woman in her early forties, her draped chador and confectionary-pink outfit all-too-familiar: my phupo on her lunch break, followed by a couple of her mousey-looking colleagues. Wonderful, I thought to myself, as she greeted us with enthusiasm, taking a few seconds to register the presence of our mamus and then, predictably, turning away. But Salaar and Alamdar Hussain were imperturbable. With a chivalrous bow, Alamdar Mamu held the door open for her and her friends. 'Durrrr-daaana!' he said with a twist of his fine mustache, flourishing his aqeeq-ringed hand in an exaggerated gesture of welcome.

C·H·A·P·TER 27

'Love is in the air!' Raza sang out gleefully, but coming from him there was no sweetness or light to it, just a sardonic roll of the eyes as he flew past us and into the main house where we were all shortly expected for dinner. 'Watch out, Fatima!' could be heard faintly through the half-open screen door, an unusual brotherly afterthought that came seconds too late as Fatima, Jamila, and I were immediately face-to-face with Aslam.

There he was, standing before us, the fine, curly hair of his virgin beard still trembling from his wild dash across the courtyard, the thinning hair on his head plastered back in an uncharacteristic effort at smartness. He was wearing a starched dress shirt and tie and his trousers were freshly ironed, the crisp folds that ran down his legs sitting neatly atop a pair of polished black Oxfords. I looked closely at his shoes and saw my own face reflected in them, only upside down, the tip of his beard growing out of my forehead. Panting, he attempted a gallant smile, his moustacheless beard giving his facial hair an air of incompleteness, as if his razor had overstepped the mark in an accidental turn of the wrist.

Fatima only had a few seconds to look desperate before Aslam, placing himself squarely before her, commented with sudden boldness, 'This is what I admire about you most – your modesty.'

'I'm not modest at all!' Fatima retorted unthinkingly. Aslam's surprise attack had put her in one of her 'moods'. I had seen all of this before. If it were not for the fact that I had actually witnessed Aslam retrieve her underwear from beneath his pillow, I would have pitied both of them equally. As things stood, however, my loyalty was unequivocal. Before anyone knew what was happening, I brought my foot down with a thud on Aslam's shiny shoes, stamping out, in imagination at least, my obsession with his beard.

'Are you crazy?' he shouted. 'Are you crazy?' He scrambled to wipe the dust off his shoes with the back of a crisp shirt sleeve, then cursed when he saw the streak of grey it left behind. 'Paagal! Crazy brat!' he hissed as he straightened himself up and looked down at his clothes. 'If it weren't for your sister…'

'Please,' Fatima interrupted coolly, 'don't stop on account of me.'

Aslam and I both scowled at her.

Putting an arm around me, she continued with exaggerated emphasis, 'Please understand that your actions, either way, have absolutely no effect on me. I'm indifferent to you.'

I noticed the skin around the curly tendrils of Aslam's beard turn, like the rest of his face, a crimson that appeared to actually emanate heat. Within seconds, he had mastered his feelings, his expression suddenly smug as he responded stiffly, 'We'll see about that,' and walked off in the direction of Dadi's house.

Fatima, Jamila, and I looked at each other as if to say 'What on earth…?'

Naturally, the furthest thing from Fatima's mind on that particular evening was the prospect of marriage, hers or anyone else's. Not that she was a stranger to the topic. In all her eighteen years, and since a diapered infant, she had heard her marriage mentioned thousands of times, generally in jest but mostly as a settled fact, a fact deferred to a future so distant that she hardly ever thought about it. Aside from the occasional literary-inspired fantasy (there was a week, I recall, where she pretended she was a desi Jane Eyre), she barely gave it a second thought, and had never – to my knowledge – had so much as a crush on a boy. But even a South Asian household as unconventional as ours was not safe from the occasional matrimonial jibe. Amma and Baba often teased her about her perfect mate – a tweed-clad professor of History or Literature. 'No way!' she would protest amid laughter as Raza did a heartless imitation of one of her trademark moves – hitching her glasses higher up her nose.

These days, Fatima was more concerned about her 'A' Level grades and the start, early next year, of university applications. Unlike the rest of us, who were busy in concocting imaginary escapes – wild flights in fragile winged ships that tottered and fell – Fatima had actually worked out a viable plan which involved straight A's, university admissions in the US, and full scholarships. The poor girl was completely unaware of the whispered conversations I

had overheard between Dadi and Durdana Phupo. Wisely,
I had kept the contents of those eavesdropping sessions to
myself, fearing that her reaction would be wilder than I could
contain. Perhaps if I had, if there had been some warning,
what happened next would not have come as a complete
shock.

Still puzzling over Aslam's odd behavior, the three of us
made our way to the main unit for dinner. As I entered the
dining room, I ran to Dada's side at the head of the table and
flung an arm around his neck. He looked up briefly from the
bowl of salaan closest to him.

'Aah, Chhoti! There's a surprise for dinner tonight.'

I peered over his shoulder and looked deep into the bowl.

'No, no – not literally!' he laughed. Then, he whispered,
'There will be a great announcement.'

I remembered the last important announcement that took
place following my disastrous exploration of the underbelly
of the family dining table: Tania Chachi's pregnancy. So
much had changed since then, I realized, as I glanced at
Dada's shiny bald head, which glistened with perspiration as
he brought a wrinkled hand purposefully down to smash the
air out of the golden roti on his plate. (Well, not in Dada's
world but certainly in the way I perceived him in mine.)
Then, scanning the table, I stopped at my youngest aunt and
uncle. There they were, the proud parents-to-be, both looking
miserable. Tania Chachi, her gigantic belly uncomfortably
wedged between her seat and the table, appeared obsessed
with the delicate matter of her stomach which, by this, her
eighth month, was an unpredictable beast. She was shifting

self-consciously in a clumsy effort to stifle its overactivity.
Shahbaz Chacha was no better. Twirling a fork like a baton
between his delicate artist's fingers, he was in dire need of
an intervention, his unshaven face an indisputable sign, in
the Mahmud men at least, of deep depression. As I looked
upon them pityingly, thinking back to just last year when
they were glamorous love birds, it suddenly struck me that
perhaps the announcement Dada referred to had something
to do with Shahbaz Chacha's parentage... But why would
Dada, of all people, be elated at the prospect of such a
scandalous disclosure?

I was still puzzling over this as I took my seat at the
children's table where Parveen, in an uncharacteristic
display of magnanimity, smiled and offered me a papadum.
She looked unusually dressed up, too, wearing a chiffon
shalwar-kameez, a head scarf wrapped turban-style around
her voluminous bun. I broke the crispy papadum in half and
shared it with Jamila, who sat quietly by her plate, staring
past and beyond us as if still dreaming of the boy she had met
at the market last week whom she told me looked just like
the bear-prince in a book of fairytales we shared.

When the family was half-way through the meal, a
sumptuous one full of treats reserved for special occasions,
Dadi's mild Lucknavi chicken biryani, shami kebabs, tangy
raita, korma and bazaari naan, I heard the scraping of a chair
from beneath the main table followed by the self-important,
deliberately exaggerated clearing of a bearded male throat.
Each and every family member, including dreamy Jamila
and a still-stricken Shahbaz Chacha, looked up in surprise

and sat quietly in the expectation of some great revelation. Even Dada put down his naan and wiped his hands on a napkin, which was surprising because he had a no-nonsense policy about meal interruptions. Something momentous was about to happen. I could feel the food that had so recently entered my stomach flip several times over before descending into a pleasant gastric tingling halfway between excitement and nervousness. It was the kind of feeling I normally experienced just before taking to the stage to receive a diploma – which, of course, I had only done once at my kindergarten graduation in Chicago but which was memorable enough to stand as a cardinal reference point for all times to come.

'My dear family,' Jamshaid Chacha began, 'may I please have your attention?'

We looked at one another, a little confused. Obviously this speech had been rehearsed. As anyone could plainly see, we were all very attentive, the room so quiet that the distant sound of Shahnaz's parents arguing behind the house came to us on a gust of sea breeze through the open windows.

'Since Bhai Jan's return from the US, we've all had the opportunity to acquaint ourselves with our American branch. The adjustments have not always been easy, particularly for Bhai Jan and his kids. I'm sorry for that.' Here, he paused and looked at us as if to take personal responsibility for our shaky cultural assimilation. 'These four children have brought much fun and mischief to our household. So much so that we have already begun to expand our clan,' he continued, glancing at Tania Chachi and Shahbaz Chacha, who were both so miserable that they barely acknowledged the reference with weak smiles. 'I think it only natural that we should find other ways of consolidating our name. And that is why we are all here today. Shahana and I would like to ask Bhai Jan's permission – formal permission – to make Fatima an even more integral part of our family, now and always. I know this fine young lady will be a wonderful sister to Parveen, a daughter to us, and…' he paused again, this time for dramatic effect, 'and a good wife to our dear son, Aslam.'

Aslam stood up and beamed. A look of complete calm had descended upon his features.

Fatima stood up as well.

I wished I could crawl under the table, but obviously that option was no longer available to me. I could only imagine what was going on in my sister's head. I covered my eyes with my hands, opening the fingers a crack to allow me to see what I needed to without being a witness to the ugliest parts, for I anticipated many.

Baba sat flabbergasted. I could see that the others' expressions were 'freeze-frame' happy, their joy suspended in mid-hurrah as they anxiously awaited a rebuttal, prepared all the while to burst into hearty congratulations should everything miraculously go as planned. I felt sorry for them. Through the slender cracks between my fingers I noticed that nearly all of the grown ups' faces expressed some kind of internal struggle, as if they desperately wanted the story to end happily but knew, given the plot and characters, that such an outcome was beyond imagining. The only other person at the adult table as delusionally happy as Aslam was Raza, of course, who delighted in his sister's distress, whatever the cause and no matter how serious, and was doing all he could to prevent himself from rolling onto the floor in fits of laughter.

Baba finally lifted his head up to speak but before he could begin Aslam announced euphorically, 'Family, this is the happiest day of my life!'

Baba cleared his throat. 'Aslam, beta, we are truly honoured to receive this marriage proposal from you and your family...'

Stop. Did Baba really understand the depth of Fatima's inexplicable revulsion for our cousin? Did he know that she woke up in cold sweats in the middle of the night strangulating a pillow that she imagined was his neck? Would he credit it possible that her entire life at home was now a checkerboard of calculated avoidances so that she could be spared his gusty 'As-salaam alaikum'? What would he do if he realized that Aslam once slept with Fatima's underpants beneath his pillow?

'But, beta, I really think,' Baba continued in a quiet undertone, 'she's a little young for marriage. She still has university to think about. I would hate for her to give all of that up.'

'Of course, of course, Aftab Taya. I'm not saying I wouldn't allow her to continue her studies once we're married.'

Baba raised an eyebrow at his choice of words. 'She's only eighteen. Still way too early to consider marriage, in my opinion.'

'Well, Shahana was eighteen when we got married...' Jamshaid Chacha pointed out.

Fatima, who was still standing, suddenly screamed, 'How dare you – how dare you even think that I'd agree to marry you!' She jabbed a finger at the air like a dagger, her expression fierce as an embattled warrior.

'Maybe a long engagement...' whispered Shahana Chachi timidly, her slender fingers playing nervously at the folds of her hijab.

'Well, Bhai Jan, she certainly knows her own mind!' Jamshaid Chacha said tersely, as he appraised Fatima anew, the disapproval in his glance indicating a subtle change in intention or, at the very least, a re-evaluation of options. 'I mean, we were even willing to overlook her unwillingness to wear hijab...'

'For God's sake, Jamshaid, that's enough!' Baba looked stern as he turned to face his brother. 'That's enough. We can discuss this later. Privately. First I need to talk to my daughter.'

'I'm all for the young people getting to know one another and then deciding. That's how it's done nowadays, even in decent households. But this, badtameezi, this rudeness? Thank God, we're all family. We won't broadcast her behaviour. If we did, she'd have precious few rishtas coming her way. Maybe this kind of behavior is acceptable in America, but over here, it's just...'

'Jamshaid, I said enough!' Baba's voice no longer sounded like his own. I squeezed my eyes shut behind my ineffectual fingers. I could hear other voices intervening:

'Bhai Jan, Jamshaid Bhai, please!'

'Boys, enough! Let's not spoil our meal over this.' There was a clatter as if someone was ladling out more salaan.

'I feel my blood pressure rising!' (That could only be Dadi.)

'If this is the way it is to be,' a tired, as-yet-unheard voice interrupted quietly, 'if the family is going to fall apart at the slightest provocation, then there really is no hope for me, is there?'

Suddenly, there was silence. Curious, I removed my hands from in front of my face. It was Shahbaz Chacha, of course. Who else could sound so forlorn among all the bluster? I turned my chair around to face the main table and sat up a little straighter.

Shahbaz Chacha, smiling wryly, spent a few seconds looking around the table at the faces that he had, for the most part, grown up with, the people whom he had always considered family. I noticed him brush away the restraining hand that Tania Chachi had placed on his shoulder. No one spoke. He passed his fingers through his curly hair much like Baba did when frustrated. Then he spoke:

'It doesn't take much, does it? A minor disagreement and we're at each other's throats. Is it any wonder that we live in such violent times – that we could be decimated by a bomb blast if we walk up the road or if we go to the market to buy fruit? I thought we always came through for each other as a family.' There was an ironic emphasis on the word. 'But since we're family, I wanted to share something with all of you – no, Ammi, please – that I recently found out about myself. I'm afraid it affects all of you, so it wouldn't be fair for me to keep it to myself.'

Dadi fell silent. Suddenly she was very still, a porcelain statue of a Lucknavi noblewoman in distress, her features hardening as she prepared herself for a potential confrontation.

Fatima and Aslam, who were both standing, sat down again, sensing, perhaps, that this announcement was about to take precedence over theirs.

'It turns out,' Shahbaz Chacha began slowly, 'it turns out that, after all these years of being a member of this family, I have now been told that I am not a Mahmud after all.'

I cast a triumphant glance around the room, then stopped. Dada, who had previously returned to the food on his plate and was lifting a forkful to his mouth, put his utensils down and stared, eyes bulging, the shiny bald patch at the center of his venerable head turning crimson. 'Wha—what bakwaas! Bloody nonsense, Shahbaz!' he scolded sternly. 'Has everyone gone mad today?' he asked the rest of the table, pausing finally at Dadi, who sat on his left.

'Eh, Zubeida? What's going on?' Dada asked, as Dadi kept quiet, her posture unyielding.

'Go on, Shahbaz,' urged Baba.

'It appears my father is none other than —'

'How dare you, Shahbaz! What the bloody hell is going on here?' It was Dada's turn to rise to his feet, although his movements were nervous and unsteady. 'What are you implying about your mother? Be careful, young man.' Durdana Phupo ran to Dada's side and gently helped him back into his seat. He looked confused again, like the lost little boy I had once had a glimpse of.

'My father was Air Commodore Rafiq Nawaz.'

'Maybe we should ask the children to leave the room first…' Durdana Phupo's mousey interjection was thankfully ignored. I suddenly made an effort to look preoccupied with the very important task of braiding the tassels on the tablecloth in front of me. One of the greatest disadvantages of being the youngest, in my opinion, was this vulnerability to forcible ejection. As soon as conversations among the adults became interesting, I was asked to leave. Little did they know that I had already guessed the substance of this revelation months ago.

'No, Abbaji. Wait. It has nothing to do with Ammi. Not directly, that is,' Shahbaz Chacha explained. 'Look, none of this has been easy for me either. I found out about this just before Uncle Raff's death. I don't know why it was kept from me – from all of us – for so many years. I don't think it did anyone any good.'

'Beta, if you would let me talk to your Abbaji about this alone first…' Dadi began, as she placed a hand on Dada's shoulder and bent towards him with a comforting nod of the head. 'It's too much for him to handle all at once…'

'Handle? Zubeida, what is it that I am supposed to "handle"? No, Shahbaz. Tell me immediately!' Dada's voice now sounded like a petulant child's, so that the difference between him, nearing his eighties, and myself, only eleven, was barely apparent. I recognized in him the signs of my own temper tantrums, the same agitation, the whining plaintiveness.

'It was a difficult year, Sikander. It was a difficult year – the war, the loneliness, the uncertainty of your return. Raff and I became friends, close friends. He helped me through many rough days,' said Dadi.

Dada waited in silence. His hands, flat on the table, trembled.

'He confided in me. He had a friend, a young Hindu girl – a lecturer at the University, bright, beautiful, too. He was madly in love with her. Then, when Dhaka began to fall apart, when the violence and the bloodshed came, the poor girl – the poor girl –' Dadi broke down and took several minutes to compose herself, during which time her children, including Shahbaz Chacha, gathered around her for support. 'Sikander, the soldiers – they sequestered the students, the intellectuals. They were merciless with the young girls... She was already pregnant – could barely hide it at that stage, but still they harmed her, kept her locked away for several days ... When Raff finally found her, she had gone into early labour. But the trauma of the last few weeks, coupled with her physical deterioration ... She died before she could properly hold the baby in her arms.

'At around the same time, Sikander, I too lost someone close to me. The baby, the one I was expecting that year, came early, too, and was stillborn. I was devastated. When Raff came to me with the request of raising his son as my own, I couldn't help but say yes. It was a way to repay all of his kindnesses as well as a balm for my own sense of loss. And that's how Shahbaz came into our lives. I should have told you, it is true. But as the months progressed, and you were already suffering as a prisoner of war, I came to believe he was my own, nursing him like only a mother could. Eventually, his origins didn't matter anymore. He was just like my other children.'

'Children,' Baba suddenly said, as if just realizing that we were still in the room, 'would you mind leaving us for a little while? Parveen, Aslam, you too, please.'

The six of us quietly walked out of the dining room.

CHAPTER 28

The four of us came directly from the 'Dining Room of Doom' as Raza called it to our secret hideout below the stairs, drawn as if by some inexplicable force to this recently disused play area, the hallowed space where not so long ago colossal creatures held trysts. Without a word, we sat down and stared, stared at the once-fantastic drawings that decorated the walls, now dusty and tattered, bloodless and discoloured and clearly what they had always been – the fleeting fantasies of children. The skin beneath my lawn kurta goose-pimpled even in the oppressive heat, and I couldn't think properly, as if my mind were sound asleep.

The others, too, were lost in thought. For once, no one dared to speak, either as themselves or as their alter egos. Disclosures like this were not meant to happen in the world we inhabited. They occurred in books, films, or play-acting as a necessary mechanism of plot, a fantastic device that magically explained away complications or created new ones. It was rarely the other way around. Who knew that our silly games would actually reveal a truth that had been kept hidden for over thirty years? Shahbaz Chacha's revelation demanded deep thought and a reverential silence. We were so quiet that all of the outdoor sounds – the crickets, the chhipkalis, the buzzing of mosquitoes – rapidly invaded our corner, their collective whirring so amplified that I shivered as I imagined the clammy damp skin and pimpled surface of a lizard's tail as it pressed against the warmth of my calves. The feeling of unease, of disconnectedness, grew as the minutes went by. From a vague sense of culpability, it became palpable, a green-skinned Frankenstein sitting in our midst and breathing hot, stale breath into our faces. There was no denying it: we had created this monster.

And then it happened. I had to speak to dispel the monsters and the lizards in the room. 'It's not fair!' I shouted.

There was an irritated chorus of 'shut ups' from the other three, who were naturally startled by the sudden interruption. 'It's not fair,' I continued, ignoring their protests. 'He was the most adorable of the lot, and now we've ruined his life!'

'Well, technically it wasn't our fault...' Fatima, ever-pragmatic, had already analyzed the consequences of our imaginings. 'Just because we guessed the truth doesn't mean that we're responsible for revealing it to Shahbaz Chacha. Uncle Raff did that.'

'But it's almost as if we willed it to happen through our games...' Raza commented, for once thoughtful, his green eyes half-closed as he leaned against the wall, his head emerging from the flames of Lady M's Crayola-induced fire. 'After all, wasn't the whole idea of our espionage to discover something sensational that would set the family at war?

Something so horrible that it would mean us packing up and leaving? Going home?'

'That's what I feel,' I concurred dully, as Jamila drew closer to rest her head on my lap. Funny how these things worked. What once seemed so important – returning to Chicago – didn't really matter that much anymore. At least not to me. I had already fallen in love with the dust and the smell, the traffic, the din and spontaneity of this city that I now called home.

'It's unbelievable,' Fatima whispered. 'Worse even than Aslam's proposal. At least I know I can refuse him. Poor Shahbaz Chacha can't change who he is.'

I wondered why he had to change. Wasn't he perfect the way he was, even though he didn't share our genes? The concept of family over here was as narrowly conservative in definition as it was wide-spreading in reach. There was, for example, the obsessive interest in the shajra or family tree, which I had seen Dada pore over many an evening, tracing with proud gnarled finger the descent of the Mahmuds from a Central Asian general of the twelfth century. Apparently this gentleman, one of a group of marauders, pillaged and plundered before settling down to domesticity with a local woman, our great-thousand-times-removed grandmother. 'That explains,' he told me excitedly, 'why we have fairer skin and slightly narrower eyes than our neighbours.' (I knew I had neither.) I looked with detachment at the spindly lines that linked branches of the tree, the difficult-to-pronounce, long-winded names and obscure dates and tried to muster a little of his passion, but to no avail. This whole exercise meant nothing to me. I could not say why, except that it was telling that our own branch of the family – the Aftab Mahmuds – had just recently been incorporated in ballpoint, a hasty footnote to a centuries' old history inserted only after Amma's death. That this figurative tree made of paper and ink was meant to bind us together, keep us whole in a world of uncertainties, was laughable to me after all that I had seen in my eleventh year. What really drew me to my grandparents in the end was not the shared blood that this piece of paper commemorated but the shared feelings.

(Ironically, this narrowly conservative interpretation of family based on the shajra demanded an allegiance to its wide-spreading branches, so that cousins who were tenth or twelfth removed could exert the same moral authority to blackmail you in the name of family as your immediate kin.)

'Why should he want to change who he is? I think he's perfect – if only he could be happy again,' I said, the tears finally coming.

'I'm not so sure Dada will see it that way. Can you imagine the shock? First, finding out your son isn't yours but your best friend's, and then finding out that he's half Hindu?'

'What's wrong with that?' I asked.

'Nothing, as far as I'm concerned,' Raza answered, 'but imagine what'll go through the old man's head! He's not exactly known for his tolerance, is he?'

I suddenly understood. Shahbaz Chacha was now a 'kaafir'. 'Wait a minute!' Laughing through my tears so that I must have looked at least half as mad as I felt, I squealed,

'Yes! He's a kaafir! And so are we! No wonder I loved him from the moment I saw him!'

And, for once, it seemed as if we had been transported back to Chicago, back to our complete and happier life there, when Amma was alive and something I said or did could send everyone into fits of laughter no matter how grim the situation. The four of us laughed more than we had done over the entire past year combined, our hysteria mirthless but strangely cathartic, so that once I had calmed down, I felt if I stood up and leaped, I could fly.

'Now,' Fatima gasped, 'how do I get that wild beast off my back?'

Raza and Jamila's peals of laughter echoed insanely in the small space that we occupied.

'What beast?' I asked.

'That dim-witted cousin of ours, who else? The "Sloth"!' More laughter at the mention of this absurd name, concocted on a whim during play.

An idea came to me, born of many months of observing the art of blackmail at work in the expert hands of a seasoned practitioner – Dadi. I had seen her use it in its most cutting form – the Emotional Blackmail – time and again, first on one son, then the other, but most of all on poor Durdana Phupo, whose celibacy was a constant source of irritation to her and against whom she employed her full arsenal of poison-tipped arrows, threatening to die of an aortic aneurysm before she had the good fortune of seeing her daughter's offspring. Though lacking all subtlety, it was a remarkably effective tactic, working in at least eight out of ten cases, especially when accompanied by alleged heart flutters, a dramatic rise in blood pressure, and the threat of fainting. As a silent observer of this drama, I had a renewed respect for the ageing human body and its potential for persuasion. I could see its effects on Durdana Phupo's anguished face: surely, if it were in her power, she would grab the next suitable man she saw (there was the caveat, for so many were *not* in Dadi's opinion) and force him to marry her if for no other reason than the health and well-being of her mother.

In addition, there was the standard-issue variety of blackmail that Dadi generally employed on the servants, who lived in mortal fear of Dada's wrath. Such were the mythic proportions of his reputation as an army man that most of the servants imagined him in uniform, medals and all, even if he were drifting off to sleep in front of the television in nothing more glorious than his fraying night suit. Everyone knew Dada was ruthless in the face of ineptitude and dishonesty. So, whether it was pilfering from our Dish antenna or gossiping about our private matters with the neighbour's servants, the threat of exposure was enough to extort a complete confession, a heartfelt apology and, on occasion, even some voluntary overtime. Not that Dadi was a paan-chewing, gun-toting, filthy-mouthed underworld don, of course. She just used this tool of manipulation much as a neighborhood witch practised her black arts on other housewives.

With my grandmother as a successful role model before me, I suggested with extreme caution that I had a way in which to silence Aslam once and for all. The solution to all my sister's problems lay in a tiny article of clothing she generally wore around her pelvis. Unfortunately, in order to outline my plan, it was necessary to admit that I had used that very same article of clothing as a mask. Her expression clearly indicated she was not happy with this, but she continued to listen patiently, and then with renewed interest when I told her of Aslam's stash of military paraphernalia. She raised an eyebrow at Raza and whispered meaningfully, 'Colonel Bogey?'

And then, when I went on to describe how I had secretly observed Aslam pull her underpants out from under his pillow, she clapped a hand to her mouth in revulsion, then instant glee. 'Chhoti, you genius! It's perfect, Raza. How will Aslam's pious daddy feel if he finds out that he likes to sleep with my underwear? Or that he was the one who wrote those vile emails to me?'

'What?' I exclaimed, shocked. 'What makes you think that?' I paused a minute. Our meeting in the courtyard was a distant memory now, but I did remember that in exchange for the key to the hoard of photographs I had given Aslam an email address – Fatima's. 'Ohhh…' I moaned, doubling over so that no one, except Jamila, whose head still lay in my lap, could see my stricken face. She looked up at me, concerned. That was one part of my involvement in all of this that I had yet to confess. Feigning a lesser degree of interest than I in fact felt, I asked casually, 'What does "Colonel Bogey" have to do with anything?'

'The anonymous villain signed all of his emails off like that. And "Colonel Bogey" is the name of a famous military march! I'm convinced Aslam wrote those emails. In any case, when I confront him, the truth will come out.'

'I—I gave him your email address!' I blurted.

'What?'

'In exchange for the keys to the photo library… A long time ago, Fatima. Please forgive me,' I begged.

Raza intervened, 'Easy on her, Fatima. She got you into this mess, but she's also found you a way out of it. And you have to admit,' he added, 'the way out will give you at least fifteen minutes of complete pleasure.'

Fatima scowled but decided – thankfully – to remain quiet, at least for the time being.

Minutes later, we had all dispersed, Raza to his room, the three of us to ours. We had had an evening of multiple revelations. I had no idea how exhausting that could be. My eyelids heavy, I struggled against the glare of the tube light in the bathroom to brush my teeth halfheartedly before changing into my cotton nightie and slipping into bed. The others took longer. I watched through half-closed lids as my sisters laboriously went through their bedtime rituals as if caught in some slow-motion reel, their movements exaggerated and weary as they, too, changed and went to sleep. Our thoughts remained with the grown ups in the dining room, partially envious that we were excluded from their discussions but mostly thankful that the painful task of unravelling then reconstituting the Mahmud family history was not expected of us, its youngest members.

✳

Unfortunately, the next morning was a Sunday.

The entire family, constrained by tradition, met in the main house for yet another communal meal, the customary late-morning brunch. The adults, silent for the most part, washed down their aloo-puri with the assistance of copious amounts of tea. Droopy eyes and dark circles were a common theme from one end of the table to the other. Poor Dada, I noticed, had lost all of his military bluster and ate his breakfast meekly, a fact unusual for him because he was known for his gastronomic zeal and his dictatorial management of meals. Today there was no shouting for more puris from the kitchen, or another round of tea, or a gruff comment on the sloppy rinsing of a spoon or fork. The servants in the kitchen were, no doubt, thankful for a peaceful Sunday. Everyone was extra gentle with Shahbaz Chacha, the conversation at the table consisting mainly of various offers to pass him something, as if this superficial tabletop politeness was enough to wipe out the memory of his unique parentage and the upheaval of the night before.

Sitting at the children's table, I attempted to keep up a steady banter with my companions to right and to left, but eventually, tired of hearing my own voice, I, too, succumbed to the atmosphere of despondence and tried instead to focus on pulling apart my puri, whose elastic viscosity provided a few minutes' distraction . Somehow it just didn't taste the same though, I thought, as I stuffed a large ball of fried bread into my mouth, almost choking as the obnoxious blare of an early-morning car horn startled me in mid-swallow. Everyone shifted uncomfortably. This was hardly the time for 'pop-ins', those heinous unexpected callers that were the plague of peaceful family-time in Karachi. Dadi's expression changed, as if she had just remembered something, and the next moment she was announcing nervously, 'I forgot … A few weeks ago I invited an old friend to come for breakfast …' There was no concealing the general irritation. Even Tania Chachi, usually so polite, expressed her displeasure through her stomach, which let out a strange protracted gurgle that added to the unanimous chorus of disapproval.

I craned over Jamila to see who had come to disturb the perfect gloom of our Sunday morning brunch and nearly fell off my chair when I smelled – there was no mistaking it – the overbearing scent of a particularly expensive perfume, which immediately took over the entire room and made the morsel in my mouth taste of bitter gardenias. Chairs shifted as the grown ups rose reluctantly to their feet, a few forced smiles and 'As-salaam alaikums' (mostly from the Jamshaids) greeting the high-bunned priestess as she swept up her drapings and sat down with dramatic flourish. She seemed disappointed by the comparatively lacklustre welcome.

'So good to see you, Aftab, and after all these years!' she said, coming straight to the point as her jewelled fingers rapidly tore through a puri.

Baba was speechless for a few seconds. Then, clearing his throat, he began with caution, 'Yes! How many years has it been…?'

'Rizwana,' Jamshaid Chacha supplied, sensing that Baba had forgotten her name.

'Now *that* I won't reveal in a room full of people!' she tittered coquettishly. 'Too long an absence, though. We should stay in touch from now on.'

Baba looked unconvinced and even a little confused by her overfamiliarity.

'Of course, of course! We're on family terms,' Dada intervened, and then went on to explain, somewhat redundantly, how he and Rizwana Hameed's father were once comrades. It was only too obvious that Dada no longer had the motivation required to matchmake, particularly as his son's disinterest was clear.

Baba merely nodded and continued his breakfast.

The four of us looked at one another smugly as we realized that Rizwana Hameed posed no lasting threat to our Baba. 'One less thing to worry about,' I thought as I wiped my plate clean and ran to him, putting my arms proprietarily around his neck and kissing his cheeks with noisy abandon.

The high priestess visibly cringed.

The breakfast could not end soon enough. Surprised by the inhospitable mood of the Mahmud clan, Rizwana Hameed suddenly found herself being ushered out the front door and then into a waiting car, the gates of C44 already wide open in anticipation of her swift departure. She barely had a chance to wave a gloved hand through the window before she was whisked away, away from us – permanently – like the evil, cackling witch of fairytales, disappearing amid a fantastic cloud of black smoke. (Alas, in her case this smoke came from a relatively mundane source – exhaust fumes from the rickety pipe of the rickshaw in front of her vehicle.)

Only her flashing image, broadcast through local television channels, remained to haunt us, triggering a faint tremor up and down my spine whenever I had a second to contemplate her as the stepmother I never had.

A few days later, a triumphant Fatima announced that she had dispatched Aslam's proposal with great efficiency and was free of him at last. Apparently waving a pair of black panties in front of him was enough of a threat to reduce him to tears. It wasn't long before he readily admitted to writing the emails, too, apologizing for their content and claiming that he wrote them in a fit of passion. Fatima left him with a stern warning never to raise the issue of marriage between them again otherwise she would tell Jamshaid Chacha all about his erratic and 'gross' behavior.

In fact, in the days after Shahbaz Chacha's revelation, strange changes took place in our household. Aslam, for one, disappeared. Technically, he was still living at C44 but he took to spending more and more time out of the house, attending meetings of a religious nature that were meant to 'distract' him from his nafs, or baser instincts. His beard grew incrementally in direct proportion to the shortening of his shalwars. When at home, he cocooned himself in his room, listening to military marches late into the night, the 'danchee-danchee-daa-daa' of the blustery strains reaching me in my sleep so that I, too, dreamed of soldiers and POW camps and a demoralized Dada sitting on a prayer mat. Even his sprightly courtyard greetings ceased, and I found myself almost missing the sound of his guttural 'As-salaam alaikum' belted out in desperation for a kind word or a passing look from my sister. Despite myself, and knowing his history, I felt sorry for him. After all, in the end, he was my cousin, and I could see he was making a sincere effort to reform. I didn't know anything about love yet, but judging by what I had seen so far, it was more of an affliction than a joy and brought little satisfaction.

The most surprising change in our household was the increasing absence of one of its most loyal and steadfast members – Durdana Phupo. I had never seen a more unlikely candidate for staged disappearances. The poor woman spent more and more time at work, causing Dadi to fly into sudden rages against her boss, the unwitting Madam Shaista, whose slave-driving ways and distinctly masculine appearance were sure signs of the makings of a megalomaniac. A suddenly more self-aware Durdana Phupo took to spending hours locked up in her little-girl room with creams, perfumes, potions and sprays housed in the most delightful bottles, the incongruous mixture of scents sending me into sneezing fits whenever I passed her door. I overheard her asking Tania Chachi (who was in no mood, of course, and who was happy these days if she had a chance to clip her toenails) for advice on personal grooming, where to go for the waxing of unsightly hair or the removal of a profuse moustache, the dyeing of greys, the purchase of new lawn prints, or a lipstick shade to lighten her sallow complexion. It was all very endearing. Even Dadi brightened at the sight of Durdana Phupo in a new outfit and matching heels. It was not until the entire family noticed the casual slipping of Durdana Phupo's chadors, the sudden and startling exposure of hair, that we realized that a truly significant transformation was taking place.

Now, if Shahbaz Chacha had suddenly grown a goatee and dreadlocks, no one would have thought twice about it. After all, he had reason. He was grappling with a new identity, searching for his roots. Contrary to expectation, he appeared to want to spend more time at C44, his afternoons and early evenings devoted to listening to Dada, Dadi, and his brothers talk about the past. On occasion, I, too, was present at these sessions, fascinated with the process, the family recollections that Shahbaz Chacha used to reconstitute himself. To their credit, the Mahmuds tried their best to convince Shahbaz Chacha that he was as much a part of the family as any of them, which in fact he was, for Uncle Raff, as Dada repeated time and again, was a brother to him, blood or no blood, shajra or no shajra.

I was proud of him for saying that.

Shahnaz, Jamila, and I sat on the floor in our bedroom. Recently, Dadi had relaxed her stringent rules about interacting with 'the servants', the need for quotation marks implied by the special way she said the phrase as if she were an anthropologist referring to a unique subspecies. At first I thought Dadi, too, had grown more liberal-minded over the year, but later I began to suspect that she had come to see Shahnaz as a useful babysitter for Jamila and myself. Regardless, the arrangement suited all concerned.

Shahnaz was not at all impressed with the news of Shahbaz Chacha's parentage. Our family secret was already known to half the neighborhood. By next week, even the dhobi and the doodhwallah would be told that Shahbaz Chacha was sired by Uncle Raff and a Hindu university lecturer. Apparently, such incidents were more common than we thought. She calmly outlined the outrageous plots of just three of the most popular TV dramas her family avidly watched each week. Nothing the wealthy did (her term, not mine) surprised the general public anymore. They wanted more scandal, more 'drama' to their drama, so to speak. Foundlings and war babies of doubtful parentage were just not interesting enough to hold anyone's attention for more than a day. Of course, being a party to the scandal, I found this impossible to believe. Nothing was more riveting to me than my uncle's predicament. I even imagined for an instant that I was him; how would I feel if my world was suddenly flipped over, turned inside out, and rolled into a ball like a pair of common socks? I couldn't imagine anyone else as my Amma or Baba. But then again, Shahbaz Chacha had probably thought the same about the only set of parents he knew – Dadi and Dada. Really, it could happen to anyone. For an instant, I panicked. Then, I remembered my best feature and tweaked that nose so like my mother's, briefly forgetting all my worries as Shahnaz, Jamila, and I played a second round of Karom.

EPILOGUE

There could be no greater testimony to the transformation that had taken place in our extended family over the last year than their willing participation in the first barsi, or death anniversary, of our mother. Baba had eagerly conceded the task of arranging the entire function to my mamus, who finally had the opportunity of honouring their sister's memory in a way that accorded with their traditions. In years gone by, Dada would have had to be bound, gagged, and forcibly transported like a cow to slaughter before he attended a majlis at an imam bargah. Now, with me perched on his lap, he waited patiently for the others to arrive so that we could make our way – a dreary Sunday afternoon cavalcade – to the north of town, where the imam bargah of my mother's childhood still stood and where the memory of her passing, like that of her parents before her, was being marked today.

As we travelled through the relatively quiet streets, I found myself wishing for manic peak-hour traffic, the commotion-filled, horn-tooting, fume-spouting aggression of trucks, the incessant whine of weaving rickshaws and motorbikes, interspersed with irate peddlers, enterprising beggars, and

342

the occasional appearance, as if from a different dimension, of the pack-animal, head down and resigned to its fate. I was desperate for anything that would slow the relentless draw of that compelling force that pulled our vehicle towards the centre of our grief, like the knots that wound endlessly in the pits of our stomachs. Again and again, I wished the day was over.

I must have fallen asleep because when next I opened my eyes it was to a different landscape altogether. I was suddenly lifted out of the car to the sight of a massive enclosure with wide open spaces. Several soaring minarets punctured the azure blue of the sky. An ornate, barred chamber with pennants or alams stood at the centre-right of the compound, surrounded by women and children. The scent of incense which, through association, now made me feel slightly nauseous, invaded my person as I tumbled out of the car and stood unsteadily on the cracked asphalt. I looked up at the sky, then quickly squeezed my eyes shut, a dance of light and shadow, image-memories, moving in quick succession across my mind.

My mother's silhouette as she bent over me flew, like a raven, across the canvas of my closed lids.

Later, close family and friends were invited back to my Nana's house, where everyone participated in the Fatiha, or prayer for the dead, and ate a simple one-dish meal which my brother and sisters and I consumed mechanically. We were surrounded by the Mahmuds but also by a multitude of my

mother's relatives whom we were meeting for the very first
time and whose greeting of choice appeared to be 'Adaab'
instead of the 'As-salaam alaikum' we were accustomed to
at C44. In fact, for several minutes all I could hear from all
sides was 'Daab, Daab', till I felt uniquely out of place among
a sea of ducks. For many, this was their first opportunity to
condole with Baba, and there were some who shared Alamdar
Mamu's proclivity to give into wild, unchecked displays of
emotion. Several older women, distant cousins of Amma,
sobbed as they leaned heavily on Baba's shoulder, beating
their chests and wailing at the sight of us. At one point, Raza
stood up and left, muttering, 'I thought we'd had enough of
this in Chicago'. Salaar Mamu, who was observing us from
afar, rushed over apologetically and urged us to climb the
winding staircase to the one-room shrine above the main
portion of the house dedicated to our poet-ancestor. There,
we sat quietly for close to an hour, completely exhausted by
the events of the day. We listlessly examined the contents of
the room for a second time: the tattered books, the Spartan
bed with the embroidered coverlet, the worn desk upon
which lay a half-scribbled sheet of poetry that Alamdar
Mamu had artfully placed there to simulate the creative
frenzy of the poet-ancestor's 'process'.

It was close to eight o'clock when I heard heavy, deliberate
footsteps on the stairs. It was Baba. He announced that most
of the family had already left for C44 with Khyber. Salaar and
Alamdar were cleaning up, assisted by Durdana Phupo, who
had volunteered to stay back and whose generally subdued
voice could now be heard from downstairs, confident and

animated. Here, Baba paused and looked at the four of us quizzically before admitting that he suspected we might have another 'interfaith' (said with ironic undertones, of course) marriage soon.

I sat up, immediately attentive, and thought about what he might mean. 'Oh...' I said, remembering our chance encounter several months ago with Durdana Phupo at the barbecue restaurant and Alamdar Mamu's elaborate greeting as he chivalrously held the door open for her. Could it be...? All of a sudden, the room in which we sat seemed brighter. Baba switched on a few table lamps, which warmed the cool grey of the tube light overhead, making the environment more inviting, the perfect spot, in fact, for storytelling, surrounded as we were by signs of literary activity – whatever the quality, alas, of its end product.

'Baba, this is the perfect time,' I said, pulling him down onto the carpeted floor beside us. 'Please, please tell us how you and Amma got married.' To my surprise, the others joined in, Raza, Jamila, and Fatima crowding around and begging Baba in exactly the same pleading tones as myself. We all sounded a little desperate. We needed this particular story to rise above the sadness that we felt after a day of mourning and remembrance. This time, Baba wasn't dismissive. He immediately understood our need to talk about Amma. Without a moment's delay, he began in that gentle melodic storyteller's voice of his to recount the curious tale, set decades ago, of our parents' elopement.

✳

It wasn't an event that Baba could have physically recreated for obvious reasons. After all, it was a marriage without photographs; even the dullest, most stereotypical ones of the period, the stiff black-and-white portraits of couples in matching cats' eye spectacles, were conspicuously absent. Despite that, I still felt as if I were truly there – as if we all were – as witnesses to our parents' union, more intriguing for being set in Karachi, a city which, over the last year, we had come to call our own and in which we had found, like millions of others, a strange kind of peace. Karachi was giving and vulnerable, intimate in the sharing of details, not only of the vibrant spontaneous moments of uninhibited joy but also of the darker ones, the eruptions of violence in a cityscape of half-finished structures, exposing the tenuousness of its hard-won struggle with itself and its far-flung parts.

So it was in Karachi on a tepid May afternoon in 1979, the 17th to be exact, that Aftab Mahmud, still undressed and unshaven, lay smiling on his bed, the sheets a mass of tangles beneath his sprawled frame. I sat beside him, privy to his thoughts, which were as confused as his bed linen, knotted, awaiting the full faculties of wakefulness so that they could be unravelled, then relished for what they signified. For today was the last day of his 'childhood' – of his life as he had known it for the last twenty-four years. He was leaving everything behind, the home he shared with his parents and siblings and the city where he grew up, to embark on a new adventure in a different country with the woman who had just agreed to be his wife. I placed a hand on his youthful brow and brushed back the curls, still a deep brown, the eyes closed in a face unmarked by age. Along with the euphoria, there was apprehension, too, a recognition that the step he was about to take was irrevocable and that both Najma and he had much to gain, but also much to lose, by setting off on their own.

Within minutes, he was up and had changed into a smart light-blue shirt, grey trousers and navy blazer. He nervously tied a newly-bought cravat around his neck, a dandyism he had never indulged in before but wanted to wear on his wedding day as a tribute to his future father-in-law and, perhaps, as a victorious slap to the dozens of young intellectuals who had vied for Najma's affections but had failed, in the end, to win her. Seeing the cravat slightly askew, Fatima stood on tiptoes and adjusted it so that its folds fell neatly around Aftab's neck, while Raza polished his shoes and Jamila laid out a pair of fresh socks. Once dressed, the four of us followed as he bounded down the stairs. He paused in the living room and placed a sealed letter next to his father's reading chair. His parents may not have noticed how long he lingered at the breakfast table that morning, relishing each bite of omelette-paratha and sips of hot sweetened tea but especially the absent-minded embrace of his mother as she walked by him. His father, the paper in front of him, spoke quietly of the day's happenings, the news rife with the hanging, just last month, of Zulfikar Ali Bhutto, and the adjustments of the new regime. Aftab listened with only half an ear, focusing less on the contents of the paper and more on his father's voice, the serious tones familiar from childhood lectures but somehow having the power, nonetheless, of making his heart ache a little at the thought of parting. As he left that morning, he embraced his parents like a little boy leaving for school for the very first time, and for minutes afterwards, his mother stood at the window thoughtfully watching the trail of smoke that rose from Rashid's car as he pulled out of the driveway and through the gates.

For Aftab had confided in one friend, his oldest friend, in fact, whom he had known since nursery school. He also owed him the confidence. How could he forget that Rashid was the one who had first spotted Najma in the library on the day that they met? He realized Rashid envied him his good luck in winning her over – they all did, those university comrades of his whose experience with women consisted primarily of limited interactions with each other's sisters, haughty, aloof girls who giggled coyly even when greeted with a simple 'As-salaam alaikum'. But Aftab knew that Rashid's jealousy was only superficial, a wistful yearning for the same kind of happiness.

'Where's your stuff, yaar?' his friend asked nervously as soon as Aftab slipped into the seat beside him.

'I took my suitcase to the University yesterday and left it with Najma. She's told her family that her class is going on a field trip to Lahore for three days. I have my passport, visa, and tickets here,' and he patted his chest for reassurance, feeling the crackle of papers shifting. Not satisfied, he pulled out his document folder and reread everything for the hundredth time. Then he took out the dark velveteen box in his breast pocket that contained the simple wedding band –

it was all he could afford right now – that was to find its way onto the slender finger of his bride.

'Are you sure about this, Aftab?' Rashid asked as they wound their way to the University, where Najma was to meet them.

'I wish it could have happened differently,' Aftab admitted, 'but, under the circumstances, yes,' and he nodded vigorously for emphasis, 'I'm sure we're making the right decision.'

His friend visibly relaxed after hearing this, and the rest of the drive was spent in discussing the logistics of the event. The four of us watched as the car veered towards the gated entrance to the University and pulled up alongside the main library building. There stood Najma, flanked by two of her closest friends, looking a little forlorn in a dark pink chooridaar pyjama and embroidered kurta. At the sight of the car, however, she suddenly smiled and waved, whatever momentary doubt she may have felt dispelled with a jaunty swipe of her hand in the air. Aftab jumped out of the car before it came to a full stop amid an expletive-filled protest from Rashid, dashed up the stairs and took the suitcase from Najma, who spent a few moments in the joint embrace of her two friends. Then, looking determined, she ran down the stairs. Aftab held the back door open for her as she pulled her slender legs in, then rolled down the window and waved vigorously to her friends as the car sped out of the University compound.

The ever-enterprising Rashid had spoken to the maulana of a small masjid in Malir, close to the airport, who had agreed to preside over the nikah. Suddenly, the car was infused with the heady scent of roses and jasmine. There, on the seat next to Najma, Rashid had thoughtfully placed two heavy garlands of flowers wrapped in newsprint which he, as the only family present, was planning to give his friends after the ceremony. Aside from the garlands and the wedding band tucked safely in Aftab's pocket, there were no other festive reminders of the day's importance – no special outfits of silk and brocade, no mehndi on Najma's hands and feet, no jewels for her, either – not even the teeka and jhoomar that her mother had worn when she had married her father. It seemed unfair, so Fatima quickly removed a locket and chain that she had inherited from Amma and gently placed it around the bride's neck, a small calligraphic 'Ya Ali' in gold and diamonds that was more lustrous now, two decades earlier, and which shone on Najma's beautiful collar bone, her sole adornment and one which she would often point to in her jewellery box as her favourite piece, despite the eventual arrival of far grander ones.

Half an hour passed before they finally drove up to the small masjid in Malir, a simple three-roomed structure painted a pastel green. Najma hastily covered her head, making sure that her cotton dupatta came down over her face in the fashion of the modest brides of the time. As she stepped out of the car, Aftab peered under her head covering and looked into her heavily kohled eyes and asked quietly, 'You're sure about this?'

'Are you?' she asked defiantly, her brows furrowed.

Aftab laughed as he led the way.

And so, in that small structure, without the fuss and fanfare of a typical Asian wedding, without the family members who make that wedding so memorable with their finger-pointing and squabbling but also with the comforting presence of their support, Aftab and Najma quietly offered their thrice-acceptance, their voices rising with conviction with each repetition of the standard 'qubool kiya'. The one familiar witness, Rashid, was joined by a bony-chested tobacco vendor from across the street whose paan-stained teeth could be seen protruding from between a sly grin, his sharp eyes registering the haste and the secrecy and assuming, correctly, that this marriage was taking place without the consent of the families. Once the nikah was over, and the document duly signed and witnessed, Rashid placed the garlands around Aftab and Najma's necks, joking that they were now officially 'yoked' together. If only he had also remembered to pick up the camera on the way out of his cluttered bedroom that morning there would have been one photograph at least: Aftab and Najma, side by side, their radiant faces framed and shoulders weighted down by thick blossoms of red and white, their hands, hidden in the folds of Najma's dupatta, firmly clasped. But even in that photograph, had it existed, there would have been intimations of flight, Aftab's eyes focused away from the lens and on the battered wall clock of the imam bargah, Najma's smile slightly forced as if her mind were already on the bare patch of land where her house in America was to be built.

Within minutes of the ceremony, the bride and groom were in the car and speeding their way towards the airport where, with a hurried farewell to their loyal friend, they suddenly found themselves on the plane, the aircraft taxiing for take off as the stewardess explained the safety mechanisms in place should they plunge, hundreds of miles down, to earth or ocean. As they rose above their city, Aftab leaned across Najma to watch with her as the dusty, sun-beaten buildings of their youth, the homes they grew up in with the people whom they loved, were pulled away, snatched by time and distance. Still holding hands, they watched as the four of us stood down below, Fatima, Raza, Jamila, and I, waving to them as they left to begin the story of our lives.

ACKNOWLEDGEMENTS

Thank you to my family for their continued love and support, to Renuka Chatterjee, my agent, for her belief in this story, to Ajitha G.S and Prerna Gill, my editors at HarperCollins India, to Bina Shah for her generous feedback, to Syeda Nazar for her careful reading of the proofs, and to Irfan Rizvi for his unwavering (and often misplaced!) faith in me as a writer.